Praise for the Novels of Whitney Gaskell

She, Myself & I

"A witty, fast-paced, and intensely entertaining journey through the lives of three unforgettable sisters. Whitney Gaskell finds the humor and the heart in each and every one of her characters, a talent that makes the pages come to life and literally turn themselves."
—Lindsay Faith Rech, author of *Losing It* and *Joyride*

"Whitney Gaskell delivers another winner. As funny as it is warm and touching, this is going on my keeper shelf along with all of Whitney's books. Filled with Whitney's trademark mixture of humor and poignancy, it made me laugh, cry, and wish I had sisters! Can't wait for the next one!"
—Lani Diane Rich, author of *Time Off for Good Behavior*

True Love (and Other Lies)

"Funny, romantic . . . an entertaining read with all the right stuff." —RomanticReviewsToday.com

"A hilarious story about love and friendships . . . breezy, delightful, and well worth reading."
—TheBestReviews.com

"Witty, honest, and refreshingly fun."
—RoundTableReviews.com

MAIN

Pushing 30

"Feisty, poignant, sexy, and packed with delicious comedy." —Sue Margolis

"Light and sweet . . . a breezy romp." —*Miami Herald*

"A sprightly debut . . . breezy prose, sharp wit . . . a delightful romantic comedy heroine." —*Publishers Weekly*

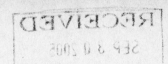
"Gaskell takes a familiar 'oh-no' chicklit theme and turns it sprightly on its ear. . . . What sets *Pushing 30* apart from others in the genre is Gaskell's sharp writing and skillful handling of many plot strands as it weaves into a cohesive, thoroughly satisfying read." —*Pittsburgh Post-Gazette*

"Gaskell's characters are funny and sexy as she incorporates serious issues of female friendships, family demands, and personal choices into her story."
—*Rendezvous*

"Witty and fast-paced, it's great chicklit."
—BookReporter.com

Also by Whitney Gaskell

Pushing 30
True Love (and Other Lies)

She, Myself & I

Whitney Gaskell

BANTAM BOOKS

SHE, MYSELF & I
A Bantam Book / October 2005

Published by
Bantam Dell
A Division of Random House, Inc.
New York, New York

Book design by Lynn Newmark

Bantam Books and the rooster colophon are registered
trademarks of Random House, Inc.

Library of Congress Cataloging-in-Publication Data

Gaskell, Whitney.
She, myself & I / by Whitney Gaskell.
p.   cm.
ISBN-13: 978-0-553-38313-3
ISBN-10: 0-553-38313-2 (trade pbk.)
1. Sisters—Fiction.   2. Children of divorced parents—Fiction.
3. Women medical students—Fiction.   4. Divorced women—
Fiction.   5. Pregnant women—Fiction.   6. Married
women—Fiction.   7. Women lawyers—Fiction.
I. Title: She, myself and I.   II. Title.

PS3607.A7854S54 2005
813'.6—dc22   2005046402

Printed in the United States of America
Published simultaneously in Canada

www.bantamdell.com

BVG   10 9 8 7 6 5 4 3 2 1

For my mother,
who makes the world a more beautiful place.

Acknowledgments

The world of publishing remains a mystery to me. I sit in my office and type up what eventually becomes a messy pile of pages, send it off to Bantam, and there they somehow magically turn it into a real, honest-to-goodness book. And so, were it not for a great many people—including my talented and always gracious editor, Danielle Perez, my terrific agent, Ethan Ellenberg, and the hardworking team at Bantam— you would not be holding this book in your hands. I owe them all my deepest gratitude for their support, their enthusiasm, and their unparalleled talent.

Many thanks also to my husband, George, who puts up with my moaning and obsessing, patiently reads and rereads my manuscripts, and holds my hand every step of the way. Without him cheering me on, I very much doubt if I'd ever have had the courage to write a single word.

Thank you to my mother, Meredith Kelly, who took Sam on countless afternoon walks so that I could fit in an extra hour of work, and to my father, Jerry Kelly, for his never-ending interest and support.

Thank you also to all of the readers who have taken the

time to write me. Your kind e-mails mean more to me than you'll ever know.

And finally, a world of thanks to our son, Sam. Without him in my life, this book would doubtlessly have been completed sooner, but I wouldn't have had nearly as much fun along the way.

She, Myself & I

Paige

Chapter One

I don't know why I got that squirmy-stomach feeling when Scott knocked on the door. It was just Scott after all—the one person who couldn't possibly surprise me any more than he already had. I took a few deep breaths to center myself, and, once I felt sufficiently calm, opened the door.

"Hi, Paige," he said.

I stared at him. Since we'd divorced, Scott had apparently stumbled onto someone else's fashion taste. Gone were the plain-front khakis, the slightly too-long floppy brown hair, the preppy tortoiseshell glasses, the quintessential boy-next-door whom most women—like me—don't notice until they hit their late twenties and start looking around for husband-type material. Now his clothes looked expensively hip, and his hair was cropped short. The tortoiseshell glasses had been replaced with sleek silver metal frames. The once soft body was now lean and muscular. He looked amazing, far better than he ever had when we were together . . . but his new look was also unmistakably gay.

Okay, I was wrong. He was still capable of surprising me.

"Hey. Come on in," I said, stepping out of his way.

I wasn't sure what the greeting protocol was supposed to be, and I could tell by the way Scott was clasping his hands together that he didn't know either. Were we supposed to hug? To exchange cheek kisses—*mwah, mwah*—like a pair of socialites? Maybe I should have written Miss Manners for the etiquette guidelines on greeting your gay ex-husband.

Dear Gentle Reader, I imagined she would reply. *What a trying situation! But now, more than ever, Miss Manners would stress the importance of conducting yourself gracefully. To wit: it is always socially acceptable to clasp hands in a firm and congenial handshake. Do not feel it necessary to engage in gratuitous kissing and grappling.*

I stuck my hand out awkwardly, and Scott stared at it just long enough to make me feel like an ass. But just as I was withdrawing my hand—*stupid Miss Manners*—Scott grabbed it and swung our arms between us.

Is there anything weirder than shaking hands with the man who once promised to love, honor, and cherish you for the rest of his life?

"Thanks for letting me visit our apartment," Scott joked, pulling his hand back and pocketing it. "I suppose this counts as a supervised visit by the noncustodial parent?"

"You agreed to the settlement," I reminded him.

"Hey, I was just kidding. And don't worry, I've learned my lesson—never divorce a divorce attorney."

Scott looked at the apartment, his expression wistful. We'd bought it together four years earlier, just after our wedding. It's located in a converted downtown warehouse, and is roomy and airy and has a fabulous view of Town Lake out of the floor-to-ceiling windows on the far side of the living room. We'd snapped it up just before the real estate prices exploded in Austin, and there was no way either one of us would be able to afford it now. But Scott's landscape architecture firm—which he'd started up after we got married, with a loan from me—had been successful. So as part of our divorce, I gave up my interest in his business, and he gave up his claim to our condo. Simple. Neat.

"You redecorated," he said, taking in the new tufted white armless sofa and matching love seat, the glass-topped coffee table, and the groovy dining table and chairs I'd gotten from Crate & Barrel. I'd really thrown myself into decorating after Scott had moved out, probably—if I were interested in psychoanalyzing myself—in an effort to stamp out any lingering presence of him in the apartment. It was easier to get rid of the memories than learn to live with them.

"Mm-hmm. I did this ages ago. You haven't been here in a while." I smiled. "Do you still have that awful sofa?"

"Of course. Admit it—you miss that sofa."

I'd hated his leather sofa. Hated it. It was an enormous brown monstrosity covered with nail-head trim, and it looked like it belonged in the office of an eccentric old man who spent his days pinning a bug collection into shadow boxes. I'd begged, pleaded, and cajoled with Scott to get rid of it when we'd moved in together, but he'd stubbornly insisted that he couldn't live without it.

"I have two things in my life that I love more than anything else," he'd dramatically declared when I'd delicately suggested it was the ugliest couch I'd ever seen and there was no way in hell I could possibly live with it. "You and this couch."

Apparently his love for the couch was more enduring than whatever it was he'd felt for me.

"So, how've you been?" Scott now asked.

"Fine. Great. I made partner at my firm," I said brightly.

"Really? Wow, that's fantastic. Good for you, it's what you always wanted," Scott said. "And how's everything else? Seeing anyone?"

"Um. No. I'm not. And I don't want to talk about it."

"Paige . . . maybe we should talk. We never really did. It might help both of us if we, you know, sat down and discussed what happened between us."

"Nothing happened. You decided—sorry, discovered—you were gay, and so we got a divorce. I think it was pretty cut and dried."

"There's more to it than that."

"And I don't want to talk about it. Really, Scott, I'm fine. I've moved on, and my life is going great. I have no complaints."

Scott looked at me, and I met his gaze straight on, keeping my face smoothed of emotion. After nine years of being a litigator, I'm well practiced at it.

"Okay," he finally said. "But if you ever want to talk, I'd be happy to. Just say the word."

"I appreciate that. But I'm fine."

"Okay. Well. Do you have that stuff for me?"

I gestured toward the cardboard document box sitting by the door. It contained the last odds and ends he had left behind when he moved out. A few CDs, his *Blade Runner* video, the collection of ugly ties my mother had given him as Christmas presents over the years.

"It's all there. I can't believe you've gone two years without seeing *Blade Runner*."

"I haven't. My . . . friend has a copy of it."

Friend.

Okay.

I had the distinct feeling that Scott wanted me to follow up and ask him about his new friend, but I just couldn't do it. Instead I smiled pleasantly at him and silently willed him to leave.

"Well. Uh. I suppose I should get going," Scott said.

"It was nice to see you," I said.

"You, too. Bye, Paige." Scott smiled, ducking his head the way he always did, and left.

Once the door latched behind him, I turned and stared out the window, trying to decide if the low, dark sky hanging over Town Lake meant it was about to storm. I decided I had time to get a run in before it rained. I went into my bedroom—I'd changed it, too, installing a Murano glass chandelier, a French armchair upholstered in gray-green silk, and the pure white bedding and walls I'd always wanted but Scott had detested, insisting that an all-white room made him feel like he was an inmate at an insane asylum—and stripped out of my suit. I pulled on a running bra, shorts, and a blue T-shirt with "University of Texas School of Law" emblazoned across the front.

I was all too aware of the potential psychological fallout of divorce—hell, it was my business—and I know for some people, women especially, it has the poisonous power to warp the rest of their lives. So when Scott and I split up, I'd been determined not to wallow. Instead I ran. It was cheaper than therapy, less numbing than medication, and had the added benefit of keeping my ass higher and firmer than that of your average thirty-four-year-old.

While I stretched my hamstrings, the phone rang. The

Caller ID reported that it was my mother, and I considered not answering. But then I wondered if maybe, possibly, my mother had somehow intuited my run-in with my ex-husband and was calling to make sure that I was all right.

I decided to take my chances, and hit the talk button.

"I'm worried about Sophie. I think she's losing it," my mother said.

I thunked the heel of my hand against my forehead. I should have known—she was worried about my younger sister. As the oldest, I'm expected to be completely self-sufficient at all times. And Sophie, my middle sister—Mickey's the youngest, the surprise baby who came along when I was twelve and Sophie was ten—was now pregnant, which made her ripe and round and bitchy as hell. The whole family was cosseting her like she was a powerful yet unstable queen who might start shrieking "Off with their heads!" at the slightest provocation.

"Hi, Mom, how are you? Me? I'm fine, thanks for asking."

"Don't be a smart-ass. I'm serious. I'm worried about your sister. I just called her, and she was sobbing hysterically. I finally got her to tell me what was wrong, and she was all upset over nothing."

"What was it?"

"The grocery store has stopped carrying those chocolate croissants she's been so obsessed with lately. She had a meltdown about it in the middle of the bakery. Don't laugh, she scared me to death, I thought something was wrong with the baby."

"Sophie's fine, Mom. She's just very pregnant, and very hormonal right now," I said, smiling at the image of Sophie

screaming at the bakery clerk, demanding pastry while banging her clenched fists on the glass counter.

"Will you go over and check on her after work tomorrow? I'd do it myself, but the garden club is coming over,
and I still have to make brownies. Do you think brownies
are enough, or should I make a sheet cake, too?"

"Mom . . ."

"Maybe I should make both. It's just the last time I
hosted, there was too much food left over," she nattered on.

"Mom!"

"What?"

"I'm on my way out to go running. I don't have time to
talk about baked goods right now," I said.

"Well, I didn't mean to bother you."

Sigh.

"Don't be mad. It's just . . . Scott just stopped by. For the
last of his things," I explained.

My mother went silent at the mention of my ex-husband.

"Hello? Are you still there?" I asked.

"I don't know what to say. How did that go?"

"Quickly. I'd already put everything in a box, he just had
to pick it up," I said. "He seemed more upset about losing
the apartment than anything else. But I guess that makes
sense. He actually loved the apartment."

"You know, I never liked Scott. I thought it was a mistake
when you married him," Mom announced for the eight hun-
dredth time.

This was an outright lie. My mother loved Scott, and had
been thrilled when we announced our engagement. Despite
her own failed marriage, she'd been stereotypically desperate

to see me wedded, to the extent that I sometimes felt like the older spinster sister in a Jane Austen novel. And I'm sure Scott had seemed like the perfect prospective son-in-law—he was kind, successful, ambitious, polished—and there was no reason to think that he was anything other than who he appeared to be.

"That's not helpful," I said.

"I don't know what else to say. Whenever I do say anything about your divorce, or Scott, you get angry at me," she said.

"I do not," I said, and I could hear the tone of my voice rising in pitch. I took a deep breath, before continuing in a calmer tone of voice. "I just wish you'd be a little more supportive. Please?"

"I am supportive. And I think the best thing to do is to just put this entire mess behind you. You should start getting out, meeting men, dating. I'm sure it will just be a matter of time until you meet someone new, get married again, and you'll forget this ever happened," Mom said.

God, I can't stand it when she gets like this. I love my mother, and at her best, she's all the things I'm not—she's vivacious, personable, a born hostess. And she has an innate ability to make everyone—well, everyone but me—feel better about themselves. But when it comes to relationship advice, she always sounds like she's quoting from a 1950s dating manual for teens.

"I seriously doubt that I will ever forget that my husband left me because I have a vagina instead of a penis," I said dryly.

"Paige!"

"Well, it's true, isn't it? And I have no plans to start

dating, so please don't start trying to set me up with any-one," I said.

"I wasn't going to," my mother said, in a tone of voice that made it clear that was exactly what she was planning to do. "But, when you're ready, I do know a few nice available men—"

"No. I'm not interested," I said, cutting her off.

"Well, maybe not now . . ."

"Not ever. I'm serious. I'm too damn old to go through this again. From now on, it's just going to be me and my work, and that's enough," I said.

"You don't really mean that. You're just upset, and under-standably so. Just give it some time, honey. You'll meet the right man, and then you'll start feeling better, you'll see," she said.

"Don't you have it the wrong way? Aren't I supposed to feel better first, before I get involved with someone else?" I asked, knowing that I was baiting her. I couldn't help myself. I was so sick of everyone presuming that the two-by-two lifestyle was necessary for personal happiness. It certainly hadn't made me or my mother or any of my countless clients happy.

"No," Mom said firmly. "I don't think that you're going to get over this until you move on and meet someone new."

"Well, that's just not going to happen," I said. "Besides, talk about the pot and the kettle. You never remarried, and I can't remember the last time you went on a date."

"I don't tell you everything, you know. And for your in-formation, I *have* been seeing someone," Mom said.

"Really? Who? And since when?"

"Don't cross-examine me. I'll tell you when I'm ready. I

have to run, I need to get the brownies started. So you'll go by your sister's tomorrow?"

I considered this. Sophie and her husband, Aidan, lived on the north side of town, so it was hardly on my way home from the office. I'd have to fight my way through grinding commuter traffic to get up there, which would take at least forty-five minutes, maybe longer. But I felt a little guilty for snapping at my mom, and I knew she wouldn't let me off the phone until I agreed. And if I had to continue the conversation about my nonexistent love life or about her apparently thriving one, I'd lose my mind.

"Fine. I'll go. Bye," I said, and then hung up and went for a nice, long, anesthetizing run.

Chapter Two

W hat are you doing here?" Sophie asked suspiciously.
Her very round pregnant shape was blocking the
door to her mammoth white limestone house. It looked so
much like every other mammoth white limestone house in
the subdivision that I'd driven past it three times before remembering that Sophie's had an heirloom-rose bush planted
under the front bay window. When it was in bloom during
the hot summer months, the almost too-sweet scent of the
roses would envelop you as you entered the house.

"Doesn't anyone in this family ever say 'hello' anymore?"

"Hello. What are you doing here?"

"Mom made me come by. She thinks you're going nuts.
Are you going to let me in?"

Sophie tottered backwards, then stood with her enormous stomach pushed out, both hands propped against her
arched back. Under one of Aidan's blue oxford shirts, Soph
was wearing a white maternity tank top and a pair of black
capri leggings. She'd caught her wild blonde curls into a low
ponytail, and her toenails were painted dark purple.

"Mom is so fucking dramatic," she said. "And I'm fine, you didn't have to come all the way out here."

"She said you had a meltdown over some pastry."

Sophie rolled her eyes. "That's such an exaggeration. I was slightly upset that the bakery has stopped carrying those croissants that I love, and yes, I might have gotten a little peeved at the manager of the store when he told me that they wouldn't even let me special order them, but I didn't have a *meltdown*. What's in the box?"

I handed her the white bakery box I'd carried in with me. "Croissants. They carry the chocolate ones at a bakery near my office, so I stopped off on my way over and got you some."

Sophie whooped with joy, and waddled toward her kitchen faster than I would have thought possible, clutching the box to her chest.

"You are the most wonderful, perfect, amazing sister in the world!" Sophie called out.

I started to follow her into the kitchen and then stopped at the door.

"Uh . . . what's going on?" I asked.

The kitchen was a disaster. All of the cupboards had been torn down, the appliances were pushed together in the center of the room and draped with plastic sheeting, and what was left of the counter was covered with a light film of sawdust.

"Didn't I tell you? I decided to have the kitchen remodeled," Sophie said. She placed the pastry box on the island and began digging out a croissant for herself. "Want one?"

"No, thanks. When did you decide to do this?"

"Yesterday. I haven't told Aidan yet. He's in Houston for some stupid business thing, and I wanted to surprise him."

My eyebrows shot up. "You haven't told him that you're tearing apart your kitchen? Isn't he going to be mad?"

"No. I don't think so. Why? Do you think he'll be mad?" Sophie asked. Her voice was muffled by the piece of croissant she'd stuffed in her mouth.

I looked at the destruction before me and just shook my head. It wasn't as though the kitchen hadn't been gorgeous before. A month after two lines appeared on the home pregnancy test, Sophie and Aidan had sold their 1940s two-bedroom cottage in central Austin for this enormous house. I couldn't decide if I loved it—it was very chichi, with ten-foot ceilings, a posh master-bed-and-bath suite, and gorgeous hardwood floors throughout—or hated it, for how conventional it was. Aidan was a project manager at Dell and had fallen in step with every other executive there by staking out a McMansion on the north side of town. And their cottage had been adorable. They'd moved into it right after their wedding and had spent every spare weekend fixing it up. It was like they'd traded in the beloved family mutt for an aloof pedigreed whippet.

"Maybe you should sit down and rest," I said, in a tone so uncharacteristically gentle that Sophie shot me another suspicious look.

"I don't need to rest. Stop talking to me like I'm an idiot child," she said, her mouth twisting into the petulant pout she'd perfected at the age of two.

"Soph, you're losing it. Did you really get up this morning and decide to knock down all of your kitchen cupboards, without so much as mentioning it to your husband first? Does that sound like rational behavior to you?"

"I didn't decide on it this morning, and I didn't do it myself. I made an appointment with a builder weeks ago, and he came over yesterday, showed me some pictures of how gorgeous he could make the kitchen, and I decided just to go ahead and have it done. I want it to look nice for when the baby arrives."

"I don't think the baby will notice the kitchen."

"Well, I'll notice," Sophie insisted. Her voice was rising in pitch, and I sensed that one of my sister's legendary hormone-induced temper tantrums was about to erupt. A few weeks earlier we'd gone to see the new Renée Zellweger movie, and I'd had to practically tackle Sophie to keep her from throwing her soda at the couple sitting behind us in the theater when they wouldn't stop talking.

"Wait. You just hired the builder yesterday, and he was able to start work today? Most reputable builders have waiting lists. Remember how long it took me to get those bookshelves installed in my apartment? What kind of credentials does this guy have? Where did you find him? Is he bonded?" I asked.

Soph rolled her eyes. "You don't have to go all lawyerlike on me."

"I just think it's odd that a carpenter would be available so quickly."

"I had a last-minute cancellation," a male voice said.

I turned around and saw a man standing there, his shaggy brown hair and faded blue T-shirt flecked with sawdust.

"Plus, Mrs. O'Neill insisted that I start immediately. She's very persuasive," he said, grinning at Sophie, who in turn blushed prettily.

"I told you, call me Sophie," she said, giggling.

I stared at my sister. Sure, the guy was sort of cute, if you could get past the grubby clothes and the unshaven face that was reminiscent of a *Miami Vice*–era Don Johnson. Not my type, although he certainly wasn't repulsive. But Sophie was happily married and extremely pregnant. I would have thought her coquette days were behind her.

"Right. Sophie," he said.

"Zack, this is my older sister, Paige. Paige, this is Zack Duncan, who came highly recommended. He did Ashley and John's den. Remember? I told you about it. They had a built-in entertainment center installed, and also put in wood floors," Sophie said, ignoring the dirty look I shot her for the "older" crack.

Zack looked at me and smiled. His narrow lips curled up and engaged hazel brown eyes that drooped down at the outer edges. He reminded me of a grown-up version of the slick, good-looking, morally deficient guy who brags about his sexual exploits with his girlfriend and then ultimately loses her to the cute, sensitive, misunderstood guy in the PG-13 movies of my youth. The character James Spader was always cast to play.

"Nice to meet you," I said, keeping my voice cool enough so that he'd know I wasn't about to fall for his act. "Aren't you working late?"

"I was just on my way out," he said.

Zack stared at me for a few beats longer than I was comfortable with, but I'd be damned if I was going to look away first. I hadn't succeeded as a litigator by allowing men to intimidate me, although enough of them had certainly tried. Some men were just threatened by strong women, and pulled all kinds of aggressive crap in order to dominate—they'd raise their voices, move toward you suddenly, try staring you down. I'd faced it all before in court. I raised my chin up a few millimeters and held his gaze.

Suddenly Zack grinned at me and winked, before turning his attention back to Sophie as she asked him about the placement of the island. I flushed and felt disproportionately pissed off. Maybe it's that I've never been able to abide winkers (I always feel like they're making fun of me), or maybe it was that I was suddenly extraneous, just standing there, overdressed and rigid, while Soph and Zack leaned over the counter to look at a sketch Zack had made on a scrap of a brown paper grocery bag. They looked like actors in a coffee commercial, all pink cheeks, gesturing arms, adorable pregnant belly.

"I'm going to go," I said abruptly.

"What?" Sophie looked up from the plans. "You just got here, and besides, you have to stay for dinner. Aidan's gone, and I hate eating alone."

"It's just . . . ," I started, and then stopped when I saw that Zack was also looking at me. His smile was pleasant enough, but I got the distinct impression that he was amused by my discomfort. Irritation rubbed at me.

"Okay. Fine. I'll stay. I need to borrow some sweats," I said, and walked out of the demolished kitchen and across the living room to Soph's bedroom before she could answer.

I rifled through her drawers and withdrew a black sweatshirt and matching cropped yoga pants. I stripped off my clothes—after first making sure that I'd shut the door firmly behind me—and pulled on the pants. The bedroom door swung open before I could shrug the top on, and I froze, clutching the sweatshirt to my chest.

"It's just me. Why are you being such a freak?" Sophie asked.

"Close the door," I hissed. With the door open there was a straight view into the bedroom from the kitchen.

"Why? Oh, Zack just left for the day, if that's what you're worried about. God, isn't he gorgeous?" Sophie said dreamily as she heaved herself down on the bed. "He looks like he should be on one of those home decorating shows on HGTV, don't you think? You know, the ones where they surprise people by redecorating their house? There's always a hunky carpenter wandering around in a skintight T-shirt. Mmmm. God, these pregnancy hormones make me so horny."

"Actually, I thought he was kind of a jerk. Very arrogant," I said. I pulled on the black hoodie and zipped up the front, then examined myself in the mirror over the dresser. I looked tired. When I was younger and still had the energy to go out to clubs on the weekend, black had been the dominant color in my wardrobe. Now it just served to highlight the dark circles under my eyes.

"Really? I don't think so at all. He seems like a really nice guy. In fact . . . I think he was interested in you," she said.

"What? Why? What did he say?"

"So you do think he's hot."

"I do not!"

"Yes you do. Do you want me to set you up?" she asked mischievously.

"No! No, no, no," I said.

"Why not? You're not seeing anyone, and I know he's not," Sophie said.

Uh-oh, I thought. Sophie had been obsessed with Jane Austen's *Emma* while we were growing up, but my sister was, without a doubt, the worst matchmaker in the history of the world. Soph never seemed to have any sense of compatibility, and always just assumed that two people she liked and found interesting just had to be perfect for each other. Even if one was a Deadhead and the other a chorus nerd. And her judgment on such matters hadn't evolved much since high school.

I hated Emma. Jo from *Little Women* was much more my style.

"Don't do that. Don't try to set me up," I said.

"Okay, fine, I won't. But just so you know, I already gave him your number."

"You what?"

"Why are you yelling at me? Your work number, I mean. He has a custody issue he's dealing with, and he needs an attorney. I told him that you're the Terminator of lawyers."

"Gee, thanks."

"I thought you'd be happy about the referral," Sophie said.

"Yeah, that's just what I need. Another obnoxious client," I said.

"Well then, if he calls you, tell him you're not taking on any new clients. God, why are you acting so weird? You're even twitchier and more argumentative than usual," Sophie said.

Why did I allow my mother to manipulate me into coming over here? I wondered. I could be home right now, watching the Home Shopping Network—my secret guilty pleasure—and painting my toenails instead of putting up with this abuse. I was going to be so glad when Sophie's hormones stabilized and she stopped being such a complete pain in the ass.

"Nothing. It's just . . ." I paused. "Mom was on a tear yesterday about wanting me to start dating again, and I told her it's not gonna happen. I thought maybe she was trying to enlist you in her campaign."

"Oh, yeah, she told me about that. Something about how you're planning on staying single forever."

"Don't roll your eyes, I'm serious. Ever since I made partner, I've been buried in work, so I don't have time to date. Besides, why is it so wrong to want to focus on my career? Men do it all the time. Why can't a woman do the same thing?" I asked.

"They can. Being a single woman in your thirties is very hot right now. It's all about amazing shoes and cocktails and sex without consequences," Sophie said.

"Yeah, right," I snorted. Sophie and Aidan had met in college, so she had no idea what it was really like out there now. "Dating in your thirties is just as bad as dating in your twenties, only the men have a lot more baggage. Ex-wives, custody disputes, and impotence. Trust me, I know. A stream of newly single men file through my office every day. And I think Austin is worse than most other cities. If I see one more guy clinging to the revolting 'I'm an evolved man' uniform of little John Lennon glasses, a goatee, and Teva sandals, and referring to everyone as 'dude,' I'm going to lose it," I continued.

"Your clients tell you they're impotent?" Sophie asked.

"No. I'm just guessing about that part from all of the Viagra commercials I keep seeing on television. There seems to be an epidemic." I smiled without humor, remembering Scott's constant stream of excuses for not wanting to have sex. He kept claiming it was natural for a couple's sex life to wane after being together for a few years. "I suggested to Scott that he try Viagra. I couldn't figure out why an otherwise healthy thirty-eight-year-old man wasn't able to maintain an erection."

Sophie grimaced. "Not your fault, Paige. You know that, right?" she said.

"Well, I'm not stupid. I know I didn't turn him off of women. But I'm tired of being told not to take it personally," I said, shrugging.

"I think you should see someone. A therapist. Your divorce and your job are making you bitter," Sophie said.

"I'm way past bitter," I said. "Way, way past it. I've also zipped past disillusioned, cynical, and distrustful."

"I'm serious. This whole thing about how you're not going to date anymore—I'm sure that's a very normal reaction after what you've gone through. And anger is healthy. But withdrawing from life is not, especially since it's been two years since you split up."

"I'm not withdrawing. I have my work and my family and friends. That's enough. Not all people have to take the same path, you know. Not everyone is cut out for marriage. In fact, it's offensive and sexist to assume that I have to be attached to a man in order to be a whole person," I said.

"I'm not saying that! I just don't think it's healthy to embrace a monastic lifestyle just because you were married to a gay man. The relationship was doomed to fail from the start," Sophie said.

I considered this. "Monastic" wasn't a particularly appealing adjective to get slapped with.

"Maybe . . . ," I said slowly.

Sophie brightened. "Really?" she said eagerly. She was so transparent, I could practically hear her mentally reviewing the list of guys she could set me up with.

"I'm through with serious relationships. But that doesn't mean I should have to give up sex, right? Confirmed bachelors don't. They have their swank apartments with mirrored ceilings and their little black books, and date all kinds of women without ever getting serious about anyone," I said, my enthusiasm for the idea growing.

Sophie looked at me blankly. "Mirrored ceilings? You're kidding, right?"

"Well, yeah, maybe about that part. But I think I'm onto something here. You were just saying that there's a renaissance of the thirty-something single woman. I could be a part of that. Why not? I could get out there, meet some new men, have some completely anonymous sex—what did Erica Jong called it? The zipless fuck? It's a fantastic idea. Maybe I'll even start with your handyman," I said, just to needle her.

"Zack? I thought you weren't interested in him."

"I'm not. That's the point. At least, I'm not interested in his mind. His body's a different story. . . ."

"Paige! You're not serious, are you?"

"What? You were just telling me I need to get back out there. Do you think Zack would be up for a fling?"

"Not Zack. I know he's a hottie, but he's a really nice guy.

Way too nice to be treated like he's disposable," Sophie protested.

"Hottie," I repeated, and snorted. "Who says that? Are you auditioning for *The Real World*?"

"That's an idea. Do you think they'd be interested in casting a thirty-two-year-old married pregnant woman? But really . . . you're just joking about Zack, right? Right?"

She looked so anxious, I couldn't bring myself to torture her any longer.

"Don't worry, I won't seduce your man candy. I meant what I said—I have no intention of ever dating again. Now, what's for dinner?" I asked, deliberately changing the subject.

"Whatever you go pick up," Sophie said, lolling back on her side, one hand resting on her huge belly. "I don't have a kitchen, and I'm too tired to move."

Chapter Three

I first met Owen Malloy in law school when he lived in the other half of a duplex I rented near campus. He was a pale-skinned, freckle-faced smart-ass with coppery red hair, which had thinned considerably in the nine years since we graduated. Owen was now an assistant district attorney for Travis County, and had worked his way up from prosecuting shoplifters to major felonies. He was also gay, and the only person outside of my family whom I'd told the real reason why Scott and I had divorced.

"I heard some gossip about your ex-husband," Owen said, looking keenly at me.

We'd met for lunch at P.F. Chang's, a Chinese restaurant near my office. I was having the Szechuan Beef, and Owen was scarfing down the Orange Peel Shrimp.

"Let me have a bite," I said, my fork hovering near his plate.

"No, go away. You know I hate sharing," Owen said. "So, you don't want to know my Scott gossip?"

I shrugged. I did, of course, but I also didn't want to seem too eager.

"Don't tell me . . . he's changed his mind and decided he's straight again," I said.

"No, it doesn't work that way. Once we turn them over to our side, they never go back," Owen said, rubbing his hands together with Machiavellian glee.

"So, tell me your gossip."

"Yeah, I knew you were just pretending you weren't interested," Owen said. His appealing grin appeared, and I thought, as I often had in the past, that while Owen was not a handsome man, his face possessed a homely elegance. "Anton saw Scott out at Club DeVille the other night. He was with Kevin Stern—the pastry chef at that new restaurant, Versa. It's very hot right now, and Kevin is considered to be quite the catch. I know four different guys who've been trying to hook up with him."

I digested this. While my love life had been labeled "monastic," my ex-husband was now sleeping with someone who could whip up a postcoital Baked Alaska. And who was considered a catch by most of the Austin gay community. I wondered if I'd ever been considered a catch, and thought probably not. I know that on days when I make an effort with my hair, makeup, and clothes, I'd be considered pretty, but my angular face and prickly nature would forever keep me out of the beautiful range.

"A catch," I repeated. I pushed my Szechuan Beef to the side, and Owen—who had no problem sharing other people's food—dug in. "And what's Kevin like? Gay all along, or did he suddenly decide to switch sides, too?"

"I don't think straight people just decide to be gay," Owen said.

"I know. That was my lame attempt at a joke, to show that I don't care anymore."

"Yeah, I got that."

"When did you first know? We've never talked about it," I said.

Owen shrugged. "As far back as I can remember. It never occurred to me to pretend to be something I'm not. But I know that's not true for everyone. There are men who stay in the closet until they're in their forties or fifties or forever. Just be glad that Scott didn't wait that long."

I tried to decide whether or not I was glad. I'd gotten past grieving for my marriage—and it obviously wasn't something Scott was dwelling on—and anyway, now that I knew he preferred men, it wasn't like that cat could ever be stuffed back into the bag. If I was still upset about anything, it was that I hadn't figured it out before he told me, before we made the enormous mistake of getting married. Because, really, how could I *not* have known Scott was gay? I was his wife, his partner, his lover. How blind could I have been?

And short of leaving around stacks of gay porn, there had been plenty of signs that later, once I knew the truth, seemed obvious in retrospect. Scott had been depressed for months, had started to shy away from any physical contact with me. And then there was the big clue, the one that should have hit me over the head like a cartoon frying pan: he'd admitted to me that he'd been with a man before, back when he was in college. Scott had laughed it off when he told me about it early on in our relationship, before we married, while we were lying in bed together and playing the dangerous game of confessing past exploits. He said it was a one-time thing, it had happened when he was drunk, and it embarrassed him to talk about it now. The way he explained it, it had sounded natural, normal even—the result of over-active hormones, too much to drink, and the hard-partying college lifestyle.

I had felt squeamish when he told me. I've always abhorred homophobia in any form, and I never thought I would be bothered by the story of a homosexual encounter. But when one of those two men was my boyfriend and later husband . . . well, it had bothered me, even if I hadn't wanted to admit it to Scott or even to myself.

I broke open my fortune cookie and read the message out loud: " 'The greatest danger could be your stupidity.' Very nice," I muttered, crumpling it up in my hand. "Just what I was hoping for today, a hostile fortune."

"Maybe you were meant to have mine: 'All is not yet lost,' " Owen read.

"Ha-ha."

"Seriously, Paige, you need to cheer up. I haven't seen you crack a smile in months. And are you ever going to start dating again?" Owen asked.

"That's all anyone seems capable of talking about lately. My mother, Sophie, now you," I said irritably.

"There's a reason why. It's time. You can't spend the rest of your life moping around over Scott," he said.

"No, it's not that. It isn't about him."

"Then what is it?"

I shrugged. It was my new favorite gesture and pretty much summed up how I felt about every aspect of my life.

"Ah, our little Paige seems to be suffering from ennui. And for that, there's only one cure," Owen said.

"Oh yeah, what's that?"

"You have to get laid. You have to fuck Scott and the entire sordid mess that was your marriage out of your memory," Owen pronounced.

"Nice mouth," I commented.

Owen snorted. "This coming from the woman who could curse a sailor under the table. But all kidding aside, it'll really work. Trust me, I'm a gay man, I know these things."

"What things?"

"Sex things."

"No, you know gay sex things, but you don't know anything about straight sex things."

"That's not true. I went through a phase in middle school where I read through all of my mother's bodice-ripper romance novels. And let me tell you, if I wasn't already gay, those things would have scared me off of women for good. All of those petticoats they had to wade through just to get to third base," Owen said, shaking his head in disbelief that any man—swashbuckling pirate or other—would want to attempt such a thing.

I stared at him. "Is there a point anywhere in there?"

"Yes. The point is, you need to reconnect with your sensual side. So go forth and find a hot guy, preferably a dumb one so you won't have to make conversation with him, and lure him into your bed. It's a surefire cure for your ennui."

"Sophie and I were just talking about this the other day. I told her I was going to have a one-night stand, but I was just trying to shock her," I said.

"See, great minds think alike."

I had to admit the idea was tempting. I did miss sex more

than I thought I would, and I'd already run through all of the new releases at Blockbuster.

"Where am I supposed to find this hot-yet-dumb guy? I'm too old for the bar scene," I said.

"Just ask, and the universe will provide," Owen said.

"That's the dumbest thing I've ever heard."

"I thought so, too, at first, but Anton has been on a real kick about the power of positive thinking and it's rubbing off on me."

Anton was Owen's boyfriend. He spent a lot of time meditating, and had a kooky New Age theory for just about everything. His life philosophy was that you should never work even a single day in a job you don't love, so he was chronically unemployed and had been mooching off Owen for years. I'd always thought that Owen could do better, but since there wasn't a tactful way for me to express this opinion, I kept my mouth shut.

"What if the universe just sends me another closeted gay man?" I asked.

"That's where it comes in handy to have a gay friend. We come equipped with Gaydar. Just point me at your man, and I'll let you know his orientation," Owen promised.

"I could have used your Gaydar with Scott," I said.

"Yeah, yeah. I think it was on the blink. But I really only met him briefly, once at your wedding and once when I ran into you at the Arboretum, and both times he shied away from me," Owen said.

"I can't imagine why," I said dryly. During the course of my marriage, I'd attempted to set up a few dinners with Owen and Anton, but Scott had always had an excuse for not wanting to socialize with them. Since I preferred to see

Owen without Anton anyway, I never pushed it, but I'd wondered at the time if Scott's reluctance to get together with
them might stem from some latent homophobia. Now I knew
it was just another sign that I should have clued into.

One of the soft cruelties of divorce is that you're forever
digging up memories and reexamining them in the light of
the split.

"Thanks for the Gaydar offer, but I don't think I'll need it.
I'll admit, the idea of a fling does sound tempting, but I can't
think of anything less appealing than going on yet another
first date with some pompous asshole who will undoubtedly
spend the entire night talking about himself, and then afterwards try to paw at my breasts in the front seat of his car," I
continued.

"Well then, stay away from the pompous assholes. Find
someone who's totally not your type, and keep it as anonymous and uncomplicated as you can," Owen said. "But I'm
telling you, you need to get laid, kiddo. You need it bad."

Chapter Four

I'm willing to chip in some for the kids, but I don't see why she should get anything. I've supported her for twelve friggin' years, while she sat at home on her ass. Mrs. Hector is . . . what do you call it? Underemployed? She's underemployed. It's time that bitch got a job and supported herself," John Hector announced, thumping his hand on the walnut conference table for emphasis.

I took a deep breath and then exhaled slowly. If it wasn't bad enough that my asshole client kept referring to his wife as "that bitch" or the slightly less hostile "Mrs. Hector," or that he was trying to wriggle out of paying child support for his own kids, it was his fault that the Hectors were getting divorced in the first place. Alicia Hector had tossed her husband out when she discovered he was cheating on her. With the twenty-year-old babysitter. While Alicia Hector was five months pregnant. Which was actually rather a fascinating phenomenon, because her husband was a short, fat, hairy little pimple of a man, and it was stunning to think that a young girl would find him even remotely attractive.

I dearly wished that Alicia had been the one to hire me,

instead of John, because I would have so enjoyed ripping him into shreds during his deposition. But such was the lot of the divorce attorney—if you only agreed to represent clients who were gracious and kind and all-around nice people, you'd quickly starve.

"Mr. Hector. I think that we should be realistic. You don't have a choice about the child support. Under Texas law, you're required to pay an amount set by statute each month. The house would fall under community property, so if we can't offset the value, we'll argue that the house should be sold and the proceeds divided between you and Mrs. Hector. However, I should let you know that she would like to retain possession of the house until your youngest child leaves for college," I began.

"What? No friggin' way! That would be eighteen years! If anyone should get the friggin' house, it should be me. And I don't see why I should have to split anything with that bitch," Mr. Hector fumed.

I indulged in a brief fantasy of leaping across the table and stabbing Mr. Hector in the eye with my silver Tiffany pen. But since I wasn't quite yet ready to be carted off to jail, I instead snapped the cap onto my pen, closed my leather folio, and abruptly stood up.

"What, are we done already?" he asked.

"Yes, I have another client waiting for me. But I'll talk to Mrs. Hector's attorney tomorrow, and get back to you next week on how the negotiations are going. Wait here, and I'll have my assistant bring you those documents after she photocopies them," I said, and then smoothly exited the room before Mr. Hector could launch into another tirade about how he shouldn't have to pay for his children's health insurance or make yet another disgusting innuendo about how much of a ladies' man he was.

I couldn't bear spending one more minute with him. Hector—and every other divorced man out there like him—was just one more reason why I was never going to get emotionally involved with a man ever again. Just thinking about it made my stomach churn with anger, and my skin felt hot and stretched too tightly over my face.

Men, I thought. Cheating, lying, shitty, asshole men. Every last one of them.

I closed the door of the conference room tightly and then paused, trying to collect myself. There was no reason to let John Hector get to me. Yes, he was a repulsive individual, but I'd dealt with clients just like him—worse even—for years, and I'd never let any of them get to me before. The only way to make it in this business was to keep a clearly defined distance from the work. You don't befriend your clients, and you also don't waste energy fantasizing about attacking them Ninja-style.

"Will you please bring Mr. Hector his papers and then see him out, Sue?" I asked, pausing by the desk of my wonderfully efficient assistant to pick up my messages.

"Sure will. And Mr. Duncan is waiting for you in your office," Sue said perkily.

Sue sported a year-round tan and wore her spiky hair short and burgundy red. She was the peppiest person I'd ever known—everything was always great, wonderful, chirp, chirp, chirp.

"Duncan? Who's that?"

"He's a new client, something to do with a custody issue.

He said he was referred by Sophie," Sue said, reading from the notes she'd recorded on the computerized calendar.

"Sophie . . . ," I repeated, and then glanced through the window of the door to my office. It was Sophie's carpenter, Zack. He was sitting at an angle, his back to the door, so I could only see a profile of his face, highlighted by the afternoon sun that streamed in.

The annoying winker, I thought, my heart sinking. Just when I thought my day couldn't get any worse.

Zack turned suddenly and looked over his shoulder.

"Oh no. Oh God," I said, and jumped back.

"What's wrong?" Sue asked, staring at me.

"It's just . . . do you have a mirror?"

Sue rummaged through her purse. "Yes, here. And you'd better take this lipstick, too. He's really cute."

"You think?" I asked, and flipped open the compact. I stared at my face, wondering if I really looked that sallow, or if it was just the effect of the fluorescent lighting, the archenemy of aging female skin. I dabbed on some of Sue's red lip-gloss, and that seemed to help. But there was nothing I could do about the dark circles under my eyes or the streaks of gray I hadn't gotten around to rinsing out of my hair.

"How do I look?" I asked Sue, who was now staring at me as though I had just sprouted an extra head. "What?"

"Nothing. You look great. It's just . . . I've never seen you like this," Sue said.

"Like what?"

"Nervous."

"I'm not! He's just a client, I barely know him. And what I do know of him, I don't like."

"Whatever you say," Sue said, and nodded toward my office. "Go get him, tiger."

I smoothed my hands over the jacket of my charcoal gray pantsuit and fretted that it was too masculine looking. And maybe I shouldn't have let my stylist talk me into cutting my dark, straight, shoulder-length hair into such severe bangs. Sure, it looked great on all of the movie starlets, but what if it made me look like a dominatrix? Or a witch? I self-consciously tucked my hair behind my ears and then changed my mind and untucked it.

I gave myself a mental shake. What was the hell was I doing? It was ridiculous worrying about what Zack thought of me. He was a potential client, nothing more, and I didn't even like him. And I'd certainly dealt with good-looking men before, without getting all fluttery and girly. In fact, I wasn't even attracted to pretty men. Not that Zack was pretty, at least not in a toothpaste commercial kind of way. But Sophie was right, he looked just like one of those quirky carpenters who provide the eye candy on home improvement shows.

I took a deep, calming breath, sucked in my stomach, and pushed the door open to my office. Zack looked up at me as I entered, and he stood, smiling.

"Hi there," Zack said.

Gone were the *Miami Vice* face stubble and soiled work clothes. Today he was clean-shaven and dressed neatly in khakis and a button-down white shirt.

"Hello," I said, and smiled coolly at him as I walked around my desk and sat down. "How can I help you, Mr. Duncan?"

"Please call me Zack."

"All right. Zack." I nodded at him, encouraging him to

continue. The sooner he told me what he was doing there, the sooner I could send him on his way.

"It's about my stepdaughter, Grace," Zack began, and then he stopped. "Or, ex-stepdaughter, I guess, since her mom and I are divorced."

"And your ex-wife is . . . ," I asked, my voice trailing off in a question, as I began to take neatly printed notes on a yellow legal pad: Zack Duncan. Divorced. Stepdaughter: Grace.

"Molly. Molly Fogel. We were married for a year, and Grace is her daughter from a previous relationship," Zack said.

"Was Ms. Fogel married to Grace's father?"

"No. And he's not in the picture."

"And is your divorce final?"

"Yes. It's been over a year. And Molly was letting me see Grace a few times a week up until about a month ago. Now she's getting married again, and she's decided she doesn't want me to have any more contact with Grace. She thinks it will complicate things if I stay in her life. That's why I'm here—I was hoping there was some way I could get a court order to see Grace. I know we're not biologically related, but I'm the only father she's known."

Zack leaned forward as he spoke, repeatedly clasping and unclasping his hands in front of him.

He's nervous. Nervous and obviously upset, I thought. My animosity toward him deflated. Who was this guy? Macho man candy, or dedicated family guy? Could he be both? Certainly not in my experience.

"How old is Grace?" I asked.

"She's four," Zack said, and he pulled out his wallet, flipped through it, and pulled out a small color photo of a smiling chubby-cheeked girl with a head full of brunette curls. The picture looked like it had been taken at one of those inexpensive mall studios, and Grace had been put in a forced pose—her head tipped to one side, resting on her hands, an ugly basket of plastic tulips in front of her.

"She's precious. Look . . . Zack . . . the custody laws in Texas, in most states, have a very strong presumption in favor of the biological parents. And since you didn't legally adopt Grace during your marriage to her mother, you just don't have any standing to seek visitation. Perhaps if your ex-wife wasn't a fit mother . . ."

"No, no. Molly's great with Grace," Zack said quickly.

"I'm sorry, I don't think there's anything I can do to help you," I said. I laid my pen down on top of the yellow pad.

"I just thought . . . it doesn't seem right that Molly could cut me out of Grace's life like that. We'd talked about my adopting Grace, but then . . ." Zack hesitated, and seemed to be weighing whether he should continue. He sighed and suddenly looked tired. "Well, there's no point in getting into it, I guess. It looks like I don't have a choice."

"I really am sorry. For what it's worth, I think it's wonderful that you want to stay involved," I said impulsively. "Too many of the divorcing parents I deal with don't seem to care about their own kids, much less try to seek visitation for their stepchildren."

I normally try to avoid making personal comments about a client's life—it was a rookie mistake I hadn't made since I first started practicing law. One sympathetic comment, and suddenly my clients would think I was their best friend/

shrink/mom, rather than a disinterested professional, and take to calling me constantly, asking for advice, divulging far more of their personal business than I'm comfortable hearing. It was much easier to keep everything on an entirely professional level, for everyone involved. But I felt unusually sympathetic to Zack's plight, perhaps because I was starting to wonder if I'd misjudged him at our first meeting.

Zack just shrugged in response, and then looked out my window at the view of downtown Austin and the tree-dotted grounds of the state capitol building. He was silent for a few beats and then glanced back over at me and said, "Would you like to have dinner with me?"

"Dinner?" I repeated. "Why?"

Zack smiled, and I flushed, realizing how ridiculous I must sound.

"It's just that we don't really know one another," I said.

"Sophie said you weren't seeing anyone, and I thought . . . well, she seemed to think you'd be open to the idea of going out with me," Zack said.

I should have known. Sophie was up to her old tricks, even after I'd explicitly told her to butt out. I opened my mouth to say *No, thank you, I'm not interested.* But something stopped me. After all, wasn't Zack exactly the kind of man Owen had urged me to have a fling with?

The thought made me swallow hard. The whole idea had just been a lark, something to laugh about with Owen . . . hadn't it? One-night stands were not—and had never been— my thing. Life was easiest when you stayed on a routine— eating the same things, working the same hours, watching the same kinds of shows on television. There was an ordered calmness to it all, and it was a sort of happiness to always know what was just around the corner. Love affairs, even if only physical, can wreak havoc on all that.

But then, wasn't that supposed to be the whole point of the no-strings fling? You get to indulge in the physical pleasure without the baggage. And if I didn't take the plunge now, when would I? Would the weak-chinned, beady-eyed tax lawyer who'd asked me to lunch last week, for whom I felt nothing but a mild revulsion, really be a better candidate?

"Sure. Dinner sounds . . . okay, why not," I said, and tried to shrug off the alarm bells that were going off inside my head.

It's just dinner, I lectured myself. If I can't go through with the strings-free sex, I just won't. I don't have to decide that now.

"Enthusiasm. I like that," Zack said, and when I opened up my mouth, gaping like a fish, he said, "Kidding. I was just kidding."

"Oh," I said, and felt absurdly stupid. This was why I hate being teased, I always end up feeling like everyone's laughing at me. Why was I letting myself be put in this position?

"Maybe this isn't . . . ," I started to say, but Zack just shook his head.

"No backing out now. A deal's a deal. Is five o'clock too early to pick you up? We're going to need a little extra time to get to where we're going," Zack said.

I stared at him, fairly sure that I'd just been outmaneuvered. It didn't happen often.

Chapter Five

"This should be an interesting evening," I muttered to myself, as I rushed into my apartment at 4:50 p.m.

I'd been planning to leave work even earlier—which was something I never did, and felt like a juvenile delinquent as I slipped out the back door of our office, looking over my shoulder guiltily while I waited for the elevator—but I hadn't been able to get off the phone with a teary client who was convinced that her estranged husband was going to get his hands on her doll collection. Now I had to hurry to change, swapping out the gray suit for a pair of boot-cut khakis and a sleek black boat-neck top.

The phone rang, and I clicked the on button, then tucked it between my ear and shoulder so I could keep my hands free for applying eyeliner and mascara.

"Hello," I said, leaning toward the mirror as I carefully smudged a black charcoal pencil along my upper lash line.

"Hey, it's me. Have you talked to Mom recently?" my sister Mickey asked.

"Where are you?"

"Where do you think? I'm at school," Mickey said. She

was in her senior year at Princeton and had already been accepted into Brown Medical School. Mickey was nauseatingly successful at everything, balancing her schoolwork and a nonstop social schedule with an effortless, offbeat charm. She was the person I wanted to be when I grew up.

"Can I call you back? I'm going out," I said.

"Ooh, hot date?"

"No. Not really. I wouldn't call it a date."

"I thought you swore off dating."

"Who told you that?"

"Mom. And Sophie. So, tell, tell. Who's your new guy?"

"No one. Really."

"So I know him?"

"No! And he's not my guy. He's just a guy. And it's not really a date, because I don't plan on ever seeing him again after tonight," I said.

"Then why won't you tell me who he is?"

"Okay, I'll tell you, but you have to promise you won't tell Sophie," I said.

"Why?"

"Promise."

"I promise. Soph is kind of scary these days, anyway. I called her a few days ago—Nick and I were going to see the new John Cusack movie, and I knew she'd just seen it, so I wanted to hear a review—and she yelled at me and told me to never, ever interrupt her when she's watching *Survivor*. So who is he?" Mickey asked.

"You don't know him. He's Sophie's contractor," I said.

"The hot one?"

"She told you about him?"

"Yeah! His name's Zack, right? He's pretty much all she

would talk about, once she stopped freaking out that I was bothering her during her precious show. I think she has a crush on him. Is that why you're not telling her that you're going out with him?" Mickey asked.

I put down the mascara wand and swished a MAC brush into a container of blush and then swept it onto my cheekbones.

"Of course not. And Sophie doesn't really have a crush on Zack, she's just a little hormonal right now."

"Then why don't you want her to know you're dating him?"

"First of all, I'm not dating him. We're just going out this one time, and it's not even technically a date. And second, I am going to tell Sophie, I'm just going to wait until after our . . . non-date thing. Anyway, I have to go, I'm running late. I'll talk to you later."

"Wait! The reason why I called: Have you talked to Mom lately?"

I frowned. "Mmm, I can't remember. I think we talked a few days ago. Why?"

"Because I'm getting a weird vibe from her. And when I called her yesterday, Dad was over at her house," Mickey said.

I dropped my MAC brush.

"What?" I asked. "But she and Dad hate each other."

Our parents' divorce had not been amicable. They'd never gotten along, bickering constantly while we were growing up, and then one day, my mother had announced that if she had to cook my father one more dinner or iron one more of his shirts, she'd—and this is a direct quote—"lose her fucking mind," and then had gone on a strike. She spent her days sitting on the couch reading astrological charts while the laundry piled up, the refrigerator overflowed with containers of stale take-out, and an aggressive mold took over the grout on the tub. A month later my father moved out, hired a cleaning lady for his new apartment, and immediately started dating one of his graduate students. This shot across my mother's bow marked the official commencement of hostilities. She turned around and sold off my father's golf clubs, his beloved collection of toy trains, and all of the clothes he left behind in an impromptu garage sale. My father retaliated by closing their joint credit card accounts. My mother changed the locks on the house. My father refused to pay for the garbage pickup. And on and on it went.

Soph and I were already out of the house by that point—I was in law school, Soph was in college—so we were spared the worst of it. But Mickey was only twelve when they separated, and so she became yet one more thing that they argued endlessly about, first directly and then through their lawyers. It was truly a miracle that Mickey was now as happy and well adjusted as she was, and I always felt a tug of guilt that I hadn't been around more to help protect her from the chaos.

"I don't think they do anymore. I know they've been talking for the past few months. Mom tried to hide it from me, but she kept slipping and mentioning things that Dad had told her," Mickey said.

"That's just so weird. Maybe it was a business thing? Something to do with the house?"

"I don't think so. Mom said she was going out to dinner, and although she didn't say who she was going with, I could hear Dad talking in the background. You don't think it was a date, do you?"

The very thought gave me shivers. After everything they'd put all of us through with the Divorce from Hell, if they even considered getting back together, I'd have to kill them both.

"Not possible," I said.

"I swear, I heard him. He was telling her to hurry up because he wanted to beat the crowds," Mickey said.

This did sound suspiciously like Dad. "Beating the crowds" had been a recurring theme of our childhood. He'd prefer eating dinner out at five in the evening at one of the least popular restaurants in town rather than risk having to wait ten minutes for a table.

"What did she say when you asked her?"

"I didn't have a chance. She just said she'd talk to me later and hung up," Mickey said. I could hear the sharp edges of panic in her voice, and it worried me.

"Try not to think about it, Mick. I'm sure it's nothing— this is *them* we're talking about—and you've got enough to deal with up there. I'll talk to Sophie and see if she's heard anything," I said. "Besides, Mom already told me that she's seeing someone else."

"That's a relief. Who is he?"

"Actually . . . I'm not sure. She wouldn't say," I said, remembering how mysterious Mom had been about her new boyfriend.

"It's Dad!" Mickey wailed.

"No, I'm sure it's not Dad. Really, Mick, you know how they feel about each other," I said.

"What should I say when Mom calls me tomorrow?"

"How do you know she will?"

"She calls me every day."

"She does? Since when?"

"Since forever."

I closed my eyes and shook my head. *Typical.* Mickey, my parents' surprise baby—they'd gone on a second honeymoon to Hawaii, and nine months later Mickey had arrived—had always been Mom's favorite. I fought off the jealousy by reminding myself just how insane it would make me if Mom were calling me every day.

My door buzzer sounded. "Crap. He's here, and I'm not ready. Mick, honey, I've got to run. I'll call you later."

Chapter Six

❧ ✿ ❧

Zack held out his hand to help me jump down out of his bright red 1955 Chevrolet pickup truck (I knew the year only because Zack had told me, his face beaming with unmistakable pride). The truck was pretty cool in a retro kind of a way, which was a very popular aesthetic in Austin, along with vintage clothing, VW vans, and record stores that still sold vinyl LPs.

We'd taken Route 2222, a lovely drive that winds through the limestone cliffs and densely wooded areas west of Austin, toward Lake Travis, and had pulled into the parking lot for the Travis County Marina. I wasn't familiar with the area, but it didn't look like there was a restaurant anywhere in the vicinity.

"What are we doing here?" I asked.

"Having dinner, like I promised," Zack said, and when he smiled at me, I briefly considered ripping off my bra and throwing it at him.

Somehow, over the course of the scenic drive, I'd fallen seriously in lust with this guy. Maybe it was because I'd already halfway made the decision to sleep with him, or maybe it was because Sophie was right—Zack was a "hottie." He was just so solidly masculine. Zack had a thick chest, sexy hips, and long, muscular legs. And he had the nicest hands—they were large and square, and when he held out his hand to help me out of the truck, I noticed they felt soft, which struck me as odd for a carpenter. I'd have expected them to be rough and calloused.

"But where?"

"That's the surprise. I brought dinner with us," Zack said, and pulled a blue cooler from the bed of the pickup.

I looked around. "Are there tables out here? Overlooking the lake?"

I had to give him points for originality. And it was a gorgeous October evening, the perfect weather for a picnic. It was warm enough that I was comfortable in elbow-length sleeves, and yet the heavy damp humidity that marked the long, uncomfortable summer had mercifully chosen not to linger.

"I thought we could eat out on the lake. On my boat," Zack suggested.

"You have a boat?"

"Come on, I'll show you."

I followed him as the pavement of the parking lot gave way to a dirt and gravel path. We wound around the main building, a rustic, two-story structure with a screened-in porch that faced the glassy blue lake, down a steep incline, and then finally onto the long, sun-bleached dock where boats were lined up smartly in their individual slips. The majority were motorboats, some tall and opulent, others squat and utilitarian. I figured Zack's would probably be one of the latter, but he surprised me by stopping at a white sailboat, small in size and impeccably maintained. The mast was up, although the sails were down, piling up on either side like a deflated parachute.

Zack hopped nimbly onto the boat and reached for my hand. The water gently lapped against the hull as the boat shifted under his weight. I hesitated, my feet firmly planted to the creaking dock.

"I have to tell you—I'm not really a boat person. I went on a cruise once, and I spent the entire time being sick to my stomach. All of the rocking and the swaying and the rocking and the swaying," I said.

Zack laughed. "It looks pretty calm out there today. Why don't you give it a try, and if you start to feel seasick, we'll come right back?"

I noticed that there was a small gap in his front teeth. And the hair poking through the open neck of his polo shirt was a reddish blond.

Yes, I thought. I was definitely up for a fling. What the hell. After everything I'd gone through over the past few years, I deserved it, didn't I?

I took his hand and step-hopped into the boat. The sailboat dipped and swayed under my weight, and I faltered for a minute—the last thing I wanted to do was fall in the lake—but Zack held on to me until I was safely sitting on the hard plastic bench built into the side of the boat. He handed me an orange pillow to cushion the seat—"It doubles as a life preserver, not that you'll need it"—while he hustled around the deck, raising the sails, releasing the rudder, and finally untying the boat. He stretched out a leg and used it to push the boat back from the deck, before nimbly moving to the stern and taking hold of the tiller. He brought the sailboat about, and we began to slowly leave the deck, helped along by the light breeze blowing from the south.

I lazed back, one hand dipped in the water, and could feel the tension leaving my body. Huh. Who would have thought I'd find boating to be relaxing?

"Are you from here?" Zack asked, keeping his eyes ahead and on the edge of the lake as the boat skimmed slowly across the water.

"From Austin? No, I grew up in Seattle. My parents moved here when I was fifteen, when my dad got a job at UT. He is—was, I should say, since he retired a few months ago—a professor at the engineering school," I said. "How about you? Are you originally from Austin?"

"Born and raised."

"You don't have a Texas accent," I remarked.

"No, my mom was an English teacher, and she drummed it out of me at an early age," Zack said, and this time he turned to look at me. As our eyes met, I felt a well-placed kick to my nearly forgotten libido, which had been numb since Scott had come bursting out of his closet.

"I've traveled around quite a bit, as an adult, but I kept on ending up back here, so I decided to stop fighting it," Zack continued.

"Where have you traveled to?"

"I spent a year backpacking around Europe and went just about anywhere my Europass took me. After college, I joined a group that sent English teachers to foreign countries, and through that I spent one year in South America and another in Japan. I still try to travel when I can, although now that my business is picking up, it's hard to get the time off," Zack said.

As he spoke I became increasingly uncomfortable with how far Zack was veering from my original impression of him. College? English teacher? Well traveled? Successful business? I'd thought he was just another typical Austin guy who had not yet evolved past his undergrad years. They were everywhere, and were pretty easy to pick out, what with their almost universal enthusiasm for live music, cycling, and "Keep Austin Weird" bumper stickers. I'd thought the retro pickup truck was a dead giveaway.

"Wow. How did you get from teaching to carpentry?"

"Now, that is a story that is very long, and not at all interesting," Zack said.

I raised an eyebrow. "Now I'm intrigued," I said.

"You really shouldn't be. Okay, I'll give you the abbreviated version. I signed up for the teaching program after my college girlfriend and I broke up, and I just wanted to get the hell out of Austin. I ended up in a town called Cochabamba."

"Where's that?"

"In Bolivia. It was an incredible experience, but also really hard. I was pretty homesick and had a hard time adjusting. So after the year was up, I came home, moved in with my parents, and started working on a master's in history at UT. I quickly realized that there weren't a whole lot of jobs out there for historians, and my parents were driving me crazy, so when the program asked if I'd be willing to take another foreign placement, I jumped at it. But while I was home, I met someone . . ."

"Ah. I should have known . . . *cherchez la femme,*" I said, and then immediately felt stupid. Who talks like that, peppering their conversation with stupid French clichés? I sounded like a complete poser.

"Yeah, well, what can I say? She and I stayed in contact while I was in Japan, and moved in together when I got back. I needed a way to pay rent, so I signed on with a local builder. I'd taken up carpentry as a hobby when I was a teenager, and I enjoyed working with my hands, and it was a natural fit. I always thought that sitting behind a desk all day sounded like a prison sentence. No offense," Zack quickly added.

I shrugged. "It's okay. I love my job. Well . . . I love practicing law. I am getting a little sick of dealing with feuding spouses. So, carry on. You moved in with your girlfriend, began working for a builder . . ."

"This is much more detail than you need. I was supposed to be doing the abbreviated version," Zack joked. "Basically, the girlfriend and I broke up. I met Molly, who worked for the same builder that I worked for—she was one of the salespeople who offices out of the model and tries to pawn off the houses on unsuspecting suburbanites—we got married, and she had an affair with our boss. So I was left with no wife, no house, no job, and ended up moving back with my parents for a few months, which gave me all the motivation I needed to start up my own business. I do a lot of carpentry, and I'm just starting to pick up some contracting work. And that's all the information I'm giving out. Now it's your turn."

"Compared to you, I'm pretty boring. I went to Georgetown for undergrad, UT for law school, clerked for a year at the Texas Supreme Court, and then joined the firm that I'm with now. I made partner six months ago, and that's pretty much it," I said, realizing that this wasn't even the abbreviated version. My life was actually so boring that if I took out the gay husband, I could sum it up in two sentences.

"Have you ever been married?" Zack asked.

"Yes, for a few years. We had an amicable breakup," I lied, and then regretted the forced, overly casual tone. But the last thing I wanted to talk about was my marriage. I know that's what people do when they first meet—they share this type of basic background information—and it was just one more reason I hadn't wanted to start dating again.

"Come on, I told you my life story. You have to give me more than that. What about your family? Do you have any other brothers and sisters? Dark secrets? Family curses? Watch your head, we're going to come about," Zack said, and pushed the tiller away from him. The boat made a swift, nimble turn, and while I ducked my head, Zack released the sail and tied it to the opposite side of the boat. The sailboat hesitated for a moment before smoothly gliding off in a new direction.

I mentally tallied another point for Zack for letting me slide on the divorce talk.

"One other sister, Mickey, who's younger than Sophie and me. No dark secrets or curses that I know of. Just the usual dysfunctional fun that every family goes through."

"Yeah, I know how that goes," Zack said. "Are you hungry?" With one hand still on the rudder, he grabbed the cooler and started to rummage around inside it with the other.

"Here, I'll do that," I said, and took the cooler from him. I popped off the plastic lid and began to pull out the goodies within. A bottle of pinot noir. A turkey sandwich on cranberry-walnut bread. Pâté and cheddar on focaccia. A plastic container of pasta salad. A bunch of grapes. Marinated green bean salad. Chocolate chip cookies.

I rummaged around, found the corkscrew, and opened the wine. I waited for a minute while the boat lapped over a wake caused by a passing motorboat, and once the water was smooth again, poured the wine into two plastic cocktail cups and handed one to Zack.

"Which sandwich do you want?" I asked.

"Whichever. Do you have a preference?"

"I'll take the turkey," I said, and handed Zack the pâté and cheddar.

We ate in a companionable silence, putting the open containers of pasta salad and green beans between us and picking at them with plastic forks. The sun had been low in the sky when we started out, and now it began to sink down into the horizon, leaving behind a gorgeous sunset of pinks, aubergines, and hazy grays. The colors reflected on the glassy surface of the water. The lights of the fine houses facing the lake were glowing, illuminating the perimeter of the lake as the sky darkened.

"It's so beautiful out here. I had no idea. I would have gotten into a boat earlier if I knew," I breathed, soaking it all in. The colors, the view, the pleasant bite to the breeze as the night cooled.

"I know. That's why I decided to build out here," Zack said.

I turned to him, surprised. "I thought you were living with your parents," I said.

"God, no. I did for a few months, but I could only take so much of listening to them having the same argument every single morning about who reads which section of the paper first. Now I'm renting a house over near Ramsey Park and trying to find the time on weekends to finish my house. I thought I was going to have a chance last week to work on it, when the job I had scheduled fell through, but your sister talked me into doing her kitchen. She can be pretty persuasive," he said.

"That's a nice way of saying that she's a spoiled brat," I commented.

Zack laughed. "No, not at all. It just seemed really, really important to her to get it done. I'm glad I could help."

"How does it look? I haven't been over there since last week. Have you finished?"

"I'm just about done with the cabinets and countertops. I'm going over tomorrow to install the backsplash," Zack said. He squinted at the sunset, and glanced over his shoulder to see how far we'd wandered from the dock. "I think that we'd probably better turn back before it gets too dark."

I considered it to be a good sign when Zack parked his car outside my building and walked me in.

This is it, I thought, my pulse picking up. I normally hate this part, the first time with a new lover. There's so much pressure. Not just performance anxiety, but having to worry about how to play it: *Is it too soon? Too late? Does he think I'm easy? Neurotic? Cold?* I think that our mother's generation had it easy in comparison—nice girls waited, fast girls put out. So all you had to do was figure out which category you were in and proceed accordingly.

But with Zack, I already knew that we weren't going

anywhere, so there was no pressure. I could be as brazen as I liked and not worry about the repercussions. I felt a surge of energy flood through me, a loosening of limbs, an openness in my lungs.

"Do you like living here?" Zack asked me as we walked through the navy blue carpeted lobby of my building and stood by the elevator bank. We looked at our distorted reflections in the brass elevator doors while we waited for the elevator to arrive. Zack hadn't put his arm around me or even taken my hand, which seemed a little odd. Most men aren't exactly subtle at this stage.

"Yeah, I do. It really suits my needs. There's a gym in the basement and a pool in the back, and I don't ever have to worry about mowing the lawn."

The elevator doors opened with a *bing,* and we stepped inside.

"The thing I never liked about apartment living was always being able to hear my neighbors walking around or fighting or having sex. When I first moved back to Austin, my girlfriend and I had an apartment near campus, and we used to call the guy who lived above us the Sixty-Second Man. It was hard to look him or his wife in the eye," Zack said.

"Ah," I said, not sure where to go with that one. Maybe this was his way of being subtle, of introducing the topic of sex in a roundabout way.

The elevator stopped at my floor, and we walked to my apartment. I pulled out my keys, unlatched the lock, and opened the door.

"Well, I had a great time," Zack said, hanging back, while I went inside and dropped my purse and keys on my front hall console table. I turned around and looked at him, surprised that he hadn't followed me.

"Aren't you coming in?" I asked.

"No. I should get back. It's getting late. But thanks for coming sailing with me," Zack said.

He hadn't even stepped across the threshold. I stared at him. Was he rejecting me? Why? What was wrong with me?

"You don't want to come in for a . . . ," I trailed off. I was going to say "nightcap," but it sounded too affected, like something out of a Doris Day movie or an episode of *The Love Boat*. And "cup of coffee" was synonymous with sex ever since the *Seinfeld* episode where George's date invited him up for a cup of coffee, and he hadn't caught on that she was inviting him to bed. Although since that's exactly why I was inviting Zack in, maybe that wasn't a bad way to go.

"Coffee?" I finished.

Zack smiled. "Rain check," he said.

"Oh. Sure," I said, crestfallen.

And then Zack did step into my apartment, until he was so close, I could see the faint white line of a scar acquired long ago under his left eye. He rested one hand on my waist, and kissed me. His lips lingered on mine, and I leaned toward him, wrapping my arms around his neck, savoring the warm bulk of him against me. But just at the point when I thought he'd step even closer and maybe reach up to cup my breasts or slide his hands down over my bottom, Zack pulled back, breaking off the kiss. My arms fell limply away from him and hung uselessly at my side.

"Do you have any plans on Saturday?" he asked.

I shook my head. Somewhere inside of me I remembered I wasn't planning to see him again, that the entire point of

going out with him this one time had been so that I could indulge in some commitment-free sex. But mostly all I could
think about was how I just wanted to kiss him again.

"Would you like to have dinner? We could go out for
some barbecue or something," Zack suggested.

"That sounds like fun," I said faintly. Barbecue wasn't
normally my thing, but hell, I'd go to dinner at the Cracker
Barrel if it ended in another one of those kisses. And maybe
next time I could talk him into coming in for that cup of coffee and get this guy out of my head once and for all.

Chapter Seven

"What's a three-letter word for 'rug in Helsinki,' ending with *A*?" my mother asked, scrutinizing the *New York Times* crossword puzzle through a pair of purple bifocals perched on her nose. Another pair of glasses was sitting on top of her head. Mom had been known to search the house frantically for her glasses while three pairs were stacked on top of her ash-blonde bob.

"IKEA," Sophie guessed.

"That's four letters," I said. "Are we going to get this over with?"

It was Saturday morning, and Sophie and I were both camped out at my mom's house. We were supposed to be shopping for a crib, but Soph was grouchy and intent on eating her way through the entire bag of sesame seed bagels I'd picked up at Central Market on my way over.

"You don't have to come with us, you know," Sophie said, blinking back tears.

I would've felt worse about making her cry if she hadn't been breaking down over just about everything lately, including most McDonald's commercials, the breakup of a couple on the soap opera she watched, and the closing of a sporting goods store near her house where she once purchased a meaningful pair of five-pound dumbbells.

"I wish Mickey were here. She's the only one of you who'll work on crosswords with me," my mother complained.

"Mom, try 'rya.' *R-Y-A*. I don't do the crosswords with you because you cheat. What's the point of working on them if you just look up every answer? Sophie, I do want to go shopping with you, but so far all you've wanted to do today is elevate your feet and snog bagels. I'd just like to get going, I have some things to do today," I said. I was thinking about buying a new outfit for my date with Zack that evening, and wanted to stop by Saks. But if I couldn't levitate Soph out of the green plaid chair and ottoman she'd ensconced herself in since arriving an hour earlier, I wasn't going to have time.

"What things?" Sophie asked.

"Rya. That fits. Good, Paige," my mom said approvingly.

"I have a . . . thing tonight, and I wanted to pick up something to wear," I said.

"A 'thing'? What's that supposed to mean?" Sophie said, looking up from her bagel.

"A dinner thing," I hedged.

"Is the word you're looking for a 'date'?" Sophie asked. The whiff of gossip had the miraculous effect of causing her to forget about her bagel, and she was now alert and upright, staring at me brightly.

"Hmm. If 'rya' is correct, then what's a five-letter word for 'lack of experience,' starting with a Y?" my mother asked.

"No, I wouldn't call it a date. It's just a . . . get-together. A dinner. Nothing serious," I said.

"So, who is it? If you're buying new clothes for your non-date date, you must be somewhat interested," Sophie persisted.

I hesitated. Since I hadn't confided in Sophie when Zack first asked me out, I felt awkward doing so now. Why, I don't know. It wasn't like we were in competition for him. But she'd been so touchy lately, and the smallest things set her off.

"Actually, it's Zack. He came to see me about a custody issue, which I couldn't help him with, and he asked me out then. We went out the other night, too," I said.

"Zack? Zack who? Wait . . . do you mean my Zack?"

"I mean your carpenter, Zack. I don't really think of him as yours, though," I said dryly.

Sophie looked confused for a moment, and when that passed, she just looked pissed off. Which was really sort of scary, considering she'd been ready to attack the checkout clerk for not properly bagging her groceries. God only knew what she'd do to someone who was seducing her imaginary lover away from her.

"You knew I was interested in him. I can't believe that you'd go behind my back that way," she said. Color rose in her face, and she glared at me.

"You're not serious? Jesus, Sophie, you're the one who suggested that I go out with him in the first place. Did you forget you're married? Don't tell me that amnesia is another fun pregnancy symptom we get to cope with?" I said, rolling my eyes.

"Ah! It's 'youth'! That fits," my mother crowed, and then looked up from the crossword dictionary she'd been rummaging through. She peered at my sister over the rims of her glasses. "What's wrong, Sophie? Are you feeling okay? You look a little flushed. Maybe you should go lie down."

"She's angry at me because she thinks I stole her boy-friend," I said sarcastically.

I knew Soph was hormonal, but the absurdity of the situation was just a little much. Sophie was both very married and very pregnant, so she wasn't exactly in the situation to be calling dibs on available guys.

"I don't feel like going shopping anymore. I'm going to go home and take a nap," Sophie said, her voice quavering.

"Don't be like that," I sighed.

"Why don't you lie down here? I don't think you should drive if you aren't feeling well," my mother suggested, get-ting up and following Sophie to the door.

"I just want to be alone," Sophie sniffed. She shot me an-other dirty look and then waddled out the door.

My mother came back into the living room and looked at me reproachfully. I knew that look. It was her signature strike-guilt-in-the-hearts-of-daughters-everywhere look, perfected after thirty-four years of parenting. I liked to think I was im-pervious to it, but it immediately made me feel like I was about twelve years old and in trouble for mouthing off.

"What? I didn't do anything."

"You shouldn't be upsetting your sister. You know how emotional she is right now," Mom said. "This pregnancy has been very difficult on her."

"It's been difficult on all of us," I pointed out.

"I know she's been a little hard to deal with. But that's normal. You'll be the same way when you have a baby," my mother said, returning to her usual spot on the end of the striped sofa. She sat down, tucking one foot beneath her, and took a sip of coffee.

"This coffee's cold," she added. "If I make another pot, will you have some?"

I shook my head, and concentrated on pushing back the tears that had started burning in my eyes at my mom's "when you have a baby" comment. I hadn't told my family about my miscarriage. It had happened just a few months before Scott made his big announcement. At first I was hopeful that I'd get pregnant again quickly, since although the pregnancy hadn't been planned, losing the baby was devastating. But then Scott had moved out, and it seemed strange to tell them then after having waited for so long.

"Paige? What's wrong? You look like you're about to cry," Mom said, her voice sharp with worry.

I shook my head again and took a few deep breaths. This wasn't like me at all. I've never been a crier. And I thought I'd put the miscarriage behind me, so to feel the loss and pain bubble back up after all this time was disconcerting. When I was sure I could speak safely, without melting down, I said, "I'm fine, just a little PMS-y."

"God help me, I'm surrounded by hormonal daughters," my mother muttered as she picked the crossword back up.

My father wandered into the living room. He was wearing a bleach-stained green polo shirt, khaki shorts that were grubby with potting soil, and garden clogs, and as he walked across the taupe Berber carpet, he left behind a trail of dirty footprints.

"For heaven's sake, Stephen, look at what you're doing. You're tracking mud everywhere," my mother said, laughing.

I just stared, first at my mother, who was giggling like a teenage girl (in complete contrast to how she surely would have responded to my father's soiling the carpet when my parents were married, which would have been to point and screech, like Donald Sutherland at the end of *Invasion of the Body Snatchers*), and then at my father, who was standing in the living room of my childhood home as though he belonged there, as though he and my mother hadn't bloodied the entire family with their messy divorce a decade earlier.

I wondered if I were going crazy, but then remembered the advice of my old therapist, Elise, who said that if you think you're having a breakdown, you're probably not. Her reasoning was that if you were alert and rational enough to question your own sanity, then chances were you were fine. Of course, this logic would also suggest that then when you feel perfectly fine, you might actually be falling apart without being aware of it, but I didn't like to dwell on that possibility.

"Hi, sweetie," he said to me. "How's work going?"

"Um, fine. You know, the usual. So why are you here, Dad?" I asked.

"I've been helping your mother out with the garden. I just cleared the summer annuals out of the window boxes and replaced them with pansies. I told her she has to fire the lawn care company she uses, because they're ripping her off. How hard is it for them to remember to water the flowers once a week? Forget about it," he said, as if this were a reasonable explanation for his presence.

"You're helping Mom," I repeated.

He nodded, and my mother beamed at him. "Can I get you some coffee, Stephen?" she asked him.

"Are you having some? Then, yes, please," he said.

My head swiveled back and forth, as though I were watching a tennis match. *Would you like some coffee? Yes, please?* What did they do with my real parents?

"Excuse me," I finally said. "Are we in some kind of a time warp? You two are still divorced, aren't you?"

"Paige," my mom said reproachfully.

"What? This is weird," I said, and suddenly remembered that I had forgotten to ask Sophie if she'd heard anything about Mom and Dad spending time together. Now I guess I didn't have to.

"No, it's not. Your mother and I can be friends. And especially now with Sophie's baby coming, we thought we should make an effort to get along a little better. That's all," Dad said. "Speaking of whom, I thought Sophie was here. Didn't I see her car in the driveway? She's still driving that gas-guzzling SUV, right? I've told her a thousand times she needs to trade that thing in for something more energy efficient, but you know how stubborn your sister is."

"Yes, I certainly do. Anyway, her head started to spin around *Exorcist*-style, so she went home to rest," I said.

"Oh," my father said. My mother shot me another look.

"She's just a little tired. It's hard carrying around all of that extra weight," my mother said.

"Yeah, that must be it," I said, heavy on the sarcasm. "Well, since we're not going to go baby shopping, I think I'm going to run over to Saks."

And then I hightailed it out of there, because frankly, the two of them were starting to creep me out, what with all of the smiling and agreeing and niceness. Could it really be true that my mother and father were becoming friends?

No. No fucking way.

Chapter Eight

Are you starving? Because I thought we could take a drive out to my house—I just put the windows in—but if you're too hungry, we could do it some other time," Zack said as he pulled out of the visitor's parking lot for my building and turned right on Congress.

"No, I'd love to see it," I said. I'd been curious about his new house ever since he'd mentioned it the day we went sailing. Before then I'd have guessed that he lived in a typical Peter Pan bachelor pad, complete with an ugly yet comfortable secondhand couch, bed linens that hadn't been changed in two months, and a light-up neon beer sign that had been filched from a bar on a drunken bet.

We took the same twisting, scenic route that leads to Lake Travis, but turned off the main road before we got to the marina, and then turned again so that we were climbing a steep and somewhat remote road, before turning yet again up a short driveway. In front of us was an extremely cool, modern two-story house, sitting on what I could only imagine was an incredibly expensive hillside lot. Dense trees surrounded the house on three sides, while I could just make out a glimpse of the blue waters of the lake behind it.

"Oh my God . . . I can't believe your location. The view from inside must be incredible," I breathed.

Zack grinned and looked up at the house proudly. It was still unfinished, but it was obvious that the house was well on its way to becoming a showplace. It had modern lines, a boxy shape, and huge windows all over to take advantage of the view.

"You want to see inside?" he asked.

"Absolutely," I said.

Inside, it was still very rough. The bones of the walls were there, but Zack hadn't put up the Sheetrock yet, and the kitchen was nothing but a shell. But the layout was open, and flowed well, and it was easy to see how gorgeous it was going to be.

"I'm doing a lot of it on my own, when I have the free time, so it's not much to look at now," Zack apologized.

I looked at him. "Are you serious? I love it. I went house hunting with Soph when she and Aidan were looking, and all of the builder houses looked so much alike, it was hard to tell one from another. And I hated how homogenous the neighborhoods are. This is so private and airy and pretty."

Zack looked pleased. "I know what you mean. I used to work for one of those builders, and I got sick of repeating the same type of design over and over. I wanted to do something different here."

"Well, you certainly succeeded," I said.

"Do you want to see the upstairs?" Zack asked, holding out a hand to me. I hesitated for a moment and then took it.

The second floor was even more incredible than the first. Zack had roughed out three bedrooms and two bathrooms, including a generous-sized master bath, but it was the view from the master bedroom that was really spectacular.

"Wow. Oh wow," I exclaimed, moving to the wall of windows that covered the back side of the room. "Your view of the lake is phenomenal! I know what this house reminds me of . . . it's a tree house. A grown-up tree house."

"That's exactly the feel I was going for. I'm going to put a patio out here, right off the bedroom, so that I can sit out here in the evenings."

"I don't blame you. I'd have a hard time leaving this view, too," I said.

We went to dinner at Fonda San Miguel, home of the city's best Mexican food. When Zack had suggested it as we clambered back into his vintage pickup, I must have looked surprised.

"Did you think I was serious about getting barbecue?" Zack asked, grinning at me.

"No, I . . . well, sort of," I admitted, and found myself grinning back at him.

"I was just teasing you. You don't strike me as the barbecue type."

I raised my eyebrows. "No? What type am I?"

"You know, I'm not sure if I know yet. I keep thinking I'll figure you out, but I haven't," Zack said.

"I could say the same about you," I replied.

"Yeah, well, I'm an enigma wrapped in a riddle," he

joked. "But really, I didn't think you even liked me when we first met."

"You winked at me," I said. "And I've never liked winkers."

"No way. I never wink at people," Zack said.

"Be that as it may, you winked at me," I said.

"No I didn't. I'm sure I didn't."

"You did," I insisted.

"Is that why you gave me such a dirty look? I thought that maybe you were worried that I was trying to hook up with your sister."

"Actually, I was more worried that she was trying to seduce you," I said.

The restaurant was located in central Austin, just off of Forty-fifth Street near North Loop. It was an elegant place decorated like a hacienda, with lovely pierced-metal chandeliers and dark rose colored walls. The food was special, too. This wasn't the place to come for greasy nachos or other deep-fried, cheese-laden junk food that was the standard fare at most Tex-Mex joints.

"I haven't been here in ages," I remarked, after we sat down and were looking over the menus.

"I try to get here once a month or so. I'm addicted to their enchiladas," Zack said.

"Mmmm, that sounds good," I said, and my stomach growled at the thought. I thought back and realized I hadn't eaten very much after having bagels at my mom's house. I'd been so busy shopping for the short-sleeved camel cashmere sweater and black wool trousers that I'd bought for our date that I hadn't remembered to consume anything other than a Diet Coke.

The waiter arrived. "I'll have the crab enchiladas and a glass of the chardonnay," I decided, and handed the menu to the waiter.

"Good choice. I think I'll go for the Cochinita Pibil. And a Dos Equis," Zack said.

The waiter returned with our drinks. Zack raised his glass, holding it toward me. I clinked my wineglass against it.

"To the future," Zack said.

"To tonight," I replied lightly. Zack looked at me quizzically, and I held his gaze, enjoying how everything around us seemed to fade away while the sexual tension leapt and flickered like a lit candle. And I knew—tonight was going to be The Night. He would be the wild fling I'd been craving, the relationship equivalent to attending Mardi Gras in New Orleans. I imagined how it would feel to have his hands running over my body, and felt a shock of excitement.

"Are you excited about the baby?" Zack asked.

"Baby?"

I'd been lost in my embarrassingly vivid fantasy, and so this question seemed to come from nowhere.

"Your sister. Sophie. She is having a baby, isn't she? Because if not, I really put my foot in it when I congratulated her," Zack said.

I laughed. "Oh yeah. And I'll be even more excited when Sophie becomes a normal person again and recovers from the estrogen-induced psychosis she's been in for the past few months," I joked.

"How about you? Would you like to have children?" Zack asked.

I blinked. The question took me off guard, as did the sudden lurch in my stomach, and suddenly I was remembering everything. The baby. Scott. Having to clench my teeth and force a smile when Soph had announced her pregnancy this summer.

I'm over this, damn it, I reminded myself.

"I . . . uh . . . why do you want to know?"

Zack shrugged. "Isn't that a normal, getting-to-know-you, second-date kind of a question?"

"It's just a little personal."

"Isn't that what we're doing here? Getting personal?" Zack asked. He reached over and grasped my hand. "Did I say something to upset you?"

"Look, can we just talk about something else?" I asked. Anything else.

"Sure. What do you want to talk about?"

"Your house. I love your house. Did you design it yourself?"

"No. My college roommate is an architect here in town, and he helped me out. I made some sketches on a napkin, and he turned them into blueprints for me. Which is good, because in my enthusiasm, I'd left out stairs," Zack said, and I laughed, and we were past the awkward moment. For now.

Norah Jones was playing on the radio as we pulled into the parking lot at my building. I was a little tired—wine always made me sleepy—but in a comfortable way, heightened by the pleasant conversation. Zack was an easy person to be with, and in his presence I was relaxing in a way I hadn't in a long time. So much so that I was surprised when Zack reached over and took my hand in his, and a jolt of excitement shot through my body. And then I remembered: this was it.

"I had a great time tonight," Zack said.

"I did, too. Do you want to come upstairs?"

"Yeah, I thought I'd walk you in."

"Actually, what I meant was . . ." I hesitated and then took in a deep breath. I'd learned that the only way to get what you want in life is to go after it, but I certainly didn't relish rejection. And while I could tell Zack was interested in me—his thumb was erotically stroking the back of my hand, and he was looking at me with obvious interest—there was always the chance that I was miscalculating things, like I had after our last date. "Would you like to come in for a while? We could have a glass of wine, or watch a video, or . . ."

Before I could complete my sentence, Zack had leaned over and caught my lips against his. His tongue flickered against mine, and I went warm and woozy. He pulled back and smiled.

"Or this?"

I nodded, my eyes large and my appetite whetted. "This would be good, too," I said. Very, very good.

Chapter Nine

The sex was like digging into an incredibly rich, gooey brownie topped with Häagen-Dazs vanilla ice cream and smothered in hot fudge after six months on the Atkins diet. Zack was athletic and commanding, and for once I actually got carried away with things, rather than just waiting for him to finish while I stressed over whether my secretary had filed all of the requisite papers for a case I was working on. Which pretty much summed up my married sex life, surprise, surprise.

"Are you going to fall asleep?" Zack asked after.

I was lying on my side, resting my head on his shoulder, my hand on his stomach. In a way, this cuddling felt even more intimate than the sex, and I worried that I was over-indulging myself. I'd heard that the trick to a successful fling was no kissing on the mouth. Wait, no . . . that was Julia Roberts's advice on being a prostitute in *Pretty Woman*. Still, I wondered if it was applicable to the present situation.

Zack nudged me. I looked up.

"You're not asleep, are you?" he asked.

"How could I be? I'm looking right at you," I said.

"Maybe you're one of those freaky people who sleep with their eyes open. Although if you are, then I think we should just end things right now, because that would really creep me out," he said, and then he leaned down and very sweetly kissed me.

I had been planning to clarify our relationship, specifically that there was no relationship, and that this was a one-off kind of a thing, but the kiss distracted me.

"Do you have Scrabble?" Zack asked.

"What?"

"Scrabble. The board game," Zack said.

"Why?" I asked.

"I feel like playing. Are you up for a game?" he asked.

"Okay . . . sure. Although I should warn you, I'm the all-time, undefeated Scrabble champion," I said.

"In the world?"

"No." I laughed. "In my family."

"As am I. So this should be quite the match-up," Zack said.

I hopped out of bed, shrugged on my red silk kimono, and went to fetch the board game from the front hall closet. When I returned, Zack had pulled on his boxer shorts and was standing in front of my open closet, hands resting on his hips. He had a nice back, broad and smooth skinned, and there was a small mole on his left shoulder. I felt an urge to walk up behind him, wrap my arms around his waist, and press my cheek against the ridge of his shoulder blade. I took a step toward him before stopping myself. The movement caused Zack to glance back at me.

"What are all these boxes for?" he asked.

Uh-oh.

"Nothing," I said, and hurried to the closet, stepping in front of Zack and closing the sliding door.

"What are you hiding?" Zack asked. He laughed and pulled me toward him, his hands strong on my waist.

"Nothing. Really. It's private," I said, trying to back up against the door, but Zack playfully swung me to the side and pulled the door back open. He reached up and pulled down one of the white shipping boxes.

"Home Shopping Network," he read, peering at the label printed in green on the face of the box. He grabbed another box. "This one, too. And this one. Are these all from the Home Shopping Network?"

I covered my face with my hands and sat down on the edge of the bed.

"This is embarrassing," I groaned.

"Why, what are these?" Zack asked as he sat down next to me.

I looked up, sliding my hands down until they were covering my mouth.

"Likshophesan," I mumbled.

"I can't hear you," Zack said. He pulled my hands down and held them in his.

"I like watching the Home Shopping Network."

"Just watching?"

"And sometimes . . . occasionally . . . I like to order things," I admitted. "Please let's not talk about it anymore."

"But these don't look like they've been opened."

"I never open them."

"Why not?"

"I don't know, I guess I just like the ordering part. When the stuff gets here, I'm too embarrassed to open it."

"May I?" Zack asked.

I rolled my eyes and gave him a half-nod. He pulled back a corner of the white box and shook out a small, clear plastic bag.

"It's a bracelet," Zach said, pulling the sparkly object out of the bag. He tipped his head and shrugged. "It's pretty. It's . . ."

"Diamondique," I said. "It's Diamondique."

"Cute name," Zack said.

"It's awful. It's truly awful," I said, palming the bracelet and staring at it with distaste. It was gaudy and chintzy and not anything I would ever wear. "Why would I buy this?"

"It's not that bad," Zack said. He plucked it out of my hand and fastened it onto my wrist, where it twinkled bawdily.

"I'm going to return it," I announced. "I'm going to return all of them."

Zack smiled. "Later. Now, I beat you in Scrabble," he said, rubbing his hands together.

We smoothed the duvet out, and then I set up the game right on the bed. "I can't believe this. I got four *O*s. Are there even four *O*s in the game?" Zack complained after we'd chosen our tiles.

I consulted the list of letters. "Yes, there are eight *O*s in total. You can re-pick if you want," I said charitably. Normally, I'm a shark when it comes to board games, and especially Scrabble—my family's vicious games of Sorry are legendary—but in my postcoital bliss, I was feeling magnanimous.

"Cheat? No, I'm not going to cheat, thank you very much. I plan on trouncing you, even with my four *O*s."

I started first, and put down "viper." "Ha-ha, look at that!

That's fifteen . . . wait, no, sixteen points, and it's doubled for thirty-two. Thirty-two points!" I crowed, marking it down on the score sheet.

"Hey, let me see that. You got 'viper' and I got four *Os*? Is this game rigged? And how do I know you're trustworthy enough to keep score?" Zack asked suspiciously.

"House rules," I said. "Come on, your time has already started to run, you'd better hurry up."

"Time? We're playing with time limits? Is that another house rule?"

"Of course! You have one minute to put down your word." I consulted my watch. "But since you didn't know, I'll let you start now."

Zack added a *D* and four *Os* to the *V* and spelled "voo-doo." "Look at that! Did you see how I'm working those *Os*? What's that . . . ten points? Almost as good as yours, oh but crap, I don't get to double it," he said. "You don't have to look quite so gleeful about that."

"Sorry," I said cheerfully. I love winning.

An hour later, we were nearly out of tiles, and Zack was beating me by twenty-seven points.

"*Grrr.* We're going to have to play again," I said.

"Don't worry, I won't gloat about my victory," Zack said modestly.

"Just because you got that lucky break with the triple 'xylem.' Otherwise, I would have won," I said.

"You shouldn't have challenged me. I told you it was a real word."

"I've never heard of it before, I was sure you made it up. Okay, you win, I give up," I said. I'd been scouring the board, trying to figure out where I could plug in the *R* and the *W*

I was still holding on to, but Zack had blocked me from the one open *A*.

Zack grinned and leaned back against the pillows, his hands behind his head, his elbows splayed out to either side. "So, since I'm the winner, you have to be my slave for the rest of the night, right?"

I stretched out next to him, lying on my stomach, resting my head on folded arms. "I don't remember agreeing to that," I said.

"Oh no? I could have sworn those were the house rules," he said. He rolled toward me and poked me in the side, catching me right on my secret tickle spot.

"Ack!" I squealed, and started to roll away. Zack caught me in his arms, preventing my escape.

"What was that?" he laughed.

"Nothing!"

"Hmmm, if it's nothing, then you won't mind if I do it again," he said, one finger poised mercilessly above my tickle spot.

"No, no, don't, please!" I begged. "Okay, so I have one very small, not-worth-mentioning tickle spot."

"Ah, so now I have power over you," Zack teased me.

I smiled back at him and relaxed in his arms.

"Just don't tell anyone," I said.

"You are so beautiful," Zack said, and all traces of laughter vanished from his face. And then he leaned over and kissed me.

A few minutes later, the Scrabble game fell to the floor, scattering its tiles across the pristine, deep-pile white carpeting and under my bed. But at that moment, neither one of us even noticed.

Chapter Ten

The next morning, we went to a little dive café on Red River, where the plastic menus were sticky with pancake syrup and you had to throw yourself in front of one of the harried, tattooed waitresses if you wanted to place your order.

"A tall stack of blueberry pancakes, two eggs scrambled, bacon, coffee, and orange juice," Zack said definitively.

"That sounds amazing. I'll have exactly the same," I said, surprising myself

Normally, I'm pretty incorruptible when it comes to breakfast—it has to be high fiber and low fat. I really did have to get this guy out of my system, I thought. If nothing else, whenever I was with him, my appetite spiked.

"I haven't been here in a while. I know it's not much to look at, but the pancakes are worth it," Zack commented, looking around. His eyes caught on something behind me, and his entire face changed. The light blew out of his eyes, and his mouth tightened. I turned and saw a family sitting in the booth behind us. The parents, decked out in sweats, were entertaining a little girl. She had blonde hair caught up in a ponytail and was wearing a purple sweatshirt and pink pajama bottoms, and she was crooning to an Elmo doll clutched in her chubby arms.

I looked back at Zack. He seemed pensive and distant, and I assumed he was thinking about his stepdaughter. I didn't know what to say. I've never been good at those Hallmark Card, heart-to-heart moments, and this problem seemed particularly complex. I tried to think of something appropriate to say, but then our pancakes arrived, and after accepting the waitress's offer of additional coffee, we began to eat in silence.

"These aren't as good as I remember them being," Zack said, pushing a piece of pancake around with his fork.

"Yeah, they're a little heavy," I said, already regretting the syrup-laden pancake I'd consumed. Two more sat on my plate untouched, turning into maple-flavored mush. I'd also lost my appetite for the eggs and too-fatty bacon.

"Sorry, this was a bad call," Zack said, and he smiled briefly and then reached forward to take my hand. "What are you going to do today?"

"Work. I have a trial starting tomorrow, and I have to prep for it," I said, catching the waitress's eye so that she'd bring us the bill.

"Trial? I thought you were a divorce attorney. Divorces don't go to trial anymore, do they?"

"Sometimes. We'll probably end up settling, but it can take the threat of court to force both sides into negotiations," I said.

"How do you do it? Deal with divorces all day long, I mean. Doesn't it depress you?"

This was something I heard all the time. Why aren't

dentists asked this about their job, or doctors, or garbage men? And what about teachers? I'd rather deal with divorcing spouses than take on a class of oversexed ninth graders any day. Every job has its downsides, and you tend to get used to them. No, I didn't love bearing witness to the ruin of marriages, and yes, the irony that my own marriage had gone down in flames didn't escape me. But having to defend my choice of careers wasn't exactly how I wanted to spend my Sunday morning.

"No, it doesn't anymore. Friday afternoons are never fun, but I've gotten used to dealing with the clients, and it's better than doing, oh, criminal law, for example. At least I don't have to go down to the county jail," I said.

"What's wrong with Friday afternoons?"

"That's the day that custody changes hands. Moms are angry when they drop off the kids and discover that Dad's girlfriend is over. Dads get angry when they go to pick up the kids and they aren't there. Then they call me, as though I'm going to mobilize the Divorce Police to enforce the custody agreement," I said.

"So what do you do?" Zack asked.

"I instruct my secretary to tell anyone who calls that I'm out for the weekend. If there were a serious problem, something we'd need to bring to the attention of the court, the earliest I could file anything would be Monday morning. And in most cases it's forgotten by then. Or, at least, it's no longer so important the client is willing to pay two hundred dollars per hour for me to deal with it," I replied. "What? Why are you looking at me like that?"

"You just seem so tough when you talk about work. You're . . . formidable," he said.

"I try to be—I owe that to my clients. Why, you don't approve of tough women?" I asked.

Zack shrugged. "No, it's not that. I just wouldn't want to have such a contentious job."

"Well then, I guess it's a good thing that you're not a lawyer," I said tartly.

"Don't get angry, I'm just trying to understand you," Zack said, and he jostled my hand gently, as though that would shake out my grumpiness.

"I'm not mad. I just get this a lot. It gets old having to defend what I do."

"Okay, sorry. Answer one question, and I'll drop the issue entirely."

"One question," I agreed.

"Is this the kind of law you planned to practice when you went to law school?" Zack asked.

I thought for a minute and took a sip of my coffee. It tasted awful, like liquid bad breath. I put the mug back down and pushed it away.

"No. I did want to go into family law, but I initially planned to be a children's advocate. In fact, my parents were going through their own bitter divorce while I was in school, so the idea that I'd spend my life dealing with people acting like my parents would have devastated me if I knew that's where I was headed," I said.

"How did you end up here?"

"There isn't exactly much money in children's advocacy. Most of the work is pro bono. But now that I'm a partner, I probably could start picking up some casework," I said thoughtfully, wondering how that would go over with the rest of the partnership. No, forget them. If I wanted to do it,

I'd just do it. They'd probably criticize me privately and then brag about it in the firm literature. "You know, that's not a bad idea. Maybe while I'm down at the courthouse tomorrow, I'll have the clerk add my name to the appointment roster. Thanks," I said, looking up at Zack.

"I didn't do anything," he said.

"Yes you did," I replied, and without thinking, I reached over and squeezed his hand.

He held on to my hand before I could pull it away, and for a moment we sat there, looking at one another. Zack had such an open face—he would have made a terrible litigator—and I saw an affectionate curiosity reflected there. I was more practiced at masking my emotions; in fact, hiding them now came easier to me than sharing. But if Zack could peer into my thoughts—a frightening prospect—he'd see the growing interest, a hazy desire to pick up where we'd left off the night before, and a growing concern that I wasn't going to be able to extricate myself from this situation as smoothly as I'd initially hoped. I felt like I should say something to clarify what I wanted—or, to be more precise, what I did *not* want.

"Zack," I began, but then the waitress appeared with the bill, and Zack let go of my hand so that he could grab it from her. I beat him to it.

"No, the bad pancakes were my idea, I'm not going to let you pay for them," Zack said.

"No way. You got dinner last night, so this is my treat," I said smoothly, and pulled out a twenty, which I left on top of the check.

"Thanks," Zack said. He smiled at me. It was the same smile that had gotten me into trouble the night before.

*   *   *

When we got back to my building, Zack started to park his truck, ready to walk me up, but I shook my head.

"You'd better not. I have to work, and you'll just distract me," I said.

"That's what I was hoping," Zack said. "But you're the boss. I'll call you tonight, and maybe we can get together tomorrow, or Tuesday."

"Tomorrow?" I repeated. My stomach pinched as I remembered what I was doing here. One night. No emotional attachments.

"Yeah, unless you're busy."

"I just think . . . Look. Zack. I'm really not looking for something serious," I said. The words made me wince. I looked sideways at him under lowered lashes and saw his naked discomfort.

"Well. I guess . . . I guess I misread things," he said.

It was painfully awkward. I had to clench my hands into fists so that I wouldn't reach over and touch his face, as I was sorely tempted to do.

"I had a good time last night, I did," I said. "My life is just really . . . crowded right now."

I braced myself, and leaned over to kiss Zack on the rough of his unshaven face. He stayed perfectly still, not turning his face so that his lips would meet mine, which I should have been glad for. Instead, stabs of disappointment pricked at me.

"Crowded," he repeated, but he didn't look at me. He was staring through the windshield, off into the distance. You could just barely make out Town Lake from the parking lot.

I hesitated, my hand on the door handle, trying to think

of what to say, overcome with an urge to take it all back, to smooth his hurt feelings, to grab back what I'd felt the night before. It had been the first pure joy I'd experienced since my miscarriage two years earlier.

I opened my mouth, but before I could speak, Zack turned to me with a small, tight-lipped smile. "Bye, Paige," he said.

The words that would make everything okay stuck in my throat.

"Bye," I said.

I got out of the car and walked into my building without looking back.

Chapter Eleven

Two weeks passed by. I tried not to think about Zack as I went about my business of ending marriages. I tried not to think about him while I took long, steady runs along Town Lake, enjoying the coolness of the late autumn air against my face. I tried not to think about him while I was sorting my laundry and found a few Scrabble blocks that had mysteriously ended up in the hamper. And I tried not to think about him as I gathered up all of the Home Shopping Network boxes, scrawled "Return to Sender" across each one with a Sharpie marker, and dropped them off at the post office after business hours. The only item I kept was the Diamondique bracelet Zack had fastened to my wrist, which I now squirreled away in the drawer of my bedside table.

Zack called me a few times, and left messages on my answering machine. I hesitated before erasing each one, not accustomed to the pang of regret I felt when hearing his voice.

Clearly, I'd made a huge mistake. The idea of a strings-free relationship sounded good in theory, but it had been a misstep to attempt it with someone I actually enjoyed

spending time with. I should have found some easily forget-
table guy, one with an irritating laugh or criminally low self-
esteem or serious mother issues—basically any guy I ever
went out with before my marriage. Had I chosen my fling
more wisely, I wouldn't be having the disconcerting sensation of missing someone whom I hadn't known for very long.

And then Soph's baby shower rolled around. Worse still, I
was hosting it. I spent an entire Saturday morning hustling
around my house, vacuuming the carpets, scrubbing the
kitchen, cleaning the bathroom. And then, since Sophie's my
sister and I love her, I put up all of the tacky-to-the-point-of-
kitsch baby shower decorations—a paper banner that spelled
out "Congratulations," balloons in the shape of storks, little
plastic rattles scattered around all of the tables. I'd picked up
trays of finger sandwiches, crudités, and cookies earlier in
the day, and I put them out, before mixing up a punch of
cranberry juice, sparkling wine, and lemon-lime soda.

My mom and Mickey, home from school for the weekend, arrived at one o'clock.

"Here, I brought some cheese and crackers, and some
brownies and lemon bars that I made last night. Michaela,
let's put out the flowers that we brought. Paige dear, where
are your vases? Are these the only ones you have?" Mom
said, looking doubtfully at the modern vase collection I'd ordered from West Elm.

"That's it," I said. I relieved Mickey of the flowers, handing them off to my mother, who began arranging them around
the living room, and then gave my little sister a quick hug.
"Hey, kiddo, it's good to see you."

"Mom's driving me crazy. Have you found anything out
about her and Dad?" Mickey whispered in my ear.

"No, she refuses to talk about it. Every time I bring it up, she says something vague about how they're 'just good friends,' and changes the subject. But I don't think it's anything to worry about. They've probably called a truce because they're about to become grandparents," I whispered back.

"Well, I guess it would be nice if they could be in the same room without killing each other. But it's just so weird, I can't get used to the idea," Mickey said.

"Have a glass of punch. I spiked it with white wine," I told her, and laughed when she said "Ooo, yum" and hustled off toward the punch bowl.

Mickey was such a goofy sweetheart of a kid. And now, looking at her, tall and slim and looking just a little awkward in her skirt and heels, envy squeezed at me. She had her whole life spreading out in front of her. All of the major decisions were still ahead: what kind of medicine she'd practice, whether she'd marry, and if so, who, where she'd live, and what kind of a life she'd lead. And even when she screwed up, it would be fine, because the mistakes you make in your twenties are always the ones that you learn from. You're still young and pliable and capable of change.

Mom fussed over the flowers—sweetheart roses and baby's breath, not my favorite, but I suppose she was going for a theme—while I put the food she brought on a plate and added it to the buffet. I swiped a brownie and absentmindedly nibbled on it while I worked.

"Since when did you start eating desserts?" Mickey asked, watching me critically.

"I don't know, I'm not really," I hedged, and then turned my back on both of them and started pulling glasses out of the cupboards. I could feel them exchange a look behind my back, and felt a surge of irritation. The truth was, I'd been eating nonstop since my night with Zack. The memory of his morning beard scratching against my face, or the way his fingers had strummed over my skin, had a way of propelling me right to the refrigerator.

There was another knock at the door, and my mom went to let Sophie in. She toddled in, out of breath and her face red.

"Hey, you! What's wrong? Did you take the stairs?" Mickey asked her, hugging her in greeting.

"Have you talked to the doctor about your blood pressure?" Mom fretted. She took Sophie's arm and guided her to the sofa, where she plopped down with a sigh of relief.

"No . . . the elevator . . . I get so winded lately. Thanks," Sophie wheezed as she accepted the glass of water I handed her. She smiled at me and almost looked like her old, affable self. "Thanks for the shower."

"No problem," I said, and tugged the end of her hair.

We hadn't seen each other since the day of my date with Zack, and had only talked briefly on the phone about shower-related things. But I could tell that the whole thing had blown over. Such was the way with sisters. Or at least the way it was with my sisters.

"So what have you been up to, Paige?" Sophie asked casually.

"Yeah, how's your love life?" Mickey asked, flopping down on my pristine white love seat, tucking one foot underneath her.

"Mick, get your feet off my couch. Nothing's up," I said, and swiftly followed Mom back to the kitchen to escape the interrogation. Unfortunately, the condo had an open floor plan, so I couldn't completely get away from my inquisitors.

"How's it going with Zack?" Sophie called out.

"It's not. We went out a few times, and that was it. No big deal," I replied. I dug out an ice bucket—one of the few wedding presents I'd forgotten to purge—and handed it to my mother.

"Oh yeah? That's not what he said," Sophie teased me.

"What did he say?" Mickey asked.

"Who's Zack?" Mom asked. She pulled the ice tray out of the freezer and dumped it into the bucket.

"Zack's my carpenter, the gorgeous one who redid my kitchen," Sophie said.

"How's the redecorating coming along anyway? What did Aidan say about it?" I asked, walking back into the living room with a tray of glasses. I set them out around the punch bowl.

"Don't change the subject. What did the carpenter hottie say about Paige?" Mickey insisted. She leaned forward, her brown eyes shining brightly, her long dark hair falling down over her shoulders. Mickey looks so much like me, although her face is softer, like Sophie's. She doesn't have any of the sharp angles that make me look like Snow White's evil stepmother when I'm angry.

I was saved by a knock at the door that signaled the arrival of our guests. A flood of blonde, perky, giggling women—it seemed all of Sophie's friends were blonde, perky, and giggling—began to pour into the apartment, each carrying a gift wrapped in pastel paper. Sophie's mother-in-law—a short, thin, manic woman with hair that had been frosted platinum blonde—and her two anorexic sisters-in-law also arrived, and my mom rallied to entertain them among the sea of strangers.

Thankfully, Sophie insisted on skipping the typical dumb shower games, and so after everyone had arrived and caught up on gossip, we filled our plates with food and settled in to watch Soph unwrap her presents. She sat on the sofa, her legs propped up on an ottoman and a few pillows (my mother, still worrying about Sophie's blood pressure, insisted that Soph keep her feet elevated), and Mickey sat cross-legged on the floor next to her, taking notes on who gave what to make the task of thank-you notes easier.

I hovered near the kitchen, filling the sandwich trays as they emptied, putting out more punch, and generally doing anything I could to avoid the tedium of watching Sophie unwrap yet another cute, unisex outfit from Baby Gap. I reached out and grabbed a mini–roast beef sandwich with cheddar cheese and horseradish mayonnaise off the tray and popped it in my mouth.

"How long do showers normally last?" I asked my mother when she breezed by me with a tray of empty punch glasses and discarded paper plates.

Mom shrugged. "A few hours. I think it's going well, though, don't you? Everyone seems to be having a good time."

I nodded, my eyes on Sophie. She was laughing, her head thrown back and her blonde curls bouncing around her face. She looked so happy, so complete. I'd thought she'd made a huge mistake getting married right out of college and an even bigger mistake when she gave up her dream of being an art photographer. I'd done everything right—I went to law school, waited until my career was established before I married. But there she was, full of light and life and surrounded by friends, her hand affectionately grazing over her enormous bump.

And here I was. Divorced, alone, and secretly stuffing finger sandwiches into my mouth.

After the horde of chattering women left, I assessed the damage done to my apartment. Mom was washing out the punch bowl, and Mickey was carefully covering the picked-over sandwich platters with plastic wrap. Sophie was still parked on the sofa, looking like she was about to fall asleep, surrounded by a sea of crumpled light pink and baby blue wrapping paper, enormous bows, and boxes upon boxes of adorably impractical baby clothes, such as a faux fur pink baby coat spilling out of a gift bag. I plucked the coat up and held it up for Sophie to see.

"What are you supposed to do with this if you have a boy?" I asked her.

"I don't know. The same thing I'll do with this necklace, I guess," Sophie said, showing me a tiny gold chain with a locket on it.

"Necklace? Do babies wear necklaces?" Mickey asked. She looked at my mom, who shrugged.

"You girls didn't. I would have worried about it getting tangled up and choking you," Mom said as she waded through the wrappings and sat down on the love seat. Mickey and I followed her, me collapsing on the other end of the sofa that

Sophie was occupying, and Mickey returned to her spot on the floor. Sophie stuck her feet on my lap.

"Will you rub my feet?" she asked.

"Ugh, gross, get them off of me," I said, pushing her away.

Sophie pouted. "But they're sore. I've been wearing heels all afternoon, and my ankles are so swollen, they look like an elephant's."

"And they smell about as bad. Stop waving them at me," Mickey said, inching away from Sophie.

"Paige. Do you think that maybe you should see a counselor?" Mom said abruptly.

"What? Why would you ask me that?" I asked, prickling.

I was tired of family members suggesting I seek out therapy. It was starting to get a little insulting.

"Well, don't get upset. But I think it would help if you talked to someone about Scott. Ever since he, um, told you about, well . . ."

"The word you're looking for is 'gay,' Mother," Sophie said without opening her eyes.

"You haven't been the same," Mom continued as if Sophie hadn't spoken. "And you've gotten so rigid about exercising, and for a while you weren't eating anything, and now you're at the other extreme, eating constantly. Do you think maybe you have an eating disorder?"

"No!" I said, dropping the cheese and cracker I'd just been about to scarf down. "Trust me, I don't have an eating disorder."

"There's a girl who lived in my dorm freshman year who was bulimic. She threw up so much they had to ask her to leave, because she was upsetting all of the other chicks with eating disorders," Mickey said, reaching for yet another brownie. She looked at me. "Do you have any peanut butter?"

"Yes, in the cupboard. Why?"

"I want to spread some on this brownie. 'Two great tastes that taste great together,' " she said, springing to her feet and heading into the kitchen.

"That's disgusting. I don't know how you can eat like that and stay so thin," Sophie said, wrinkling her nose. She looked over at me. "What's wrong with you?"

The sandwiches and cookies and brownies and chips and dip I'd been downing all day were starting to catch up with me. My stomach had started to heave, and I sat still, breathing deeply, hoping it would pass.

"Look how pale she is. Paige, I think you must be coming down with something," Mom said.

"Either that or she's pregnant. That's how I spent the first fourteen weeks of my pregnancy," Sophie said, resting her hands contentedly on her massive abdomen.

Mickey, who had returned from the kitchen with a jar of peanut butter and a knife, giggled. "Well, we know she's not pregnant. Right, Paige?"

My mom laughed, too. "That's just what I need right now."

I frowned. "So, Sophie gets pregnant, and we all have to suffer through yet another party thrown in her honor, but if I do, I'm just a burden to the family?" I asked.

"That's not what I meant. And you're not pregnant . . . are you?" my mother asked.

"Don't you have to have sex in order to get pregnant?" Mickey asked.

"Why do you find it so unbelievable that I'd have sex?" I asked, rolling my eyes.

"I don't know, I just can't picture it," Mickey said.

"God, Mick, I don't think you're supposed to picture your sisters having sex," Sophie said.

"Well, I can totally imagine you and Aidan doing it," Mickey said.

"Really?" Sophie asked, looking so pleased by this that I just rolled my eyes again.

"Will all of you please *shut up*!" my mother yelled.

We all turned to stare at her. My mother is not prone to screaming "Shut up." This was the woman who advised me when I was a child that it was much more polite to say "I don't appreciate the exuberance of your verbosity" than the easier "Shut up" or more satisfying "Shut your face." I had to look up "exuberance" and "verbosity" in my children's dictionary to understand what the hell she'd been talking about.

"Thank you. Now, Paige. Let me get this straight. Are you pregnant?"

"No," I admitted. "At least, I don't think so."

"Good," my mother said, looking relieved. In fact, insultingly so.

"Why would it be such a bad thing if I were pregnant?" I asked her.

"I just don't think that would be the best thing for you right now. Do you?" she asked. "You're not married or even in a relationship, you work long hours, you've gone through a difficult last couple of years."

"Yes, but . . . ," I started, and then I frowned, biting my lip. "Maybe that's what I need. Marriage didn't work out for me, but that doesn't necessarily mean that I can't have a baby. I could always go to a sperm bank."

"Good Lord," my mother said weakly. She picked up her glass of wine and downed it in one long gulp.

"But you don't like babies," Sophie said, eyeing me critically.

"Of course I do! Why would you think that?" I asked.

"You just never seemed to have any interest in kids. Even when you were married, I just assumed that you'd be too caught up in your career to have a family," Sophie said.

"Plenty of women balance a career and kids," I said.

Sophie shrugged. "I know, it's just a big sacrifice." She looked around my apartment at the white sofas, and the glass coffee table with the hard sharp corners, and the bar against the wall that had wineglasses hanging from the underside of the cabinet, and I knew what she was thinking: this wasn't a kid-friendly place.

"It's not like I'm going to have a baby right this second," I said irritably.

"Thank God for small favors," my mother said. "Mickey, would you pour me another glass of wine?"

"Even if I did get pregnant right away, there would be nine months to get ready. I could sell this place and buy a house. And maybe I could cut my hours back at work, or work out of the house part of the time," I mused.

"You've got to be kidding me," Sophie said, rolling her eyes. She struggled to get up off the couch. "Just a few weeks ago you were saying that you were never going to date again. And now you're all of a sudden going to have a baby? On a whim? Having a baby isn't something that you just casually decide to do, and it isn't something that's going to be a Band-Aid for everything else that's going wrong in your life."

"It's not just a whim," I said, choking on my anger. How dare Sophie, she who had everything—the doting husband, the baby on the way, the knack of being the center of attention at every single social gathering she'd ever been to—tell me that I can't have a child? "As a matter of fact, I was pregnant once already. And then I miscarried, and then my marriage turned to shit, but before that, before I knew about Scott, all I wanted was to get pregnant. In fact, sometimes I wonder if I had . . ."

My voice trailed off, and I clapped my hand over my mouth. Salty tears stung at my eyes and spilled over onto my cheeks. Sophie, Mickey, and Mom were all staring at me.

"Oh, Paige," Mom said, and she leaned over and put her hand on my leg. "Oh, honey, I'm so sorry. Why didn't you tell us before?"

"If you had, maybe Scott wouldn't have left you?" Sophie asked, finishing the thought that I hadn't been able to bring myself to complete.

"No. I mean, yes, I wonder what would have happened. I'm not saying I think a baby would have saved our marriage. There was that one rather large problem that he wasn't attracted to me, or anyone of my gender," I said. "But I wish I'd been able to have that baby or that I'd gotten pregnant again. I want a family."

"But you've said you don't want to get married, or even date again," Sophie said carefully. We'd suddenly swapped roles: I was emoting, she was analyzing.

"I don't know what I want," I said miserably.

Chapter Twelve

W hat do you think you should do?" Elise asked.

"Don't do that. Don't get all shrinky on me," I groaned.

God, I hated therapy. It always seemed so self-indulgent to me, wasted money and wasted time. I'd first seen Elise several years ago, when Scott and I had been married for about six months and I'd been struggling with a low-grade depression that I couldn't seem to shake. One year and a grossly large amount of money later, we'd discussed every-thing from the competitive nature of my relationship with Sophie to the many issues stemming from my parents' acri-monious divorce to the distance I sometimes felt from my new husband, and I was no closer to uncovering what had been bothering me. So I stopped going.

But now that I was wading through this postdivorce swamp, I for once decided to take my mother's advice and called Elise for an appointment. I figured that now more than ever I probably needed a neutral opinion on how to proceed. Should I call Zack? I hadn't been able to stop think-ing about him, but the idea of getting further involved with him terrified me. What if he, too, was gay, and I was some-how doomed to a life of dating and marrying closeted men? And was it really so crazy to consider having a baby on my own? Or were my baby pangs the result of loneliness and grief?

"Okay, here's my non-shrinky answer for you: you're really screwed up," Elise said, peering at me through her thick, tortoiseshell-framed glasses.

"What? You're not supposed to say that," I protested. "You're supposed to be supportive and kind."

"Whenever I try to be supportive and kind, you accuse me of being shrinky," Elise pointed out. Accurately.

"True, but I don't think you should go around telling your clients that they're screwed up. At least give me some hope."

Elise looked at me thoughtfully. But then, Elise did every-thing thoughtfully. She probably peed thoughtfully and went through thoughtful labor with her children. She even looked like a therapist, with her tasteful brown pageboy haircut and her gently rounded face.

"I didn't say you're *irredeemably* screwed up. If you wanted to, you could overcome it," she offered.

"With another year of therapy spent discussing why my mother always felt she had to befriend my friends?" I asked, and crossed my arms.

"No, that's not what I was going to say. But I'm not going to tell you if you're just going to sit there and be sarcastic," she said.

"You can't do that! I'm paying you for this!"

"Paige, you are not the craziest client I've ever had, but I think you might be the most stubborn. Which is not neces-sarily better," Elise sighed.

I bit my lip. I was a little intrigued. "Okay, I won't be sarcastic. Tell me how I can unscrew myself, ha-ha."

Elise shook her head, obviously not appreciating my shrink humor. "Okay, here it is: stop being so fucking closed off."

Fucking? I'd never heard Elise swear before. It was like hearing your parents curse for the first time—it was both titillating and disillusioning, and not at all what you expect to come out of the mouth of someone wearing a long flowered skirt and matching pink sweater set.

"Fucking?" I repeated.

"Yes. Fucking. I'm not denying that you've had a tough time, and I can understand how having to cope with the loss of your pregnancy, the loss of your marriage, and finding out that your partner was not the man you thought he was would be overwhelming. And it does take time to get over those kinds of traumatic events, absolutely. But you're not trying to heal. You're just closing yourself off and making stupid declarations about how you're never going to risk getting involved in another relationship again," she said.

"Are you just going to mock me, or is there some advice coming my way?" I asked.

"Here's the advice: trust yourself. Yes, Scott deceived you, and yes, I can see how it would make you question yourself. But as a closeted gay man, Scott had a lot of practice getting by with his sexuality undetected. And maybe he didn't even consciously know that he was gay. I wouldn't be surprised if he thought his attraction to other men was just an impulse he could control, and that living life as a straight man was just a matter of discipline. But in the end, that doesn't matter. What matters is that you get to the point where you can

accept that there is nothing flawed or wrong with you because you didn't know the truth," she said.

"You make it sound so easy. But you can't guarantee that
the next guy won't be seriously screwed up in some way, or
the one after him, or the one after *him*. What am I supposed
to do, just leave myself open to getting kicked in the teeth
over and over again?" I asked.

"No, I'm definitely not saying it's easy. You trusted someone you loved, and he deceived you, and it's only natural
that it's going to be harder for you the next time around. But
you're taking it to an extreme. You're not just saying, 'I want
to take some time off of dating so that I can heal, but I fully
plan to get out there again.' Instead, you're deciding that you
don't want to get close to anyone ever again, because you don't
want to add any complications to your life. And I think that's
why you're suddenly so eager to have a baby on your own.
You're craving the intimacy of a loving relationship, but
you're too frightened to put your heart on the line, and a
baby will love you unconditionally. And to answer your earlier question, no, I don't think that right now is the best time
to make that decision. I'm not saying that you should never
consider it, or even that doing it on your own is an objec-
tively bad idea. And I'm certainly not saying that being single is a bad thing. But you shouldn't make those kinds of
decisions because you're afraid of the alternative, afraid of
opening yourself up to the possibility that there is someone
out there for you."

"Like Zack, you mean."

"I don't know," Elise said, and she shrugged again.

Considering I had gone to her for some solid, orderly advice, all of this shrugging was not comforting.

"He could be the right one for you, or maybe he's not. You hardly know him, other than to discover that your first impression of him wasn't accurate and that he might have more to offer than you first thought," Elise continued.

"So . . . you think I should call him," I surmised.

"It's up to you whether or not you choose to see him again," she said. "I can't decide that for you. Whatever you decide to do, though, just make sure you're not letting your fear control you."

"Huh," I said. "I guess I can see that."

Elise's eyebrows arched.

"What? I'm open to personal growth. I'm here, aren't I?"

"Always an important first step," Elise said.

"That's right. And as long as I'm here, I do have one other tiny issue I wanted to talk about," I said.

"What's that?"

"The Home Shopping Network. Is it a bad sign if someone—not necessarily me—shops there? A lot?"

Chapter Thirteen

ello."

"Hi. Zack. It's Paige," I said. I turned my chair around and stared out my office window at the back of the capitol building. It was a grand building that mimicked the architecture and style of the United States Capitol. I'd always thought it looked out of place in Austin, like the poser girl everyone knows in college—usually a drama major—who shows up at keg parties in her prom dress.

"Hi," Zack said in what might have been a cool tone of voice. I couldn't be sure—I'd called him on his cell phone, and the line had that tinny quality that took all the nuance out of a person's voice.

"We went out last month," I clarified.

"I know who you are," Zack said. This time I knew I wasn't imagining the curt tone—he was miffed.

"I'm sorry I didn't return your call before this," I began.

"Calls," Zack said.

"What?"

"Calls. I called you more than once. I left several messages for you, both at your office and at home," Zack said.

"Right. Calls. It's just . . . well, things were kind of hectic here at work, and then I had Soph's baby shower, and I, well, just sort of lost track of time," I finished lamely.

Zack didn't say anything.

This wasn't going as well as I'd hoped it might.

"So I was wondering . . . uh . . . would you like to have dinner with me? Maybe tonight, or if you already have plans, later in the week?" I said. I rested the palm of my hand against my forehead and waited.

Zack still didn't say anything.

"Hello?" I asked.

"I don't think so," Zack said.

"You don't think you can tonight?" I asked.

"I don't think dinner would be a good idea," Zack said firmly.

"But I thought . . . when you called me so many times, I just assumed . . . I thought that you wanted to get together again," I said, stumbling over the words.

I'd been so focused on trying to overcome my fear of getting involved with Zack, I hadn't considered the possibility that he no longer wanted to see me.

"I did . . . but not anymore. I don't like the way you treated me," he said.

I was so completely and totally mortified by this succinct rejection that it took me a few beats to get to the point where I could respond.

"I, um . . . don't know what to say . . . I didn't mean to be unkind. I'm sorry if I was."

"Thank you."

"So . . . do you think we could try again?"

Zack paused again, and my heart stalled.

"No," Zack said. "I don't think so. Bye, Paige."

And then he hung up on me.

"Un-fucking-believable," I said, and slammed my phone down.

I'd done exactly what Elise had advised me to do—I'd taken a chance on a relationship, put myself out there, and look what happened: complete and total rejection. And humiliation. Okay, maybe it was a little shitty of me not to return his phone calls. Maybe a lot shitty. But how could he not give me a second chance?

"Asshole. Jerk. Creep," I muttered as I slammed client files around on my desk, for no other reason than that it made me feel better.

"Um, Paige? Is everything okay?" Sue asked.

I looked up and saw my assistant hovering by the door, looking a little nervous. I paused, holding a file in midair, and suddenly realized that I was turning into a scary, crazy woman. Sort of what Soph had been like for the past seven months, but I didn't have the excuse of being pregnant.

I very calmly set the file down on my desk and smiled at Sue.

"Why are you smiling like that?" Sue asked suspiciously.

"What do you mean? How am I smiling?" I replied.

"Like you're planning to kill me. What did I do wrong?"

Argh. I tried to focus on remaining calm and exuding a Zen-like patience.

"Nothing, of course not. Did you need something?" I asked sweetly.

"Yes, here you have to sign these." Sue darted into my office, dropped a stack of letters on my desk, and then backed away slowly. "And your sister's on line two." Sue scampered out of the office as though she were afraid that I might swarm and attack.

I rolled my eyes and punched the line-two button on my phone.

"Hi," Sophie said. Her voice was thick and heavy.

"Hey. Is everything okay? You sound like you just woke up," I said.

"Yeah, I was taking a nap. I went to the doctor today, and he said my blood pressure was too high. He's putting me on bed rest," Sophie said, and then yawned loudly. "Mom said she'd stay here for a while, since I can only get up for ten minutes every two hours—can you freaking believe that? I have a baby *sitting on my bladder*. I have to pee every ten minutes. What am I supposed to do?"

"Ugh, I don't know. Maybe use a bedpan?" I suggested.

"Yuck."

I placed a hand on my flat, as-yet-unfertile belly and realized that if I did decide to go ahead and get pregnant, this was the direction I was heading in. Uncontrollable urination and possible bed rest. And then, after the baby came, there'd be the late-night feedings, the stitches on the most delicate area of my body, the sore nipples, the general fatigue that every new parent is cloaked in. Sophie had Aidan, and apparently Mom was ready to sign on as a nanny. What would I do if I needed help? Sure, my family would probably help out, but most women who go through this have a partner. And, unlike Sophie, I'd have to juggle motherhood with my career.

"I don't think I can cope with Mom being here full-time. I wanted a bowl of ice cream earlier, and do you know what she did? She brought me some *fucking frozen yogurt*," Sophie said. Her voice was shrill with outrage. "She actually suggested that I'm putting on too much weight. Can you believe that? I'm growing a child *inside my body,* what does she think, that I'm going to look like a stick-thin model?"

"I'm sure she doesn't—" I began.

"And then she *confiscated* my secret stash of peanut M&M's. I don't know how the *hell* she found them, because I hid them in the freaking garage, but she did, and she actually *threw them away*. I swear, if I could get up, I'd kill her," Sophie raged on.

"Is she there now?" I asked.

"No. Dad came over and the two of them went off somewhere and left me here alone until Aidan gets home," she said.

"Don't you think it's a little strange that the two of them have been spending so much time together?"

"Tell me about it. Have you talked to Mom lately? She's all 'Your father said this' and 'Your father thinks that.' They used to hate each other, it was the natural order of things. Wait!" Sophie gasped.

I nearly had a heart attack. "What? Are you going into labor?"

"Do you think Dad had Mom turned into a Stepford wife?"

"Jesus, Sophie, don't gasp like that again unless the baby is actually in the birth canal, sticking his or her hand out and waving at you. You scared me to death," I said.

"Well, what do you think?"

"Do I think Dad had Mom killed and replaced with a robot? No, that's highly unlikely."

"Maybe you're right," Sophie said. She sounded unconvinced.

"I am," I said. "So, to change the subject . . . I called Zack today."

"Really? What did he say?" Sophie suddenly sounded wide-awake.

"That he didn't want to talk to me, and that he doesn't want to see me ever again. So much for hanging it all out there and taking a risk on romance."

Sophie gasped. "No! Are you serious? Why?"

"He's angry that I didn't return his phone calls sooner. Which I do understand. But I apologized and asked for a second chance, and he just said no," I said, feeling a stab of self-pity.

"But . . . he was just asking me about you the other day. I can't believe he wouldn't accept your apology. Does he know about your history?"

"You mean about Scott? No!"

"Why not?"

"It's not exactly a great selling point for me. It makes me sound . . . damaged."

"That's ridiculous. You should call him back and explain your history and tell him that's why you got freaked out and treated him like shit on a stick," Sophie said judiciously.

"I wouldn't exactly characterize it that way," I said.

"Are you going to call him back?"

"Why, so he can just hang up on me again?"

"He *hung up* on you?"

"Practically. It was very clear that he wanted nothing to do with me," I said.

"Still. I don't think you should give up on him. He's a really sweet guy, and I think that if he knew your history, he'd be much more forgiving," Sophie said. "Maybe you could send him a letter. Or I could tell him, if you want."

"No! That's a terrible idea!"

"Which one? The letter or my telling him?" Sophie asked.

"Both! I don't want you to tell him, that's ridiculous. I can speak for myself. And what am I going to do, pass him a note like we're in junior high?"

"Do you remember doing that? You'd write the cute boy in math class a note on a folded piece of paper that says 'Do you like me? Check box.' And then there'd be a 'yes,' 'no,' and 'maybe' listed below," Sophie said, giggling.

"Can you imagine doing that now?" I said, and couldn't help laughing at how ridiculous it sounded. Had I ever been that young, or that open with my feelings?

"So what are you going to do?" Sophie asked.

"For now, nothing. What else can I do?" I asked. "I have to go, though, I have a pile of work to do."

"Okay, I'll talk to you later. Wait, Paige?"

"Yeah?"

"Are you sure it's not possible for Mom to be an evil robot? Because I swear, she had a really strange look on her face when she was over here earlier," Sophie said.

I was guessing that the strange expression probably had a lot more to do with what an enormous pain in the ass Sophie was being than anything else.

"Yes. I'm sure she's not a robot. Good-bye."

"Okay, bye."

Chapter Fourteen

Did you mean it when you said that if I ever wanted to talk about . . . you know, why we divorced . . . we, um, could?" I asked Scott over the phone.

"Talk?" he asked, sounding surprised and a little wary.

"I just want to clear some things up. Try to understand everything better."

Scott was quiet.

"But every time I tried to talk to you, you shut me out," he finally said.

"I know. It's taken me a while to get to the point where I can deal with it," I said.

"Okay. I'll come over," he said.

"When? Now?" I asked, suddenly feeling a surge of panic at the idea. The first step had been reaching out to him, and I'd had to psych myself up for that. I didn't know if I was ready for the one-on-one encounter yet.

"I'll be there in twenty minutes," Scott said.

And exactly twenty-one minutes later, there was a knock on the door. I opened it, and Scott was standing there, looking like a Banana Republic model in dark-rinse jeans, a stylishly untucked striped shirt, and a blue cotton blazer that was nipped in at the hips. On his feet, he wore a pair of rounded black oxford shoes, the very kind that I remember him making fun of the college kids for wearing. I looked him up and down.

"I can't get used to your dressing like this," I said. "It's so weird."

"I know, I was always the dirty-jeans-and-T-shirt kind of a guy in my straight days," Scott said. This time he moved toward me as if to hug me, and then hesitated when I froze. It was just so bizarre, feeling this awkward around someone I had once thought I knew better than anyone. I put an arm around him and patted him on the back, and he kissed me on the cheek.

"This is strange," I said, and rested my head on his shoulder for a minute.

"Totally weird," he agreed, and then we both laughed, and then everything suddenly felt familiar. Even if the clothes and hair were different, the face was still the same: the eyes that were just a smidge too far apart, the long, prominent nose, the wide mouth that smiled easily. It wasn't a handsome face, but it was kind. I had always loved that about him.

He stepped into the condo, shutting the door behind him. "And it's so surreal to stand out there in the hallway and knock on the door. I almost reached for my keys when I got here," Scott said.

"Where are you living now?" I asked.

"I've been—we've been—renting a house in Hyde Park," he said shortly, which didn't explain much, but at the same time said everything.

We walked into the living room, and Scott sat on one of the white sofas.

"Do you want a glass of wine?" I asked.

"Probably more than one. I have to admit, I'm a little nervous," he said, and then he ran his hand over his head. His hair was cropped so short, I could see the vulnerable whiteness of his scalp underneath.

"Yeah. I know; me, too," I said, and I poured him a glass of wine from the bottle I'd opened a minute after I got off the phone with him. "But don't worry, I didn't ask you over here to yell at you."

I handed him his glass, and then poured myself one and sat across from him on the love seat. I'd put out a dish of cashews on the coffee table before he arrived, and I slid it toward him. He nodded toward the framed picture of Sophie, Mickey, and me on the side table.

"How's the kid?" he asked.

"Mick? She's doing great. She's graduating this spring and going to medical school next year," I said.

"No way. I can't believe it. They're going to give her a license to practice medicine?" Scott said.

"You should call her, I know she'd love to hear from you," I said, surprising myself. I hadn't asked my family to cut off contact with Scott, but I also hadn't encouraged them to stay in touch. I knew how much Mickey loved Scott, and our divorce had deeply upset her. It suddenly occurred to me how selfish I'd been not to encourage her to continue a relationship with the man who'd been like a big brother to her for so many years.

"Yeah, I should do that. I miss letting her beat me in chess," he said.

"Yeah, right. She always beat you fair and square," I said.

"Don't remind me. And how's the prom queen?"

"Pregnant, and due in a few weeks," I said.

"Good for them, but . . . that must be hard for you."

I shrugged and didn't answer. Instead I took a sip of my wine and looked at the flickering freesia-scented pillar candle sitting on the low coffee table. The white wax ran down one side and pooled by the base, hardening almost immediately.

"Boy or girl?" Scott asked.

"They're not finding out. I wish they would, it makes shopping hard, but you know how stubborn Sophie is," I said.

"It's a trait that tends to run in your family," Scott said, and he laughed.

This is bizarre, I thought. Scott sitting again in the living room, teasing me, poking fun at my sisters. It was as though my life had suddenly looped backward.

"So. How's work going?" I asked.

"Same as usual. Busy. You?"

"Pretty good, I guess. I'm not so sure anymore. I'm getting a little tired of spending all of my waking hours destroying people's marriages," I said.

"That's just one way to look at it. Maybe you're helping people get fresh starts," Scott said quietly.

"Like with you," I said.

He nodded. "I hope that for both of us."

I sipped at my wine and looked at him some more, and realized for the first time that I truly wasn't in love with him anymore. I hadn't thought about it in a long time—there'd been hurt and anger and numbness to distract me—but I now knew for sure that the man sitting across from me wasn't the one that I was supposed to be spending my life with. My lungs felt open, and as I inhaled, the breath rushed through my body.

"Well, that brings me to my first question. Did you know? When we got married, did you know that you were gay?"

Scott shrugged and looked down at his wineglass. "It depends. I knew that I was different, and I knew that I wasn't feeling all of the things that I should. Certainly I knew that I was drawn to men, and you were the first woman I'd ever had a strong attraction to. But no, I didn't have any clarity about being gay, and the idea of living any kind of a life other than as a heterosexual man would have terrified me, if I'd allowed myself to think about it. And I did love you, and was in love with you when we married. You know that, right?"

"It's one of the things that I've wondered about. Not knowing just how much of it was fake, how much of it was real," I admitted.

"That's fair. I really fucked everything up. I could bear screwing up my own life, but dragging you into it . . . that was the worst part," he said. "And I even thought that maybe I could keep going on the same way, and never tell you . . . but then that didn't seem fair to you, fair to either of us. Maybe it would have saved you the unpleasantness of learning the truth about me, but it also would have prevented you from pursuing a relationship with someone else, someone you could be real with."

"And if . . . the baby had made it?" I asked. I nearly choked on the words, but I had to know. I needed to stop playing the "what if" game in my head: what if Scott had never figured out he was gay, what if we were still together and raising our child, what if everything in my life hadn't been turned up-side down.

"I don't know what would have happened. I think I would have tried to stay, but . . . I don't know how long I could have pulled it off. It's like I was wearing clothes that didn't fit," he said. "I know, I'm crap at analogies, but try to understand: I was living a life that was a lie in almost every way. And once I realized that, it was never going to work."

I nodded. His wineglass was empty, so I gestured to him with the bottle, and he held his glass out so I could refill it.

"How are you doing? I mean really doing?" he asked. He'd always been great at this, the listening part.

"It's been hard. I haven't been dating much. It's hard to get back out there again. I don't really . . . trust myself," I admitted.

"Don't do that. Don't punish yourself just because I let you down. When we met and got married, I thought I was straight. So if I didn't know, how could you?"

"No, I get that. And I know that you didn't mean to hurt me. But there's also no guarantee that I won't be hurt again," I said.

"Oh God, I did this to you, didn't I?" Scott said, and he slouched down on the sofa, looking miserable. "You didn't use to be this guarded."

"I'm not that bad, really. I've started seeing my therapist again, and I did go out with a guy last month."

"Yeah? How'd that go?"

"Actually it was pretty great. I didn't think he was my type at first, but I really liked him," I said.

"Are you still seeing him?"

"No, I messed it up. I got kind of freaked out and didn't

return his phone calls. I called him yesterday to see if we could try again, but now he doesn't want anything to do with me. That's actually what prompted me to call you. I thought if I could get past everything that happened between us, then maybe I wouldn't screw things up next time," I admitted.

"You deserve to be happy," Scott said. "I'm really sorry, Paige. For everything."

"I know. But as far as you and I are concerned, we're okay," I said. "Who knows, maybe we can even be friends again."

"I'd like that," Scott said. His eyes were moist with emotion. "It's been so strange not having you in my life."

"Yeah, I know, it has been weird. So . . . what about you?"

"What about me?"

"You asked about my nonexistent love life, now what about yours?"

"Are you sure you want to talk about this?"

I nodded.

"Well . . . it's not nonexistent," Scott said. "I met someone."

"Is this the chef?" I asked.

"So you've been keeping tabs on me? Yeah, he's a pastry chef, his name is Kevin. And he's pretty great. In fact, he's introducing me to his parents this weekend. I haven't had to go through that since you took me home to meet Blair." Scott laughed, and I did, too.

Scott had been so nervous meeting my mother, he'd barely said two words at that first dinner. She concluded that he was a drug addict. Why, I don't know, because I'm pretty sure my mom doesn't know any drug addicts, and certainly not any mute ones. Later she fell in love with him, but that first meeting had been uncomfortable. Mom later claimed, with typical revisionist clarity, that she'd had a feeling that night that Scott was gay.

"Speaking of whom, how are your parents? Do they still hate me?" Scott asked.

"They're fine. And apparently best buddies all of a sudden. But no, I don't think they hate you. Of course, you're also no longer their favorite son-in-law."

"Yeah, I can see that. My parents aren't too thrilled with me either," he said.

"They're not being supportive?" I asked.

"They just pretend that it's not happening. I tried to tell Mom about Kevin, and she just acted like she didn't know what I was talking about. And my dad won't look me in the eye," he said.

My heart squeezed. "That doesn't sound like them . . . they never struck me as intolerant people," I said.

"Yeah, well, it's different when it's your own kid, I guess. I think they'll come around. It's just been a tough couple of years for all of us," Scott said. "You, me, them, your family. We'll all get past it eventually."

"I hope so," I said.

Chapter Fifteen

Thanksgiving was only a week away, and promised to be especially grim this year. I was still divorced, Sophie was on bed rest and crabby as hell, and my parents were acting so strangely they had all of us on edge. On the bright side, Mickey had come home a few days early—no doubt with an enormous garbage bag full of dirty clothes and a bottomless appetite—and our resident court jester always lightened the mood of the family. She called me the day after she arrived.

"What are you doing tomorrow night?" Mickey asked.

"No plans. Why? Do you want to catch a movie or something?"

"I'm at Sophie's right now, and she wants us all to have dinner over here. But we can rent some videos if you want," Mickey said.

"Well . . . is she still being scary?" I asked.

"Give me the phone. Hey, I heard that," Sophie said. "You have to come over, Paige. Mom and Dad are coming, too."

"I thought Mom said she was staying with you," I said.

"I couldn't take it anymore, so I kicked her out. If she asked me one more question about her stupid crossword puzzle, I was going to sit on her. And that's a real threat coming from a woman who's about to give birth at any minute," Sophie said.

The idea of a family get-together was sounding less and less attractive.

"I think I might be having a migraine on Saturday," I said.

"Don't even think about it. You have to come, there's no way you're going to leave Mickey and I to deal with them alone," Sophie huffed.

"Okay, fine, I'll come," I said.

"Good. Would you mind picking up the pizzas on your way over? And maybe you could make a salad or something, too," Sophie said brightly. I heard Mickey shout in the background, "And Mickey wants some cheesecake. Mmm, that sounds good."

"Let me get this straight: You're inviting me over for dinner, and you want me to bring the dinner? And the dessert?" I asked.

"And although I can't have any, you might seriously want to consider bringing a bottle of wine, too. Who knows how long Mom and Dad will be able to stay in the same room without going for each other's throats? Truce or no truce," Sophie said.

I arrived at Sophie's with three large pizzas—one veggie, one pepperoni, and one with everything—and also a store-bought salad, cheesecake, and two bottles of wine. Everyone was already there, and Sophie had descended from her bedroom for the occasion. She was lying regally on her Pottery Barn sectional sofa with a cranberry chenille blanket draped over her huge belly. Mom and Mickey were huddled on the couch together, looking at some photos, and they looked up when I came in.

"Hi, honey," Dad said, and he stood up to kiss me on the cheek.

"Hi," I said, hugging him. "Hey, everyone. What pictures are those?"

"Hey!" Mickey said, and she jumped up and started rummaging through the shopping bags I'd brought.

"They're from Sophie's shower," Mom said. "Here's a good one of you, Soph."

"No, I don't want to see them. I'm sure I look enormous in every single one," Sophie said. Her face lit up when she saw the pizza boxes in my hands. "The food's here! Will you put it in the kitchen? Mick, help Paige get everything out. There are plates in the cupboard to the right of the sink . . . wait, never mind, I'll just do it."

"No!" everyone shouted, and Sophie slumped back on the couch.

"I'm sick of lying down," she said pitifully.

"You promised you'd stay off your feet. If you don't, you're going to have to go back upstairs to bed," Mom admonished her.

Sophie rolled her eyes. "I'm not five years old, you know," she complained, but she stayed down.

I walked into the kitchen with Mickey. Aidan was there, sitting at the kitchen table, drinking a beer straight from the bottle and reading the sports page of the paper. Aidan had been a quarterback in high school, and twelve years later, like most ex-jocks, his body had thickened while his hair thinned. Still, he was an attractive guy with an amiable face and brilliant blue eyes.

"Are you hiding?" I asked him.

"Hi, Paige. No, not hiding, just came in to get a beer," he said, smiling, and pecked me on the cheek before sidling out of the kitchen.

"I think we scared him off," Mickey whispered in my ear, and we both laughed. Aidan was unfailingly polite to all of us, but he always found a reason to disappear when our family descended upon him.

"Wow. The kitchen looks fantastic," I said, looking around at the gorgeous cherry wood cabinets, the new granite counter-top, the stainless steel backsplash and appliances. The floor was tiled in a slate gray, and the walls were a lighter dove gray. It looked like something out of an interior-decorating maga-zine. "Did Zack do all of this?" I wondered out loud.

"Yup. Except for the floor—I had my tile guy do that," a male voice said from behind me. I whirled around, and there was Zack, standing in the doorway of the kitchen, just as he had been the first time I saw him.

I gaped at him, feeling like the breath had been sucked out of me. After Zack's brusque refusal to have dinner with me, I'd fantasized about how fabulously cutting I'd be if and when I ever did see him again. But now that the moment was here, all I could do was stand there, feeling the sting of just how firmly he'd rejected me.

"What are you doing here?" I asked.

"Your sister wanted me to install some built-in book-shelves in the nursery. And she was very insistent that I come over tonight to measure for them. I just got here. I thought I recognized your car when I pulled up," Zack said.

"Are you Zack? Hi, I'm Mickey," Mickey said, and she held out her hand. Zack grinned at her, and Mickey colored. She turned to me and mouthed, "He's hot," and then scampered out of the room.

I bit my lip, and considered throttling Sophie, since she'd obviously ignored my strict instructions not to interfere and I was now in the mortifying position of having to make small talk with the guy I'd had a one-night stand with. At least he seemed pleasant enough, and the curt edge had disappeared from his voice.

"I didn't know you'd be here," I said, and paused. There were two courses of action open to me: I could take advantage of Sophie's meddling by asking Zack for another chance, or I could turn around and walk away. I made my decision. "But actually, I would like to talk to you, if you have a minute."

Zack hesitated for a second, but then nodded. "Sure. Did you want to talk here, or . . . ?" His voice trailed off in a question mark.

I looked over my shoulder and could see Mickey trying to look inconspicuous as she eavesdropped from the hallway. I rolled my eyes.

"Not here," I said firmly. "Let's go outside."

We walked out of Soph's house. I was glad that I hadn't taken my coat off yet, as the wind that had been blowing all day had picked up a sharp bite now that the sun had set.

I followed Zack to his vintage truck, and he opened up the passenger-side door for me.

"It would probably be warmer if we got in," he said. He smiled, but his eyes were shuttered, so I couldn't tell if he was still feeling hostile toward me. Or if he just wasn't feeling anything at all.

I climbed up into the cab of the pickup, and watched through the window as Zack walked around to the driver's-side door, and tried to figure out what in the hell I was going to say to him. I could always fall back on the eighties pop song lyrics of my youth: *I want you to want me,* or *If you leave, don't leave now,* or *I'll stop the world and melt with you.*

Oh no, it's happened, I've actually lost my mind, I thought. I balled up my hand and rested it against my forehead.

Zack opened the driver's-side door, letting in another blast of wind, and then slid in next to me and started the engine. He smelled wonderful, a combination of aftershave and freshly cut wood. And he looked distressingly handsome in his faded Levi's and a dark blue T-shirt underneath a heavier plaid shirt.

"So. What did you want to talk about?" Zack asked, glancing in my direction. He fiddled with his car keys, jingling them in his right hand.

He's nervous, I suddenly realized. He wouldn't be nervous if he didn't care about me at all . . . unless of course it stemmed from a fear that I was going to start screaming at him or turn into an obsessed stalker.

"Just that I again wanted to say that I'm sorry. About everything. I don't know why I didn't return your phone calls earlier . . . wait, no, that's not true," I said, deciding that since I knew I didn't have much of a chance with Zack anyway, I might as well be honest.

"The reason I didn't call you back is that I had intended for that night that we slept together to be a one-time thing. I was trying to prove something to myself, and I didn't stop to consider your feelings. Or my own," I continued.

"Which were?"

I took a deep breath and then forged on.

"I was trying to convince myself that I could have a relationship with a man that was purely physical, with no emotional attachments, because . . . well, you know that I'm divorced. But I didn't tell you why. My husband left me because he was—he is—gay. And since then I've been wary of getting involved with anyone," I said, and squirmed a little at this last part.

"Actually, I already knew that, about your husband and how it had messed you up," he said.

"Well, I wouldn't say it messed me up. I was just a little . . . sideways. Anyway, who told you? Sophie, I assume? Right. After we finish here, I'm going to go inside and kill her."

"Don't be too hard on her. She was trying to help. But that's not what I mean, anyway. You said you didn't stop to consider your feelings, and I wanted to know what those feelings are," he said.

I looked down, examining my hands. They were dry and needed moisturizing lotion. And the sensible beige polish had chipped away at the edge of the ring finger of my left hand.

"Does it matter?" I asked quietly.

"It matters to me," Zack said, and he reached out and

took my hand and cradled it between both of his. He didn't seem to notice the dry skin or the chipped polish.

"Well. I . . . I haven't been able to stop thinking about you," I admitted.

I looked up at him, and he leaned forward and caught my lips on his. His mouth was warm and sweet, and then he was cradling his hand against my neck, pressing me closer to him. It rated as one of the all-time greatest kisses of my life.

"I really hope that wasn't a good-bye kiss," I said when we came up for air.

"Nah. I have to give you another chance to beat me at Scrabble," Zack said, and he kissed me again.

"No time like the present," I said, grinning at him until the skin at the corners of my mouth was sore.

"Don't you have to go back in there and do family stuff?" he asked.

"Well, no, but I should probably tell them I'm leaving. I don't want them to think you've abducted me," I said.

I climbed out of the truck and let myself back into Sophie's house through the garage. I passed through the laundry room and opened the door into the kitchen . . . and walked right in on my mother and father. Mom was leaning back against Sophie's new granite-topped island, and Dad had his arms around her, and—oh God—he was sticking his tongue down her throat.

"Ack!" I said.

They jumped apart like teenagers caught necking when they're supposed to be studying for midterms. My mother turned around, and when she saw me standing there, my mouth wide open, she blushed.

"Uh . . . Paige," she said delicately.

"This isn't what it looks like," my father said. My mother's cherry red lipstick was smeared all around his mouth, and his glasses were askew.

"Don't tell me, I don't want to know," I said, raising both hands in front of me.

"But honey—" Mom said.

"Nope, nuh-uh, not interested."

"Um, guys, I think you'd better get in here," Mickey yelled from the living room. "I think Sophie's going into labor."

I dashed to the living room, my parents right behind me. Sophie was standing up, looking behind her at the couch.

"Shit. My water broke on my brand-new couch. Mom, do you think that's going to stain?" she wailed.

"Sophie, sit down. Mick, go get Aidan, I think he's up-stairs. Dad, you'd better drive Sophie's car, Aidan will proba-bly be too nervous. Mom, Mickey and I will meet you at the hospital," I said.

"Stop being so bossy," Sophie grumbled, but she sat down heavily, her hands resting on her giant bump, and Mickey went flying out of the room. I could hear the thump-thump-thump as she ran up the stairs.

"Are you having contractions, honey?" Mom asked, sit-ting down next to Sophie and putting an arm around her.

"No, I'm not feeling anything yet. Other than hunger. I'm going to go get a piece of pizz—Yow! Oh . . . dear . . . God, what the hell was *that*?"

"It's probably a contraction. Stephen, are you wearing a watch? Start timing how long until her next contraction," Mom said.

"Are you okay, Soph?" I asked.

"No, I'm not okay! That fucking hurt! I . . . I don't think I can do this," Sophie said, shaking her head from side to side and rubbing her hands over her swollen belly.

"I think it's a little too late for that now," I said wryly.

"What the . . . Now? Is it . . . Oh my God," Aidan said, running into the room, Mickey behind him. "Car. We need a car. Where? I should drive. Keys. I need my keys."

Aidan just stood there, raising and then dropping his hands helplessly, his eyes unfocused. Clearly he would not be any help.

"Do you have a bag you'd like me to bring?" I asked Sophie.

"No, it's already in the back of my SUV. Aidan, the keys are in my purse, but Dad's going to drive," Sophie said calmly. "Mom, help me up. And Paige, will you help Aidan, he seems a little . . . out of it."

I gently held my brother-in-law's arm. "Why don't we go out to the car," I said to him.

"I have to prepare. Shouldn't I be boiling some water or something?" Aidan said. "Or ripping sheets?"

"Don't even think about it. The sheets have a six hundred thread count, and they cost a fortune," Sophie said.

"I know! I'll call an ambulance," Aidan said.

"We'll just drive you guys to the hospital," I said.

"I should change," Sophie said, turning on her heel and marching out of the room. "And I need to paint my toe-nails."

"What? Sophie, you look fine," I said, running after her. She moved fast for a woman in labor, and I didn't catch up to her until she was already in her walk-in closet, pulling clothes off hangers.

"I'm not going to go to the hospital wearing sweats.

Where's my Mimi Maternity dress? The black one with the flowers on it?" Sophie asked.

"Here, just wear this," I said, holding up flax linen overalls.

"No way. I look like a clown in that," Sophie sniffed. "Here's the dress."

She pulled off her purple T-shirt and stepped out of the gray cotton maternity sweatpants, and then pulled the sundress on over her head, exposing her enormous, round stomach. Standing in front of the mirror, she pulled her blonde curls forward into two low pigtails and fastened them with elastics. I had to admit, she did look better.

"Okay, now I need to do my toenails," she said, walking past me out of the closet and then turning left toward the en suite bathroom.

I scrambled after her. "Have you lost your mind? Your water broke, we have to get you to the hospital," I said.

"No, we have loads of time. I've only had one contraction, we don't even have to go in until they start getting closer together," Sophie said.

"And what if we get stuck in traffic? Or if it all starts to happen quickly?"

"Well then, help me. The faster we do this, the faster we'll get out of here," Soph said. She handed me a bottle of bright red nail polish and then sat down on the rim of the bathtub.

"I can't believe I'm actually doing this. If you weren't in labor . . . ," I muttered, but I kneeled down in front of her and unscrewed the top of the nail polish bottle. I dabbed the brush in. "This is a pretty color."

"Isn't it? I just bought it the other day. I was saving it for when I went into labor," Sophie said, beaming.

I knelt down and dabbed the brush over her shell-shaped nails.

"Okay, nutty girl, that should do it. I think I did a pretty good job. I guess if I ever tire of practicing law, I can always get a job giving pedicures," I said, sitting back to admire my handiwork.

"*Oh shit!*" Sophie exclaimed. She went pale and bent over, clutching her stomach.

"Mom! Sophie just had another contraction," I yelled. "How long was that?"

"Eight minutes," my mother called back. "Come on, we'd better get her to the hospital."

"Can you walk? Here, let me help you get up," I said, and heaved Sophie up onto her feet. "Do you want to lean on me?"

"No, I can walk, but wait . . . Paige? I'm scared," Sophie said, her voice wavering. Her face was small and pale, and I was reminded of when we were little and Sophie broke her leg skiing. She'd been determinedly cheerful right up to the point when she was wheeled into the hospital.

"I know, sweetie. I know. But just think, when it's all over, you'll look down and see your daughter's face for the first time, and it will all be over," I said.

Sophie looked at me sideways. "How do you know the baby will be a girl?"

"I'm just getting a strong female vibe," I said.

"Do you promise me that you won't leave me?" she asked, grabbing my hand as we started to walk out of the bedroom.

I suddenly remembered Zack was outside in his truck, waiting for me to sneak off with him. The promise of sinking into his arms—he was a world-class hugger, pulling me close to him until our hearts lined up and his arms were wrapped all the way around me—was snatched away.

For now, I reminded myself. Just for now.

"I won't leave you, no matter what," I promised.

Mom, Dad, Mickey, and Aidan were all standing by the front door, looking excited and worried, with the exception of Aidan, who seemed a little woozy. But to his credit, he came forward and put his arm around his wife.

"Are you okay?" he asked her softly, and she just rested her head against his shoulder for a minute.

"We're ready to go," Sophie said brightly, rallying back, just as her eight-year-old self had done when it was time to set the broken leg.

"Baby, I'm going to drive you and Aidan. Mickey and Paige will go with your mother," Dad said.

"Actually, I have a ride. I'll meet you there," I said, and although Mickey shot me a curious look, everyone else was too busy scrambling out the front door and into the assortment of cars to pay much attention.

I watched while Aidan carefully helped Sophie into the backseat of her Tahoe and then crossed himself before climbing in after her (I hadn't known he was religious, but perhaps the birth of a child was atheist-free in the same way that foxholes were said to be). And then I turned and walked over to Zack's truck.

"Is everything okay? I got worried, you were gone so long," Zack said.

I leaned over and kissed him firmly on the lips. Zack smiled, even as our lips were touching, and threaded his hands through my hair.

"I thought you might have been running away again," he said.

"No. Definitely not. But there's been a slight change in plans," I said. And then I sat back in the seat and turned to pull on my seatbelt. "I'll tell you about it on the way to the hospital."

Sophie

Chapter Sixteen

I knew the moms' group wasn't going to work out the moment Lucille's eight-year-old daughter Olivia yanked open her mother's denim shirt, unfastened her bra, and proceeded to nurse while leaning over her mother's breast like it was a drinking fountain.

I really didn't need to see that.

I also didn't need to know that Lucille had nipples that were roughly the size of coasters.

Why was a child who was old enough to fix herself a peanut butter and jelly sandwich still breastfeeding? Will she expect her mother—or, more specifically, her mother's breasts—to accompany her to college? I wondered, and was suddenly gripped with insecurity. The pediatrician had recommended that I nurse Ben for one full year, and while I struggled with a bout of mastitis, blocked milk ducts, and sore nipples, the remaining eight months were yawning ahead of me, a seemingly insurmountable task. Wasn't one year good enough anymore? Was I supposed to play the part of a human cow until my children were in grade school?

"I thought Olivia had weaned, love," Velvet said. She was

dressed in all black and had henna tattoos covering her hands, and even though she was American, peppered her speech with British colloquialisms. Velvet was studiously ignoring her twin eighteen-month-old boys, Atticus and Macaulay, while they tore apart the den.

"She did. But after Griffon was born, Olivia was so jealous of her brother when he nursed, she asked if she could start up again. I had to teach her how to do it, but she picked it up again quickly," Lucille said, beaming down at her daughter.

Olivia finished gulping, smacked her lips, and ran off. Lucille didn't bother to button up, and instead took the opportunity to lift her baby son up to the exposed gargantuan nipple.

The mothers' group was meeting at Lucille's house. Also in attendance were Missy and her two-year-old daughter, Jade. Missy wore hemp overalls and insisted that the Wiggles were right-wing extremists trying to brainwash tots into embracing the evils of capitalism. Then there was Sonya—who never smiled—and her equally serious son, Quentin, whom Sonya claimed liked to meditate with her in the mornings. Rounding out the group were Velvet and Lucille and their kids.

And then there was me, perched on a sagging orange corduroy couch that had tufts of batting poking through the holey upholstery, cradling four-month-old Ben in my arms. Ben was a roly-poly Gerber baby with a dimple in his right cheek and round blueberry eyes. In fact, he was a composite of circles—the round cheeks, snub nose, tiny paw hands, fat little feet.

"How's he sleeping?" Missy barked at me, and I winced. The woman's voice was like sandpaper.

"So-so. He's slept through the night a few times, but most nights he still gets up once or twice," I said, and I leaned down and kissed Ben on the cheek.

I found that I kissed him constantly. One afternoon, while Ben napped, I absentmindedly leaned down and kissed the armful of laundry I was carrying.

I was guarding Ben on my lap largely because the thin, anemic-looking twins were playing a game that involved screaming at the top of their lungs, rushing each other like jousting knights, and then crashing to the ground with an audible cracking of bones. Every once in a while they'd miss each other and take down a sour-faced Quentin instead, who would promptly burst into tears and scream until his mother picked him up. In the middle of this chaos, Jade was running around giggling hysterically and clad in only a bulky cloth diaper that sagged at the bottom, a look that reminded me of a baby version of those wife-beater tank tops that the people being arrested on *Cops* were always wearing.

"You're co-sleeping," Missy pressed on. It wasn't a question, it was a declaration.

"No, he sleeps in his crib," I said, smiling pleasantly.

All of the mothers stared at me as though I'd just admitted to regularly holding Ben upside down out of a window, dangling him by his toes.

"Bloody hell. You put your baby in a cage?" Velvet asked, her blackened lips forming a surprised O. I wondered how a mother of twins had the time to also put on black eyeliner, mascara, white pancake makeup, and the glittery beauty mark in the shape of a star pasted to her cheek. Since Ben's arrival, I hardly had time to comb my hair, and my highlights hadn't been touched up in months.

"Crib, not cage. Crib," I said. I over-annunciated the words.

"That's what a crib is. A baby cage. I've never understood how any mother could do that, just leave her baby all alone. In a cage. In a dark room," Missy boomed. The word "mother" was a curled lip sneer. She glared at me, furrowing her small dark eyes over a pugnacious nose.

My skin felt tight over my face, and white flashes of light began to cloud my eyes. I struggled to swallow my anger, not wanting to launch into a rage right in the middle of my very first moms' group meeting.

"I don't think a crib is a cage," I said.

"Hi, everyone, sorry I'm late," a very tall, very thin woman said, walking into the den.

The newcomer was a pretty woman, with small sharp features and a skinny, pipe-cleaner body. She was wearing tight cropped denim capris and an orange tube top, and had an enormous pair of lightly tinted Chanel sunglasses pushing back her teased inky black hair. A baby who looked to be about the same age as Ben was nestled in her arms. I hoped to God that the child was adopted, because otherwise I was going to spin into a shame spiral. My postpartum body was still lumpy and swollen, a jiggling mass of angry red stretch marks and loose drooping skin, while this woman looked like she was ready to model for a *Sports Illustrated* spread.

Immediately, instinctively, I didn't like her. If the perfect body hadn't done it, the tube top would have. My boobs were so stretched out and deflated from nursing that if I tried to wear one, it would have slithered off my breasts and settled around my hips.

"Hi, Cora," Velvet said.

"This is Sophie, she's our newest member," Lucille said.

"Hi, nice to meet you," I said, smiling my nicest, fakest smile perfected after three years of college sorority rushes.

Cora smiled at me and shifted her sleeping infant in her arms.

"This is Beatrice. Your son is gorgeous. What's his name?" Cora asked kindly.

"Ben, short for Benjamin," I said, and my smile relaxed into its more natural state. Maybe she wasn't so bad after all.

"We were just telling Sophie about co-sleeping, and how beneficial it is. It facilitates bonding for the entire family. Our kids have never slept apart from us, and we just love it," Lucille said, smiling beatifically.

She'd finally buttoned up her voluminous shirt, which I was glad for. I want to be supportive of other women nursing in public, but I was having a hard time getting used to all of the spontaneous nudity. I hadn't yet gotten up the courage to nurse Ben in front of my mother-in-law—who was as anti-breastfeeding as these women were for it, and had widened her pale eyes with shock when I'd told her at my baby shower that I was planning on nursing Ben—much less whipping out my nipples in front of a roomful of strangers.

"You co-sleep with both of your children?" I asked, eyeing Olivia, who was walking around on her tiptoes, wielding a Popsicle and loudly bossing the other children. She was topless and a red smear ringed her mouth. Olivia had already tried to steal Ben's stuffed Manhattan Whoozit toy, and I'd had to wrestle it out of her sticky hands when her mother wasn't looking.

"All three of them. We have another daughter, Jordan, who's in the fourth grade," Lucille said.

"You must have a really big bed," I joked, and laughed nervously.

All of the women just stared at me humorlessly, with the exception of Cora, who snorted.

"The thing I've never understood about co-sleeping is how do you have sex? Do you just do it with your kids right there next to you?" Cora asked.

"Well, not while they're awake, of course," Lucille said, emitting a tinkling little laugh.

Literally every word the woman said made my skin itch. She was so goddamn patronizing. I felt like stomping her on the foot and marching out of her house. But I was pretty sure that wasn't acceptable playgroup etiquette.

"There are other places in the house to have sex," Missy said.

"We never have sex in the bedroom," Velvet interjected. "After the boys go to sleep in our bed—we have to lie down with them and sing until they drift off—we do it in the kitchen, or the loo, and every once in a while on the stair-case."

I stared at her. Freaky Fake British Goth chick had sex on the staircase? Even Missy the Troll was doing it? Was I the only one whose sex drive had withered up and blown into dust following Ben's birth? Between my nipples, battered from the constant nursing, to the fat deposits padding my stomach, ass, and thighs, to the exhaustion that seeped

through me, the last thing I wanted to do was have sex. Ever
again.

"We never had Beatrice in our bed with us. When we
brought her home, she spent a few weeks in a bassinet in our
room, but she's a really loud sleeper, and all of her snorting
and heavy breathing was keeping Jason awake," Cora said.

I nodded along while she spoke. "Same here. And I
wouldn't have felt comfortable having Ben in bed with us. I
was on pretty strong pain medication after my C-section,
and it really knocked me out. I would have been too worried
that I'd roll over and smother him," I said.

"You had a C-section?" Sonya gasped.

"How terrible. I would have been devastated if I hadn't
been able to deliver using the Bradley method," Lucille
tutted.

"I didn't have a choice. Ben was failing to progress," I
said, feeling ridiculous that I felt I had to explain it. Why
was it any of their business anyway? Who were they, the
Labor and Delivery Police? And the memory of that other-
worldly day—the loud shouts of the nurses as they rushed
me to the OR, the frightened look on Aidan's face, the cold
sterility of the bleached white operating room, the plastic
mask covering my face while the anesthesiologist instructed
me to count to ten—caused the surgical scar that cut horizontally under my pubic hair to twinge. I shoved the recol-
lection aside, before an acid-laced panic attack could start
roiling in my stomach, squeezing my chest and filling my
lungs until my breath could only escape in short, desperate
puffs.

"That's because you delivered in a hospital," Velvet said.
"Hospitals are so litigation adverse that they'll cut you open

at the slightest provocation. That's why I had a home birth. It was important to me to have the right birth experience."

"Birth experience?" I repeated.

"Oh, I agree. And I read somewhere that children born by C-section have problems bonding. It's really a travesty," Lucille continued. "Do you know that something like ninety percent of all C-sections are preventable?"

"At least! And then there's the too-posh-to-push women," Sonya said. "You know, the ones who actually request to have a C-section because they don't want to go through labor."

"You should have insisted on having a vaginal delivery," Missy barked, glaring at me. "You put your son at unnecessary risk. What if they had cut him while they were operating? That happened to someone I know, the scalpel went right through the uterus and nicked the baby's ear."

"I didn't have a choice," I bleated.

Labor had been progressing normally. Then, all of a sudden, Ben stopped moving. I'd pushed and pushed and pushed, until I thought I'd literally melt away into the rough, hospital-issue white sheets. When my doctor finally arrived—silly me, I'd had the strange idea that the doctor would just stay there the entire time I was in labor, not swan in and out like a socialite making the rounds at a charity event—he stuck his hand up my crotch, rooted around for a moment, and then shouted a curt "Prepare her for surgery" to the nurse. And then all of a sudden nurses were rushing around, shaving me, making me drink a nasty-tasting salty liquid out of a plastic cup, wheeling me down the hallways into the too-bright, freezing-cold operating room.

"I don't think it's anyone's business how Sophie had her baby," Cora interrupted me, before I could explain.

"Too many women follow their doctor's advice blindly instead of doing what's right for their baby," Missy continued.

"I have to go," I said, standing abruptly. I heaved my enormous black nylon Baby Gap diaper bag onto my shoulder and balanced Ben in my arms. He reached out and grabbed onto a piece of my hair and pulled it hard. My eyes watered, and I grappled with him, peeling his fingers off my hair. "Ouch."

"Ouch, Beatrice does that to me all the time," Cora said. "Here, I'll walk out with you. I was just stopping by for a minute, I can't stay."

The others didn't seem all that disappointed to see us go.

"Thank you for coming," Lucille sang out in her annoying, saccharine voice.

"I think C-sections should be outlawed," Missy was saying to Velvet, who was nodding along in agreement.

"It's just one more example of how Western medicine has gone wrong," Sonya opined. I slammed the door behind me, cutting off whatever other brilliant insights they might offer up.

"Don't let them get to you," Cora said as we walked out together, our arms full of babies and diaper bags. I always felt like a pack mule doing this, but Cora looked elegant and together with her Kate Spade bag tossed casually over her shoulder and her fresh-faced daughter cuddled up against her. Was I the only mother who rushed madly around the house before going out, stubbing my toe on the leg of the changing table, dropping my keys when I picked up my sunglasses, and then dropping the glasses when I bent over to retrieve the keys, and in the process forgetting to replenish the wet wipes in my diaper bag, or to pack a freshly laundered onesie or Ben's sun hat?

"What *was* that? A moms' group or a cult of Moonies? While I was in there, I was lectured on how I gave birth, where my child sleeps, and what my child eats. And when I admitted that Ben was circumcised, Sonya actually started to cry. She likened it to the mutilation of female genitalia that's practiced in some cultures," I ranted, and at the end of this my voice cracked and tears stung at my eyes.

We paused at the curb, where a fleet of minivans were parked. I felt a stab of pride when I saw my Tahoe, the only SUV there. I *love* my SUV. Aidan had tried to talk me into trading it in for a minivan—a.k.a., a dorkmobile—but I'd flat out refused.

"Don't let the Mother Superiors get to you, they're always like that. You should hear how they go after me. I once said I didn't see anything wrong with teaching Beatrice to self-soothe, and they practically had me stoned for it," Cora said, laughing. She kissed her daughter's smooth forehead and then rested her cheek on the cloud of dark downy hair. Beatrice was a miniature version of her mother, from the serene dark eyes to the tiny cleft chin.

"Why are you a member of the group, then?"

"Velvet and I go way back, from before she was doing her Vampire Queen act," Cora said.

"What's up with all of the 'bloody hell' and 'loo' stuff? Is she trying to be British?"

"I don't know, she must have just started that. I haven't heard her doing it before. When I met her, she had pink hair and worshipped Madonna. She talked me into joining the group after I had Beatrice, so I gave it a try. Today was the final straw, though—I'm not going back. I'm just not into the whole attachment-parenting thing," Cora said.

"I don't know what I'm into," I said honestly. I reached into my diaper bag for my keys and felt something cold and slushy in the pocket. When I withdrew my hand, I discovered the remains of a cherry Popsicle, now mostly melted. I had a vague memory of Olivia hovering near my diaper bag.

And then I actually burst into tears. I leaned against my car, heaved Ben up to my shoulder, and let my tears soak into the fuzz that masqueraded as his hair.

"Shit. I think this calls for a caramel macchiato. Follow me, there's a Starbucks down the street," Cora said.

Chapter Seventeen

"Hey," Aidan said, walking through the garage door into our remodeled kitchen.

The room was still a sore subject between us, even though the renovations had been completed months ago. He'd been furious that I'd hired Zack to tear apart a kitchen Aidan insisted was perfectly acceptable. When I'd tried to pretend that I'd done it to surprise him, he'd just looked at me and said flatly, "Do you really think I'm that stupid, Soph?" Now nearly every time his eyes took in the gorgeous cherry cabinets, granite countertop, and professional stainless steel range, his expression soured.

Don't start a fight, don't start a fight, don't start a fight, I told myself.

I thought that maybe if I repeated the words often enough, it might actually work. Lately everything about Aidan—from the pinched-up corners of his eyes to the tightness of his jaw—irritated me. Had he always been wound this tight, and I just hadn't noticed?

"Hi. How was your day?" I asked as I sliced into an onion.

Ben was lounging in his vibrating bouncer seat next to my feet and drowsily staring at the attached mobile. Every once in a while, he'd reach out and bat at the brightly colored plastic balls.

"Crap. This department reorganization means that I suddenly have three different bosses, and they each seem to think that I should be doing work only for them," Aidan said. He rummaged through the cupboards. "Isn't there anything to eat? I'm starving. I thought you were going to the store today."

"I didn't have time. I had my moms' group, and then I went out for coffee with one of the women I met there," I said proudly, as though I were eight years old again and had succeeded in wooing the popular Jenny Wells into sitting with me at lunch, sipping our silver Capri Sun drink packs and playing with our Strawberry Shortcake dolls.

"Must be nice," Aidan said. He found a nearly empty box of graham crackers, fished one out, and popped it into his mouth. He made a face. "These are stale."

Don't start a fight, don't start a fight, don't start a fight.

"Why don't you just tell your bosses to talk to one another and work out amongst themselves who you're supposed to report to?" I suggested.

"I can't do that."

"Why not? It's unreasonable for them to expect you to answer to three different people. It's not good management skills. You'll be stretched too thin, and you'll never do a good job for any of them," I continued.

I finished chopping the onions, stopping to sniffle into a tissue—onions didn't make me cry, but they did cause my nose to run—and scraped them off the wood chopping block into a frying pan along with a tablespoon of chopped garlic and a pound of spicy Italian sausage.

"They don't care about any of that. They just want their projects completed on time," Aidan said.

I noticed that he still hadn't said hello to Ben. I tried not to let this bother me. If I commented on it, Aidan would get defensive and we'd spend yet one more night avoiding one another while we watched the same television shows in separate rooms. That's what had happened last night, when I suggested—okay, maybe not using the nicest possible tone of voice—that Aidan should give Ben his bath, since he hadn't been spending much time with him lately. And three nights earlier, when Aidan miraculously did get Ben ready for bed without my having to ask him, but dressed him in an expensive velvet romper, and I'd groused at Aidan for not knowing what pajamas looked like.

His fumbling approach to parenting was seriously starting to push me over the edge. It wasn't like I had any experience with babies either, and pregnancy hormones didn't program me with instructions on what kind of diaper rash balm to apply to Ben's bottom. The first time Aidan was left alone to change Ben's diaper came when I was sitting on the toilet, sobbing my way through my first postpartum bowel movement (*What to Expect When You're Expecting* hadn't mentioned that this would be nearly as painful as giving birth, although to be fair I'd tossed out my copy when it piously preached limiting sugar in your pregnancy diet). Aidan had stood outside the door asking me what side of the diaper the tabs were supposed to fasten on and was it normal for Ben's poop to be neon green and where could he find extra wipes, until I snapped, and screamed, "You have a fucking MBA, figure it out yourself!"

But I knew that the only way we were going to get out of this negative pattern was if I stopped focusing on everything Aidan did wrong with Ben and instead approached problems from a position of unity. This job dilemma was an excellent opportunity to practice.

"I think that's really unfair, but I don't blame you for being upset," I said, careful to make "I" statements, just like the expert on *Oprah* had recommended (for example, *I appreciate how hard you work to support us, but I'd really like it if we could spend more time together as a family,* rather than, *You never help out around the fucking house, you selfish bastard*). "But I think that if you could talk to all of your bosses, or maybe just the most senior one, and explain that you can't work effectively if you're taking orders from more than one person, they'll figure out they're overloading you."

"Jesus, Sophie, you just don't get it. I can't do that. That's not how men work. My bosses just want the work done, and they don't want to hear any bitching. They don't fucking care if I'm overloaded, or if their counterpart in another department is throwing work at me. It's not like one of your moms' groups, where everyone sits around sharing their feelings and being supportive of one another."

"Do not swear in front of the baby. And don't talk to me like that in front of him, either. You're supposed to be a role model for Ben on how to treat his future partner," I hissed. I glared at Aidan—if I was barred from telling him to fuck off, I wanted my eyes to communicate the sentiment for me—and then glanced quickly at Ben, hoping that he wasn't going to be scarred by witnessing this exchange.

"Fine. Whatever. I'm not hungry anyway. I'm going up-stairs, I need to work tonight," Aidan said.

"Are you kidding?" I asked. "I'm making baked ziti, and now you're not even going to eat it?"

"I'll just have some cereal or something. I need to go over some reports, and if I don't get started, I'll be up all night," he said.

I could tell that he was just being mulish from the way he was pressing his lips together so tightly they were flat and ringed with white. He only did that when he was irritated, and it was an expression I'd become all too familiar with lately.

His face had once been so dear to me.

Now I was starting to wonder if I was still in love with him.

"Fine," I said shortly. I pulled the frying pan off the stove and, with a flip of the wrist, neatly emptied the contents into the garbage. I dropped the pan into the sink with a loud clatter.

"God, Soph, you don't have to get so mad. I have to work, why are you getting pissed off about that?"

I leaned over and plucked Ben out of his vibrating chair. He smiled at me with a pure and untempered joy, and I kissed him on the pink roundness of his plump little cheeks.

And then I walked by Aidan and out of the kitchen without another word.

"What are you doing?" I asked Paige over the phone a few hours later.

Ben was nestled up in his crib, sleeping. Aidan had

emerged from his study long enough to give Ben a bath and lather him up with lavender-chamomile baby lotion and then wrestle him up into his blue-striped Carter's footie pajamas with the fuzzy frog on the front. I hadn't thought Aidan would put Ben to bed after our fight, and had been gearing up for an even bigger blowout over it—I was planning on pointing out how Aidan was becoming just like the dad in the "Cat's in the Cradle" song. Now I was a little miffed that I didn't get to use my "Cat's in the Cradle" line, and hoped I would remember it the next time he pissed me off.

"Zack's over, we just finished dinner," Paige said. She sounded happy, a marked change from the months following her separation and divorce.

When Paige had first told me about Scott, I'd been horrified and angry on her behalf, and at the same time, a little smug that I'd been wiser when choosing my mate, especially since Paige had always been so much more successful than me when it came to school and work. But now here I was, stuck rattling around a house we couldn't afford—an interesting little nugget of information Aidan had only let me in on after we'd bought the place—living with my sour-faced husband, while Paige was moony-eyed in love with Zack the Hottie, living in a condo she owned outright. Every time we got together with them, Paige's hair was mussed and her eyeliner smudged, as though they'd rolled out of bed just moments earlier.

I'd wondered—probably too often—what would have happened if I'd been thin and single when we met Zack. Would he have picked me over Paige? I'd always been considered the prettier sister—Paige was the smart one, and

Mickey, who was smarter and prettier than either of us, was so much younger she escaped the inevitable comparisons. I'd lain in bed, my hugely pregnant stomach propped up on a pillow. And fantasized about Zack leaning toward me, his eyelids heavy, his lips firm as they nibbled at me, savoring the taste of my skin.

And early on, I'd thought that Zack was flirting with me. Only later, after he and Paige had gotten together, did I realize that Zack was just naturally as friendly as a freaking Labrador retriever, that he treated everyone with the same grinning affability, and he hadn't been interested in me at all. I'd seen him look at my sister with awestruck reverence, and wondered when—if ever—Aidan had looked at me like that.

It wasn't fair.

"Want to hear about my day? Ben got up at five a.m. and wouldn't go back to sleep, so I got all of four hours of sleep last night. And then I was verbally assaulted at my moms' group. And then when my asshole husband got home from work, he barked at me for not going to the grocery store, refused to eat the baked ziti I was making for dinner, and then shut himself up in his office for the rest of the night," I said bitterly.

"Well, don't forget, he only got four hours of sleep, too. And he had to work all day, so he's probably exhausted," Paige said.

"So, what, you're taking his side? You know, I work all day, too. It isn't exactly easy taking care of a baby. Do you want to know how many times Ben pooped today? Six times. I had six shitty diapers to change. And I've already nursed him eight times today, and I had to deal with his meltdown when he didn't nap for long enough," I said, warming to my subject.

Paige sighed the sigh of a martyr. Saint Paige, the put-upon eldest sister, having to endure yet another temper tantrum from her bratty little sister. It didn't matter that we were adults, she still treated me with the same supercilious condescension she had when we were eleven and thirteen. She was forever the bossy big sister, Lucy Van Pelt from *Peanuts*.

"Why are you yelling at me? I know that it's hard taking care of a baby," she said.

God, I hate it when she talks to me like that. As though she's the rational one and I'm always teetering on the edge of a nervous breakdown.

"Don't patronize me," I snapped.

"Soph, take a deep breath. Inhale, exhale. Good. Now, why are you picking a fight with me?"

"I'm not. Okay, maybe I am a little. I've been a bit irritable lately," I admitted.

"Well, that's normal, right? The hormones, the lack of sleep. Do you think that maybe you're dealing with some postpartum depression?"

"No! No. Absolutely not."

"How can you be so sure?"

"Because I don't feel depressed. Grouchy, yes, but not suicidal or anything. And I don't feel like running away from Ben . . . although right now I wouldn't mind getting some time off from Aidan," I said.

"Is it that bad?"

"It's pretty bad. We're fighting a lot, and he's always working, and then when he is home, he spends all of his time in his office upstairs."

"Do you think it's possible that fatherhood is stressing him out, making him feel like he's under more pressure to be a provider? That could be why he's working so hard," Paige suggested.

I considered this. It was true, Aidan had gotten freaked out when I first told him I was pregnant. Within days, he'd purchased additional life insurance and was poring over college savings plans. And then he insisted that we leave our rehabbed cottage in central Austin and move out to the suburbs, claiming it was safer and the school districts were better. I still resented the move. I hated the cookie-cutter neighborhood we were in, and having to check with our omnipotent homeowners' association before I could do something as simple as plant bougainvillea down by our mailbox. Not to mention the exorbitant mortgage that made Aidan's eye twitch whenever the monthly bill arrived.

"I suppose. But even if he is stressed out, that doesn't give him the right to take my head off over every little thing," I said.

"Maybe you guys just need some time together, so that both of you can decompress. When was the last time you two had a romantic night together?"

"The night Ben was conceived. And I'm only halfway joking," I said.

"Why don't you plan a date for Saturday night, and I'll come over and watch Ben," Paige said.

"Oh . . . well. I suppose we could," I said. My stomach rippled with anxiety at the idea of leaving Ben at all, even with someone as trustworthy as Paige. "I haven't been away from Ben since he was born."

"Really? Never?"

"I made a quick run to Babies "R" Us for breast pads once

while Mom watched him, but I was only gone for about a half an hour."

"Then it's time. Saturday night. Zack and I will come over, armed with popcorn and movies, and you and Aidan can go crazy. Go out to a nice dinner, catch a movie, fool around in the backseat of your car," Paige teased me.

"Maybe. I'll ask Aidan. But I think what I'm feeling is more than just not spending time with Aidan or being tired from the baby. It's bigger than that. It's just . . . ."

"What?"

"My life isn't what I thought it would be."

"How so? I thought this was what you wanted—marriage, kids, day trips to IKEA."

"It is what I wanted. It's just . . . different. Some of it's better than I ever imagined, like having Ben. I thought the first few months after he was born would be awful, like baby combat duty. But it wasn't like that at all. Some days are hard, but really, not as bad as I thought it would be. But then other parts . . . like my marriage . . . it's not all bad, but it's hard. Harder than I thought it would be," I said.

"Yeah, tell me about it," Paige said. "Relationships, and marriage especially, are never clear-cut. What did you think it would be like? Your wedding day?"

"The day Aidan and I got married, Mom got tipsy at the reception, dirty-danced with each of Aidan's groomsmen, and then told Daddy—who spent the entire day telling anyone who'd listen, including my new husband, that he thought marriage was a sham institution—that he was 'damaged,' " I said wryly.

"God, I'd forgotten about that," Paige moaned.

"So, no, not my wedding. My romantic expectations were set high by the movie *Say Anything*. John Cusack playing "In Your Eyes" underneath my bedroom window," I said.

"Great scene," Paige sighed. "But completely unrealistic. You expect Aidan to dig out a boom box and play old Peter Gabriel songs for you every time you have a fight?"

"One time. I'd settle for just once. And maybe flowers once in a while. Or making an attempt to actually seduce me, rather than just rolling over in bed and pressing his erection against my back," I said.

"That's really more information than I needed to know."

"You know what I was thinking about today? I love Ben more than I love Aidan. If I was forced to choose between the two of them, you know, a scenario where one would live and the other would die, I'd pick Ben," I said.

Paige went silent.

"What?" I asked.

"You've thought this through? And how exactly would this scenario come to pass?"

"It happened in *Sophie's Choice*," I said.

"That was a fictional story set in the Nazi concentration camps. I don't think it's something you're going to have to worry about in present-day Austin," Paige said.

"Well, just say that it did happen. An armed crazy man could break in, or maybe a terrorist," I said. "And he'd tell me I had to choose, one or the other. I wouldn't even have to think about it, that's how easy the decision would be for me. It would be Ben."

"This is what you think about during the day?"

"I have a lot of time on my hands. I spend most of my day sitting at home with milk leaking out of my boobs, lucky if I can fit in a shower, while everyone else is out living their lives, all of them filled with a sense of optimism and hope and a greater purpose."

"Soph, don't be so maudlin. No one goes through life always filled with optimism and hope, it's just not normal. Everyone has a hard time, everyone struggles. And I think that if you're feeling down all of the time, then you should really talk to your doctor about it. Postpartum depression can be treated, you shouldn't just let it go," Paige said.

"No, because then they'll just prescribe me an antidepressant," I said. A sickly feeling spread through me at the idea.

"But if it would help . . . ," Paige said.

"No, I can't take anything. I'm breastfeeding. And I know they say it's safe to take medications while you're nursing, but how do they really know? Besides, I'm fine, I'm not depressed," I said.

"You just said that you sit at home, feeling like life is passing you by. How is that not depression?"

"I don't want to talk about it anymore."

"I think you should at least call your doctor. Do you want me to call for you?"

"No! Stop being so bossy," I said.

"I'm worried about you. You don't sound like yourself," Paige persisted.

"Let's just talk about something else. Anything else. Have you and Mom had The Talk yet?"

"You mean the one where she tells me that she wants us to be supportive of her insane decision to get back together with Dad? Yup, we had it yesterday. She's upset that none of their children are happy for them," Paige said, snorting.

"Can't imagine why she'd think that. Just because they dragged us all through a horrible divorce and made nasty little comments about the other at every possible opportunity, and then refused to show up at any function the other was attending, so that we had to do two celebrations for every single holiday, birthday, and graduation for the past ten years . . . and now we're supposed to be thrilled that they've 'reunited, 'cause it feels so good,' " I said, breaking into the old Peaches and Herb song.

"I've always hated that song," Paige said, and we both laughed.

"What are you doing?" Aidan asked, sticking his head in the bedroom door.

"Talking to Paige," I said, and then—forgetting that I was supposed to be freezing him out—I smiled at him.

"Say hi for me," Aidan said, and he blew me a kiss before withdrawing his head and disappearing from sight. I felt that old rush of affection I used to feel every time I saw him. It had been dwindling lately, but apparently it was still there, hibernating.

A date night. Who knows, maybe it would help.

Chapter Eighteen

Y ou did what?" I asked, hoping that I'd misheard him.

"I told my parents we'd have dinner with them Saturday night. Why are you getting so mad?" Aidan asked.

We were sitting at the round cherry table—another point of contention, I'd bought it to match the new kitchen cupboards, and Aidan had fumed over it, insisting that we couldn't afford it, although he shut up when I pointed out that we'd somehow been able to afford the new golf clubs he'd just purchased—eating dinner. Or I was eating. Aidan was unenthusiastically poking at the tuna noodle casserole I'd made.

"Because Paige said she'd babysit Ben Saturday night, and I thought that you and I could go out on our own. Do something romantic," I said. Tears began to sting my eyes at the enormity of how unfair he was being.

"How was I supposed to know? You didn't say anything to me about it before, so when my mom asked us over, I said sure. Besides, I think we should go. My parents haven't seen Ben in two weeks," Aidan said.

"And that's my fault, I suppose."

"Jesus, Sophie, I wasn't criticizing you. But you never

want to go over to their house anymore, and my mom's been bugging me about it," he said. The cross look had returned to his face. It made me want to kick him in the ankle.

"I don't want to go over there because your mother constantly criticizes how I take care of the baby. And why can't they come over here if they want to see him? Why do I always have to go over there?"

"God, Soph, do we have to fight about everything? All of the time?" Aidan asked, and suddenly he didn't look cross at all. Just tired. Which made me a little nervous. I figured as long as we were fighting, at least we were still emotionally engaged. The fights that stopped only because we'd run out of energy were a bleaker reality.

I sat on the vinyl-upholstered bench in the pediatrician's waiting room, with Ben strapped to my chest in his Baby Bjorn carrier. He was facing outward and smiling his gummy grin at everyone who made eye contact with him. Ben was a gregarious baby—one of his many nicknames was Mr. Vegas—but this sometimes freaked me out. I kept worrying that some baby-snatching nut job was going to think that she (maybe this was sexist of me, but I tended to think of baby-snatching as a female crime) had a special connection with Ben, and would grab him when I wasn't looking.

"Mrs. O'Neill? Come on back," the stout, clipboard-wielding nurse who guarded the door said.

I struggled to my feet—even at four months, Ben was chubby—and followed the nurse back through the door. She showed me into the patient's room, and after I unsnapped Ben from the harness and undressed him down to his diaper, she measured and weighed him. He was seventeen pounds and twenty-seven inches.

"Is that normal? How does it compare to his two-month visit?" I asked.

"Everything is fine. But Dr. Prasad will go over all of it with you," the nurse said.

"Dr. Prasad? Who's that? We see Dr. Madden," I said anxiously. Finding a pediatrician had been a laborious effort—I'd interviewed five before I found one that I felt comfortable with. Now they were pulling a bait-and-switch on me?

"Yes, I know, but Dr. Madden is out sick today, and so Dr. Prasad, who just joined this practice, is taking over his appointments. If you'd like to reschedule . . . ," she said, her voice trailing off disapprovingly, as if to say that only the most neurotic of mothers would insist on having a specific doctor handle a well-child visit.

I was annoyed and yet chastened at the same time.

"No, I guess it's fine," I said, and the nurse bustled out of the room.

I lifted Ben up to look at the mobile hanging in the corner of the room. Blue squares, red triangles, green circles, and yellow moons dangled from lengths of string. Ben reached his hands toward it and cooed.

"Look at that, Ben baby," I said.

There was a short rap on the door, and I spun around to see a tall man of Indian descent entering the room.

"Hello, I'm Vinay Prasad. And you must be Mrs. O'Neill," he said, smiling, holding out his hand to me. He spoke with a British accent. "And who is this young man?"

I froze. Good God, he was gorgeous. He had almond-shaped tortoiseshell eyes, a long aquiline nose, and the kind of high cheekbones and Cupid's-bow lips that a silent-screen starlet would lay down and die for. I reached for his hand, and as we touched, a warm rush flooded through me.

It was just how I'd felt the first time I met Aidan.

"Sophie. Please, call me Sophie," I stuttered, desperately—stupidly—wanting to distract him from the "Mrs.," although the one-and-a-half-carat diamond engagement ring twinkling rebelliously from its position on my left hand treacherously threatened to give me away. "And, um, this is Ben."

"And hello to you, Ben. You're a handsome little fellow, aren't you?"

Ben beamed at the doctor and stuffed his chubby hand into his mouth. Dr. Prasad smiled back, and I quickly sat down and held Ben in front of me, hoping that my son would camouflage the jiggling baby flab still parked on my ass, hips, and stomach.

"Are you having any problems? Is he sleeping well?" Dr. Prasad asked me.

"Well. He sleeps, but he's still getting up a few times a night," I said.

"He's getting old enough that he should be able to sleep for longer periods of time. Oftentimes with babies this age, they're not getting up because they're wet or hungry, they just want to socialize with their mum," the doctor said. "Are you still breastfeeding?"

"Mm-hmm," I said, flushing red and hoping he wouldn't notice. It was, after all, a normal topic for a pediatrician and parent to have. But I'd never before had a conversation about the fluid leaking out of my breasts with a man I found attractive. Other than Aidan, of course.

"How is that going?"

"Fine, fine. It's going fine. Normal," I said, and decided I'd just save all of my blocked-milk-duct questions for my ob-gyn.

"Good. We normally advise you to hold off on solids until about six months, although it's up to you. If you want to start him on some rice cereal or mashed banana in a few weeks, that would be fine. Just take it slow, and let him guide you. All right now, let's see. His height and weight are excellent, he's in the ninetieth percentile for each. And his head circumference is in the fiftieth percentile," Dr. Prasad said, consulting the charts attached to Ben's file.

"What? But his head was in the seventy-fifth percentile at our last visit. Is that normal for it to shrink?" I asked. I peered worriedly down at my son. Did he have a freakishly small head, and I'd just never noticed?

"No, it didn't shrink," the doctor said, laughing gently. "See here, this is where we chart his growth. See how it went up from his two-month visit?"

"So he isn't abnormal?"

"No, he's absolutely perfect," he said, resting a reassuring hand on my shoulder. I was startled by the sudden contact and flinched nervously. Surprise registered on his face.

Oh no, I thought. He's going to think that I'm repulsed by him. Maybe he'll even think that I'm bigoted against Indian people. What can I say to make this less mortifying? *The reason I jumped is that I know we just met and all, but I think I already have a massive crush on you.*

Hardly. Gah.

"Thank you, I think he's pretty special," I simpered, hating myself for how stupid I sounded.

"Is it all right if I look him over now?" Dr. Prasad asked. I held Ben out, and the doctor took him from my arms, laid him down on the padded waist-high bench covered with thin paper, and checked him over from head to toe.

"He has a bit of a skin irritation here, underneath his armpit," the doctor said, showing me the bright red spot, the size of a penny, under his left arm.

"He does? I hadn't . . . noticed," I said.

I was the worst mother in the history of bad mothers. How could I not have noticed my son had a rash? Oh my God, would the authorities take Ben away from me? And then I remembered . . . I hadn't been the one to give Ben his bath. If anyone was neglectful, it was Aidan, not me.

"I didn't bathe him last night, my, er, husband did," I said. "I'm sure that if I had, I would have noticed that he had a sore spot."

"Don't worry, it's very minor, easy to miss," Dr. Prasad said. His voice was cool and deep, and very reassuring. It was a good tool for a doctor to possess. If I weren't so attracted to him, I'd probably find him a very calming person to be around.

Suddenly I imagined what life would be like if I were married to him instead of Aidan. I bet Dr. Prasad didn't return home at the end of the day in a bad mood, squirreling himself away in his office to surf the Internet or zone out in front of the television. He was probably the kind of man who liked to savor a glass of wine with his partner while they—although to be honest, I was thinking "we"—talked about work, and then enjoyed a simple, gourmet meal involving fresh pasta and cilantro. He would probably even offer to do the dishes afterwards, so that I could take a bubble bath.

I wondered if he was married. He wasn't wearing a ring, but not all husbands do.

"Are you married?" I asked abruptly, and then died inside as I heard just how inappropriate this sounded. "I'm sorry, I don't meant to be intrusive. . . ."

"No, no, not one bit. And no, I'm not married," he said, and smile his wonderful smile at me. His teeth were straight and white.

Dr. Prasad handed Ben back to me, and then turned to the sink to wash his hands before writing out a prescription of hydrocortisone cream for Ben's rash.

"Just apply this to the irritated area twice a day, and it should take care of the rash. The nurse will come back to give Ben his vaccinations. There are three shots this time, and I like to be long gone when she comes in wielding her needles. Sophie, it was so nice to meet you and your charming son," Dr. Prasad said, and he extended his hand.

I took it, clasping my fingers against his, this time managing not to flinch.

"Nice to meet you," I said faintly.

"And unless that rash gets worse, which I don't expect it shall, come and see us again at six months. Any questions before I go?"

Mutely, I shook my head. He smiled again and inclined his head.

"Good-bye," he said.

"Bye," I squeaked as the door shut behind him.

"I think we've found you a new doctor, kiddo," I whispered to Ben.

Chapter Nineteen

So help me God, if your sisters start in on me about my weight, I'm going to tell them to—" I couldn't complete the sentence with the words I wanted, because Ben was strapped into his car seat in the backseat of my Tahoe, "—go to hell."

"Don't curse in front of the baby," Aidan said severely.

"What? I didn't."

"You said h-e-l-l."

"Is that a bad word?"

"When you use it pejoratively, yes."

Great. One more bad-mother strike against me. The way I was going, Ben was going to end up as one of those foul-mouthed, ecstasy-dropping, skateboarding youths who go around with their pants hanging off their asses.

We were en route to Carmello's, an Italian restaurant on West Sixth Street, to meet Aidan's parents, two sisters, and brother-in-law for dinner. These excruciating family get-togethers always seemed interminably long, and I couldn't even amuse myself by downing too much red wine, because I was breastfeeding.

There was no end to the sacrifices mothers have to make.

"I mean it. Every time I see Allison, she asks me if I've lost weight. The next time she does it, I'm going to stick a fork in her hand. What? I didn't use any naughty words," I said, exasperated at the martyred expression on Aidan's face.

"Just try to get along," he said.

"I always do! They're the ones who pick at me, I'm always nice to them. God, you always take their side," I said, crossing my arms tightly over my chest. And there were the tears again, pricking hotly behind my lids, threatening to spill out and ruin my makeup.

"No I don't. I'm on your side. Come on, Soph, I don't want to fight," Aidan said, and we spent the rest of the drive in an uncomfortable silence, broken only by the ring of Aidan's cell phone when his father called, wanting to know where we were. The rest of his family was already at the restaurant. They're always ten minutes early, we're always five minutes late, and they always call to make sure we're coming. This is just one of the many things about his family that drive me crazy.

"I'm pulling into the parking lot now," Aidan assured him.

We unloaded Ben out of the car. He'd fallen asleep on the way over, but I jostled him as I unbuckled him from his car seat, and woke him up. Ben's face crumpled, and he started to cry. I lifted him into my arms, savoring the warm heft of his solid little body as he cuddled into me. Ben relaxed for a minute and then began mooching around near my boobs.

"I think he's hungry," I said.

"Now? But we're already late," Aidan said, looking at his watch.

"I can't control these things. Do you want to tell your four-month-old son that it isn't a convenient time for him to be hungry?"

"What do you want to do?"

"Just go ahead. I'll sit in the car and nurse him, and we'll be in when he's done," I suggested.

I was losing my timidity about nursing in public, especially since Cora had popped out a boob in the middle of Starbucks without blinking an eye. I didn't even have to be that brazen, I could simply camouflage the latch-on with a strategically placed receiving blanket. And it might be fun to shock my prudish mother-in-law, whose babies were all formula fed and who viewed breastfeeding as unnatural and borderline obscene. But by pleading modesty, I could eke out a final few moments of solitude, away from the sharp, critical eyes of my in-laws.

I lifted up my shirt and unsnapped my milk-stained cotton Bravado nursing bra, and Ben eagerly lifted his head, his mouth greedily seeking out the nipple. After months of this routine, my nipples had finally started to go numb, which was a relief. Although he was still toothless, Ben's gums were extremely sharp.

"My little boob shark," I said. I caressed the back of his head, noticing that the last of the dark hair he'd been born with had fallen out. He was now nearly bald, although fine downy hair was just starting to sprout. It looked light, almost white. Excellent. This would help me perpetuate the lie that I myself was a natural blonde.

Once Ben had his fill and was starting to sag against me, heavy with sleep, I sighed and buttoned back up. I flipped down the mirror on the back of the car visor to assess what my makeup looked like. Staring back was a too round face, pale from a winter spent indoors, and eyes darkly ringed from lack of sleep. My eyebrows were growing out of control—I hadn't gotten to the salon to have them waxed since before Ben's birth—and even the addition of eyeliner, cream blush, and rose-hued lip gloss didn't do much to spruce things up. I was ugly.

Sometimes it seemed like the rosier Ben's skin glowed and more brightly his eyes shone, the more my skin and hair dulled and diminished. It was like I passed on a little more of my life force to him every time he suckled.

I climbed out of the car, Ben in one arm, my diaper bag in the other, and lugged them both into the restaurant. He was dozing again, but as soon as my mother-in-law, Eileen, clapped her rolling blue eyes on us, she shrieked and he startled awake.

"Where's my grandson? I haven't seen him in ages—oh, look, he's awake. Hello, precious boy, come see your Momo," she crooned, wrenching Ben from my arms. He scowled up at her. "Sophie, you look tired."

I tensed. And so it began. *You look tired* was Eileen-speak for *You look like shit*.

"Hi, honey," Ron O'Neill, my father-in-law, said, kissing me on the cheek.

"Hi," I said. "Hi, Allison, Melanie. Where's Alex?"

Allison and Melanie were my sisters-in-law, and they were locked in a fierce battle to see which one could waste away to nothing first. Put them together, and they still didn't make one normal-sized woman.

"He went out with his friends tonight," Melanie said, and I could tell that Aidan was purposefully avoiding my glare. Alex was Melanie's husband, and so the only other outsider at these O'Neill affairs, and if he was allowed to skip it, then why the hell did I have to show up?

"May we have a highchair please?" Eileen asked the waitress.

"That's okay," I said, shaking my head at the waitress. "Ben is too little for restaurant highchairs. He can't sit up well enough yet. I'll just hold him on my lap."

"We'll just try it and see," Eileen overruled me.

"No. Really. He's too small," I said. I shook my head at the waitress, who despite my protestation had started to pull over exactly the kind of small wooden highchair that Ben would certainly topple out of if she put him in it.

Eileen smiled at the waitress. "First-time mother," she said apologetically.

The waitress, who looked like she was about thirteen years old, seemed confused.

"So you don't want the highchair?" she asked.

"No," Aidan said. He rested a hand on my thigh—whether this was meant to comfort me or silence me, I didn't know. "So, Mom, Ben went to the doctor yesterday, and he's in the ninetieth percentile for height and weight."

"He's such a big boy," Eileen said, holding him up so that my father-in-law could tickle his stomach. "Don't you want to hold him, Ron?"

"Come to Grandpa," Ron said, reaching out. He cradled Ben in his arms, holding him horizontally in the traditional "Rock-a-bye Baby" pose. Ben loathes to be held that way, unless he's nursing. I could tell from the cross look on his face that if Ron didn't whip out a lactating breast, Ben was about to pitch a fit.

Aidan also noticed the storm clouds gathering on the small round face of our son.

"Dad, you'd better hold him upright," Aidan warned.

"I know how to hold him. You're not the first parents in the world to have a baby, you know," Ron snapped.

Ben immediately burst into tears, sticking his lower lip out as far as it would go in between wails. Ron panicked and held Ben out, pushing him back into Eileen's arms. He did not, of course, apologize for upsetting the baby in the first place. But then, O'Neill men weren't known for admitting when they were wrong.

"Maybe he's just hungry," Eileen suggested. She tore a piece from her roll and offered it to Ben. He just screwed up his face and screamed louder.

"Don't give him that. He'll choke," I said sharply. "Ben hasn't had any solids yet."

"No solids? Why not?"

I plucked Ben out of Eileen's arms. He immediately stopped crying and snuggled up against my shoulder. I was so warmed by this act of loyalty, I didn't even mind the quarter-sized dollop of regurgitated milk that he deposited on my black cashmere sweater.

"The doctor said that I could start giving him a little cereal in a few weeks, but I'm supposed to hold off on most solids until he's six months old," I said. As irritating as it was that my parenting decisions weren't simply respected and followed, and had to be reinforced by trotting out the pediatrician's recommendations, I knew that it was the fastest way to get Eileen to shut up.

"That's not how we did things in my day. But then, new

mothers always think they know best," she said, shrugging and laughing.

I let this obnoxious comment go and instead focused on the laminated menu, searching for something to eat that wasn't fattening, and getting increasingly panicked when I saw that every entrée was described as being topped with cheese or swimming in a cream sauce. Or both.

The waitress reappeared, and the Dueling Anorexics each ordered a small dinner salad for their entrée. Allison ordered hers with the vinaigrette on the side, so Melanie one-upped her by ordering hers with no dressing and no tomatoes.

I ordered the veal piccata with a side of pasta and Caesar salad.

"Have you lost weight?" Allison asked as she handed her menu to the waitress.

"No," I said shortly, feeling even fatter in my stretchy-waist maternity khakis—I still couldn't fit into my regular clothes, and I refused to buy anything new in my current size—and the black sweater that was straining against the volume of my newly enlarged breasts.

"Don't worry. I'm sure it will come off eventually. Although my friend Jordan—the one who has two-year-old twin boys—said that she could never get the last ten pounds off. Some women just can't. In fact, she just had liposuction and a tummy tuck a few weeks ago. I'll give you her phone number, if you want to talk to her about it," Allison said.

I stared at her. "Are you suggesting I get plastic surgery?" I asked.

"Allison, back off," Aidan said.

"I wasn't saying that, I just meant—" Allison started to protest.

"Just drop it," Aidan said again, and then he rested his hand on my thigh again, this time giving it a little squeeze.

A few hours later, when we were safely home, my duty to my in-laws discharged for at least a fortnight, I was lying in bed feeling like a beached Orca whale.

"I shouldn't have eaten so much," I groaned, holding on to the gelatinous mound of skin and flab that used to be my stomach with both hands. I had meant to eat sparingly, but Allison's comments pissed me off so much I spitefully ordered a tiramisu for dessert and consumed the whole damned thing.

Aidan entered the bedroom, wearing only his light blue boxer shorts. He paused to admire himself in the mirror— I could tell from the way he contracted his abdominal muscles—and then hopped into bed next to me. Unlike most nights, when he immediately switched on the television set and zoned out to the white noise of *SportsCenter,* Aidan rolled over on his side, propped himself up on one elbow, and rested his hand on mine. I jumped and pushed it aside.

"Please don't touch my stomach," I said.

Undaunted, Aidan lowered his hand to my upper thigh.

"How are you feeling?" he asked.

Oh no. He was in the mood. The last time I was interested in sex was right around my sixth month of pregnancy, when the hormone influx made me hornier than a sixteen-year-old boy, and I'd had to beg Aidan to sleep with me. As I got bigger and bigger, he'd looked increasingly panicked at the idea.

"Um, not very good, actually. I think I'm getting a sinus infection," I said.

"Are you sure? Maybe if I gave you a back rub, you'd feel better."

Actually, a back rub sounded nice. But since he'd probably expect at least a blow job in return, I decided not to risk it.

"Thanks, honey, but I think I'm just going to read for a few minutes and then go to sleep," I said, and I rolled over and pretended to read my book.

Aidan flopped onto his back, gave an exasperated sigh, and then just lay there sulking. I waited patiently, and a few minutes later, as expected, he started to snore softly. I folded the corner of my page down and turned off the light. And then I thought about what it would be like to kiss Dr. Prasad—the soft pressure of his lips against the curve of my throat, his elegant fingers brushing the hair back from my cheeks, the ripples of muscles on his taut stomach—until I drifted off to sleep.

Chapter Twenty

I pulled into my mother's driveway, right behind my father's black Volkswagen Passat.

Oh shit, I thought.

I considered putting the car in reverse and getting the hell out of there, but before I could, the front door opened and my mother appeared, dressed in a red cardigan sweater and denim skirt. She'd cut her hair since I'd last seen her, trading in the smooth bob for a short, choppy style that showed off her long neck. Standing behind her was my father, looking exactly the same as he had for the past twenty years—balding, paunch-bellied, and dressed in his traditional dad-wear of a golf shirt and khakis. And, if I wasn't mistaken, he had his hand firmly planted on my mother's ass.

I parked my Tahoe and climbed out.

"Hi, Mom. Hi, Dad," I said, and waved weakly at them before unloading Ben out of his rear-facing Britax car seat. He broke out a gummy grin, which made his round face look like a jack-o'-lantern, and kicked his feet happily.

"Ben, I apologize in advance. Your grandparents—all of them—are insane," I whispered into his tiny shell-like ear.

"Where's my Ben baby?" Mom said, walking down the short driveway and reaching out for Ben. I handed him over to her, and she bundled him close against her, resting her cheek on the top of his head. "Mmm, he smells so good. What kind of lotion do you use on him?"

"I don't know, just the normal stuff," I said, following her into the house.

"Hi, baby," my dad said, grabbing one of Ben's chubby little bare feet. Ben squealed with laughter.

"He's such a happy baby," Mom said.

"That's because of his mom. Happy mother, happy baby," my dad said proudly.

"Erm, I don't think it works like that," I said, flopping down on the cream wing chair. "Aidan's dad said that he thinks all babies are just born with the personality they have, and nothing the parents do makes any difference."

"Your father-in-law is a jackass," Mom sniffed. She looked at me, her eyes narrowing. "You look tired. Are you sleeping?"

Sigh.

"Here, I brought you copies of some pictures I took of Ben," I said, trying to ignore that my parents had arranged themselves side by side on the green plaid sofa. They were holding Ben between them, smiling down into his round pumpkin face and tickling his feet. He grinned back at them and grabbed for his toes. I handed them the photos, and my mother balanced Ben in her left arm in order to examine the pictures.

"Sophie, these are wonderful! Here, Stephen, will you

hold them up for me? I don't want the baby to bend them," Mom said.

"This one is terrific," my dad said, holding up a black-and-white shot of Ben lounging in his baby bathtub, a mound of bubbles piled up on his head.

"Look at this one of Aidan holding Ben. The composition is just gorgeous. I love how they're both wearing white T-shirts against the dark background," Mom said.

"I like that one, too. I also like the one where he's asleep in his crib. I love how plump his cheeks look when he's sleeping," I said. Warm satisfaction curled within me. They were good photos, far better than the ones I'd had taken of him at the mall last month, where Ben was posed against an ugly yellow backdrop and ended up looking jaundiced in the final prints.

"Why did you ever stop pursuing your photography?" Mom asked.

"I haven't. Obviously," I said.

"No, you know what I mean. Those arty photos that you used to take in college. Do you remember, Stephen, that exhibit they had of Sophie's prints?" Mom said.

"Oh, right. The black-and-white close-ups of the leaves and flowers," Dad said.

"It wasn't really an exhibit. They just hung some of my pictures at the Fine Arts Building," I said.

"Don't run yourself down, honey, it was a wonderful show. I wish you hadn't given it up," Mom said.

I felt a flash of irritation. "I told you, I haven't. I took the photographs that you're holding in your hands."

"I know, honey, and they're beautiful pictures. Look, isn't

Ben's smile in this one sweet? All that child does is smile. What I mean is, I wish you'd been able to pursue it professionally," Mom said.

"Why didn't you? I can't remember now," Dad said.

That's because you and Mom never asked, since you were going through your divorce and didn't pay attention to anything other than who was going to get their hands on the ugly avocado-green dishes, I thought. In fact, the photography exibit they were now fondly reminiscing over had been a logistical nightmare for me. There had been a short cheese-and-wine reception on the opening night, and I'd had to hustle Dad and the date he'd insisted on bringing—I could still remember her, she was an associate professor in the English Department, and had a long, horsy face and an annoying yawning laugh—in and out early so that he wouldn't be there by the time Mom arrived.

"Because I couldn't find anyone to hire me after I graduated. I ended up having to take that job answering phones at the insurance company. Remember? I quit two months later because my boss was sexually harassing me."

"But I thought you did get a job working at a gallery downtown. Didn't you?" Dad asked.

"That was an internship. An unpaid internship. And it was only for one summer, after my junior year," I reminded him.

"Well, it's too bad you never pursued it. You have such a good eye," Mom said.

I shrugged, pretending it was no big deal, but the stab of regret cut deeply. I'd always seen myself running a studio out of a downtown office space—exposed brick walls covered with white-matted black-and-white photographs. I'd do all of the high-end weddings in town and would be known for my stunning and unexpected shots. A stark close-up of the satin-covered buttons running down the back of a wedding gown, a black-and-white of a bride wiping confetti from her new husband's hair, the bittersweet pride in a father's eye after he'd completed his duty of giving his daughter away.

But after college graduation, I'd been in the thick of planning my own wedding, and then buying and remodeling a house, and then trying to get pregnant, and over time the idea of starting my own studio had just faded away.

I stood up abruptly. "Well, this trip down memory lane's been fun, but I have to go. We need to stop by the grocery store on our way home," I said, retrieving Ben from my mom's arms.

"You just got here," Mom protested.

"Yeah, why don't you forget the store and eat here? We're going to order a pizza and then watch *Out of Africa*," Dad said.

He moved his hand to my mother's knee, and she curled her hand over his, interlacing their fingers together.

"No, sorry, I can't," I said, shouldering the ever present diaper bag.

"Wait, I'll walk you out," Mom said.

I didn't wait, wanting to flee the nauseating sight of their newfound lovey-dovey domesticity. How long had it been since I'd seen my parents demonstrate affection toward one another? Fifteen years? Longer? Certainly the end of their marriage had been one long sparring match, and canoodling had been conspicuously absent during those final years.

"Sophie, stop," Mom said, catching the screen door before it could bump shut behind me.

"What? I really need to get going," I said, shifting Ben to my right hip.

"Why are you and your sisters being so unsupportive of your father and me?" Mom asked, folding her arms in front of her.

"That's exactly the same thing you said during the divorce. That we weren't being supportive enough. As though we were supposed to cheer you on while you dismantled our family," I said.

"So then why would it upset you that we're becoming close again?"

"Because it would mean that you put us through all of the pain and trouble for nothing. It's like you want just one big do-over, where everyone's supposed to forget that the two of you have hated one another for the past ten years. That we had to have separate Christmases and birthdays and graduation dinners, all because you guys couldn't stand to be in the same room. And now you want to say 'Oops, our mistake, let's take a mulligan,' " I said.

Ben frowned at the shrill, angry tone of my voice, and he reached out a chubby little finger to touch the side of my cheek with his hand. I grabbed his hand and kissed the palm to reassure him.

"Can't you understand that being apart has caused us both to change? It wasn't until recently that we've both been able to accept our individual responsibility in the failure of our marriage."

That was rich. Ever since the day my dad moved out, my mother never shrank from the opportunity to delineate to anyone who cared to listen just how my father was singularly responsible for the collapse of their marriage. And according to my father, my mother's personality was so shrewish, no man could ever make her happy. Now they were suddenly ready to accept joint responsibility for their actions? What was next, acknowledging a higher power and asking for forgiveness from the people that they'd hurt?

"And what happens when you break up again? You're just going to drag us into another big messy fight. We don't deserve that. And do you really think Mickey can handle it? She gets flipped out when characters on a television show break up," I said.

"We'd never do anything to hurt any of you," Mom said.

"And yet you're both so good at it," I said. And then I banged down the wooden front steps and stomped over to my Tahoe.

Having a baby does make it harder to storm off, since I had to wrestle him into his car seat. But my mom didn't approach me again. She just stood on the front porch, her arms wrapped around her, watching me. I climbed into my vehicle, waved once, and then backed out of the driveway.

Chapter Twenty-one

Cora looked awful. Her eyes were ringed with dark circles, and her hair was flat and oily. Her clothes—dark-rinse jeans and a white T-shirt emblazoned with the words "Rock Star" in purple glitter—were as skintight as ever, but her face was bare, making her look younger and more vulnerable than she had when she was dolled up with sparkly green eye shadow and mascara so thick her eyelashes looked like asparagus stalks. I hated to admit it, but seeing her like this made me like her even more. Women who can tend to a baby and look perfect are so unnatural they're almost creepy. Give me a real, milk-stained, belly-pouched, bedraggled mama any day.

"I haven't slept in forty-eight. Beatrice has her days and nights mixed up," Cora said, glaring at her daughter, who was napping peacefully in the car seat carrier, despite the din in the Starbucks where we were meeting for coffee. Cora took a long draw on her fully caffeinated double espresso.

"The nurse at the hospital told me to sleep when Ben sleeps. Maybe you should go home and lie down," I suggested.

"Ha. I wish. I'm drinking so much coffee to stay awake that when she finally does drift off, I'm too hopped up to get any sleep," Cora complained.

I nodded sympathetically. "The other night, Ben woke up four times. By the fourth time, I just wanted to hide under the covers when Aidan brought him in," I said.

"Your husband gets up with the baby? Jason is a shitbag. He hasn't gotten up with Beatrice once. Not once! And then he had the nerve to try to touch my tit last night. I nearly broke his wrist twisting his hand off of me," she said, still glowering at the memory.

"Oh God, boobs are off-limits. The first few weeks, my nipples were so sore from nursing, I could barely stand to have my bra touch them. Now I just have no sensation there at all," I said.

"The other day, Beatrice clamped down so hard while she was nursing, I nearly dropped her. And then Jason had the fucking gall to tell me to be careful," Cora said.

I glanced at Ben, who was happily sucking away on his pacifier. We had a policy of not swearing—and not allowing others to swear—in front of the baby, but I'd feel like a drip asking Cora to watch her language. And while I knew that I shouldn't back down on this—after all, if it were my in-laws, I'd be ripping into Aidan to keep them in line—I didn't want to alienate Cora. She was the one person in my life who understood why I counted it a good day when I managed to change out of my pajamas into real clothes.

Besides, Ben wasn't old enough to understand what Cora was saying. And if his first word was "fuck," I'd just blame it on Eileen. Whenever she has too much wine, her language gets salty.

"I read somewhere that breastfeeding suppresses your sex drive. But Aidan's getting frustrated with me. He doesn't seem to understand that after being on call all day for Ben, and the endless diaper changes and nursing sessions, that I just want to relax and have some time to myself. Not that I don't love taking care of Ben—I do, of course I do—but I need some time to myself, too," I admitted.

"I know. And after holding Beatrice all day, I'm all touched out. I just want to be left alone. And besides, how am I supposed to feel romantic with a man who refuses to change a shitty diaper?"

"He won't? And I thought Aidan was bad."

"Jason has been annoying the crap out of me lately. Everything he does and says makes me want to scream," Cora said.

"I'm so glad to hear you say that. I've been feeling the same way. I thought it was just me," I said.

"No, it's normal. My mother said that for the first year after my older brother was born, she announced about once a week that she was leaving my dad. She'd even pack a bag for her and the baby, and would stand in the kitchen, saying, 'I'm going, I mean it, I'm really leaving this time.'"

"But they were okay in the end?"

"No, they divorced right after I was born. My dad was turned off by all of the weight my mom gained during her pregnancies, so he had an affair and left her for another woman," Cora said nonchalantly. She broke off a piece of blueberry muffin and popped it into her mouth.

I'd already eaten half of my peanut butter cookie, and pushed the rest off to the side. I didn't particularly like

Aidan right now, but I also didn't want him to be so grossed out by my baby fat that he'd end up leaving me.

"That's depressing," I said. I picked up my Mocha Frappuccino—made with whole milk and topped with whipped cream, I didn't want to even think about how many calories I'd just consumed there—and noticed that it was empty. "I'm going to get some herbal tea. Do you want anything?"

"No, I'm all set," Cora said.

Ben had fallen asleep, his eyelashes curled over his plump round cheeks, so I left him in Cora's charge while I went to place my order. There was a college-aged girl behind the counter. She was pretty in a grungy sort of way—lots of long straight hair, petite features, a skimpy tank top paired with a cutoff jean skirt. As I handed over my money to pay for the tea, I noticed that she still had bar stamps on the back of her hands, and her baby blue nail polish was chipping away.

"When's your baby due?" she asked, handing me back a handful of change.

"What?"

"Aren't you, like, pregnant?"

"No. I just had a baby," I said. My body went stiff with fury—how dare she!—and my eyes flooded with the hot, stinging tears of mortification. Four months postpartum, and she thought I was pregnant?

"Sorry," she said, smirking.

"Excuse me?"

"I said I was, like, sorry," she said, the sneering smile still pasted on her skinny, anemic face.

Who the hell was she? Just some stupid little coed who

spent her weekends killing brain cells with bong hits and Jell-O shots, who had probably never contributed anything to the world in her entire insipid little life, and she had the utter gall to judge me?

"Yes, I just had a baby and I still haven't lost all of the weight. Thank you so much for pointing that out to me. But I'll have you know, that I am a mother, a . . . a . . . *vessel of life,* and that's a beautiful thing. So what if my body has changed? The stretch marks and extra weight are badges of honor, not something that I should be ashamed of or ridiculed for," I informed her.

"Oh yeah, I totally agree. I have a little boy and twin girls," she said.

"You do?" I asked. I eyed her narrow, boyish hips doubtfully. How was it possible that she had carried three children—twins!—in that tiny little body? Was I the only woman in the world who gave birth and whose body didn't snap right back? Was I going to retain this gourdlike shape for the rest of my life? I'd seen women like that, women whose bodies softened and spread after having kids, whose stomachs forever stayed pushed out like a Buddha's. Was that my destiny?

"Try Pilates. It, like, totally flattens your stomach out," she advised, handing me a paper cup of steaming-hot jasmine tea.

Later that day, I put Ben in his bouncy chair, set it to vibrate, and while he blissed out to repeated choruses of "Three Blind Mice," I unwrapped the plastic off a Pilates DVD that I'd picked up at Target and stuck it in the DVD player.

The graceful blonde instructor on the video suggested that I watch the entire class first before attempting the exercises on my own, but I decided to disregard this advice. Ben would only tolerate the bouncy chair for so long, and I wanted to squeeze as many ab crunches in as I could in the short time that I had.

"Lie down, keeping your body in a straight line and your core strong and responsive," the blonde chirped.

I lay down on the carpet, my legs straight in front of me and my arms stretched over my head.

"Now, breathing deeply, pull your body up, using your core to lift you. Don't arch your back, just lift up through your core and touch your toes, like so," the Barbie-shaped, leotard-wearing instructor commanded. And then she lifted up in one effortless swoop, leaned forward, and touched her toes.

I tried to engage my core—or what I thought she meant by that, because really, who the hell knows?—and lift up, but nothing happened. I grunted and strained, and still nothing. There was absolutely no way the stretched-out muscles of my "core" were going to lift anything anywhere. In the time that the instructor had bobbed up and down five times, I managed to roll on my side and shove myself up with both hands, sweating with the effort.

Obviously this first exercise was a bit advanced for abdominal muscles stretched out by pregnancy. So I sat and waited patiently for her to move on to the next exercise.

"Now, for position two, we're going to lean back, raise our legs in the air so that our bodies form the letter V, and then we're going to flap our hands to the side while breathing deeply. Don't forget to engage your core and keep breathing," she chirped. And then she contorted her body into the letter V and began flapping away.

I leaned back, raised my legs in the air, and immediately fell backwards.

"Oof," I grunted.

I pushed myself back up, raised my legs lower, so that instead of a V, I looked more like a wonky L, and then, resting one hand on the carpet—which I noticed needed vacuuming—I flapped the other hand. I tried to engage my core, but nothing seemed to be happening.

"Now, keeping this same pose, take each leg and make wide circles. First one way and then the other," the instructor commanded, swooping her legs around in wide, graceful circles.

I collapsed back on the floor, lying with my arms splayed to either side, hyperventilating, while the instructor continued to swoop away.

"That's just unnatural," I muttered. "No human can move like that."

Ben began to hoot with displeasure and kick his feet against the brightly colored circles and squares on his bouncy seat. His round face crumpled into a scowl. I punched the stop button on the remote to switch off the Gumby-esque blonde, heaved myself up off the ground, and then plucked the DVD out of the player and Frisbeed it into the garbage can. And then I swooped Ben out of his seat, and together we wandered into the kitchen to forage for brownies.

Chapter Twenty-two

Thanks for coming to the gym with me. It's my first time, and I'm nervous about leaving Ben here," I said as I ushered Mickey—who was home on spring break—past the front desk of my new gym and down the industrial-carpeted hall to the nursery.

The muscle-bound sales representative had assured me during his go-go sales pitch that the gym's baby-care facility was very clean and very safe. And when I checked it out during the tour he gave me, I'd had to admit it looked like a nice place. There was an indoor jungle gym, a television playing Disney videos, and padded baby corrals filled with every plastic toy ever made by Fisher-Price. It seemed so easy—I just had to hand Ben over to the smiling, clean-cut attendant and then have a carefree hour to myself to work out and get back into shape.

But now that I was actually here, clutching Ben to my chest, I couldn't bring myself to do it.

"I don't think this is a good idea," I whispered to Mickey.

"It'll be fine," she said, pushing me forward toward the

sign-in area, where a pretty, petite Asian girl was sitting. She looked like she was about fourteen years old.

"Why don't you just go ahead and exercise, and I'll stay here and play with Ben," I hedged.

"It'll be fine, Soph," Mickey repeated. She turned to the nursery attendant. "We'd like to leave my sister's baby here while we work out."

"Have you been here before? No? Okay, I'll need you to fill out this paperwork. And the same person will have to sign him in and out, and show a picture ID each time," the girl said. There was a plastic name tag pinned to her red polo shirt. *Kim*.

"I've been worried that some crazy, desperate person will notice how cute Ben is and try to grab him while you're not looking. It's been freaking me out," I admitted.

"No, we're very careful with security here. An alarm goes off whenever the nursery door opens, and no one is allowed to leave with a child they didn't sign in. And we always keep our eyes on all of the children," Kim assured me.

Mickey looked at me like I was nuts. "Who's going to kidnap Ben? He poops five times a day," she said. "And he has bad breath. It smells like sour milk."

"Ha-ha, very funny. You're off the godmother short list," I said.

"I didn't know I was on it," she said. "Come on, let's go."

I stood there, stubbornly clinging to Ben. I knew that I was overreacting, and probably looked ridiculous to both Kim and Mickey, but I couldn't seem to loosen my grip on the baby.

"He'll be fine, I promise," Kim coaxed me, flashing a toothy smile. She looked like she could be a spokesgirl for Noxema.

"Do you mind if I ask how old are you?" I asked.

"I'm twenty-seven. I just look young. People are always telling me that," Kim said.

I finally allowed Ben to be gently pried from my arms and handed over to Kim. As Mickey dragged me out of the nursery, I looked back and saw Ben grinning up at his new best friend and trying to grab onto the end of her long, sleek ponytail. I was completely unprepared for the shock of jealousy I felt. My son. In another woman's arms. Smiling at her.

Maybe I should start being nicer to Aidan, I thought. I might be able to live without him, but I didn't think I could handle his introducing a stepmother into Ben's life.

Mickey and I retraced our steps back to the main lobby and then veered off to the left, through the open door to the women's locker room.

Just inside, a naked woman stood at the mirrored vanity counter, blow-drying her hair. It always unnerves me how comfortable some people are with their own nudity. Even if I had a body like a supermodel, I don't think I would ever be comfortable standing stark naked in a room full of judgmental women.

"Did you see her pubic hair?" Mickey murmured in my ear.

"No, I didn't look down! Why?"

"She didn't have any! I think she waxed it all off."

We dissolved into immature giggles. I was glad to see Mickey smiling. She'd been uncharacteristically quiet ever since she'd gotten home. She was sleeping on Paige's couch—like the rest of us, she didn't want to deal with Mom and Dad's rekindled romance—and Paige said that all Mickey had been doing since her arrival was lying around, watching an *I Love the 80s* marathon on VH-1.

"Why didn't Nick come home with you? I thought you

two were going to spend a few days here and then go camping," I said as we stuffed our bags into a locker.

"We broke up."

"What? When? Why didn't you say anything?"

"I don't know, I guess I just didn't feel like getting into it," Mickey said.

"What happened?"

Mickey shrugged. "Nothing dramatic. We've been growing apart for a while, and we're graduating in a few months. It was just time to move on."

"No, you're going to have to give me more details than that. Are you seeing someone else? Is he? Who broke up with who?"

We walked into the large room that housed the aerobic and weight machines, and each climbed on a treadmill. After first making sure that I had a good view of the front door, so I could see if anyone was trying to smuggle Ben out of the gym, I set the speed to a brisk walk. Mickey put hers on a slow jog.

"It was mutual. I think I brought it up, but he agreed with me. It wasn't one of those awful breakups that go on for hours. Instead it was really very civilized. And no, I'm not seeing anyone else. He wasn't while we were together, but I heard that he's started dating someone."

"Already?"

"It's not a big deal. Actually, if he's happy, I'm happy for him."

"How can you be so magnanimous? You guys were together for years, since like the first week you got to college," I said.

"Halloween our freshman year. We met at a costume party."

"It's freaking me out that you're so calm about this. It's like you're channeling Paige. And that's not a good thing," I said.

"I was sad for a few days, but then I just mainly felt relieved. I love Nick, but I'm not in love with him anymore. And everyone seemed to think that we were going to get married, which is just insane. I'm way too young for that," Mickey said.

This stung. Aidan and I got engaged the weekend we graduated from college, and were married a year later. We were the first of our friends to take the plunge, and the build-up to the wedding had been so exciting. I'd had four bridal showers, an engagement party, and four hundred people attended the wedding and reception at the country club. At the time, I'd felt like the fairy princess—even wearing the stupid, big puffy white dress—and now, looking back, it all seemed so ridiculous. I'd been playacting the part of Princess Di in the fairy-tale wedding, and look how it turned out for her. Besides, I was one of those people who thought that Mickey and Nick were on the cusp of announcing their engagement.

Although maybe she was right—maybe twenty-two was far too young of an age at which to select your life partner. I'd been so sure that Aidan and I were soul mates back then, and look at us now, barely able to hold a civil discussion over dinner.

"What do you think is going to happen with Mom and Dad?" Mickey asked. She turned the dial up on her treadmill and started to seriously run—arms pumping, legs churning. It didn't seem to affect her ability to carry on a normal conversation.

"I don't know. I don't know why they think they can make a relationship work now, when they were so miserable at it when they were married. And it's hard to believe that after all of the years of hostility, they can just forget it all and move on as though it never happened," I said, the words coming out in short puffs of air as I walked.

"Paige said that she went over to Mom's last weekend, early in the morning, and Dad was there. She thought he had slept over," Mickey said.

"I so did not need to know that. Ew."

"Tell me about it."

"They're spending too much time together. They'll get sick of one another, or one of them will say something to piss off the other one, or they'll start trotting out their old fights. Really, I can't believe—" I began, but then I broke off.

Dr. Prasad—my Dr. Prasad—was on the other side of the gym, doing bicep curls with a set of hand weights. My stomach clenched and my heart started to race, the same combination of queasy excitement that would hit me when I was in high school and would see the lacrosse player I had a crush on in the cafeteria.

Should I go talk to him? Looking like this, with my hair up in a knotted ponytail and absolutely no makeup on, and wearing an old T-shirt of Aidan's over a pair of ratty nylon shorts? But if I didn't talk to him now, then when would I have the opportunity again? And would he even remember me? If I walked all the way over there and initiated a conversation with him, and then had to remind him who I was, I would die of mortification.

"What?"

"Huh?"

"You were in the middle of saying something, and you just stopped talking," Mickey said.

"I can't remember."

"You said that you can't believe something about Mom and Dad," Mickey reminded me, sounding exasperated.

"Oh. I don't know what I was going to say. Do you see that guy over there? The Indian man in the black running shorts and gray T-shirt?"

"Where? Over there by the machines? Wow, he's hot! Do you know him?" Mickey asked, perking up.

"He's Ben's pediatrician. I just met him for the first time the other day. Do you think he's cute?"

"I wouldn't say cute, no. Puppies are cute, Ben is cute. That man is hot, sexy, and drop-dead gorgeous. Is he single?"

"I think so."

"Want to introduce me?"

I looked at my little sister, who had at some point over the past few years blossomed into a long-legged, lithe beauty. Next to her, I looked like even more of a cow than usual. In fact, I *was* a cow, I was Ben's cow. Moo.

"No," I said firmly.

"Oh no. Don't tell me you have the hots for him," Mickey said much louder than necessary.

"Shhh!"

"You do! You do! How can you have a crush on your son's doctor? I don't think that's even ethical," Mickey screeched.

"Mick, so help me God, if you don't lower your voice, I'm going to flatten you. There is nothing unethical going on. I'm not sleeping with him, he's just Ben's doctor, and yes, I suppose he's attractive. I can't exactly discriminate against him because he's good looking. Should I only take Ben to ugly doctors?"

"Yes. You should," Mickey said severely.

"That's completely unreasonable. If everyone acted like that, attractive people wouldn't be able to run businesses, or medical practices, or . . . or . . ." I tried to think of someone else who would be discriminated against using Mickey's model.

"Not everyone. You. Because you're happily married, and yet you keep getting crushes on every cute guy you meet."

"Name one!"

"Zack. That cute doctor. The guy who prepared your taxes," she began listing.

"I did not have a crush on our accountant. He's a complete dork."

"Aha, but you do have crushes on Zack and the doctor! Gotcha!"

I turned off the treadmill and tripped as it came to an abrupt stop. I climbed off of it and snapped my towel back over my shoulder.

"Where are you going?"

"Away from you," I said huffily.

"Don't be that way," Mickey called after me.

I walked over to the drinking fountain and took a long sip of cold water while I planned my next move. I could either head back to the locker room, raid my makeup bag, and repair my face as best I could with the lip balm and concealer I kept stashed there. Or I could forget the makeup, figuring that exercise was supposed to make me look healthy and flushed. No, that was crazy, I'd better freshen up. When you're twenty years old, a scrubbed face and ponytail says *Sassy Nature Girl*. When you're thirty, it just says *I'm depressed and have given up on life.*

I stood up and turned around, using my forearm to wipe the excess water off my upper lip, and bumped right into Dr. Prasad. I froze, arm still lifted to my lips, mortified to realize that not only had I been caught in an indelicate position, but—even worse—I'd forgotten to put on deodorant before leaving the house. I now stank.

Dr. Prasad smiled at me politely as though he recognized me, but couldn't place me.

Unlike me, he looked great in his workout clothes. The charcoal gray V-neck T-shirt showed off his muscular shoulders and the elegant line of his neck.

"Hi," I said, lowering my arm slowly so as not to bring quick attention to either my face-wiping or my body odor.

"Sorry, have we met?" he asked.

"Um, yes. My son—I have a baby—he's a patient of yours. Well, not exactly yours, he's actually a patient of Dr. Madden's, but you saw him last week for his well-child visit. But I was thinking of changing from Dr. Madden to you, because I really liked you," I said, while thinking, *Good God, Sophie, you're babbling. Shut the fuck up.*

"Of course. I remember. How is your son?"

"He's fine. He's here, in the nursery. It's the first time I've left him. Well, not left him alone. I mean there's someone in the nursery watching him, of course. Do you think that's okay? I'm worried that he's going to pick something up in there," I said.

There seemed to be no stopping my mouth from blurting out every thought as soon as it popped into my head. Give it long enough, and I'd be telling him that I fell asleep every night fantasizing about making out with him.

"I'm sure he'll be fine. Children do pass things on to other children, but unless you keep your son in a bubble, he'll be exposed to germs," Dr. Prasad said, in his incredibly sexy English accent.

"Yeah, I guess," I said. "So, do you come here a lot?"

"I try to work out a few times a week. Sometimes when work gets hectic, I can't. And you?"

"I just joined, this is my first time," I said. I was smiling so wide and hard, my cheeks felt stretched out. I wondered if it made me look crazy.

"Well, it was nice seeing you again," Dr. Prasad said.

I could see that he was about to edge away, so I tried desperately to think of something to keep the conversation going.

"Juice?" I asked.

"Pardon?"

"Um. There's a juice bar over there," I said, pointing weakly. "I was wondering if you were, um . . . thirsty."

"As much as I would love to, I'm afraid I have to get back to work. I'm the junior doctor, so I've been delegated to cover the hospital rounds this weekend. Perhaps another time?" he asked.

"Oh. Sure. Yeah. Whatever," I said, continuing to smile widely while I died inside.

For some unearthly reason, I had basically just asked the

man out on a date (sure, it was just a trip to the juice bar, but come on, my motives must have been transparent). And he had shot me down. What was I doing? First of all, I was married, although I comforted myself with the knowledge that no one could possibly consider having a juice at the health club with your baby's pediatrician to be an infidelity. Second, I had a baby who was his patient. Third, my body was still jiggling with so much postpartum fat that when I sat down, my belly rested on my thighs. Fourth, I was losing my looks. Obviously. And fifth . . . what else did I have going for me? I didn't have a career or anything that would make me remotely interesting. I was just another woman on the wrong side of thirty, with a tired face and an expanding body, and nothing to talk about other than the merits of the latest Baby Einstein video.

"Are you going to be here next Saturday? I usually get here around noon, after the morning rounds, and then work out for an hour. We could catch up with one another then," he said.

The clouds parted, the sun beamed down on me, and Madonna's "Like a Virgin" began to play on the soundtrack of my mind. No, wait, "Like a Virgin" was actually playing on the club's sound system.

"Yeah, I'll probably be here. I'll look out for you," I said giddily.

I sashayed away, in what I hoped was a flirtatious, sexy way . . . until I caught sight of myself in the mirror and saw the pasty paleness of my skin and that my hair was frizzing up from my head. Not a pretty picture. Ugh.

"So how's the doctor?" Mickey said, suddenly appearing beside me, radiating with disapproval.

"Why are you looking at me like that?"

"You know why."

"No, I don't. I didn't know it was a crime to talk to your child's pediatrician," I retorted.

"You weren't just talking, you were flirting."

"I was not."

"What do you call this?" Mickey flipped her hair back over her shoulder and bared her teeth in a sharklike smile. "Ooo, Doctor, can you examine me?" she purred, cocking her hip and resting a hand on it.

"Stop it," I hissed. "What if he hears you?"

"He's not here. I just saw him leave," she said.

"Thank God. And I didn't do that. We were talking about medical stuff—whether it was safe to leave Ben in the nursery. I'm worried that he's going to catch tuberculosis from all of the germs floating around down there."

"Mm-hmm."

"Just forget it. Let's just finish working out," I said.

"Okay. But promise me you won't do anything stupid," Mickey said.

"Mick, you're completely overreacting."

"Just promise."

"Fine. I promise I won't do anything stupid," I said.

Just to be contrary, I crossed my fingers behind my back as I said it.

Chapter Twenty-three

"Can you talk?" Paige asked when I answered the phone.

I considered this. I was lying in the bathtub, soaking in the hottest water I could stand, and surrounded by mounds of verbena-scented bubbles. It was the first moment of peace I'd had all day. Ben's first tooth was coming in—months ahead of schedule—and he'd been a grouch. He wasn't coordinated enough to hold a teething ring, so all I could do was dope him with baby medicine and rub his sore gums, and even that didn't keep him from sobbing pitifully. When Aidan got home from work, he gave me a kiss and took over the baby duty, and I'd escaped to the bathtub with a glass of cold chardonnay.

"Mickey said you're having a fling with Ben's doctor," Paige said.

"That's a vicious lie!" I exclaimed. "I ran into him at the gym, and said hello, and she completely overreacted."

"Don't forget, Mick's sensitive when it comes to that sort of thing. First Mom and Dad divorced, and then Scott and I broke up," Paige said.

"Well, Aidan has been annoying the crap out of me lately,

but it's nothing serious. All couples go through this after they have babies," I said, feeling like an authority on the subject after my talk with Cora. And, of course, omitting the part where I'd been engaging in my favorite fantasy of Dr. Prasad kissing me on the neck with his fabulous, full lips right when Paige called.

"Okay, good. But anyway, that's not the reason I called."

"What's up?"

"It's Zack. He's getting a little . . . weird on me, and I need a second opinion," she said.

"How is he being weird?"

"I don't know exactly. Everything's been fine. Better than fine, it's been wonderful. But lately, he's just been so . . . I don't know. I can't explain. It's nothing that he's done, really, I'm just getting the feeling that he's getting serious," Paige said.

"That's normal. It's been, what, five months? And you're not seeing anyone else," I said.

"I think he wants to move in together," Paige said.

"Why do you think that?"

"Because he suggested it over breakfast this morning."

"Would that be a problem? Isn't he always staying over at your place anyway? It seems like he's there whenever I call," I said.

"It's more complicated than that. Where would we live? Sure, he could stay here, but he's building that house out by Lake Travis. Would he want me to give up my apartment and move in with him? I *love* my apartment," Paige said.

"How do you feel about Zack?"

"I . . . love him."

"More or less than the apartment?"

"Ha-ha. I just don't know if I'm ready to take that kind of step right now. Things are going so well, why not just leave it the way it is?"

"Because that's what people do. They take the next step. Get married, have kids, lose all interest in one another, bicker, grow apart, and then retire to Boca. It's the normal progression of things."

"Or you get married, find out your husband is gay, and end up going through a gut-wrenching divorce," Paige said.

"Zack isn't gay," I pointed out.

"I know. But something else could happen that would ruin everything. The way we are right now feels good. And safe. Taking the next step, any step, just seems like I'm risking a lot for nothing."

I thought of how it felt when Aidan took me into his arms, rubbing his cheek against my wavy hair. And then I thought of Ben, and how after he finished nursing, he'd stretch his neck out like a turtle and then snuggle up into a round baby ball. And how even on the days when my shoulders were stiff with tension and the thought of facing one more overflowing poopy diaper was enough to make me run out of the room screaming, and when Aidan bristled with tension until my stomach curdled, that it was hard to imagine a life that didn't revolve around my two guys.

"It's not nothing," I said.

"I think I'm pregnant."

This made me sit up in the tub.

"What? Why? Did you take a test?"

"No. But my period's late. And I've been feeling really tired lately, which is exactly how I felt when I got pregnant the last time," Paige said.

"Go get a home pregnancy test. Go now," I said.

"I don't want to. I'm afraid."

"Wait . . . I thought you wanted to get pregnant. A while ago you were talking about going the single-mom-sperm-donor route," I reminded her.

"I know, I know. But that was before. Now there's Zack, and our relationship, and shit, Sophie, I don't know what to do. What if I were pregnant and then Zack and I broke up? I'd have to deal with him for the rest of my life," Paige said.

"Now you're breaking up?"

"It could happen! A baby is a big responsibility, and a lot of stress for a new relationship."

"But you want the baby."

"Of course. Yes. I think so."

"Then go take a test. There's no point in worrying about the long-term consequences when it could just be nothing," I said.

"And if it's not nothing?"

"Then it'll be okay. You'll have Zack, and me, and Mickey. And if Mom and Dad ever stop acting so insane, you'll have them, too."

"I know, but still. And there's something else . . . I've been thinking about leaving my firm," Paige said.

"You mean not being a lawyer anymore?"

"No. I just don't want to handle divorces anymore. It's too toxic. I was thinking of starting a practice that focused on child advocacy. The only thing is that it'll be financially risky, and even if I could get it off the ground, it would never pay as well as divorces," she said. "That didn't matter so much when it was just me, but add in a baby, and I don't know if I can afford the salary cut. Especially if I end up doing this on my own."

"What does Zack say?"

"He's been really supportive of the idea, but that was before. I haven't told him yet that I might be pregnant," Paige said.

"Paige! How can you not have told him?"

"What's the point until I know for sure? I don't want to scare him or get his hopes up if it just turns out to be early menopause," she insisted.

"No way, you're too young for that."

"I guess. I don't know what to do. It's too much to think about. But you know what?"

"What?"

"It's sort of exciting. The very idea that there could be a little person growing inside of me," Paige said.

When I swiped at the tears, I rubbed verbena bubbles into my eyes.

"There's nothing more wonderful in the world," I agreed.

"Guess what?" I said to Aidan later that night. He was already in bed, dressed in pajama pants and no top. My skin was still flushed red from the hot bath, and I was wearing a white T-shirt and a pair of Aidan's red plaid boxer shorts.

"What?"

"I'm not supposed to tell you."

Aidan put down the sports magazine he was reading and looked at me.

"Okay, I'll tell you," I said, and I climbed into bed next to him. Paige had sworn me to secrecy, but I think she was more concerned about my telling Mickey or our parents. Surely she hadn't meant Aidan, even if she did say "Promise me you won't tell anyone, not even Aidan." Because I had to tell someone. There was no way I could keep it in.

"Paige might be pregnant. She's not sure yet, she hasn't tested or anything, but she thinks she might be," I announced.

"Oh yeah? That's nice," Aidan said. And then he picked his creased copy of *Sports Illustrated* back up.

"Are. You. Kidding. Me?" I said. Gone was the cozy good fun of sharing a secret. Rage erupted inside of me.

"What?"

"What do you mean *what*? I tell you that my sister is pregnant, and your response is 'That's nice'?"

"What do you want me to say?"

"I don't know. Nothing specific. But some sort of a reaction would be nice. God! Why can't we ever just talk anymore? Why does everything always have to be a fight?"

Aidan put down the magazine.

"Do you really want to know?" he asked.

"Yes."

"You've been acting a little nutty ever since Ben was born. Before then even. Ever since you got pregnant. You freak out at the smallest little things. Look at tonight. I've been working all day, and then I took care of Ben this evening to give you some time off, and this is the first moment I've had all day to relax. And you start screaming at me because I didn't react the way you expected me to when you told me some family news," he said, sounding irritatingly reasonable.

"It's big news!"

"What? The news that your sister may or may not be

pregnant? So basically you're reporting that what, your sister's period is late? Tell me—what would be the appropriate amount of enthusiasm for me to show? Should I pump my arm in the air and yell 'Way to go, Paige'? Or are you waiting for me to ask for a more in-depth analysis of her menstrual cycle? Because I have to say, hon, I'm just not ready to go there. And I don't think you're going to find many guys who would," Aidan said.

"Now you're making me feel stupid," I muttered.

"Yeah, well, the one thing you've made clear lately is that pretty much whatever I do, it's wrong," Aidan said.

"That's not fair. I don't criticize everything you do," I protested, stung at this accusation.

"This morning you accused me of burning your toaster waffle on purpose. Last week when I had a sinus infection, you insinuated that I was faking it to get out of taking care of Ben," Aidan said.

I lay back on the bed and stared at the ceiling fan circling above me. It went round and round and round, so fast that I couldn't count how many blades were on it. Aidan turned over on his side so that he was facing me. He reached over and poked me in the side.

"Don't poke me."

"Then say something," he said.

"I know I've been touchy lately. I don't mean to be, I just can't help it. Between the hormones and the lack of sleep and taking care of Ben—as much as I love him, it can be really hard. Like today. He didn't nap, and he was crying on and off all day. All day! It's hard to deal with," I said.

"But you don't have to deal with it by yourself. When I'm home, I help," Aidan said.

"I know. You've just been working so much lately."

He shrugged. "I can't help that. It's not like I'm working for fun."

"I know. But it's like that song, 'Cat's in the Cradle.' You need to spend more time with Ben."

"I am not a 'Cat's in the Cradle' dad, and I spend plenty of time with Ben. What I need to do is to spend more time with you. We used to laugh and hang out together every night, and I can't even remember the last time we slept together."

"When I was six and a half months pregnant with Ben," I said.

"You came up with that answer pretty quickly. How do you remember?"

"Because I had to beg you. Wait, though . . . are you saying that you wish Ben hadn't been born?" I asked.

"No! Of course not! But I think we need to spend some time together on our own, too," Aidan said.

"I tried to set that up last week. Remember? You made plans to have dinner with your family instead," I said.

"Don't remind me," Aidan said. "Can we try again? Maybe see if one of our moms or sisters will babysit this weekend? What are grandmothers for, anyway?"

I nodded and took the hand that he was extending to me. "Maybe we should ask your mom. I think Paige has her hands full right now, and I'm trying to avoid my mom."

"Your parents are dating," Aidan teased me.

"Ugh, don't remind me. And don't joke about it."

"Your parents are dating. Your parents are dating," Aidan sang out obnoxiously.

"I can't hear you, I can't hear you," I said, and clapped my hands over my ears. "Nananana, I can't hear you."

"Not only are they dating, they're probably having sex," Aidan said.

"Ack! How can you say that?" I shrieked, and I rolled on top of him, straddling his body. "Just for that, I'm going to tickle-attack you."

I dug my fingers into his ribs and tickled him until his eyes watered up and he begged me to stop.

"Okay, okay, I give up. I promise, I'll stop talking about your parents having S-E-X," he said, and then he reached up and grabbed my wrists. "Speaking of S-E-X . . ."

"What about it?"

"Do you feel like having it?'

"I don't know. Maybe."

"Come here," Aidan said.

And he pulled me toward him, and we kissed. He struggled to get my T-shirt off over my head.

"Wait," I said.

"Oh no," Aidan said.

"No, I want to, it's just . . . I don't want you to see me naked," I said.

"Well, I know it's been a while since we did this, but if memory serves me, I think that nudity is sort of a requirement."

"Can't I just leave my shirt on?"

"Why? I love seeing you naked," Aidan said.

He log-rolled me over and began nuzzling my neck.

"I'm embarrassed."

"I have seen you naked before, you know."

"But my stomach is all flobby now."

"I don't think that's a real word."

"The skin is all loose and pouchy. It's embarrassing."

"Let me see."

"No!"

"Come on, let me see." Aidan pulled my T-shirt up, exposing the jiggling looseness of my stomach. He leaned over and tenderly kissed it. "I think it's beautiful."

"No you don't. I have stretch marks, and my belly button is black from all of the dead skin cells. And I'm fat," I said, and I tried to stretch the T-shirt back down, wanting to hide the disgusting mess that was my body.

"Hey," Aidan said softly. He reached over and placed his hand on mine. "That's where you carried our son. It's beautiful. You're beautiful."

I rested a hand on the side of his face, trying to remember what it was about him that had been irritating me so much lately.

"Okay," I said, sitting up and peeling off my shirt.

"Hot damn!" Aidan said.

Chapter Twenty-four

❧ ✤ ❧

"Thanks for coming over," I said, opening the door for Cora and Beatrice.

"No problem. She's asleep. Can I put her down somewhere?"

"Sure. Ben is napping in his room, but I have a Pack 'n Play set up in the family room. Is that okay?"

"Sure. Wow. Your house is gorgeous. Who took these pictures of Ben for you?" Cora asked, stopping by the matted, framed black-and-white photographs I'd hung in the front hall.

"I did."

"Are you serious? They're amazing! Are you a professional photographer?"

"God, no. I majored in photography in college, but I never did any real work. Just artsy stuff for class. Most of it's awful—extreme close-ups of leaves, and pretentious stuff like that," I said.

"Well, I think you're really talented. You know, people would pay you a lot of money to take pictures like this of their kids," Cora said.

"No. Really? You think so?"

"Yup. In fact, I'll be your first customer. Would you photograph Beatrice? In black and white? I'll pay you."

"Of course! But you don't have to pay me, silly goose," I said.

"Yes I do. And then you can use Ben's and Beatrice's pictures to start a portfolio. They're having a baby expo at the convention center in a few months. I went last year when I was pregnant, and there were a ton of photographers there displaying their work, and none of them were as good as these," Cora insisted.

"I don't know. That sounds like a lot of . . . trouble," I said.

Cora shrugged. "It's up to you," she said.

I felt the regret catch in my chest. Why had I said it would be too much trouble? My hesitation flowed from a wild-eyed fear that if I did try to make something of what had once been my passion, and had in recent years dried up to a part-time hobby, I would fail.

"Well, maybe I should try," I said lamely, but Cora just smiled, and it seemed like the moment—and the opportunity—had passed.

After Cora had settled Beatrice into the Pack 'n Play, and accepted the coffee I'd made especially for her—I'd never seen anyone ingest as much caffeine before in my life—I said, "The computer is upstairs, in Aidan's office."

"Okay, cool. I just can't believe you don't know how to use the Internet."

"I don't. I don't even have e-mail."

"You do know you can shop online, right?"

"You can?" I asked. "No, but if I had, I would have done this sooner."

We walked up the open staircase, and once upstairs, I pushed open the second door on the right.

"Sorry it's such a mess in here. This room sort of became the dumping grounds for all of our random stuff when we moved in," I said, waving my hand to indicate the boxes of files, Aidan's golf clubs, the treadmill I'd insisted on buying and had only used three times. "I don't even know how to turn the thing on."

Cora settled in behind Aidan's desk and hit a button on the computer. I stood behind her, leaning over her shoulder. The computer began to whir and beep, and a minute later, the blue desktop screen appeared.

"You have a high-speed Internet connection, so all you have to do is open the browser—that's this button here—and voilà! Here's the Internet."

"You make it look so easy."

"It is. Now, to research something, you just have to type it here in the search box. What did you want to look up? Cruises?"

"Yeah, I'm going to surprise Aidan with a trip. There are some weekend cruises that depart from Houston, and I thought it would be fun for us to get away together," I said.

"Are you going to bring Ben?"

"I'm not sure. My mom said she'd watch him, but I'm nervous at the idea of leaving him. Do you think I should take him with us?"

"Hell, no. Have a romantic weekend, you guys probably need it. Ben will be fine. Okay, here are some websites where you can book cruises. This one here is a discount travel website, where they have cruises that have been marked down, and this one is a general travel site, which is going to have everything," Cora explained.

"How do I find these websites again?" I asked.

"You right-click on 'Favorites' and then scroll down to 'Add to Favorites.' There, it's right . . . oh."

"What?"

"Um. This is your husband's computer?"

"Yeah, why?"

"Well. This is really none of my business, but most of the websites he has marked as favorites look a little . . . porny," Cora said.

"Porny? What do you mean?"

"Look: pussygalore.com, boobweb.com, Hustlervip.com, cumshots.com . . ."

As she read the list of websites, nausea began to roll and gurgle in my stomach. I closed my eyes, wanting to blot this moment out of my memory. But I could tell by the way everything seemed too bright, too loud, too in focus that it would stick, just like the night when I was a freshman in college and walked in on my roommate, Meryl, giving my boyfriend, Brad, a blow job. On *my* bed, so that her sheets wouldn't get sticky.

"I take it you didn't know about this," Cora said.

"That my husband's a porn freak? No, I did not know that," I said thinly.

"It's not a big deal. Jason buys *Playboy* every once in a while. I found one in his briefcase, and he trotted out that lame-ass excuse about only being interested in the articles," Cora said.

"Are there articles on those websites?"

"I don't know. Let's look and see."

Cora scrolled the mouse down the list of marked websites and clicked on one. Immediately the screen was full of naked women—naked women masturbating, naked women kissing other naked women, naked women performing blow jobs on faceless men, naked women posing in fuck-me heels with come-hither pouts stretched over their plastic faces, all set against a bright pink background with coy captions in a juvenile bubbly font: *Blonde hotties work a cock! College girl spreads her pussy! Big titted girl sucks and fucks!* The copy for the site depended heavily on multiple exclamation points, the letter *X*, and advertised videos, photographs, a live chat, and something called a "dorm cam."

"What's a dorm cam?" I asked faintly.

"Erm. I think it's where they put some cameras around a house, filming the women 24/7. You know . . . having sex, showering, going to the bathroom," Cora said.

"Ew! Going to the bathroom? Aidan watches women going to the bathroom? I think I'm going to be sick," I said.

"No, I'm sure he doesn't. He probably just watches the movies and looks at the pictures," Cora assured me.

As though the image of my husband masturbating to naked sluts writhing on his computer screen would be comforting.

Suddenly a small window popped up on the screen, announced by an electronic beep. At the top, in white type against a blue background, it read, *Instant Message,* and below, against the white background of the text box, were the words: *Cherry: hi big boy. wanna play?*

"Who the hell is that?" I asked.

Cora was silent. I took in her pale, pinched expression and her obvious mortification at tripping into another couple's marital mess, and suddenly knew.

"It's a woman, isn't it? Someone who knows Aidan," I said, the nausea spreading outward into my limbs. My chest constricted, and dagger-sharp pains prickled down my arms. Was this what it felt like to have a heart attack? Wasn't I too young for the chest-clenching symptoms normally reserved for fifty-year-old men with rolls of belly fat and a habit of washing their fillet-o-fish sandwiches down with beer?

"I think I'm having a heart attack," I said, and I leaned back against the wall.

"No, you're not. It's just anxiety," Cora said.

"I've had panic attacks before. This is different," I gasped.

Cora fished around in her diaper bag and retrieved a brown prescription pill bottle. She spun open the top and tapped out a small white pill into the palm of her hand. "Here, take one of these."

"What is it?"

"A Xanax."

"Can I take this while breastfeeding?" I asked, swallowing the pill before she could answer.

"Well, technically, no, although it's a pretty low dosage. But if you're worried, just pump and dump your breast milk," Cora said.

The computer emitted another beep. Cora and I peered at the screen. Another message had popped up: *Cherry: R U there? I'm hornee.*

"A slut who can't spell 'horny,' " Cora murmured.

"Should we respond?" I asked.

"Absolutely," Cora said.

She began typing: *Who are you, and why are you sending whorish messages to my husband?*

When the message popped up in the dialogue box under Cherry's two messages, the sender was listed as "12inches."

"At least he's lying to her, too," I quipped—*How can I be making jokes at a time like this?*—and Cora snorted.

We waited a minute, and then a message popped up: *Cherry: Who r u calling whore bitch? I'll kick your bony little ass.*

"Obviously she doesn't know me," I said tightly. "Bony little ass. I wish."

"What should I say?" Cora asked. "Do you want information from her, or do you want to insult her?"

What I wanted was to kick Aidan in the balls. Hard. A clichéd response to a husband's infidelity, yes, but oh so satisfying. I looked down at my hands and noticed they were shaking, but I couldn't figure out if it was from shock or rage. The first was starting to ebb, while the other leapt like a flame.

"Insult her," I said.

Cora began to type, her long red fingernails rapping against the plastic keys. Ratta-tat-tat. She hit the Enter key, and her instant message appeared in the window.

12inches: What else would I call the pathetic slut who has Internet sex with my husband? Are you really that desperate, you $3 hooker?

We both leaned in, shoulders hunched and eyes riveted to the screen, while we waited for her reply.

Cherry: Maybe if you kept your man happi he wouldn't be loking for a women who could.

"I'm going to get her now, the little bitch," Cora said, and she began to type furiously.

"No . . . don't bother. She's right, actually. Maybe if I hadn't gotten so fat, Aidan wouldn't have felt the need to seek out porn," I said. I turned away and stared out the window at the view of our street—an uninspiring view of lifeless suburban homes—and wondered just when my life had turned to shit. When I was little, I always believed I was special and destined for great things, like Dorothy Hamill twirling on the ice or Carrie Fisher sassing her way through *Star Wars*. Never would I ever have imagined I'd end up here, a soft suburban mom stuck with a philandering asshole for a husband.

"Fat? You just had a baby. *His* baby. If that asshole is turned off by the weight you put on while you were pregnant, then you're really better off without him," Cora fumed.

"I know!" I agreed, deciding to put aside for the moment the small fact that Aidan hadn't actually ever commented negatively on my weight gain. Besides, if he was attracted to me, why would he be having Internet sex with Cherry the Whore? And then an awful thought occurred to me. "Oh my God. What if this isn't just dirty talk and a porn obsession? What if Aidan's cheating on me? I mean for real, what if he's actually meeting women in real life that he meets online?"

"Don't overreact. I'm sure it hasn't come to that," Cora said.

"How can you be? For all I know, he meets Cherry the Whore on his lunch hour," I said.

"No, you would have noticed it on the credit card bill if he was charging hotels or expensive lunches," Cora said.

"I never look at the bill! Financial stuff stresses me out, so Aidan handles it all," I wailed.

Cora looked at me. I could see the pity plainly written there, alongside concern and relief. Seeing the messy innards of another person's life always makes you feel better about your own warty existence.

"You'd better talk to him," Cora said.

"Yeah. Unless I kill him first," I said.

I'd planned to have Ben in bed by the time Aidan came home from work. It was bad enough that Ben was going to be the child of a broken home, I didn't want him to have to witness what was going to transpire between his parents that night.

But Ben's afternoon nap had worn on for hours. I went to bed, too, although I didn't sleep. Instead, I lay on top of the bed, sinking into the fluffy down comforter, the Xanax making me feel unnaturally calm. By the time Ben finally did wake up, his left cheek red and creased from the sheet and his sleepy little body smelling sweetly of grape lollipop, he shrieked until I stumbled into the circus-themed nursery and rescued him. When Aidan arrived home an hour later, Ben was lying on his Gymini play mat, giggling at the stuffed animals dangling over him. He waved his arms, batting an elephant with a sparkly pink belly.

"How's my little guy? What did you and Mommy do today?" Aidan asked, playfully swooping Ben up into his arms and kissing him on his nearly bald, egg-shaped head.

I sat in the red leather armchair, my body folded up, my arms wrapped around my knees, watching this happy domestic scene—a besotted father kissing his son. How sweet.

Aidan glance at me. "Is everything okay, hon? How was your day?"

I stared at him. The bile churned in my stomach, shocking me with just how much dislike I could feel for a man who only the night before had made love to me. And right now I was really wishing I hadn't faked my orgasm just to give him the ego boost.

"Soph? Honey, what's wrong?" Aidan asked. He sat down at the ottoman by my feet, Ben perched on his knee.

"What did I do today?" I repeated, ignoring his last question. "What did I do today. Let's see. I took Ben for a walk, showered, we went to the grocery store to get dinner. Then Cora came over to help me make online reservations for a cruise—I was going to surprise you with the trip. But then we were interrupted when Cherry the Whore started to send you private messages about how horny and lonely she was. Oh, and we also uncovered your online porn stash. Let's see: walk, shower, grocery store, Cherry the Whore, porn. Yup, that pretty much sums up my day."

Aidan's expression did not change, although his skin turned gray.

"I don't know what you're talking about," he said.

"Please, you're going to have to do better than that."

"You don't know how to use the Internet. You probably just typed the wrong word into the search box and ended up on a porn website by mistake," Aidan said.

"If you keep lying that way, lightning is going to come through that window and strike you down. And just because I'm not computer savvy doesn't mean I'm stupid," I said.

"I didn't say you were. I just don't know what you're talking about."

"I'm talking about the porn sites that you've saved under your Favorites section on the computer. The ones featuring lesbians and teen cheerleaders. Freak."

"I don't think you should talk like this in front of Ben,"

Aidan said severely. It was so typical of him. As soon as he started to lose on the merits of the fight, he'd immediately start arguing about the form or manner in which we were fighting. It's the same kind of sneaky lawyer thing that Paige does, and it's always irritated me.

"Okay. Then why don't we talk about Cherry the Whore, and why exactly it is that a married man and father is exchanging raunchy e-mails with another woman," I said, much more calmly than I felt.

Aidan stood up and shifted Ben up into the crook of his arm.

"I'm not going to talk about this with you now in front of Ben. Why don't we wait until he goes to bed and you calm down," he said, turning to leave the room.

His cool reaction was stunningly insulting. I'd caught him with his pants down—almost literally—and he was yet again insinuating that I was out of line. There goes Sophie again, overreacting. Ever since she had the baby, she's been so irrational. Must be the hormones, must be the lack of sleep.

If he hadn't been holding our child in his arms, I would have picked up the ugly crystal candy dish his alcoholic aunt had given us as a wedding gift and chucked it at his head.

"Get out," I hissed.

Aidan stopped and turned around. His eyes were dark and angry, and his mouth flattened into a severe line. If I really gave a shit how he was feeling, I might have been worried.

"Sophie, I really don't think you should act like this in front of Ben," he said.

"Give me Ben. And then go upstairs, pack a bag, and get out," I said.

Aidan stared at me as the impact of my words hit him. Perhaps in the past I had been overly emotional and hormonal, going back to the beginning of my pregnancy. Once I had a screaming fit when it took him two weeks to get around to setting up the crib after we bought it, even though Ben wasn't due for another two months. I'd started to cry in the middle of the grocery store when I found out that they'd run out of Dove bars on a night when nothing else would do. And when he'd interrupted a romantic—and rare—dinner out to take a cell phone call from one of his annoying friends, I might have been guilty of grabbing his phone and turning it off in the middle of the call. But I'd never before, even during one of my hormonal rages or sob-fests, asked him to leave.

"Just go," I said again.

"No," he said softly. "I'm not going anywhere."

"Fine. Then we will," I said wearily.

Chapter Twenty-five

By the time I parked my Tahoe in my mother's driveway, it was already dark out. The lights of Austin reflected off the low clouds in the sky, casting a greenish glow over the city. It was such a cozy time of night—children were doing their homework at the kitchen table while marinara sauce bubbled on the stove, couples were reuniting over glasses of red wine, the comforting deep voices of the news anchors were calmly running down the various conflicts and traumas in the world.

And I had left my husband and my home. This realization hit me in waves, and I leaned forward, resting my head against the steering wheel, waiting for the sour sickness to pass. Why hadn't I asked Cora for an extra Xanax or twelve? It was the one upside to playing the role of the scorned wife—the ability to indulge guilt-free in pharmaceutical crutches.

My dad's Passat wasn't in the driveway, but for all I knew he'd gotten garage privileges back, so when I rang the doorbell I braced myself for another meeting with the happy couple. I had thought of going to Paige's just to avoid this, but if

Zack was there—as he always seemed to be these days—I would have to act sanely in front of him. And right now, I just wanted to let it all hang out, in the messy, slobbering way you reserve for your family.

The door swung open.

"Sophie. What's wrong?" my mom asked, taking in the baby in my arms and the overnight bag and folded-up Pack 'n Play at my feet.

"I've left Aidan," I said.

"You what? Why? What happened?"

"Well . . . God, I don't want to go through it all right now," I said. I suddenly felt exhausted, like I could sleep for a week. "Can I stay here for a few days?"

"You don't have to ask," Mom said, and she opened the screen door for me and drew me in. "Here, let me take Ben. Has he had his bath yet? No, I'll do it. You go sit down, pour yourself a glass of wine, and we'll talk once the baby's down. It's good to see you, honey, I've missed you."

When she kissed me, her lips felt like paper against my cheek, and then she took Ben out of my arms and whisked him upstairs. I lugged the Pack 'n Play up after her, and while Ben splashed around in the tub, I set it up in Mickey's room, which looked pretty much exactly as it had when she was in high school. There were posters of Sugar Ray and Lenny Kravitz tacked to the wall, and the plastic horses she had loved so much when she was a kid stood head to tail along the built-in bookshelves. A cheap felt pendant featuring a lion, her school mascot, was tacked to a corkboard, surrounded by photos of her and her friends at track meets, in their prom dresses, standing in lines with their arms around each other's necks. A faded pink bedspread, nubby from use, was draped over the narrow twin bed.

"Here he is. He loves taking baths, doesn't he?" my mother said, appearing with Ben wrapped in a towel. He looked happy, but his eyes were rimmed with red, which meant sleep was not far off. I pulled diapering supplies from my overnight bag, and we kitted Ben up into his nightclothes, and then I kissed him on the cheek before laying him in the Pack 'n Play.

"I love you," I breathed into his fine wisping hair.

And only then did I—the woman who had been known to become weepy at McDonald's commercials—begin to shed tears for my marriage.

My mother was fantastic. For the next few days, she took care of both Ben and me, cooking all of my favorite foods— risotto, brownies, lasagna—and watching over Ben in the afternoons while I napped. Months of exhaustion seeped through me, and no matter how much I now slept, I was still achingly tired. When I told Mom what Aidan had done, she was properly outraged. So much so that when he called her house periodically, wanting to speak with me, she put him off and told him that I'd get in touch with him when I was ready to talk.

"But you are going to have to talk to him eventually. He wants to see you and the baby. You can't hide from him for- ever," Mom said, as she hung up the phone.

"If Ben and I are so important to him, why is he screwing around?" I asked, my lip curling indignantly.

"Does what he did really count as screwing around? Not that I'm taking his side, but I thought that when people had Internet sex, they just typed things out to one another while masturbating. Am I wrong?"

"Ew! I don't want to think about it. And I certainly don't want to talk about it with my mother," I said.

But mostly, returning to the nostalgic comforts of my mom's house meant that I was able to put Aidan, and Cherry the Whore, and all thoughts of my broken marriage aside. I didn't even mind it so much when Dad came over and we popped popcorn and watched the first Harry Potter movie on HBO.

"Isn't it weird being around them?" Paige asked one night while we were talking on the phone.

"No, it's really not. I'm sort of getting used to them being together again. Although Dad stayed over last night, and that was a little weird at first. It's been so long since I woke up in the same house as him. But then Mom made scrambled eggs, and they worked on the crossword puzzle together, and it was actually sort of nice," I said.

"Oh no, they've gotten to you. You've been brain-washed."

"I have not. It's actually been cathartic. The last time I lived at home, it was so chaotic here. All of the fighting and turmoil. But now it's kind of nice how sweet they are with one another. It's like I wish it had been when we were grow-ing up," I tried to explain.

"But doesn't that piss you off? That they're capable of be-ing kind and loving to one another, and yet they didn't do that when we were younger?"

"It did before, but I think I've gotten over it. And it's good for Ben to have his grandparents together. I guess that's probably it—it's more important to me that he's able to experience that, than it is for me to be angry with them about the past. Oh! I totally forgot! What ever happened? Did you get your period?"

"No."

"Did you take a home pregnancy test?"

"Yes," she said.

"And?"

"And I'm pregnant."

"What! Oh my God! That's so exciting! It is good news, right? It's what you wanted?"

"Well, now that the shock has started to wear off, I am getting excited. And Zack is thrilled. Although he's getting on my nerves. I agreed to let him move in for a trial period, and he's overdoing the protective male routine. He keeps trying to stop me from running, or working late," Paige complained.

The thought of Zack attempting to stop Paige from doing anything made me smile. He might as well go bang his head against a wall.

"But other than that, how is cohabitating?" I asked.

"I have to admit, I kind of like it. And Zack was already over here all the time, so it hasn't been a huge change. He keeps talking about marriage, though, and that freaks me out," Paige said.

"Yeah, I bet. But you don't have to decide that now."

"I know. But the house he's building is going to be ready in a few months. He wants us to get married, sell this place, and move in there to have the baby. In fact, he has this whole picture in his mind of Pottery Barn meets Norman Rockwell," Paige said.

"That's not such a bad thing. No matter what you decide to do, it sounds like your baby is going to have a good daddy. Unlike my son, who has an asshole for a father," I said.

"I take it you haven't yet forgiven and forgotten," Paige surmised.

"And I don't plan to do either."

"So, that's it? You're just going to throw it all away?"

Fear swarmed me, prickling at my skin, unsettling my stomach.

"He's the one who threw it all away, not me. And I don't know what to do. Aidan keeps calling here, and I talked to him for a few minutes last night. I told him he could see the baby tomorrow, but I think I might leave when he comes over here," I said.

"Did he tell you about what happened between him and that woman he was talking to online?"

"No. I haven't wanted to talk about it."

"You can't hide from it forever."

I snorted. "You're one to talk."

"Actually, Scott and I have seen each other a few times. He's met Zack, and I've met his partner, Kevin, and we all get along really well. I think we have one of the healthiest post-divorce relationships possible," Paige said smugly.

"Well, goody for you. I'm not quite ready to become newest, bestest friends with Aidan."

"I know. But you should still talk to him."

"Why?"

"Believe it or not, I actually wish I had talked to Scott

about things earlier. I just froze him out, and I don't think it helped anything," Paige said.

"Did you just admit to being wrong about something? Because if so, we're going to mark this day on the calendar," I said.

"Don't tease me, I'm feeling nauseated and crabby."

"Okay. That gets better, by the way. The nausea anyway. I was crabby for the entire forty weeks."

"No kidding."

"Paige?"

"Yeah?

"I really am happy for you. And whatever you decide to do about Zack and the baby, you know I'm here for you."

"Thanks, Soph."

Chapter Twenty-six

As I walked into the gym Saturday morning, duffel bag slung over my shoulder, new sneakers squeaking against the tile floor, a warning rolled through my head: *Dr. Prasad probably won't even be here. It was just a casual suggestion to meet up, not a firm date. He knows you're married. Just get a workout, and if you see him, great, if not, no big deal.*

Still, after I'd tossed my gym bag into a locker and touched up my lip gloss, I started to scout around for Dr. Prasad. I tried not to be too obvious about it—I walked over to the water fountain, which afforded me a pretty good view of the Nautilus side of the room, and after taking a drink, I casually scanned the room. Nothing. Next I canvassed the treadmills and bikes, faking an interest in the elliptical cross-trainer, and then finally checked out the juice bar. When I still didn't see him, I was faced with a quandary. Rather than throw on sweats and head to the gym with bed head, I was freshly showered and wearing just enough makeup to look dewy skinned and bright eyed. If I started to work out, I might end up sweaty and stinky by the time he showed up. But if I sat in the café, perched prettily on one of the high stools that faced the juice bar, I'd look ridiculous.

"Sophie?"

I spun around. And there, looking gorgeous in a white T-shirt and navy shorts, was Dr. Prasad. Excitement jittered through me.

"Hi. Did you just get here?"

"Yes, just a few minutes ago. I was hoping I'd see you here," he said.

His smile was warm, and completely focused on me.

"Did you want to get something to drink?" I asked, gesturing toward the juice bar.

"Yes, absolutely," he said, and we walked over to the counter.

"I'll have a large orange juice, and what would you like?" Dr. Prasad asked, turning to me and resting his hand on my lower back. About an inch up from my butt.

"Ah. Um. I'll have a Berry Berry Smoothie," I stuttered.

All I could think was: Dr. Prasad's hand. Is right near. My ass.

"That'll be five fifty," the teenage boy behind the register said.

"Here, put it on my account," Dr. Prasad said, handing over his laminated membership card.

"Oh no, you don't have to pay for me," I protested.

"I insist."

"Thanks," I said, ducking my head down.

This was fun. The conspicuous absence of flirting was one of the suckier aspects of marriage, right up there with the end of first kisses. Nothing beats a really great first kiss, and when you've been kissing the same man for ten years, it begins to lose its charm. Especially when said man is a complete fucking asshole who surfs porny websites when he's pretending to work.

"Is something wrong?" Dr. Prasad asked as we sat down at a table.

"What? Oh no."

"You were frowning."

"No, no. I was just . . . remembering something I have to do. Anyway. Um. So how are you?" I asked.

"Very good. And how is little Ben?"

"He's great. I thought he might be coming down with an ear infection this morning—he was grabbing his ear—but maybe it's just another tooth coming in. Is that normal? Oh no. I'm sorry. I don't want to harass you with medical questions," I said, blushing.

The question had just sort of gushed out on its own volition. It was as though the Mommy part of me was trying to wrestle the femme fatale part for control of the conversation.

"No, that's quite all right. It could just be teething pain. Why don't you watch him for the next few days, and if he starts to run a fever or seems less animated than usual, bring him in to see me," Dr. Prasad said. "And please, call me Vinay."

"Okay. Vinay," I said, testing it out.

"So, tell me about you," Vinay said.

"Me? What do you want to know?"

"Do you work? Not to suggest that being a mother isn't work," he said, smiling.

I wondered if his shiny hair was as soft as it looked. I had to fight back an urge to touch it.

"I haven't been, but I'm about to open a photography

business specializing in baby portraits," I said, surprising myself with this announcement. When had I decided that? Or had I just made it up to sound more interesting?

"Are you an accomplished photographer, then?"

"Yes," I said, holding my chin a fraction higher. "I majored in it in college, and have been planning to open my own studio for a while."

"Where are you going to have your studio? At home?"

"I haven't decided yet," I said. "But probably not at home. My husband and I are separated, so I'm not staying there now."

I struggled to stay calm and serene with this admission. If I let on that I was still spitting mad at Aidan, so much so that I launched into a white-hot rage whenever I pictured his sordid little get-togethers with Cherry the Whore, Dr. Prasad—Vinay—might conclude that I hadn't reached closure on my marriage.

"I'm sorry," Vinay said. "Actually, no, bugger that. I lied. I'm thrilled to hear you're available."

And then he smiled so charmingly, I gurgled with laughter.

"Would you like to have dinner with me tonight?" Vinay asked.

It had been a long time since I'd gone out on a first date, but from what I could remember, you're supposed to play somewhat hard to get. Never accepting dates on short notice, for example, and not rushing to bed.

And then I remembered again: Cherry the Whore. The porny websites. Aidan masturbating in a darkened room. Anger whirred in my ears.

"I'd love to," I said. "I just have to make sure my mom can watch Ben for me."

*   *   *

I found out too late that Mom and Dad had tickets to the ballet. When I got back from the gym, Dad was there, and Mom
was making grilled cheese sandwiches and heating canned
tomato soup. I picked up Ben and shifted him onto my hip.

"Who am I, Ben? Oo, oo, oo," Dad said, opening his mouth
wide and scratching under his armpits. "I'm a chimpanzee!"

Ben giggled. Dad had finally found an appreciative audi-
ence for his repertoire of dumb jokes.

"The ballet?" I asked doubtfully.

"Don't ask. I can't believe how much they charge for the
tickets now. Forty years ago, you could buy a used car for
that price. Nowadays, forget about it," Dad said.

"Your father surprised me with tickets! It's something I've
always wanted to do," Mom enthused. She no longer seemed
annoyed by Dad's "forget about it" rants. It used to make
her apoplectic when he went off on one.

My mom put a plate down in front of me, and I shook my
head. "I shouldn't. I really need to lose some weight, and I
don't think bread and cheese fried in butter is the best way
to go about doing that," I said.

"It will come off eventually. And I think you look beautiful. I was just noticing that you have some color back in
your cheeks. Did you sleep better last night?" Mom asked.

"Erm, yes. Do you know if Paige has plans tonight?"

"I don't know, give her a call. Where did you say you were
going to go? Out with your friend Cora?"

"Yeah, she wanted to have a girls' night out," I lied.

I had decided that it might not be the best idea to tell my
family about Dr. Prasad. Vinay. They might not think it wise,
considering Aidan and I had only been officially separated

for six days. Or unofficially. Whatever. So I'd told them a little white lie. It was a useful technique most daughters perfect during their teenage years, and if it had been a while
since I'd trotted it out, at least my skills weren't rusty. No
one seemed suspicious.

Six hours later, Paige showed up. She looked pale and tired,
and a minute after she arrived, she flew into the bathroom. I
heard gagging sounds, and when she emerged, she looked
like she was going to pass out.

"Estrogen poisoning," she gasped. "What's that smell? It's
making me sick."

"I think Mom's roasting a chicken for lunch tomorrow, is
that what's bothering you?"

"Chicken." Paige turned around and rushed back into
the bathroom. She refused to come out until I retrieved the
chicken from the oven and tossed it into the garbage can in
the garage, and then opened up all of the downstairs windows so that the chicken odor would dissipate.

"For me it was spinach. If it so much as touched my
tongue, I'd gag and throw up," I told Paige, once she finally
staggered out of the bathroom and collapsed on the green
plaid couch. Ben was sitting in his swing next to the couch
and looked like he was close to drifting off.

"Don't talk about spinach. I can't deal with chicken, or
spinach, or pretty much any meat or vegetable," Paige said
weakly.

"What can you eat?"

"Crackers and lemonade. And tuna fish sandwiches," she
said.

"You can't stand the smell of chicken, but you can handle tuna?" I said.

She shrugged. "I can't explain it. It's out of my control. Where are you going with your friend?"

I hesitated, and considered telling Paige my real plans. But she was so out of sorts, telling her the truth might prompt a lecture on why dating now was an altogether bad idea. She might even refuse to watch Ben, which would force me to cancel.

"Just out for a bite. In fact, I better go, I'm supposed to meet her in a few minutes," I said.

"I think it's great that you're getting out. After Scott and I split up, I spent every weekend at home, moping around, watching videos. And you look so pretty. Is that outfit new?" Paige asked.

I ran my hands down the front of the sheer navy blouse that showed off a cream camisole underneath and the pencil denim skirt, all of which I'd picked up at Banana Republic on my way home from the gym. I knew that I shouldn't be shopping—Ben's and my future was up in the air enough as it was already—but I figured this was an emergency. Plus I charged it to the credit card that I shared with Aidan, which seemed a poetic justice.

"No, it's just something I had," I said. "So, do you think you'll be okay? Is Zack coming over to help you?"

"God, no. I need a break from him. Every time I turn around, he's there trying to help me with something or telling me that I need to get off my feet. Is it normal that I'm so irritated with the father of my child? Oh . . . I'm sorry, that's probably not the best thing to be asking you right now," Paige said.

"Totally normal. I wanted to kill Aidan the entire time I was pregnant. Everything he said or did made me want to throw heavy things at his head," I said.

"When did that stop?"

"Never," I said. I leaned over to kiss Ben good night on his chubby cheeks, now slack with sleep. His grapey scent filled my nose, and for a minute I wanted to grab him up against me and stay that way for the rest of the night. I could change into my soft cotton knit pajamas with the pink flowers on them and watch movies with Paige, and just check out of life for another day. "Do you want me to settle him into his crib before I leave?"

"No, you better get going. Go on, have fun. We'll be fine," Paige said.

"Okay." I stood up reluctantly. "I just nursed him an hour ago, but he'll probably wake up before I get home and want a bottle. There's one in the fridge. Heat it up by running it under some warm water, but don't put it in the microwave, 'cause it'll scorch."

"Go. Have fun," Paige said.

"Bye," I said.

I glanced back at Ben one more time before I left. And then I walked out of the house and out to my Tahoe, while the cicadas sang to the setting sun.

Chapter Twenty-seven

Vinay was already at the Hyde Park Bar and Grill when I got there. I had a last-minute attack of nerves when I saw him standing at the bar, holding a glass of red wine. He was wearing a white button-down shirt tucked into Levi's, and the outfit set off his wide shoulders and tapered waist. He turned and smiled at me, and I raised my hand up in a nervous greeting.

"Sophie," Vinay said. He leaned over and kissed me on the cheek. His lips felt warm, and I could smell the merlot on his breath. "Can I get you a glass of wine?"

"Yes, thanks. I'll have what you're having," I said.

He retrieved a glass from the bartender and turned to hand it to me.

"Cheers," he said, lifting his glass, and I clinked mine against his before lifting it to my lips.

"You look beautiful," Vinay said, his eyes drifting over me.

"Thanks," I said, blushing, but beginning to enjoy myself. Under his appreciative gaze, I felt beautiful for the first time since I'd had Ben.

"Is your party complete? Then come right this way," the hostess said, appearing behind us.

I turned to follow her, and as I did, Vinay rested his hand on my waist, guiding me in front of him. I could feel the warm pressure of his fingers through the sheer fabric of my shirt.

As we sat down at a corner table, I suddenly realized that no matter how smitten I was, there wasn't a chance in hell I could let this man see me and my flobby stomach naked. And my milk supply was still unpredictable . . . all I had to do was miss a feeding and my breasts would swell up into enormous, hard bowling balls. One touch and milk would squirt everywhere. What had I been thinking? How could I take this baby-stretched, milk-excreting body out on a date?

This was bad. Really, really bad.

"Is everything all right?" Vinay asked. He leaned his head toward me, his dark eyes fixed on mine.

"Mm-hmm," I said. I opened my eyes wide nodding vigorously. I grabbed for a glass of water and took a big gulp, realizing too late that I'd picked up my wine instead.

"Mpfh," I sputtered, as the too-large gulp burned against the back of my throat.

I set the glass down and focused on the menu.

"Have you ever been here before?" Vinay asked.

"Aidan and I used to come here all the time before we moved out to the burbs," I said, and then did a mental head slap. Although I hadn't been out there long enough to know the ground rules, I was pretty sure that mentioning your maybe-soon-to-be-ex-husband was a no-no on a first date.

"What do you recommend?" Vinay asked, graciously ignoring my gaffe.

"The sirloin burger. And they have the best fries in Austin," I said.

"Is that what you're going to have?"

I thought again of my flobby stomach, and then of my judgmental, stick-thin sisters-in-law.

"No . . . I think I'll just have a salad," I said.

"Absolutely not. Two sirloin burgers, and one very large order of chips," Vinay said to the waitress, who'd appeared at the table. I noticed that she was staring at Vinay with an undisguised interest. She was about four sizes smaller than me, and her ass was as high and round as a supermodel's.

"Chips?" she repeated stupidly.

"He means french fries," I said, handing her the menus. "And I'll have another glass of merlot, please."

"French fries, right. I always forget that," Vinay said, grinning at me.

"Is Austin a temporary move, or are you in Texas permanently?" I asked, once the flirty waitress had moved on.

"Permanent. Well, permanent for now, if that makes sense. I went to medical school at Tulane in New Orleans, and ended up in Houston for my residency. I decided to specialize in pediatrics, and was casting around for a job, and then one opened up here, so I thought I'd try it out," he said.

"Where are you from originally? Where in England?"

"London."

"Really? And you'd rather be here than there? I've always wanted to go there, it seems like such an amazing city. And so much more interesting than Austin," I said.

"I imagine I'll move back there someday. My parents are there, as are my brothers and sister," Vinay said.

"Are they upset that you're staying in the U.S. for now?"

"Yes and no. I think that if I married a nice Indian girl, settled down, and started having babies, they wouldn't care if I lived on the moon."

"And what's been holding you back?"

"I just never met the right nice Indian girl. It's silly, really, how hung up they are on it. But they emigrated to Britain from India in the sixties, and still live near and socialize with other Indian families, so they have a hard time getting away from traditions," Vinay said.

"What do your parents do?"

"Both doctors. My mother is a psychiatrist and my father is an anesthesiologist."

"Wow. And they're still married?"

"Yes. Are your parents divorced?"

"Sort of. They divorced when I was in college, but they just recently got back together. They're dating now, if you can believe that," I said.

"Bloody hell. That must make for interesting family get-togethers," Vinay said.

"You have no idea," I said.

The waitress arrived with our hamburgers and two more glasses of wine, and dinner passed in a pleasant haze of good, greasy food and amiable conversation. The wine was making me light-headed, but in a pleasant, loose-limbed kind of way. And it seemed from the way that Vinay was smiling at me that flobby stomachs were the last thing on his mind.

Maybe he's the one I'm supposed to be with, I thought. Maybe Aidan was just the wrong man for me all along. I couldn't remember when—if ever—Aidan's touch had made my heart speed up or if his smile made my senses hum with possibility. Sure, maybe back in the beginning it had been like this, but if it was true love and meant to be, would those feelings really have eroded over time, a mortgage, and a baby?

Yes, another part of me—apparently one unaffected by winsome smiles, candlelit dinners, and the rich timbre of a British accent—said. It's entirely normal. The heightened senses and sweet obsessions of early love never last. It morphs and changes and grows. And even if my frayed bond with Aidan has snapped for good, and this flirtation with Vinay grows into something meaningful and permanent, the flutters that I get when he smiles at me across the table will eventually dissipate, too.

I couldn't decide if this thought was comforting or depressing.

Vinay paid the bill, slipping his gold American Express card into the plastic billfold, and the annoyingly thin waitress tried to catch his eye as she returned the receipt for his signature. I felt a stab of triumph when Vinay responded to her coy smiles and hair flips with a polite disinterest.

We walked out of the restaurant, and unseasonably chilly air rushed by us, eager to pass into the warm recesses of the restaurant. I hadn't thought to bring a jacket.

"Brrr. When did it get so cold out?" I asked. "Wasn't it in the eighties today?"

"I'll keep you warm," Vinay said, wrapping an arm around my shoulders.

For the first time, I felt a little uncomfortable with him. It was a borderline-smarmy line, just one step removed from the horrible yawning-then-arm-stretching-then-boob-feeling move my freshman high school boyfriend actually tried on me.

"I'm parked right over there," I said, pointing at my SUV in the alley at the side of the restaurant.

"Did you want to get some coffee somewhere, or maybe we could rent a movie and take it back to my place?" he said. He rubbed his thumb against my shoulder in a repetitive motion that irritated my skin.

"I wish I could," I said. "But my sister is sitting with Ben, and she's expecting me back."

"You could call her, see if she'd mind staying a little later," Vinay said, stepping closer to me.

I knew then that he was going to kiss me, and every last inch of my body went on high alert.

"No, I can't. She's pregnant and hasn't been feeling well," I said.

He was now standing so close that I had to tip my head back to see him. The glow of the streetlights cast a bluish light over his face, and he looked so different than he had in the restaurant. I wondered if I did, too. Candlelight is so much more flattering, more seductive.

And just as I was thinking that this could be the most ingenious invention of modern mankind—some sort of device to secure a candle under your chin, so that everyone could walk around in dark rooms with their faces glowing in the light (and yes, the high rate of singed hair and stubbed toes might be an issue, but it was still a brilliant idea)—Vinay leaned forward and pressed his lips against mine.

The pressure was soft but insistent, and as he kissed me, he rested a hand gently on the back of my neck to draw me closer to him. I closed my eyes and leaned into the kiss, catching my breath as the tip of his tongue flickered against my lips. And I waited for the falling-from-a-high-height-while-simultaneously-melting first-kiss feeling to hit me.

It didn't come.

I'd always loved first kisses when I was single—they were what made the horrors of first dates worthwhile. Nine times out of ten, you wouldn't click, but on those rare occasions when you did, the first kiss was the jackpot payoff. So I gave it another minute, forcing my body not to tense up, and instead rested my hands on his waist, where I could feel warm skin through the heavy cotton of his shirt.

Still nothing.

Instead, I was starting to become all too aware of the hint of onions on his breath. And that the fine hairs on his upper lip were tickling me. And then his other hand was suddenly on my lower back, teetering on the brink of heading toward my too-large bottom. That was it. I didn't mind letting the lukewarm kissing go on for a while—maybe I was just out of practice or too stressed out to enjoy it—but I wasn't about to let him get anywhere near my ass. I took a step back, breaking off the kiss.

"I really should get going. Thanks again for dinner," I said.

Vinay looked at me, and his dark, still eyes were so kind, I started to think that maybe I should give him a second chance on the kissing. For all I knew, he was the best kisser to have ever puckered lips, and the lack of reaction on my part was just one more lovely little postpartum side effect.

"Are you sure?" he asked. He ran his hands up my arms until they were both resting on my shoulders. A few hours earlier, the very thought of this sort of close proximity to him, this casually intimate touching, would have thrilled me. Now I just felt tired and wanted to retreat back to where it was safe and quiet.

What I really wanted to do was to go home. Not to my mother's house, but to my home, the one I shared with Aidan. And suddenly, just like that, I was missing my husband. I missed the soapy scent of his aftershave, the way he always closed his eyes and took a deep breath when he cuddled Ben, and Saturday afternoons spent lazing around the house in our sweats together, watching videos and screening phone calls. I missed that he knew I never drank coffee at night since it keeps me up. I missed how he always made sure my gas tank was full and my cell phone charged. I missed how he always got up with Ben in the morning, and carried him into the bedroom, so that the first thing I saw every day were my two smiling, sleepy-eyed guys.

"I really have to. But, I mean it, thanks. This meant a lot to me," I said.

"Right then." Vinay cleared his throat and thrust his hands in his pockets. "I take it there's not going to be a second date."

"I haven't been completely honest with you," I said. "My husband and I are separated, but only just recently. I still don't know what's going to happen with my marriage. But it's probably a little early for me to start dating."

"I understand. And I don't want to sound as if I'm rooting for the collapse of your marriage, but if things don't work out, why don't you give me a call," he said.

I felt a burst of affection for him, and immediately began to think of someone I could set him up with. There was Vicky, one of my few remaining single friends, but then again, she was a depressive. And then there was Allison, my sister-in-law, but no, no way was I going to hook her up with anyone, not after her tummy-tuck comment. Mickey, maybe? She'd be home for the summer soon, and since she was headed to medical school, they'd have that in common.

"My little sister is graduating from college in two months and then will be home for the summer. If you want, I could introduce you to her. She's absolutely amazing—she's funny, smart, beautiful. And she broke up with her boyfriend a few weeks ago, so I know she's available," I said.

"It's got to be the ultimate rejection when your date tries to fix you up with someone else—her sister no less—at the end of the night," Vinay said wryly, and I must have looked stricken, because he laughed, and tapped me on the arm. "I'm just kidding. Is your sister as pretty as you are?"

"Prettier. And she's much nicer than I am," I promised.

"All right then. You're on," he said.

Chapter Twenty-eight

I've never felt more lonely than I did as I drove back to my mother's house. Lonely and tired. My fantasy about Vinay had been just that—a fanciful break from the cold reality that the rest of my life was in tatters. I didn't have a home or a job, my marriage was likely shattered beyond repair, and I was just sitting around waiting for everything to sort itself out on its own, which apparently wasn't going to happen.

First, I had to talk to Aidan. I was angry at him, but we had a child together, and if there was any way we could salvage our marriage, we had to try. For Ben's sake. The kiss with Vinay had made me realize something—as angry as I was at him, I was still in love with my husband.

And no matter what happened with my marriage, it was time to get serious about my career, time to do something about starting up my photography studio. I needed to network with other moms, and maybe offer to do some free sittings so I could build up a portfolio. And I'd look into going to the baby expo that Cora had told me about. Where I was going to run my business, I had no idea—if Aidan and I were going to permanently separate, we'd have to do something about the house—but that was more decision making than I was up to facing tonight.

I turned onto my mom's street, and started to pull into the driveway, before I realized that it was already full. My dad's car was there—they must have returned from the ballet already—and Paige's car . . . and Aidan's car. My stomach jolted with nerves, but then I remembered that he was here to see Ben, not me. In the excitement over my date, I'd completely forgotten. I put the car in reverse and parked on the street.

I walked up the driveway, wondering what was going on inside the house. Mom and Paige knew about the porn incident, which meant Dad probably did, too, even though I'd been too embarrassed to tell him. I wondered how they'd reacted when Aidan showed up. Were they being hostile to him? Or chillingly polite? I hoped that they weren't being too hard on him—it was important that he feel comfortable when seeing his son.

But wait, I thought. Why did he come over this late? Ben must be asleep by now, Aidan knows that.

"Sophie," Aidan said, and I started. I hadn't noticed that he was sitting on the darkened front steps, lit only by the small lamp beside the front door. He was slumped forward, his long legs sprawled out in front of him.

"Hi," I said, but he didn't respond. It wasn't until I took another step forward that I saw he'd been crying.

I had never seen my husband cry before. Not once.

Did he know where I'd been? Had my mother or sister somehow figured out and told him, or had he maybe followed me? Although I would have thought he'd react to the news that I was dating—or had gone on a date—with anger, not tears.

"What is it? What's wrong?" I asked, and I sat down next to him on the step.

"I screwed everything up. For you, for Ben, for me. I was such an idiot. I don't blame you for hating me," Aidan said.

"I don't hate you," I said softly.

"You don't?"

"No. I'm pretty ticked off at you, though."

Aidan nodded, and he clasped his hands in front of him. "I know," he said.

"Are you having an affair?" I asked. My throat felt raw and itchy as the words squeezed out. It was a question I had to ask, I knew, even if I wasn't at all sure that I wanted to hear the answer.

"No. I never touched another woman. Not even a kiss," Aidan said, and I felt a rush of guilt.

"What was going on with that Cherry woman?" I asked.

Aidan sighed and rubbed his hand over his mouth. "Nothing. Well, not nothing nothing, just . . . sending each other private messages that were . . . sexual in nature. It's really embarrassing, but . . . I don't know. I don't want to justify it, because I can't, but you and I had become so distant, and every time I tried to touch you, you'd move away, and I was just trying to fill the space. But it was a stupid, juvenile thing to do, and I'd do anything to take it back," he said. "Anything."

"You were still cheating on me," I said.

I couldn't help picturing Aidan sitting in his darkened study yet again, looking at pictures of naked women or exchanging lascivious notes with Cherry the Whore and getting off on it. The thought sickened me. I'd never understood what was remotely sexy about a close-up of a cheesy, mustachioed man penetrating a silicone-injected, hard-faced woman. It always seemed so impersonal and sordid, and the idea that Aidan would find it so arousing disturbed me.

"I'm so sorry. I never wanted to hurt you."

"Are you going to stop doing it?"

"Yes, absolutely. I've already canceled my memberships to those sites and cleared it all off of the computer. It's gone," he said. "Does that mean that you'd consider giving this . . . us . . . another try?"

I looked down, and remembered how it had felt to drive home alone, leaving behind the man who had been my fantasy. Were my daydreams of Vinay really all that different from Aidan's porn surfing? Wasn't I just as guilty of looking outside of our marriage for fulfillment? And then I thought of Ben and Aidan, and how even if things didn't always function perfectly, on the nights that they did—when we were all sitting together on the couch, and Aidan and I were smiling down at our son, charmed by whatever his most recent accomplishment was—that it really couldn't get any better than that. And I wanted us to be together, to be a family again.

"Yes. But I think that we need some help. Maybe we should start seeing a marriage counselor," I said slowly.

"Anything. Whatever you want," Aidan said, and he took my hands in his and then brought them to his lips. "I love you. I won't let you down again. Oh shit!"

"What?"

"I totally forgot. Wait here," he said, and then he jumped

off the step and bounded down to his car, opened the door, and got in.

"Aidan? Where are you going?" I called after him.

"Just wait one second," he said, and then he started his car. I could see him leaning forward, fiddling with something on his dashboard. And then there was a burst of music, a pause while Aidan fiddled some more, and then suddenly a familiar song was started up. *"Love I get so lost, sometimes . . ."*

Aidan turned the music up and then walked back up the path toward me, looking shy and pleased with himself.

" 'In Your Eyes,' " I said. "How did you know?"

"Paige told me. She said you'd always wanted someone to play it for you," Aidan said.

"Not someone. You. But you're supposed to be standing under my window, in the rain, holding a radio up over your head," I said.

"I knew I'd get it wrong," he said, and looked so let down that I stood up and wrapped my arms around him.

"No, you didn't. You got it just right."

Mickey

Chapter Twenty-nine

I honestly meant to tell my parents the truth when they picked me up at the airport. I figured, I'd just get it out of the way early, so I wouldn't have to spend the entire summer pretending that I was about to launch on this great future. The lie was getting out of hand.

I'm not even sure exactly how it happened. At some point I mentioned that I might possibly be sort of interested in maybe considering attending medical school, and I even went so far as to take some preliminary steps, such as sending out some applications and taking the MCATs. But then I got my acceptance letter to Brown, and everyone started congratulating me, and the whole thing got away from me. Suddenly, my entire life had been decided for me—the years of studying, a sleep-free residency, hours of mind-numbing scut work. And my parents were telling everyone they knew that my getting into medical school was a dream come true for all of us, an announcement that I couldn't seem to argue with. Instead I just smiled and said thank you when people gushed on about how wonderful it was, and tried to ignore the sluggish sickliness that washed over me whenever I let myself think about it.

I don't think you can even be a doctor when the sight of blood makes you woozy. A sloppy, drunk girl in my dorm sophomore year stepped in her shower basket and cut off the top of her big toe on her razor. She was screaming, there was blood everywhere . . . and when I saw the sticky red trail she left behind as she limped to the health center, I felt so nauseated I thought I was going to hurl. I spent the rest of the night curled up on my military-style cot bed in the fetal position. Which is just not doctor material. Obviously.

And seriously, there are a lot of careers out there that don't require you to take a class where you cut into dead people, which I can almost guarantee I would not survive. In every television show I've ever seen about medical school, there's always that one loser who faints during a surgical instruction, and if I did end up in medical school, that loser would undoubtedly be me.

And that's what I fully intended to tell my mother and father when they met me in the baggage claim area at the Austin-Bergstrom International Airport. I was not, nor would I ever be, matriculating at Brown Medical School.

But my parents weren't there.

Instead, bizarrely, my ex-brother-in-law Scott showed up, dressed in a tight black T-shirt and black leather pants.

"Let me guess. You're running away to join a motorcycle gang," I said.

"Ha-ha. You just wish you were as hip as me," Scott said. He folded me into his arms. "Hey, kid. It's been a long time."

"No kidding. Paige told me you two are talking again. I

was really glad to hear that. I've missed you," I said, punching him lightly on the arm. "So, are you coming or going?"

"What do you mean?"

"You do know you're in an airport, don't you?"

"I'm here to pick you up. But keep up with the wise-cracks and it'll be a long walk back to the city," Scott said.

I looked around for a sign of the Cassel family. But among the harried parents herding their little ones, seniors in jogging suits, and clusters of college students milling around, all waiting for baggage, I didn't see any familiar faces.

"You came by yourself?" I asked. "Where's everyone else?"

"Your parents are tied up with something, Paige wasn't feeling well, and Sophie had to deal with the baby. So Paige called and asked if I'd swing by and scoop you up. Are all of these your bags? God, what do you have in here?" Scott asked, straining to lift my luggage into a cart.

"Books," I said faintly. This was weird. I'd just talked to my mom last night, and she hadn't said anything about Scott coming instead.

What was it with my family? In other families, when people get divorced, they go off in different directions. Now my parents were dating, and Scott was my airport shuttle. I suppose it was better than all of the acrimony, but still—weird.

"Right. I should have known. No, don't worry, I've got these. Just follow me," Scott said.

We walked out to the garage and after a few minutes of searching, found Scott's pickup truck. My bags were heaved up into the bed, alongside bags of soil and assorted gardening tools, and then we climbed into the cab. The truck and dirt seemed incongruous with Scott's outfit.

"Is the black leather meant to be a marketing gimmick, like Chippendale Landscapers?"

"No, but that's not a bad idea, kid," Scott said, grinning at me.

"How is business going?" I asked him as he pulled out of the garage and headed out toward the freeway.

"Crazy busy. I have more work than I can handle this summer, even without your brilliant marketing hook. Do you have a summer job lined up yet? Because I could use an extra set of hands. And I figured you'd probably want the extra cash to take to med school with you. Congratulations on Brown, by the way," Scott said.

"Er. Thanks. And thanks for the job offer. But I was thinking . . . I think I want to get a job in a restaurant," I said.

"You mean waitressing? Like at Chuy's or something?"

"No, somewhere nice. But I was hoping that maybe I could be an assistant or gopher to the chef," I said. "Or, if not, I'd wait tables."

"I don't know about the kitchen work—I think most of the chefs in the high-end places are professionally trained—but I could see if my boyfriend's restaurant is hiring, if you're interested," Scott said.

"Really? That would be great! Do you think they are?"

"Yeah, actually I think they might be. Kevin said a waiter was fired the other night for smoking a joint in the bathroom in the middle of a shift. But why so excited about waiting tables? Is it really that much better than planting flowers for me?"

"You have no idea," I said, grinning happily.

*   *   *

I should have figured out that something was up when Scott insisted on walking me into my mom's house rather than just dropping me off. He did it under the pretense of helping me carry my luggage in, and I slowly trailed up the paved walk behind him, dreading how the big reveal would go when I told my parents my decision. Would Mom cry? Would Dad turn red and get that awful crease in his forehead?

If I don't step on any cracks, they'll just be happy for me and not at all angry, I thought, and then almost immediately stepped on one. And then another.

I decided the game of not stepping on cracks in the pavement was juvenile and beneath me.

Scott was waiting by the front door, looking expectant.

"Just go in," I said. "Here, take my key."

"I think we should ring the bell," Scott said, pressing the doorbell with his thumb.

"What? Why? I never ring, and it doesn't look like anyone's home."

The house was dark and still, and the driveway was free of cars.

"Okay then, go ahead in," Scott said, stepping out of my way.

"What's going on?"

"Nothing. What do you mean?"

"I know you. I can see it in your face. Something's up." I crossed my arms and stared at Scott defiantly. "I'm not moving until you tell me what's going on."

"Christ, you sound just like your sister," Scott said wearily.

"Which one?"

"It doesn't matter. You're all equally stubborn. Okay, fine, I'll tell you, but you can't tell that I told." Scott bent down, and with his lips so close to my ear, I could feel the warmth of his breath, he whispered, "Surprise party. So try to look surprised."

"Oh no. No, no, no," I said, shaking my head. I took a step back from the door and looked around, trying to find an escape route. Up the street, I could see a couple dozen cars lined up by the side of the road.

"What's wrong?" Scott asked.

"I'm so not up for this right now."

"Go on, it'll be fine," Scott said, pulling my arm gently.

"No, you don't understand . . . ," I began, about to tell him about how I wasn't going to medical school, and that I had to tell my parents before anyone else, and that I couldn't bear spending one more night lying to everyone.

But before I could blurt any of it out, Scott opened the door and gently herded me inside the dark house. And then suddenly the lights were turned on, and the fifty assorted guests were yelling surprise, and everyone was laughing and hugging me and asking me if I was truly surprised.

I pasted a smile on my face, while the crowd—family, friends of my parents, a few kids I'd gone to high school with—pushed forward, swarming me with congratulations and the inevitable questions.

Yes, I'm excited about Brown. No, I don't know what specialty I'm going into. Yes, I've heard that dermatology pays well. No, I have no idea where I want to spend my residency.

Somehow I managed to work my way through the crowd of well-wishers, accepting hugs and kisses on the cheek. I stole a few minutes to say hello to my sisters, cuddle Ben, and pat Paige's budding pregnant belly, before my mother dragged me off to talk to another one of the ladies from her garden club and yet again go through my repertoire of canned responses to the set of inevitable questions.

I felt like I was suffocating.

And then it got really bad.

My mother started tapping her fork against her wine-glass, until everyone quieted down.

"Thank you all so much for coming tonight. We're just thrilled that you're here to celebrate Mickey's college gradu-ation and acceptance into Brown Medical School with us," Mom said in a news-anchor voice that made me cringe.

Mom held her glass up toward me, and stood there poised until everyone else followed suit. My cheeks flamed as I felt the weight of attention focused on me. Unlike Sophie, who would happily have a party thrown in her honor every week, I loathe being the center of attention. It made my nose feel even longer, my hair that much stringier. And everyone else was dressed up—strappy sundresses, crisply ironed shirts, mingling perfumes. I was wearing baggy Levi's and a white T-shirt that I'd spilled Coke on when my plane was somer-saulting through some turbulence, and my hair was scraped back in a messy, uncombed ponytail.

"To our Mickey, the future doctor. Wishing you joy and success in all that is before you," Mom said.

"To Mickey," everyone chimed in, before lifting their glasses to drink.

I worked the corners of my mouth up into a smile and tried to avoid eye contact.

"Thanks, everyone," I mumbled.

"And while we have everyone here, Stephen and I have another announcement to make," Mom continued. Dad moved to her side and, looking proud and sheepish, clasped her hand in his.

I froze, my glass to my lips, and looked around for Sophie and Paige. Sophie was standing next to Aidan, holding Ben in her arms. Paige, wearing an elegant black slip dress, was ladling some punch into her glass. Their eyes were riveted on Mom. We could all feel the disturbance in the Force, and we all knew to brace for whatever it was that was about to come spilling out of Mom's red-lipstick-ringed mouth. The hair on the back of my neck actually stood up.

"After spending many years together raising our family, and then working through some time apart, Stephen and I have managed to find one another again. Last week, Stephen asked me to marry him, for a second time, and I've accepted. We're having a small ceremony and party here at the house at the end of the summer, and we'd be overjoyed if all of you would join us," she finished, smiling radiantly.

My father kissed Mom's hand, and they beamed at one another like a pair of love-struck adolescents while people applauded and called out their congratulations. My mouth sagged open, and I was overwhelmed with the vertigo feeling that stress sometimes brings—the room was loopy and off balance, my stomach was queasy, my chest felt tight.

"Mickey, are you okay? You look like you're going to be sick," Paige whispered in my ear, appearing behind me. She grabbed my left elbow and guided me out of the room, down the slate-tiled hallway and out onto the front porch. I sat down heavily on the same wooden front steps that I'd spent hours of my childhood playing on. This was the very spot where Barbie had dumped Ken so that she could pursue her dream of riding on the Olympic cross-country equestrian team without the distraction of his plastic sculpted hair and paper white teeth.

"Just take a deep breath. I know it seems bad, but it will be okay, I promise," Paige said, sitting down next to me and rubbing my back in a circular motion.

"Married? What . . . are . . . they . . . thinking?" I gasped. "And I have to live here this summer with Mom while she plans her fucking wedding? Just when I thought things couldn't get any worse."

"Do you want to stay in my apartment?" Paige asked.

"You don't have room for me," I said, although spending two months sleeping on her sofa did sound better than staying here. I just didn't want to impose on her and Zack, especially while they were in the midst of new-relationship flutterings and baby preparations.

"I won't even be there. I'm moving into Zack's new house on a trial basis. This would actually work out perfectly, because it would give me a good excuse not to give up my apartment," Paige said. "Now that I'm starting my own firm, I've been having a hard time justifying the additional expense. But if you were there, I'd get to keep it. You'd be doing me a favor."

"Why do you want to keep it? Don't you think it's going to work out with you guys?" I asked.

Paige sighed and rested her hands on her baby bump. "Some days I think yes, this is it, this relationship will last forever. And then other days . . . I don't know. I don't know how sure I'm supposed to feel," she said. "But maybe it's just my mood right now. Zack and I got into an argument on the way over here about which route to take. Honestly, it's my mother's house, does he really think I don't know the best way?"

"That's normal though. Soph and Aidan bicker all the time, and they have a strong marriage," I said.

Paige didn't comment on this. I had the distinct feeling that she knew something about Soph and Aidan that she wasn't telling me.

"Oh God. Oh no. Don't tell me they're breaking up, too," I said, and the world started to veer around again. I rested my head on my hands and stared down at the stone-paved path that connected the driveway to the front porch. One of the stones by my foot was loose, and I wedged my toe against it until it popped out of place.

"No, they're fine. Really. They went through a rough patch this spring, but they're doing better now," Paige said.

"Yeah, I thought she seemed really happy tonight. She told me she and Aidan are going on a cruise in September. I think they're leaving Ben with Mom. Or Mom, Dad, and me," I said bleakly.

"Don't worry, you'll be long gone by then. When does med school start? Right around Labor Day weekend?" Paige asked.

"I guess."

Oh shit. Medical school. I'd forgotten about that in the aftermath of our parents' announcement. I could have kicked myself for not telling them the previous week, when everyone was up at Princeton for my graduation.

"And you can stay in my apartment until then."

"Are you sure you don't mind?"

"Of course not. I don't want to sell it right away, not until

I'm sure about Zack and me, and this way I have an excuse to hang on to it," Paige said.

"Here you are. I was wondering where everyone ran off to," Sophie said. She let the front door slam behind her. "So, what do you think about those crazy kids? Getting married and not a care in the world."

"They certainly don't seem to care what we think," I said.

Sophie plopped down next to us.

"I think it's sweet. And so romantic," Sophie said.

I stared at her. Normally Sophie's the one flying off into a tizzy about things.

"You can't be serious," I said.

She grinned and swatted me on the arm.

"Let's just not make a big deal out of this, and see how it goes. Knowing them, they'll probably end up getting into a huge fight and call it all off, so there's no sense getting worked up about it," Paige suggested. "And besides, we all have a lot on our plates right now. And . . . oh . . . um . . ."

"Actually, there's something I have to tell you guys . . . ," I began.

"Paige, are you okay?" Sophie interrupted me.

I looked at my older sister and saw that she was holding her head in her hands, swaying slightly from side to side.

"Kack," Paige gagged.

"Are you feeling sick? Okay, come on, I'll help you to the bathroom," Sophie said. She grabbed Paige's hand and hauled her up to her feet.

"Is she okay?" I asked, alarmed.

"Yeah, she'll be fine. This is normal," Sophie said.

"I thought morning sickness was supposed to go away once you get to the second trimester," Paige groaned. Her face was pinched up and had turned a sickly shade of greenish white.

"Only if you're very lucky," Sophie said.

She held Paige's elbow, as though our older sister was an elderly woman. I scrambled to my feet and held the door open for them as they hobbled slowly through.

I trailed behind my sisters and then turned into the dining room. On the table there was an enormous sheet cake that had "Congratulations Mickey!" scrawled across it in blue icing, and what I think was supposed to be a frosting-rendered stethoscope snaking around the "Mickey." It was my favorite kind—chocolate with mocha butter cream frosting, the kind that's so sugary it gives you the shivers. And after I ate two pieces, I felt a little better about things. But then, cake usually does help.

Chapter Thirty

T hanks so much for helping me get this job," I said, nervously running my hands down over my starched white apron, which, along with a white button-down shirt and black trousers, was the uniform for my new waitressing job at Versa.

"No problem, glad to help. Nervous?" Kevin asked.

Scott's boyfriend wasn't at all what I thought he'd be. I'd been expecting . . . well, I don't know what I was expecting. I suppose a male version of Paige—type A personality, goal oriented, takes no shit from anyone, every last item of clothing ironed to perfection. But Kevin looked like he'd rolled out of a Seattle coffee shop circa 1991. He had longish scruffy brown hair, kind hazel brown eyes, and he'd forgotten to shave that morning. While we talked, he was pulling a denim blue chef's coat on over a stained Nirvana T-shirt.

"No. Well. I wish they had some sort of a training program, because I have no idea what I'm supposed to be doing," I said.

"Yeah, it's sort of sink-or-swim here. But I'm sure you'll be fine. Scott told me you're going to medical school this fall," Kevin said.

"Um. Well. That remains to be seen," I said.

I considered—and decided against—telling Kevin my supersecret plan: I was planning to enroll in culinary school. I'd taken a few off-campus gourmet cooking courses from a chef in Princeton—one in basic techniques, another in baking bread, and a third in sausage making—and had fallen in love with everything about the craft. It appealed to my chemistry background, just as medicine had, but it also allowed me to be creative and original. I knew it was crazy—the late nights, the silly hat, the dorky uniform—but the more I thought about it, the more I just knew this was what I was meant to be doing with my life. And so I made my decision. It was too late to register for fall courses, but I'd already talked to the admissions office at the Culinary Institute of America and was in the process of completing the paperwork to enroll there for the spring semester.

But if I told Kevin, he might tell Scott, who would tell Paige, and she'd almost certainly snitch me out to our parents. And I had to tell them myself, which I would do just as soon as I could stomach talking to them again.

Kevin looked at me quizzically, but then the head waiter, Adam—who was tall and gangly—called out for the waitstaff to gather round.

"Come on, guys, hurry up, don't keep Chef waiting," Adam now said, sighing with irritation.

"Does he mean you?" I asked Kevin.

Kevin shook his head. "I'm only the lowly pastry chef. The head chef is Oliver Klein."

"Is he scary?"

"A little. He acts like a rock star," Kevin said. "Before he came here, he worked in Miami and was starting to get semi-famous. There was even talk that he was going to star in a restaurant-based reality show."

"That's impressive," I said, and was about to ask him how the chef had ended up in Austin, when Oliver Klein walked into the room.

There wasn't any doubt about who he was, even if he was dressed only in white cotton pants and a white V-neck undershirt, with no sign of the Pillsbury Doughboy hat or traditional white coat. The entire kitchen reacted, everyone quieting down and turning toward him, faces expectant and eager. Kevin was right, it was just as though a rock star had rolled onto a stage. He even looked the part, with thick dark hair that curled down over his high forehead, brilliant blue eyes, a wide nose flattened across the tip, and a slightly lopsided mouth, so that when the full lips smiled—as they did now, at one of the waitresses who was laughing at him flirtatiously—they curled slightly, Billy Idol–style. He was lean but muscular, with the build of a runner.

"Wow," I breathed softly.

Kevin looked at me, alarmed. "Oh no. Trust me—he is not someone you want to mess with," he whispered.

"Why not?"

"He's married. Well, at least he was. When he moved here, his wife and kid stayed in Miami, so they might be officially separated. I heard a rumor that he left Miami because a hostess at his restaurant was threatening a sexual harassment lawsuit against him. Of course, I also heard that their relationship was very consensual, and she was just mad because he dumped her. And I know for a fact he's already slept with one of the waitresses here. I saw her coming out of his office the other day, crying," Kevin said.

"How do you know they slept together?"

"Word gets around. You have to be careful. The restaurant business is like high school. Everyone knows everyone, and everyone gossips," Kevin warned.

"I'll keep that in mind," I said, and then edged closer to the rest of the waitstaff gathered around the stainless-steel-topped table.

With one hand resting on his hip, Oliver cleared his throat and began to speak.

"Here are tonight's specials. Write them down, because I don't plan on repeating myself. Appetizer: seared Hudson Valley foie gras, with a caramelized-apple sauce. Salad: jumbo lump crab with coriander and honey-cured carrots. Entrée: milk-fed veal served with crispy sweetbreads and a rosemary demi-glace. Dessert: espresso soufflé. Any questions? You, New Girl, did you get that?" he said. The words were firing out of his mouth so quickly, it took me a minute to realize he was speaking to me.

Everyone turned to look at me. I could feel my cheeks heating to a red stain.

"I . . . uh . . . I think so," I said weakly.

"That's not good enough. You have to know it, and know it cold. Tell me without looking down at your paper, what's the entrée?" Oliver barked.

I stared at him and shook my head mutely.

"Sarah, tell her," Oliver said.

Sarah—who, it turned out, was the coquette who'd been flirting with the chef—looked at me and said, "A milk-fed veal served with sweetbreads and rosemary demi-glace."

I wondered if Sarah was the waitress who Kevin saw crying over Oliver. She had sallow skin, mean eyes, and her face was hard, but a lot of guys go for that type. I think it's a regression, a feeling of inadequacy left over from high school when they were too intimidated to ask out the bad girls who wore too much black eyeliner and smoked cigarettes in the school parking lot. So maybe it was her. Or it could have been Caitlin, a short, chunky waitress with sexy blonde ringlets and enormous breasts, or Opal, a black woman with sharp, high cheekbones who walked like a ballerina, with her toes pointed out.

My cheeks burned, even as the mocking eyes of my new co-workers slid over me, obviously amused at seeing the new kid getting hazed. I scowled at Oliver, but he'd lost interest in me. He turned his back dismissively on the wait-staff and asked his sous-chef for an update on the dinner prep.

"Don't worry. He picks on a different server every night," a voice murmured in my ear. I looked up and saw that it was Opal, her eyes narrow and lips pursed. "I got it yesterday. Oliver's an asshole. I'm thinking about quitting, I don't need his shit."

"Is he really that bad?" I asked. Unease snaked through me.

"He yelled at one of the girls the other day for mixing up an order. It shouldn't have been a big deal, but he belittled her in front of the whole kitchen staff. She quit that night. I saw her coming out of his office in tears," Opal murmured.

So maybe *she* was the crying waitress Kevin had seen. Maybe it had nothing to do with sex after all, and everything to do with Oliver's nasty temperament.

He was still talking to his sous-chef—Ansel, I'd met him

earlier, who had the long, stretched-out body of a basketball player—but his demeanor with the kitchen staff seemed much friendlier. Ansel continued to work while they talked, prepping for the shift ahead—setting out his knifes, checking on the levels of chopped garlic and minced shallots, dicing mushrooms into a neat, rounded pile, and occasionally barking out an instruction to one of his three underlings to fetch something from the cooler. I got tingly just watching him, knowing that's where I wanted to be. Someday.

But Oliver, in contrast, was still and calm, exactly like a musician resting before a big concert. He stood with one hand leaning on the stainless steel counter. My eyes inadvertently dropped down, and I looked at his square hips, at the front of his white chef's pants, and suddenly an unexpected image popped into my head of what he'd look like naked and aroused.

Oliver looked in my direction. I started and dropped my pencil. It bounced and fell with a muted clatter.

"Is everything okay?" Opal asked, peering at me.

I bent over to retrieve the pencil and dared another glance at Oliver as I stood back up. He was laughing again at one of Ansel's jokes, completely ignoring me. I turned away, ducking my head and smoothing my apron.

"Yeah, I'm fine. Just a little nervous."

"Don't worry. This job is a piece of cake. Just stay calm, and go over your checklist: greet, beverages, order, serve, check back every ten minutes, dessert, check. And try to stay as organized as possible," she said, repeating what I'd learned from the paltry manual Adam had given me in lieu of any real training.

*   *   *

My first shift was a nightmare. From the moment my first party sat down to when the bell on the door tinkled, signaling that the last guest had left the restaurant, I ran. Not literally, of course, since sprinting through the chicly understated dining room of gray walls, modern paintings, and Asian paper lamps would have ended my career as a Versa server. But it was back and forth, hurry, hurry, don't forget this, oh God I forgot that, get the food, place the order, ignore Adam's supercilious smirk, laugh at Ansel's jokes. Everything was flying by me, and I was falling back, scrambling to keep up. I'd always thought that waiting tables was a dignified and gracious occupation at these high-end restaurants, one that required a subtle understanding of the melding of flavors in fine cuisine and detailed knowledge of the wine list. It shocked me to find out it was mostly physically exhausting labor, involving lap after lap through the kitchen.

After hearing Kevin's warning about Oliver's libidinous interest in the waitstaff, I would have liked to have had the opportunity to ignore Oliver's interested gaze just to get back at him for yelling at me earlier, but he paid no attention to me. Instead he turned his narrow focus on what he was sautéing in his pan, or building on a plate, or sniffing as he waved his hand to waft the aroma up toward his face.

He was beautiful while he worked. And I couldn't stop watching him.

The only time he noticed me was at the very end of the shift, when the tension in the kitchen had mellowed out—while the dinner rush was on, Oliver yelled at Ansel, who in turn yelled at his assistants, who screamed at the waitstaff, who got temperamental with the busboys—and the kitchen staff was popping bottle caps off sweating beer bottles and laughing at a goof-up that the grill cook had made in the middle of the shift.

"Hey you, New Girl," I heard, and when I turned, Oliver was smiling at me. He'd taken off his white coat and was again wearing only his white T-shirt, now damp with sweat. I thought chefs normally wear those dorky black-checked outfits, but Oliver's garb looked like medical scrubs.

"Me?" I asked, feeling like I was about ten years old.

"Yeah, you. How did your first night go?"

"Um. Fine."

"And what was the special tonight?" he asked. Although he was smiling, the squinting eyes were challenging me.

I hesitated.

"Veal. With sweetbreads and demi-glace," I said.

"What kind of a demi-glace?"

"Um. Rosemary."

Oliver nodded. "Very good," he said. And then he turned away, walking into his office. He left the door open, and although I pretended to organize my credit card slips, I watched him covertly while he shucked off the soiled T-shirt. Fine dark hair covered his chest, thinning as it dipped below his nipples and streamed down over his flat stomach.

"How'd you do?"

I spun around and saw Kevin standing there. He too had lost his chef's coat, and was back to just the stained Nirvana T-shirt, although his shaggy hair looked like it had grayed in the past few hours. I looked closer and saw that it was just a light dusting of flour.

"Fine. Great," I said brightly. "Where've you been all night? I've hardly seen you."

"I stay in the back room, partly to stay out of Oliver's way and partly because I can. I do most of my heavy lifting before the shift starts. Once dinner's under way, it's only about presentation and monitoring the soufflés," Kevin said. "I'm heading out. Need a lift home?"

"No, thanks, Opal said she'd drop me off," I said.

Kevin hesitated for a minute and looked like he wanted to say something. But then he seemed to change his mind. "Okay. See you tomorrow," he said.

Chapter Thirty-one

I don't see why you'd rather stay at Paige's tiny apartment than at home with me," Mom said querulously. "I was looking forward to spending the summer together."

I shifted the phone to my left ear, balancing it against my shoulder while I raided Paige's fridge. A few months ago, the pickings would have been scarce—nonfat yogurt, skim milk, a few bananas. But now it held a bountiful crop of cheeses, containers of commercial ranch and black bean dips, break-and-bake cookie dough, ice cream sandwiches. Thank God Paige got knocked up, I thought.

"Mom, I told you. I'm closer to my job down here. And Paige needs me to stay here so I can look after the place," I said.

"But why? She has a doorman. It's not like anyone's going to break in."

"Other stuff can happen. Remember Rory, my friend from Princeton? When she and her parents went to Vail for Christmas? Their ice maker leaked and flooded the whole house," I said.

I settled on a jar of natural peanut butter and plucked it

from the refrigerator door. After swinging the door shut with my hip, I grabbed a loaf of bread from the bread box—my anal-retentive older sister was the only person I'd ever met who actually had a bread box, although admittedly it was a really cool stainless steel one—and set about making myself a sandwich.

"But you don't have a car. How do you get around? And get groceries?"

"Paige picks me up on her way home from the office and drops me off at the restaurant. And Sophie said she'd take me shopping this weekend," I said.

"How do you get home from work? Don't tell me you walk by yourself at that hour," Mom said.

This was exactly what I'd done the night before when I couldn't mooch a ride home from anyone.

"No, I always get a ride from one of the other waitresses," I lied.

"I'm going to talk to your sisters, and see if they know anyone who can lend you a car for the summer. If not, you can just take mine."

"Mom! No."

"Why not?"

"Because then you won't have a car. Look, I have to go," I said. And then, remembering that I'd promised myself I was absolutely, positively going to tell her about med school the next time we talked, I continued, "But wait, before you go, I have to tell you something."

"Did I tell you I got my dress?" Mom interrupted me.

"What dress?"

"My *wedding* dress."

At this I lost my appetite, and shoved my peanut butter

sandwich to the side. I was suddenly envisioning horrible poofy sleeves, a Scarlett O'Hara hoopskirt, and a long train that I'd be expected to hold up behind her as she pranced down the aisle. The very idea was nauseating.

"I really should go," I mumbled.

"It's very elegant. It's a cream raw-silk sheath with just a spattering of sequins across the bodice, and a matching jacket. Although I think it might be too hot to wear the jacket in August, don't you? Anyway, I got it at Talbot's, and just wait until you see it, you're just going to love it," she continued.

"Sounds great," I said, the words curdling in my mouth. "But I really have to go."

"Do you want to come over for dinner this weekend? Your dad and I are going to grill some steaks, and we'd love to see you," Mom said.

Guilt competed with annoyance; the irritation won out.

"I can't. I'm working. Look, I have to get ready for my shift, or else I'm going to be late. I'll talk to you later," I said.

It was only after I hung up that I remembered I once again hadn't told her about medical school.

"Why does this have to be so hard?" I asked Paige's empty apartment. My voice sounded odd and flat, and when there was no response, I got up from the table, tossed the sandwich into the garbage, and got ready for work.

"Mickey, you're such a slob. How can you live this way?" Paige asked, looking crestfallen as she took in the mess I'd made out of what had once been her pristine apartment. She'd stopped by to take me to work, but instead of pulling up to the curb outside her building like she normally did, she came upstairs to pick up some of her things. If I'd known the control freak was going to be making a surprise inspection, I would have made an effort to pick up the place.

"What do you mean?"

"The clothes everywhere, the empty Diet Coke cans, the dishes in the sink. There's dried ketchup on my counter. I'm going to get bugs," she said.

"I don't think so. The exterminator came by the other day and sprayed," I said. "Any cockroach who tries crawling in here will face certain death. If the apartment gets infested with anything, it's more likely to be mice. Or rats."

"Thanks, that makes me feel loads better," Paige said.

After she shoved a pair of my Levi's to one side to clear a space on the sofa, she sat down and looked around.

"I miss this place," she said mournfully.

"You've only been gone for a few days," I said.

"Ten days. Ten long, long days."

"Things aren't going well with you and Zack?"

She shrugged. "No, he's fine. We're fine. I'm used to living with him. It's just that now that we're in the house, he wants to start shopping for nursery furniture," she said.

"Well, you are having a baby, aren't you?"

"That's not the point. I just think it's a little early in our relationship to be picking out a crib together," she said.

"I guess," I said.

"It's just too much, too soon. We were just getting used to living together here in my apartment—*my* apartment, where I was still in charge—and now all of a sudden we're in a house. *His* house," she said darkly.

"Does he say that? Act like it's his house and you're just a guest?"

"No, just the opposite. He keeps saying it's our house, my house. It's just too weird."

I had no idea what was upsetting her, but I had a now slightly fuzzy memory of Sophie acting like this when she was pregnant. I'd thought it was just Sophie, who had a tendency to veer toward the dramatic, but apparently all pregnant women lose their minds.

"You're upset that things are moving too fast?" I guessed.

Paige shrugged. "No. Yes. I don't know. Zack proposed to me last night. Officially this time," she said abruptly.

"What happened?"

"I didn't say yes," she said.

"Why not?"

"I wanted to, I was going to accept. You should have seen him, Mick. We were out on the back porch, looking out at the most beautiful sunset over the lake, and he actually got down on one knee and gave me the most beautiful ring. It was a sapphire, with two diamonds on either side. It was perfect. And then I ruined it," she said, her voice breaking.

I looked at her in alarm, and saw fat tears rolling down her cheeks.

"What happened?" I asked.

"I said I'd have to think about it. You should have seen his face, he looked like he'd been punched in the stomach. He just got up, and said that was fine and to please let him know when I'd decided, and then he went inside and made dinner. And I just sat there like an idiot. I wanted to go after him, but I just . . . couldn't. It was like all of my muscles were frozen," she said.

"Do you think it means that you don't want to get married? If that was your first reaction?"

"No! Don't you understand? I do want to marry him," she cried.

"But . . . isn't that good news? He wants to marry you, you want to marry him," I said, feeling a little like Alice must have after she tumbled down into the White Rabbit's wonky hole, and everything that was supposed to be big was suddenly small.

"I just don't know if I can be married again. I think I'm defective. I'm missing the wife gene."

"You're not defective. You're just a little gun-shy."

"Either way, it's bad. What should I do?"

"Why don't you say yes? If that's what you want, I mean," I said, looking at the clock nervously. I had to be at work in ten minutes. If I was even a minute late, Oliver would know, and I'd have a big target on my forehead during the pre-dinner meeting.

"I guess I should. I know I probably sound crazy to you. I sound crazy even to myself," Paige said. "I think it must be work stress."

"Yeah, well, I'm used to crazy women. I grew up in this family, after all," I said. "But look, we really should get going. I can't be late for work."

"Sometimes I really envy you, Mick. You're on the cusp of this incredible new life and embarking on a new career, and you get this one last summer of freedom and zero responsibility. That must be so . . . liberating," Paige said, completely ignoring what I'd just said about getting to work on time. It was eerily like something Mom would do, but I refrained from pointing this out to Paige. She seemed pretty fragile, and comparisons to Mom might drive her over the edge.

"Erm, I guess," I said, trying to shrug off the stabs of guilt, wondering if I should just tell Paige the truth. It would feel so good to tell someone, to not keep the secret swallowed up inside. But I hesitated. Of my two sisters, Paige would almost certainly make me tell our parents. Immediately. No, if I was going to confess, it would have to be to Sophie. "I don't think I'd call waitressing 'invigorating.' It's actually pretty tedious. And they hate it when you're late," I said instead.

"Tedious? Really? I guess. Kevin's nice, though, don't you think? Zack and I had dinner with him and Scott on Friday."

"Wasn't it weird for you to double-date with your ex-husband? And his boyfriend?"

"No. I know it should be, but it wasn't. I think it feels less weird than it would be to go out with Scott and another woman," Paige said. "And it's hard not to love Kevin. He's a sweetheart."

"Yeah, he really is. And much nicer than the head chef," I said, without meaning to bring up Oliver, who seemed to be sidling into my thoughts too often for comfort.

"Kevin told me about him. Told me he was glad you were staying away from him," Paige said.

All senses went on high alert. "What? Why would he say that?"

Paige shrugged. "It wasn't a big deal. He just mentioned that the chef has a reputation of being a womanizer and has been known to target pretty waitresses. He just said he was glad you weren't among the hunted."

"Maybe Oliver doesn't think I'm pretty," I said.

"Come off it, you're gorgeous. He probably just knows he doesn't have a chance with you. You're too smart to get involved with a guy like that," Paige said.

Yeah, that must be it, I thought. I'm just too damned smart.

Chapter Thirty-two

My first few weeks at Versa were exhausting. Each shift was a whirlwind, and although I tried to keep my mistakes to a minimum, I still made plenty. Like the time I didn't realize the couple sitting ignored at table four were mine. Or when I put in a party's entire order at the same time, which meant their entrées came out at the same time as their starters. Or when I turned a corner too quickly and slipped, spilling two glasses of red wine down the front of my formerly pristine white shirt.

But I learned quickly. I learned how to move gracefully through the dining room with a tray balanced on my shoulder, and how to scan my tables, assessing and anticipating the patrons' needs. I retrieved bottles of wine, filled bread baskets with piping-hot rosemary-infused rolls, and whisked away credit cards as soon as they were snapped into the leather billfolds. I befriended Calla, the zaftig hostess, so that she'd steer higher-tipping parties into my section (businessmen always tipped the most, senior citizens the least, and Calla took great pleasure in sitting the latter at Adam's tables).

And I watched Oliver. I wasn't even sure I liked him, and I certainly resented how he indulged his bad moods by stalking around the kitchen, barking orders at his underlings (we all quickly learned that the curled-lip grin would signal a good night, the dark scowl a bad one). But despite this, I was uncomfortably aware of Oliver, of where he stood, whom he talked to, the way he shrugged his white chef's jacket on just before he turned his focused attention to the food.

But other than occasionally being the target of the pre-shift specials quiz, Oliver didn't pay much attention to me. The rest of the cook staff would tease and flirt with the waitresses, but once the kitchen got busy, Oliver was always too immersed in his work to talk to any of us, even Sarah, who found every excuse she could to fling her skinny body into his path. Instead, he chopped, tasted, stirred, and sautéed, spinning out dish after tantalizing dish. I kept hoping that I'd learn from watching him, but his movements were too quick, too subtle for me to follow.

One night, after I'd cashed out and was counting how much I'd made in tips, Adam tapped me on the shoulder.

"Need a ride home?" he asked.

My lack of a car was starting to become a problem. The other servers were friendly enough, but I knew they were getting sick of my mooching rides, and Opal now rolled her eyes whenever I approached her at the end of a shift. So while I didn't relish having to deal with Adam for even the relatively short ride home, I didn't have much of a choice.

"Um. Yeah. That would be great," I said, mustering up a half-smile for him.

"Come on, my car's out back."

I trailed after Adam through the kitchen. Rob, one of the line cooks, noticed us leaving.

"What do we have here? Love in the workplace?" he said, leering.

I opened my mouth to protest, but then I saw that Adam was shrugging with false modesty. *Oh no.* Did Adam think that this ride home was some sort of a date? My first thought was Oliver, and I quickly looked around, hoping he wasn't there to see Adam and me leaving together. But when I glanced into his office, Oliver was sitting there with his feet up on his metal desk and the phone to his ear. He was looking right at me, eyebrows raised.

"No," I said as loudly and clearly as I could. "Adam and I aren't seeing one another, he's just giving me a ride home."

"Right, that's what they all say," Rob said, laughing. Justin, one of the other line cooks, cackled appreciatively.

I glanced back at Oliver, but he was no longer looking at me.

Shit.

"How have you been enjoying your job, Michaela?" Adam asked.

I glanced at him. One of my friends in high school insisted that men always look sexier when driving stick-shift cars. I wish she could have been here with me now, because short of an extreme makeover, nothing could have made Adam more attractive, and certainly not his manual-transmission baby blue Civic.

"Mickey," I said. No one calls me Michaela.

"You're settling in all right?"

"Yup. I'm doing great."

"Good. Because if you need anything—a shift off or if one of the kitchen guys is bothering you—let me know, and I'll take care of it for you," Adam said.

In my peripheral vision, I could see his ferretlike eyes seeking me out. I turned away, staring out the window at the storefronts, all closed and dark with the exception of a bar so crowded, people were spilling out of the open doors. In front, a young blonde woman wearing a T-shirt with Greek letters embroidered on the front was leaning over, hands braced against her knees, puking on the curb.

"Sure. Thanks," I said.

I could sense that Adam was leading up to asking me out, and I was hoping that by keeping my voice flat, my demeanor cool, I could squelch the impulse before he said anything. And for a few minutes, I thought that my strategy had worked. The rest of the drive home was mostly quiet, other than Billy Joel's "Scenes from an Italian Restaurant" playing on the radio and my occasional direction of "Turn here" or "It's the parking lot up ahead on the right."

Adam pulled up in front of my building. A light rain had started to fall, and he flicked his wipers on. They squeaked rhythmically back and forth. As soon as the car jerked to a stop, I hit the button on my seat belt and had one hand on the door latch.

"Thanks for the ride home," I said.

"Anytime. In fact, there's something I wanted to ask you," Adam said.

My heart sank. We weren't going to avoid this after all. I looked over at him. His face was partially lit by the parking lot lights, giving his oily skin a ghastly yellowish pall.

"Can it wait until tomorrow? Because I'm exhausted," I said, feigning a loud yawn.

"I was wondering if you'd be interested in going to see that new space alien movie with me on Monday," Adam said.

"Um. I don't think that would be a very good idea," I said. "I mean, you're sort of my boss. I don't think it would be professional for us to get involved."

"I checked the employee manual, and there isn't a policy forbidding the waitstaff from dating. Although, you're right, I am your superior, so maybe I should check with Mr. Kramer, the owner. You know, I don't mean this to be sexual harassment or anything," he said self-importantly.

"Oh, I know, I know," I assured him.

"Okay. It's no big deal. I just thought . . . well, okay."

"Thanks for the ride," I said, opening the door, and swinging my legs out. I couldn't get away fast enough, wanting to leave the scene before Adam figured out that my excuse had been a poorly disguised rejection.

"Sure," I heard him say, before I swung the door shut and hurried toward my building.

Chapter Thirty-three

"A dam's such an asshole," Sarah muttered under her breath while we worked side by side setting the tables. We draped them with stiff white linens and lined up the flatware, shining now that Opal and Caitlin had polished the water spots off it. Sarah's small, sharp features were pinched with irritation, and her dark hair swung as she moved. We were supposed to wear it up while we worked, but I'd noticed that Sarah left it down until the diners arrived. When she flirted with Oliver, she liked to twirl one of the locks between her fingers, or toss it back over her shoulders in a casually calculated way.

"Why? What's going on?" I asked.

"He just posted a notice saying that no one's leaving after a shift until he personally inspects all of the service stations and okays them. Power-hungry little prick," she said, banging down empty water goblets so hard I was surprised they didn't shatter. She glanced up at me. "He always pulls this crap when he's in a bad mood. I guess you shot him down last night, huh?"

"What? How did you know . . . oh," I said, remembering

Kevin's warning about how gossipy the restaurant world was. "*Nothing* happened. He just drove me home, and that was it."

"Don't look so surprised, Adam always hits on the new waitresses. He thinks that if he keeps throwing his shit out, it's got to eventually stick somewhere. Did he try to kiss you?"

"No! Why?"

"I let him kiss me when I first started here. It was awful, it felt like there was a slug rooting around in my mouth," she said.

"Ew!"

"I know. But I was worried that if I didn't, he'd stick me with a bad shift. That was before I found out that Oliver's the one who handles the waitstaff schedules, and so when Adam cornered me in the walk-in freezer, I told him if he ever tried to touch me again, I'd kick him in the nuts. He's barely spoken to me since," she said gleefully.

"So . . . what's going on with you and Oliver?" I asked.

"Why? What did Caitlin tell you?" Sarah hissed. She reeled around and stared at me. "I'm going to kill her!"

"Nothing, she didn't tell me anything. I've just seen the two of you together, and you seem . . . friendly," I said innocently.

"Do you think he likes me? He flirts a lot, but he hasn't asked me out yet. I keep hoping that he will," Sarah said. "Oh God, don't tell anyone. Caitlin's the only one who knows. Do you think anyone else knows I like him?"

Everyone knows, I thought. It's so obvious. But, interestingly, Kevin was wrong. Oliver doesn't hit on all of the waitresses.

"No, I doubt it. I thought maybe you were just good friends," I assured her.

At the end of my shift, Adam made a big show of pointing out that the extra napkins in my station weren't folded just so, and that one of the saltshakers needed to be filled up, and that I'd forgotten to empty a water pitcher. By the time I ran back and forth, fixing these and a half dozen other transgressions, I realized that Opal, Sarah, and the others had already left for the evening.

Shit, I thought. Shit, shit, shit.

I pushed the swinging door into the kitchen and saw Adam heading out the back. I considered and quickly discarded the idea of asking him for another ride, and hung back until I saw the back door close behind him.

I'd rather walk home, I thought, although my feet ached at the prospect.

But it seemed to be my only choice. The kitchen was deserted. Even the dishwasher—a sweet, quiet teenage boy—had left.

"You're still here," a voice commented.

I spun around and saw Oliver standing in the door to his office. He was wearing a navy blue V-neck T-shirt and his white chef's pants and was holding a bottle of beer in his hand.

"Yeah. I was just about to go," I said.

"You want a beer before you leave?"

"Um. Sure. Why not," I said, and Oliver stepped back inside his office. I assumed that I was supposed to follow him, but I hesitated for a minute. He'd been sort of moody during dinner, which muted the usual mischievous atmosphere in the kitchen, and I was afraid that he was going to yell at me. Or fire me. Or both. I tried to remember—had I screwed up more than usual tonight? I'd brought a plate of lamb chops back to him, because the customer had insisted they were too raw.

"They're perfect. You're supposed to eat them rare," Oliver had snapped, but he tossed them back into the sauté pan for a few minutes and then handed the plate back to me without further comment.

But that wasn't my fault, was it? Or did he take it as my criticizing him?

"Are you coming?" Oliver called, and so I stepped into his office.

He was sitting behind a steel desk that reminded me of the indestructible ones my high school teachers had used.

"Take a seat," he said. He popped the cap off of a bottle of Amstel Light and pushed it across the desk to me. I grabbed it and dropped into the visitor's chair.

"Thanks," I said, and took a long draw.

"Your boyfriend left without you?" Oliver asked.

"I don't have a boyfriend."

"I thought you left with Adam last night."

"He was just driving me home. I don't have a car. But there's nothing going on between us," I said.

Oliver looked at me for a few beats longer than I was comfortable with, appraising me with his dark eyes, and I wondered if he thought I was lying. Maybe that's why he asked me in here, I thought. Maybe he just wanted to find out what was going on within the waitstaff ranks.

"Good. That kid's a putz," he finally said. He shook his head and drank some beer.

I laughed and tried to relax—it didn't seem like he was planning to fire me after all—but being this close to Oliver filled me with nervous energy. I looked around his office and saw some framed awards and diplomas on the wall, between the pair of frosted windows.

"Where did you go to school?" I asked.

"Paris. Le Cordon Bleu," Oliver said.

"I'm in the process of applying to the Culinary Institute of America," I said.

Oliver's eyebrows went up. "You want to be a chef?"

"Yes. I mean, I think I do. Do you think . . . should I try to go to school in France instead?" I asked anxiously, not wanting to screw up my career before it even began.

Oliver shrugged and took another drink. "It doesn't matter so much. But I wouldn't rush off to school if I were you. I'd take a year, try to get some apprentice work, and see how you like it. If it still seems like a good fit, then go next year."

"Really? Because I thought you couldn't get any work in a kitchen until after you graduate from culinary school."

"Probably not paid work, no. But you should be working back in the kitchen, not up front in the dining room. Take whatever tasks are given to you, and if you're lucky, you'll find a chef who's willing to take you under his wing as an apprentice," Oliver said.

The thought of not going to culinary school—a path that I'd been clinging to as an acceptable and responsible alternative to medical school—scared me. And if I told my parents I was giving up Brown Medical School to be an unpaid kitchen lackey, I imagined it wouldn't go over well.

"You need a ride home?" Oliver asked abruptly.

All thoughts of parents and career vanished from my thoughts, and my breath caught in my throat as I nodded. I was going to be alone. With him. In a car. We were alone now, but it was basically still just work, in the brightly lit office among indestructible industrial furnishings. But being in a car at night, seated just inches away from one another, was far more intimate.

"Okay, let's go," he said.

We walked into the kitchen and dropped our bottles—his empty, mine still half full—into the large green plastic trash can, and then I followed him outside. His BMW was parked right by the back door, and after he unlocked the doors with his remote key, I slid into the passenger seat, praying that the stink of kitchen smoke and sweat wasn't clinging to my hair and body.

I gave Oliver directions to Paige's apartment, and he pulled out, driving with the same efficient, silky motions that he used while cooking.

"Do you like Austin?" I asked him.

He shrugged. "It's all right."

"You used to live in Miami, right?"

He nodded, but didn't say anything, so I, too, lapsed into silence, my feeble attempts at conversation having so dismally failed. Thankfully, the drive was short, and within moments, he stopped in front of my building.

"Thanks for the ride," I said.

"Do you have any plans tomorrow night?" Oliver asked.

The restaurant was closed on Mondays. It was the only day off most of us had.

"No," I said, shaking my head.

"I'll teach you how to make an omelet. The right way," he said.

"What?"

"You said you wanted to be a chef. The first thing every student learns is how to make an omelet."

"Okay. Um, where?" I asked.

"My apartment. I'll pick you up here at seven," he said.

"Okay," I said again, trying to ignore my heart, which was thudding in my chest, as heavy as a potato.

And only after I'd climbed out of the car and watched him drive off did I wonder, Was this a date or a teaching exercise? Either way, I didn't care. I'd take whatever I could get.

Chapter Thirty-four

W hat are you looking for?" Sophie asked me.

I'd lured Sophie away from her budding photography business for the afternoon, and convinced her to come to the Arboretum with me under the pretense of catching up. What I really wanted was advice on how to handle the whole Oliver situation. And whether buying black stockings and a garter would be overkill for a first date.

We'd eaten subs, and stopped in at Gymboree, where she bought Ben a T-shirt with dinosaurs on it, and the Gap, where I picked up a skirt on clearance, and then I steered her toward Victoria's Secret. Sophie was pushing Ben in a stroller, and he'd fallen asleep, his head lolling to one side. His navy blue hat was tipped forward, covering his face.

"I'm just browsing," I said.

"Do you need panties?"

"Actually, I'm looking for something a little more . . . sophisticated."

"You mean like a thong?"

"Maybe a matching bra-and-panty set. Or maybe a teddy," I said, trying to sound casual.

"A teddy? Mickey," Sophie said, grabbing my arm and turning me toward her. "Who is he?"

"Who?"

"Whoever it is you're sleeping with," she hissed.

"I'm not sleeping with anyone!"

She looked at me, head tipped to the side, eyebrows arched. "Yeah, right. You're just shopping for a teddy to what, wear around the house? I don't buy this stuff, and I'm married."

"Okay, fine, there is someone. Nothing's happened yet, but he's invited me over to his place for dinner tonight," I said.

"Your first date, and you're already shopping for lingerie? Don't you think that's a little fast?"

"Don't you think that's a little judgmental?"

"I'm your big sister, it's my job to be judgmental. Seriously, are you really going to go bed with him so soon?"

I shrugged. "I don't know what's going to happen. I'm not even sure it's a date," I said, turning away from her so that I could browse through a rack of silk nightgowns. They were in pretty jeweled colors—deep purple, azure blue, crimson—but definitely not what I was looking for, unless I showed up for dinner wearing one under a raincoat. Definitely overkill.

"If a guy cooks you dinner, that's a date. No, it's more than a date, it's a seduction ploy," Sophie said.

"We work together. He's the head chef at Versa. It could just be a collegial thing," I said.

"Yeah, right. How hot is he?"

I sucked in my breath. "Really, really hot," I admitted.

"So it's a date. Shoot. I had a really nice guy I was planning on setting you up with," she said, pausing to pick out some gray cotton briefs from a round table in the middle of the store. She held a pair up to me. "See, this is what you wear when you're old and married. God, I feel fat."

"I think you look great. Haven't you lost weight?"

"A little. At least I'm not wearing my maternity pants anymore."

"Who did you want to fix me up with?"

"Ben's pediatrician."

"The sexy Indian guy from the gym?"

"Mm-hmm."

"The one you have a crush on?"

"I don't have a crush on him. I told him all about you, and he asked me to give you his number," she said.

"Paige warned me that if you ever tried to set me up with anyone, to run very fast in the other direction," I said.

"Very funny. And I can't believe she's complaining, since I was the one who set her up with Zack," Sophie said.

I pulled a corset-and-garter set off of a rack and held it up. "What do you think of this? Too much?"

Sophie considered it and then nodded. "Yeah, you don't want to look like you planned this out. If things go in that direction—although I think you should wait a little longer and go out with the guy a few times, that's all I'll say—you want it to look more casual. Like you just happen to be the kind of woman who always wears sexy underwear. You want something that says, *I'm a fascinating, erotic woman.* The corset says, *I'm going to an S&M club after our date.*"

"Point taken," I said, and put down the corset.

Sophie wheeled Ben over to a rack of bras and rummaged through them for a few minutes, before pulling out a black lace push-up bra. "This is what you want. Simple yet devastating. What size are you?"

"Um, 32B."

She checked the tag. "Here you go. And these panties, too," she said, handing me the bra and a matching pair of black bikini panties. "Unless you want the thong."

"I'll take the panties."

"Do you want to try the bra on?"

"No, let's just go. I'm sure it'll fit," I said, suddenly feeling shy and strange shopping for lingerie with my big sister. Up until now, I'd always bought my underwear at Target, the cotton kind that comes in a six-pack. My college roommate had been into the more exotic fare, and often announced that she felt underdressed if her bra and panties didn't match—"I'm a set girl," she'd giggle—but I'd always thought it was just an affectation. Maybe she had a point. She certainly got laid more than I did, even during the years when I had a steady boyfriend.

I paid for the underwear, and the salesclerk handed me back a pink-striped shopping sack. Sophie and I headed back to her SUV, loaded Ben in—somehow he stayed asleep even when Sophie lifted him from his umbrella stroller and buckled him into his car seat—and then climbed in. Sophie pulled out of the parking lot and turned onto the access road for the highway.

"Have you talked to Paige recently?" I asked.

"Not for a few days, no. Why?"

"Zack asked her to marry him," I said.

Yes, I was aware that it probably wasn't my place to tell Sophie this news, but this is what sisters do. Paige had to have known she was taking the risk when she told me.

Sophie screamed, slammed on the brakes, and yanked the SUV over to the shoulder.

"Jesus. What the hell are you doing? Are you trying to get us all killed?" I asked, grabbing onto the side of the door, as though this would protect me if an eighteen-wheeler slammed into us.

"Tell me everything," Sophie said. "And don't swear in front of Ben."

After my adrenaline level returned to normal, I gave her the highlights, and when I was through, Sophie looked more worried than excited.

"I hope she doesn't screw this up. Zack's the best thing that ever happened to her," she said, flicking on her turn signal and pulling back out onto the highway.

"That's so sexist."

"I'm a woman. I can't be sexist."

"Of course you can. And Paige is an incredible, accomplished person in her own right, with or without a man in her life."

Sophie shrugged. "I don't mean it that way. Zack makes her happy. Happier than she ever was on her own. It's like that line in *Jerry Maguire*—he completes her," she said.

Sophie pulled up in front of my building, and I leaned forward to gather up my packages.

"Coming up?" I asked.

"I'd better get going. I still need to edit the photos I shot yesterday. Mick, you should have seen this child, she was the homeliest baby I have ever seen. I tried putting a headband of flower petals on her, I tried soft-lighting her, I even tried making the photos slightly out of focus, but nothing helped."

"All babies are beautiful."

"I know that's what you're supposed to say, but it's just not true."

"Well, Ben's pretty cute," I said, looking back over my shoulder. I could just see the top of Ben's head over the rear-facing car seat. "Thanks for going shopping with me."

"Call me tomorrow and let me know how your date went. And seriously, at least consider taking it slow. I'm not saying you have to be a prude, but sometimes it takes a few dates to get the measure of a guy and figure out if he's really the kind of person you want to get involved with," she said.

"Okay, I will. Think about it, that is. Hey, Soph? Before you go, can I ask you a question?"

She rolled her eyes. "Like you have to ask."

"No, never mind. I know that you have to get going."

"I'm fine, don't worry. What is it?"

"Um. Would you think less of me if you found out I wasn't going to medical school next year?"

Sophie didn't even pause to think about it, she just shook her head and said, "No, of course not. Why?"

I hesitated and took a deep breath. "Because I'm not going."

"What? Are you crazy?" she yelped.

"You just said you wouldn't think less of me!"

"I don't. I just . . . why?"

"It's not right for me. I know it will sound crazy to everyone, but what I want to do is become a chef," I said.

"Wait . . . you said the guy you're going out with tonight is a chef," Sophie said, narrowing her eyes. "Is this just to impress him? Like when I pretended to like football when Aidan and I first started going out?"

"No, absolutely not. I made this decision before I graduated. That's why I wanted to work at a restaurant this summer," I said.

"I can't believe you're doing this. You never do things like this. You're always the good one."

"It's not that big of a deal."

"You're kidding, right? It's a huge deal. Huge. And I take it you haven't told Mom and Dad?"

"No. I keep trying to, but all they ever want to talk about is their stupid wedding," I said.

"They're going to flip when they find out."

"You think?" I asked. My stomach shifted nervously.

"Oh yeah. Big-time. And you have to tell them now. Dad's selling off some of his stocks to help pay your tuition," she said.

"What? Shit! Why would he do that without telling me?"

"Don't swear in front of the baby. It was supposed to be a surprise," she said.

"Okay, okay, I'll tell them. But promise me you won't say anything. Not even to Paige."

Sophie hesitated.

"Promise me!"

"Fine, I promise. But Mick, you have to tell them. And do it soon, okay?"

"Okay, okay. I guess I should go up, I have to get ready for tonight."

"You know, I got you the cake," Sophie said. I glanced over at her, and saw that she was frowning.

"Cake?"

"At your party, the one with the stethoscope on it. I got that for you."

"Thanks," I said.

"If I'd known you weren't going to med school . . ."

"What, you wouldn't have gotten me a cake?"

"I wouldn't have gotten one with a stethoscope on it."

"Sophie, no offense, but that really seems sort of . . . unimportant right now."

"Sure, you'd say that. You don't know what I went through to get it. I had to find a picture of a stethoscope, which wasn't exactly easy. . . ."

"Didn't you just look online?"

"No, I don't like that Internet thing. Anyway, I had to find a picture of a stethoscope, and take it all the way into the bakery before they could decorate the cake," she said.

"Well . . . I appreciate that."

"Do you?"

I stared at my sister. "Are you seriously mad at me about this?"

"No. Of course not. I'm just saying, I thought you should know."

"Okay. Now I do."

"Okay, then. Bye."

"Bye, Soph."

Chapter Thirty-five

Oliver's apartment was utterly charmless. Located downtown, just off of Congress Avenue, it basically consisted of two stark white rooms plus a tiny kitchenette and bathroom, and was carpeted in industrial beige Berber. There were no pictures on the walls, nor the normal debris of everyday life—stacks of J. Crew and L.L. Bean catalogs, carelessly dropped sneakers, a discarded newspaper. The apartment contained only the most utilitarian furnishings—a love seat upholstered in navy blue duck cotton, a tan recliner, a pine coffee table, a small television set perched on a metal cart, a cheap dinette set.

"This is . . . nice," I lied, standing in the middle of the main room and looking over his dreary home.

"It's a shit box. And it's temporary," Oliver said, and when he smiled at me, I wanted to fold into myself with happiness.

It was the first time I'd seen Oliver in street clothes, and it was a little strange. Tonight he was wearing faded Levi's and a black T-shirt, and he looked so . . . normal. Like any other guy you might run into at the market or video store. Maybe his chef's outfit was like a superhero's costume—

Super Chef!—and this was his meeker alter ego, like Peter Parker and Spider-Man. And I could tell he'd just gotten out of the shower before he picked me up—he smelled like Irish Spring soap, and his hair was still damp.

He thought I was worth showering for, I thought, pleasure curling through me.

"Where are you going to move to?" I asked.

Oliver shrugged. "I don't have definite plans yet. My wife and I are separated, so it depends on how that's resolved," he said. "But we'll have to sell the house we own in Miami, and once we do that, I can look into buying a place here."

Ah. The first mention of The Wife.

"I'm sorry. About your wife, I mean," I said, hoping I didn't sound as disingenuous as I felt. "Are you getting divorced?"

"It looks that way," he said shortly. "Can I get you something to drink? Wine?"

"Sure, wine would be great," I said.

He moved into the kitchen, and I heard the rattling of glasses and the pop of the cork. I felt out of sorts, not sure what I should do with myself, so I sat on the edge of the love seat. Oliver had said something about cooking omelets for dinner, but the shabby little table wasn't set, and there weren't any obvious signs of dinner preparation taking place.

Oliver returned with the wine and glasses. He poured out two glasses and handed one to me.

"Mm, thanks, this is good," I said, sipping the chardonnay.

"Are you ready for your lesson?" he asked.

"Sure. But just so you know, I already know how to make an omelet," I said.

"I'm going to teach you how to do it the French way. The

way I learned at the Cordon Bleu. It's always the first lesson you learn at school. Trust me, if you practice and perfect this technique, you'll be miles ahead of your classmates. Come, I'll show you," he said, standing up.

I followed him into the tiny kitchenette, carrying my wineglass.

"The first thing to remember when making an omelet is to pick the right pan. It must be heavy, flawless, scrupulously clean. I prefer a stainless steel pan, like so," he said, reaching into a lower cupboard and retrieving just such a pan.

He held it up to me, and sensing that he wanted me to say something, I said, "It's pretty," and then cringed at how stupid I sounded. A pan, pretty? Oh yes, and the whisk is *so sexy*. Gah.

"Crack the eggs into the bowl—I use two, some chefs use three, I think my way is better, but it's really just personal preference—and beat them until they're frothy," he said, demonstrating the moves while he spoke. I peered into the bowl, expecting to see something magical, but no, they looked like average beaten eggs to me.

"And then you add some clarified butter to the pan—and this isn't going to be perfect, because instead of a professional-grade gas cooktop, I have to use this shitty electric range—and add the eggs. Stir the eggs slowly, lifting the edges so that the liquid will run underneath. And here's the real technique—you move the pan like so—and there you have it," he said, neatly rolling the omelet onto the plate without the aid of a spatula. "Now you."

"Oh, no. I'll just watch," I said quickly. The last thing I

wanted to do was have his sharp eyes on me while I tried to mimic his demonstration.

"Here, take these eggs and crack them in the bowl. I'll monitor the heat for you," he said.

I dutifully cracked two eggs into the glass bowl, and of course, tiny fragments of shell toppled into the bowl.

"Shit," I said, reaching in to pick them out.

"No, no, no, don't touch them. The oils on your hands will keep the eggs from frothing."

I beat the eggs until my hand hurt, dropped some clarified butter in the pan, and then turned back for the bowl. The butter sizzled and browned, and when I poured the eggs in, they too began to turn brown. I could feel the weight of Oliver's eyes on me, although I didn't dare look at him. I'd heard him berate Ansel for far less serious transgressions.

"Shit, shit, shit," I breathed, stirring and lifting as Oliver had done, but unlike his graceful execution, the eggs stuck and lumped up in some places, thinned and broke in others. Finally, mercifully, it was cooked, and using a spatula to scrape it, I turned it onto the plate next to the other omelet. It broke midway through and landed with an unappetizing thunk.

"Now we taste," Oliver said, holding up a fork.

He cut off a piece of my omelet and held it up to me, feeding me as though I were a baby bird.

"How is it?"

"Okay. Not great. Sort of like dried-out scrambled eggs," I said.

"Now try mine," he said, lifting the fork to my mouth again.

"Wow. It's . . . succulent. I didn't even know eggs could be succulent," I exclaimed, and then smiled ruefully. "I'm awful at this."

Oliver smiled back. "No, you did fine for your first time. Just practice, and it will be better every time. Cooking's the same as playing a musical instrument or painting. Keep practicing, and you'll improve slowly."

"And what if I don't?" I asked, the anxiety needling at me. My whole life, I've been the straight-A student, but it was all just book learning. It's easy to be good at that. Everything's already written down, and all you have to do is learn how to study it, commit it to memory, and then regurgitate it back up at test time. Cooking was different. It was all about sensing, tasting, anticipating, creating. What if I never got the hang of it? What if, for the first time in my life, I was a complete and utter failure?

"You will," Oliver said, and he put the plate down on the counter and kissed me.

My shock over this sudden move quickly dissipated, and I kissed him back, savoring the taste of his mouth, the soapy, clean scent rising off his body, the feel of his foreign body as it pressed me back against the kitchen counter. Oliver deftly unbuttoned my black stretch oxford shirt. He slid it off my shoulders, and then broke off the kiss while he gazed down at my newly exposed cleavage nestled snuggly in the black lace push-up bra. The bra pushed my small breasts up and together, creating a pronounced décolletage. Earlier, when I first tried it on, I'd turned around and around in front of the mirror, delighted at the difference it made.

Murmuring his approval, he slid his hands down my

shoulders, and then up my sides, and cupped both of my breasts. Whenever Nick was in this area, he would squeeze and knead at me until I could diplomatically find an excuse to move his hands away. But Oliver's touch was firmer, more precise, and as he played with my nipples through the satin of the bra, pinching, coaxing, stroking, all I could do was hold on to his shoulders and make mewing sounds.

"You like this?" Oliver whispered in my ear. "How about this?"

I just nodded, and swayed, and any thought I might have had of entertaining Sophie's advice on playing hard-to-get dissipated immediately. Although when he reached behind me to unhook the bra, I stopped him. I'd gone to the trouble of buying a matching bra-and-panty set, and damn it, I wanted him to appreciate it.

"Wait," I said, and I unbuttoned my Gap khaki skirt. I slid it off my hips and onto the floor. I couldn't bend over to pick it up—Oliver had me boxed in against the counter—so I stepped out of the skirt and kicked it away.

Oliver looked me up and down, taking in the over-the-top sexy underwear, his eyes heavy-lidded with lust. And then he smiled wolfishly, which probably would have frightened the old Mickey, but in my new rush of sexual awareness, it only turned me on even more.

Oliver rested his hands on my waist and lifted me easily up onto the counter, so that I was sitting with my legs dangling and pushed apart by his waist. He reached behind me and unhooked my bra and slid the straps off my arms, before curling his mouth around one exposed nipple. I nearly died with pleasure.

I plucked at his T-shirt, wanting to pull it off over his head, but Oliver caught my hands in his and said, "No. In my kitchen, I'm always in charge."

And then he went back to licking and sucking at my nipples, this time also sliding his fingers under my panties, up into me, until I was grabbing fists of his T-shirt in my hands and breathing in shallow puffs of breath.

It was our first time together, and I was naked and trembling before Oliver, who was still fully dressed and in complete control.

The next morning, I woke up with that slightly euphoric, slightly off feeling I always get when I'm seriously sleep deprived. I rolled over and stared at Oliver's bare back. We'd been up half the night, making love and eating a Papa John's pizza with extra garlic-butter sauce that Oliver ordered in. The night before seemed like the most romantic thing in the world, but in the harsh naked light of the morning, it felt a little sleazy, especially looking around at the starkly empty bedroom. Oliver didn't even have a real bed, he just slept on a mattress propped up on a metal frame. My freshman-year dorm room had been more posh.

I slipped out of bed and padded to the bathroom. I had to pee and my breath was foul. I've never understood how in movies couples wake up and stare dreamily at each other first thing in the morning, falling into one another's arms before they use the bathroom or gargle mouthwash. Was I the only person who woke up with a mouth that tasted like something had died in it, and the feeling that my bladder was about to burst?

After I went to the bathroom and helped myself to Oliver's toothbrush, I stared at myself in the mirror, hoping that I didn't really look as strung out as the mirror was reflecting. I combed my fingers through my hair and pressed my hands to my cheeks.

God, I wish I had a car, I thought. I could get out of here and just go for a long drive by myself. It didn't matter where I went, but Seal would be on the radio, turned up as loud as I could stand it. I'd sing along, hitting the high notes, tapping out the beat against the plastic steering wheel and not caring what any passing motorists thought when they saw me. And I'd swing by the Wendy's drive-through, and get two large orders of fries with extra ketchup and a chocolate Frosty. Pure bliss.

I flicked off the buzzing bathroom light, returned to the bedroom, and slid back into the rumpled sheets. The room smelled stale, and I felt hot and sticky. I thought about taking a shower, but then suddenly felt shy, as though it would be overstepping the bounds of propriety. I guess it was one-night-stand logic: it was one thing to have a man's penis inside of you, and altogether another thing to use his shower without permission.

I scooted over closer to Oliver and wrapped my arms around his waist. He had done the same to me at some point in the middle of the night, kissing my neck, reaching around to caress me, and finally rolling me over. Now, feeling the warmth of his body against mine, my urge to get away was replaced by a stronger impulse of wanting to be close to him, so close that I could reach up and feel his chest rise as he breathed. But as I tried to snuggle up to Oliver, he grunted and shifted away from me in his sleep. I rolled back on my back and stared at the ceiling, wondering how long I'd have to wait until he woke up.

I must have drifted off to sleep, because the next thing I knew, my eyes fluttered open again and Oliver was up and out of bed, dressed in white briefs and pulling a T-shirt on over his head. His curly hair was wet from the shower.

"Hi," I said, sitting up, wondering if he had been planning on waking me up, or if he would have just left me here.

"Hey. Are you as tired as I am?" he asked.

I nodded, drew my legs up so that they were bent in front of me. "I didn't really sleep much," I confessed.

"I know," Oliver said, and then shook his head, a half-smile on his face. "I should have known better, I'm getting too old for this."

He sat down on the edge of the bed with his back to me and pulled on his jeans.

I swung my legs out of bed and reached down for my discarded underwear next to the bed. I didn't see my clothes, and then remembered they'd been left behind on the kitchen floor.

"Are you taking off?" he asked, watching me as I self-consciously pulled on my panties and bra, like I was doing a backwards striptease.

"I don't have a car," I said. "Can you give me a ride?"

"Right, I forgot. I have to go down to the restaurant and meet the supplier, so we'll have to hurry. Although if you keep prancing around in that getup, I'm going to be really late," he said, suddenly smiling and reaching for me. When he kissed me, his tongue slid easily into my mouth and I could taste the mint of toothpaste on his breath.

His hands slid down, discarding my underwear and then

guiding me by the hips back onto his bed. We were back to where we'd been last night.

Oliver wasn't rejecting me, I thought. This wasn't going to be just a one-night stand.

As he parted my legs and eased into me, I knew with absolute certainty that he wanted me.

Chapter Thirty-six

Come on, everyone, we're going over the specials. Front and center," Adam called out. "Mickey, get over here, you can polish silverware later."

I gave Adam a dirty look when his back was turned, but left behind the flatware I'd been rubbing water spots off of and walked over to the steel-topped worktable where everyone was grouped, waiting for Oliver to appear.

My stomach shifted nervously, and I rubbed my palms against my starched white apron. This was the first time since we'd been together that I'd be seeing Oliver at work, in front of everyone. I'd asked him about it while we were parked in front of my building, eating Egg McMuffins in his car, the greasy wrappers perched on our knees.

"You sure know how to treat a girl," I teased him. "Pizza last night, McDonald's this morning. And here I thought getting involved with a chef would mean round-the-clock gourmet meals served by candlelight."

"Well, if you hadn't distracted me, we would have. But you're right, I owe you a dinner cooked by the best chef in Austin," Oliver replied.

"Where are we going? The Four Seasons?" I asked, laughing, and Oliver pretended to look injured, until I leaned over and kissed him.

"You'd better get out of here, before I'm any later than I already am," Oliver said.

When I got back to Paige's empty apartment, I wrapped my arms around myself, grinning stupidly and remembering our exquisite first kiss, until the oily hangover from the Egg McMuffin forced me to search through the medicine cabinet for Pepto-Bismol.

Now, seven hours later, I half listened to Caitlin's bawdy tale of her night off—"Ohmigod, we were, like, totally wasted," she giggled—alert for some sign of Oliver. Suddenly the door to his office swung open, and he came striding out, laughing as he talked to someone on his cell phone.

"Yeah? Love it. That's perfect. Okay, I have to run, I'll talk to you later," he said, before snapping the phone shut and dropping it on the counter.

Who was he talking to? Another woman? His wife? I wondered, hating how the cold fingers of insecurity were grabbing at me.

"All right, specials tonight. Hot and cold oysters for the starter. Salad of aged Serano ham, shaved fennel, and baby vegetables with a saffron vinaigrette. Entrée is duck with a rhubarb and cherry compote, and seared foie gras. And for dessert, Kevin has prepared a very nice apple and pear tarte tatin to be served with caramel ice cream. Any questions? No?"

"How about giving us a taste of everything," Sarah said, leering at Oliver as she leaned forward, giving him a clear shot of her nonexistent cleavage.

"How about this. The server who performs with the least amount of mistakes tonight will have the duck special for dinner at the end of the shift," Oliver said.

The servers murmured with appreciation, and I heard Opal say to Jasmine, "He's in a good mood tonight." My cheeks stained with pride. I tried to catch Oliver's eye. We'd agreed that morning—or, to be more precise, Oliver had insisted—that we not tell anyone at the restaurant about our relationship. But I was hoping that he'd give me some sort of a sign, a smile or wink or sustained eye contact, so that I'd know I was in his thoughts as much as he was in mine.

Once he'd finished running the specials, he turned to Ansel, joking about something that had happened when they went out for a beer after work the previous weekend. I'd already heard all about it from Sarah: Ansel had gotten drunk, hit on a coed, and they'd ended up making out in the middle of the bar. Now Ansel was ducking his head and grinning sheepishly while Oliver reenacted how the coed had closed her eyes with drunken abandon while grabbing Ansel's narrow ass with both her hands. The kitchen staff roared with appreciation.

Oliver completely ignored me.

I turned away and walked out to the front dining room to inspect my tables.

And it only got worse. Not only did Oliver continue to disregard me as the night went on, he seemed to be going out of his way to pick on me. When Sarah or Caitlin swung through the kitchen, he flirted with them—reaching out to pull the end of Caitlin's curly ponytail, teasing Sarah about her love life until she was practically bursting from the attention. He normally ignored the waitstaff, unless he was yelling at one of us for not standing at attention, waiting with an arm outstretched the second a dinner order was up.

But everything I did was wrong. Oliver sighed with irritation when my starters sat under the heat lights for two minutes, even though he knew I was running entrées out to my eight-top. He blamed me when Ansel screwed up and put out my entrées before another table had gotten their salads. And he outright yelled at me when a persnickety woman sent back her tuna not once, but twice, insisting that it was first underdone and then overdone.

"Jesus, Mickey, did you tell her that's what the fucking tuna is supposed to taste like?" he said, throwing a slotted metal spoon onto the counter with a loud clatter.

"I did. She said she wants something else," I said through clenched teeth.

God, he was such an unbearable shit, I thought, trying to hold back tears while I snatched another plate up and stormed away.

I planned on leaving as soon as my last table departed. I'd finish my shift, get the hell out of there, and then send him an e-mail in the morning announcing that I'd quit. Or maybe I'd just tape my apron to the glass front door of the restaurant, with a note that simply said: *Fuck you, Oliver.*

But then my last table dawdled over coffee and dessert, and I had to stand there, arms crossed, waiting for them, while Opal, Caitlin, and Sarah all finished and took off, chattering over their plans to meet up at the Apple Bar for a beer.

And then just to be an asshole, Adam made me run the carpet broom around the entire dining room, even though the cleaning crew would be coming in overnight. By the time I finished and my table had cleared out, the entire place was empty. All of the servers had left, and as I pushed open the swinging door that led to the kitchen, I saw that the kitchen was empty, too. Only Oliver was still there—I couldn't help myself, I snuck a peek into his office as I walked by—sitting behind the brushed-steel desk, talking on the phone. I heard him laugh and say, "Yeah, that figures. Hold on . . . hey, I've got to go, so I'll call you back."

I squared my shoulders and lifted my chin, and walked by his open door without making eye contact.

"Mickey, come in here," I heard him call out, but I decided to ignore him. No way was I going to be summoned after being ignored all night.

I continued stomping toward the back door, and just as I had my hand on the doorknob, ready to swing it open, a hand grabbed onto my left arm, spinning me gently around.

"Where are you going?" Oliver asked, looking down at me.

Gone was the sighing irritation. Now his mouth curved in a gentle smile, and his blue eyes were warm with interest.

"Home. I'm going home," I said sullenly, pulling my arm away from him and trying not to think about the long walk I had in front of me.

"You seem angry," Oliver said.

"Very perceptive."

"What's going on?"

"You haven't noticed you've been treating me like shit all night?" I asked.

"I thought we agreed we weren't going to let anyone here know we're involved," Oliver said.

Involved. The delicious intimacy of the word sucked the force out of my anger.

"We did. But you were going out of your way to be horrible to me tonight. The way you yelled at me about the tuna, and the salad mix-up, and you were nice to everyone else. Sarah even noticed it—she asked me why you were gunning for me tonight," I complained, folding my arms in front of me.

"Hey, come here. You're all crossed up," Oliver said, laughing softly, and shaking my arms gently apart, so that he could wrap his arms around my waist. "I'm sorry. I was worried that someone would figure out what's going on between us, so I guess I overcompensated in the other direction."

I could feel my resistance weakening, especially when my cheek was pressed against the soft cotton knit of his T-shirt. He smelled of sweat and olive oil, which probably shouldn't be appealing, but somehow was.

"I can understand not wanting people here to know, you know—I feel the same way," I lied.

What I wanted was for Oliver to pull me to him, just as he was doing now, and kiss me in front of Sarah, so that she'd stop leaving the extra button on her shirt undone to flaunt her cleavage.

"But you don't have to be mean to me, either. Can't you just treat me like everyone else?" I continued.

"Absolutely not," Oliver said, laughing down at me. And then he kissed me, and I forgot all about being mad.

* * *

When I walked into my apartment and flipped on the lights at 2 a.m., I was so tired, I didn't notice the bulging tote bag leaning against the wall in the short front foyer, nor the carton of ice cream sitting on the kitchen counter, slowly melting into butter pecan soup. I'd walked all the way into the living room, carelessly flipping on lights, distracted by thoughts of Oliver and our lovemaking, and wondering if his excuse for dropping me off back home rather than inviting me to spend the night at his apartment—"I need to get up early to go to the produce market, and I'll sleep better if I'm alone"—was really as lame as it sounded, before I noticed the pregnant woman sleeping on the sofa.

"Oh, dear God," I said, starting violently.

Paige groaned, opened one eye, and then heaved herself up into a sitting position. Behind her the television glowed silently.

"What are you watching? Is that the Home Shopping Network?"

"Where have you been?" she asked. "What time is it? Have you been having sex?"

"What? No. How can you tell?"

"Your hair's all messed up."

"Oh. No. That's just from work. But wait, what are you doing here, and why are you sleeping on the couch?" I asked.

"Zack and I got into a fight, and I left," she said briefly.

"You left him?"

"I left the house. I'm not sure about him yet."

"Do you want to talk about it?"

"Not really," Paige said, yawning. "I'm beyond tired."

"Okay, but go sleep in your bed, I'll take the couch," I said.

"Are you sure?" she asked.

"Yeah, I'm not about to deprive a pregnant woman of her bed, for God's sake," I said. "I'll just grab a shower and then sleep out here."

"When was the last time you changed the sheets?" Paige asked.

"Uh, never," I said.

"Gross, Mick. I'll get a fresh set out of the linen closet," she said.

"You have a linen closet? That sounds so . . . grown-up," I said.

"Sweetie, I am a grown-up. Want to know something even scarier? You are, too," Paige said. She stood up, stretching her arms and yawning loudly.

"Shut up, I am not," I said.

"Not only a grown-up, but a soon-to-be doctor," Paige said, smiling and ruffling my hair as she passed by on the way to her bedroom.

"Yeah. How 'bout that," I said weakly. "Here, I'll help you make up the bed. Where is this linen closet you speak of?"

Chapter Thirty-seven

I'm far too old and pregnant to be a bridesmaid," Paige complained as she and I walked into the cheesy bridal boutique, Happily Ever After. The theme was carried throughout the store, from the grotesquely ornate crystal chandeliers to the liberal use of the color pink to the over-the-top swaths of rose velvet drapes. The look was Cinderella-meets-French-bordello.

"It's unnatural to be attendants at your own parents' wedding," I agreed. "It's like those families where the mother and daughter are pregnant at the same time, so that the mother's baby is an aunt or uncle to the daughter's baby. It's all wrong."

"What are you talking about? How is this anything like that?"

"It just is," I said.

Sophie and Mom were already inside. Sophie was sitting on a pink satin slipper chair, with Ben beside her in his stroller, and Mom was standing at the counter, explaining to the tiny, dark-haired salesclerk what she was looking for.

"I'll be wearing a tailored suit, and I want the girls in simple sheaths, fitted through the bodice and then going out like this to an A-line skirt," Mom said, demonstrating with her hands while the salesclerk nodded.

"Hey, Soph. Hi, Mom," Paige said. "How's Ben?"

"Teething," Sophie said. I looked down and saw that Ben was sucking on his hand, looking cranky. "I told Mom that today wasn't a good day for this, but she insisted."

"There will never be a good day for this," Paige whispered, collapsing into another chair. Then, louder, she said, "Mom, make sure that you pick out something a pregnant woman can wear."

"Pregnant? We don't carry many maternity styles," the salesclerk said doubtfully, looking at Paige's still-tiny belly. "How far along are you?"

"Four months," Paige said. "But I'm getting hungry, and plan on being good and fat by the time the wedding rolls around."

"Why, what's going on?" Sophie asked.

"Zack and I broke up. I don't want to talk about it," Paige said, reiterating what she'd been saying to me for the past three days.

She also had no interest in talking to Zack, who had taken to calling the apartment four hundred times a day. When she made it clear she wasn't going to take his calls, Zack began leaving detailed messages on the answering machine, reminding her to take her prenatal vitamins, not to forget her obstetrician appointment, and pleading with her to give up running until the baby arrived.

"What did he do?" Sophie gasped.

"Why do you assume he did something? What, do you think it's my destiny to get dumped by men? Maybe I just changed my mind," Paige snapped.

"It's just the hormones," Sophie said sagely. "When I was pregnant, everything Aidan did irritated the crap out of me."

"I don't want to talk about it," Paige said.

"Mickey, come here and try these dresses on," Mom said, holding up a half dozen satin dresses in a range of grotesque sorbet colors.

"Why me?"

"Because Paige is pregnant, and Sophie's taking care of Ben," Mom said.

"Luckies," I hissed at my sisters.

I grabbed the dresses from her—I could already tell I hated all of them, especially the shrimp pink one—and stalked off into the dressing room. I hung the dresses up on the hook and pulled off my shorts and T-shirt, and then slipped into the first. Horror. It was light green crepe and chiffon, and had wide horizontal satin stripes around the bodice, and even worse, there was a long scarf thingy that you were supposed to drape around your neck.

"Mickey? Do you have a dress on?"

"Yes, and I'm not coming out. It's awful," I said.

"Come on, honey, just let us see."

I closed my eyes, gritted my teeth, and then stalked out to the sitting area where my mother had joined my sisters. They were all drinking glasses of water with slices of lemon.

Sophie laughed when she saw me, and Paige grimaced.

"No way, Mom. That's awful. And I'll look like a Granny Smith apple in that color," Paige said, looking at me.

"The choices are limited because of your . . . condition," the salesclerk said delicately.

"Well, the next time I have an unplanned pregnancy, I'll try to arrange it so it won't affect my parents' wedding," Paige snapped.

"Paige, honey," Mom began, but I retreated back to the dressing room before I heard her complete the thought.

The rest of the dresses didn't fare any better. Sophie and Paige rejected each one—the color was wrong, the fabric was unacceptable, the bodice made my boobs look weird.

"Hey," I said to this last one, lifting my arms to cover my chest.

"No offense, Mick," Sophie said. "But you're the skinny one, so if it doesn't look good on you, how do you think it's going to look on Paige or me?"

"This is the last one," I said, peering down at the ugly pink satin dress. It did make my breasts look odd. They were pushed apart and then up, like torpedoes about to be launched off my chest.

"I don't know what to do. Maybe we should just get the blue one, so that we have something," Mom said.

"Ugh. Absolutely not," I said. The powder blue one had a Juliet-style empire waist and looked like a prom dress circa 1978.

"Mom, that was the worst one," Sophie agreed. "There's no way that one will fit me through the hips."

"I think it's fine," Paige said unexpectedly.

"Really?" Sophie asked.

"No. I just don't want to have to spend one more minute trying on dresses," Paige said.

"You didn't try them on. I did," I said. The synthetic fabric was making me hot and cranky. I lifted my hair up off the back of my neck. "Is the air-conditioning on in here?"

"Fine, if that's how you feel, then you don't have to be bridesmaids at all," Mom said, her voice high and thin.

"Really?" Paige asked, brightening for the first time in days.

Mom burst into tears and stormed out of the boutique.

Paige, Sophie, and I all looked at one another, shame-faced.

"I was just kidding. Sort of," Paige said.

I ran after Mom, although when I got to the door, the salesclerk started shrieking, "You can't leave the store wearing that dress."

"Okay, I won't," I told her, and so stood in the doorway. "Mom! Please don't leave. We were just joking."

"It isn't funny. This wedding is important to me, and it's important to me that you girls be there," Mom said. She was struggling to unlock her car door and ended up dropping her keys. "Shit!"

"Come on, come back inside. We'll look at the rest of the dresses. Maybe there's something pretty we haven't seen yet. Please."

Mom hunched over, grabbed her keys, and then looked up at me. "Is it really so awful I'm marrying your father? Is it really so unbearable that you girls have to act like this?" she asked. The points of her cheeks were unnaturally red.

I hesitated, and pushed my hair back from my face, while the absurdity of the situation sank in. My mother had to pick a public place to throw a hissy fit, and now I—standing barefooted in the doorway of a strip mall, wearing shrimp pink satin, with the owner of the store standing about an inch behind me, prepared to tackle me if I tried to shoplift the hideous thing—was the one who was going to have to placate her with soothing promises that my sisters and I would be more enthusiastic about wearing insipid brides-maid dresses the color of after-dinner mints in front of every-one we knew. All the while, people were staring at us as they streamed in and out of the Radio Shack and laundromat lo-cated on either side of the boutique.

"Mom . . . I don't want to yell across a parking lot. Just come back inside, and we'll talk about it," I begged.

"No. I've had it with the three of you," Mom said. She climbed into the car, threw it into reverse, and screeched out of the parking lot, leaving behind a pungent wave of gaso-line and hot rubber.

"Really, I must insist that you come back inside. You're going to get the dress dirty. Please at least lift the hem up off the ground," the shop clerk said.

I shuffled back into the store, plucking the skirt up.

"What did Mom say?" Sophie asked.

"She's mad we're not being more enthusiastic about the wedding. I think we should probably follow her home and talk to her," I said, sighing.

"Okay. But can we get something to eat first?" Paige asked. "I'm starving."

"Maybe we should have been a little nicer to her about doing this," Sophie said. "I didn't mean to be bitchy, I'm just so tired. Ben was up half the night, and this was after I'd worked all day. And yesterday really sucked. I left Ben with the sitter for a few hours while I worked, and he sat up for the first time while he was there. I missed it."

"I'm sure he'll sit up again," I said, trying to be supportive.

"Well, *obviously*. It's just he won't sit up for the *first time* again," Sophie said. Her face crumpled. "I'm a bad mommy."

"You are not a bad mommy, and you'll be there for plenty of firsts," Paige said, going to Sophie's side and wrapping her arm around her.

"I'm almost always with him, and I leave him for three hours, and he has to go and reach a milestone without me," Sophie said, her voice soggy and muffled against Paige's shoulder. Paige stroked her head and made soothing sounds, and I stood there watching them.

"Are we getting something to eat?" I asked.

"Yes!" Paige and Sophie yelled simultaneously.

We thanked the salesclerk—who seemed miffed that after all of that we were leaving empty-handed—and walked out to where my sisters' cars were parked. We agreed to meet up at a coffee shop down the street.

"Mick, why don't you ride with me?" Sophie said, shooting me a meaningful look.

"Why don't you be a little more obvious that you're going to talk about me behind my back?" Paige said huffily as she opened the door of her car and eased inside.

"We're not talking about you, silly. I want to find out the dirt on Mickey's new boyfriend," Sophie said.

"Good luck. I haven't been able to get a single piece of information out of her. All I know is that she's out late with him every night," Paige said.

"How do you know? You're always asleep when I get in," I protested.

"I get up to pee ten times a night. You're never home at

my two a.m. pee, but you're usually in by the four o'clock one," Paige said.

I rolled my eyes and climbed into Sophie's SUV. Once Soph had Ben buckled in and started the car up, she turned to me and said, "Okay, now tell me what's going on with Paige and Zack."

"I don't know," I said honestly. "He calls a lot, but she won't talk to him. I have a feeling this is about his proposing to her last week. It really freaked her out."

"Yeah, that's what I thought," Sophie said. "We're going to have to get involved."

"And do what?"

"I don't know. We'll have to get them together. Or do some kind of an intervention," Sophie said. She turned around and looked over her shoulder as she backed her enormous Tahoe out of the parking spot.

"How do you ever see anything behind you in this thing?" I asked.

"I don't. If I hit something, I stop," she said.

"That's comforting."

"I'm guessing that you haven't told Mom and Dad about medical school yet," Sophie said. "Since I haven't heard any high-pitched screaming from that direction."

"You guessed right. And please don't lecture me, Soph, I know I have to tell them. I've just been busy, and haven't been spending much time at Mom's," I said.

"She's upset about that. She asked me why you're avoiding her," Sophie said. "Is this the coffee shop you two were talking about? Yup, that's where Paige is turning."

"Every time I've been to the house, Dad's always there,

and all they want to do is talk about the wedding. And I don't want to deal with it. I don't want to hear about her dress, or be a stupid bridesmaid, or read poetry at the ceremony," I said, slumping forward.

"I know, I used to feel the same way," Sophie said, pulling into a parking spot and coming to an abrupt stop.

"But not now?"

"No. I'm okay with it. I mean, it isn't really about us, it's about them. And strange as it may be, they make each other happy now," Sophie said.

"Why couldn't they make each other happy when I was growing up? I had to shuttle back and forth between Mom's house and Dad's apartment like I was some kind of a pet dog. I had to deal with their constant fighting, and their dating other people, and all of the ugliness, and now that I'm grown up and on my own, they just *now* get it together? It sucks," I said.

Sophie nodded. "I know, but we don't have any more control over how they act now than we did back then. So there's no point in getting upset about it. And at least the screaming fights have stopped."

"For now," I said bleakly.

"I think things will be different this time. Did I tell you they asked me to take photos at the reception? It will be my first wedding, and I'll be able to start a portfolio. I think I'm going to shoot it all in black and white," she mused.

"Great," I said without enthusiasm.

We climbed out of the Tahoe, and Sophie untangled Ben from his car seat. "Mick, you really should tell them soon. I know you're angry at Mom and Dad about the wedding stuff, but not telling them about medical school is just wrong."

"What about medical school?" Paige asked. She appeared behind us.

"Nothing," I said brightly.

"Mick," Sophie said.

"Nothing," I insisted, giving Soph the evil eye and mouthing, *You promised.*

Sophie shrugged. "Fine. But you know my feelings on the subject."

"You two are going to have to tell me what's going on," Paige insisted.

"Okay. We'll tell you as soon as you tell us what happened between you and Zack," Sophie said sweetly.

"On the other hand, sharing is overrated," Paige said and she turned and walked into the coffee shop ahead of us.

Chapter Thirty-eight

How come we never go anywhere?" I asked Oliver.

We were lying in his bed, naked, watching a boring Jackie Chan movie on television. Oliver was very still, and his eyes were slitted, so when he didn't answer, I thought he might be asleep. I was wide awake, my body curled around a flat, musty pillow. I wanted to stretch my body against the length of his and slide the flat of my hand over the hair on his chest, but I didn't want to risk waking him. Instead, I picked up the remote and changed the channel to an old rerun of *Friends*. It was the one where Rachel loses Ross's monkey. A classic.

"I was watching that," Oliver said.

I sighed and changed the channel back to Jackie Chan.

"Why don't we ever go anywhere? All we do is hang out in your apartment," I said.

"Where else can we go? I thought you said your sister moved back into your apartment," Oliver said.

I gazed at him, thinking how beautiful he looked lying there. I've never thought men's bodies were all that attractive—too much hair and weird dangling parts. But

Oliver was lithe and muscular, and his olive-toned skin was supple to the touch. I rolled over and rested my head on the crook of his arm, and when he wrapped his arm around me, I sank against him with pleasure.

Was this love? I wondered. Sometimes, as I felt his chest rise and fall, the heat of his skin on my face, I thought yes, absolutely. Then other times, when we were at work and pretending not to know or care about one another, the charade would suddenly seem real.

Did Oliver ever think about me when we were apart? I wondered. Did the scent of rosemary remind him of my shampoo? Did he smile to himself as he recalled a joke we'd shared?

"She is. We can't go there," I said. "But I mean, why don't we go out? To dinner, or a movie or something."

"God, Mickey, what do you want from me? I spend more time with you than anyone else. We're together almost every night, and we work late. What, do you want to go out to dinner at midnight?"

I could feel him shifting away from me, irritated, crowded. I panicked. That was how I used to feel when Nick would bring up getting engaged, or moving in together after graduation. It had felt like the whole world was closing in on me, and I'd be stuck staring at him for the rest of my life. Living in suburban Pittsburgh—his hometown, where he'd always been clear he wanted to return to—in a horrible split-level ranch with brown linoleum kitchen floors, a plastic swing set in the backyard, and Sunday-night pot roast at his parents' house. And all the while, I'd just feel more and more trapped.

"No. I mean . . . I don't know. I just thought it would be

fun to go out. But we don't have to, we can just keep doing this," I said, trying to keep my voice light, wanting to placate him.

"Do you have any idea how much pressure I'm under right now?" Oliver asked. He sat up abruptly, bending over to retrieve his underwear from the bedroom floor. "I have to turn Versa around. You know the last chef nearly drove the restaurant into the ground."

"I thought business was going well."

"For now. But things could change just like that." He snapped his fingers. "And if that happens, then there goes all of my profit sharing. If I'm ever going to open my own restaurant, I need to take a profit out of this place."

"I understand," I said, reaching out to rest my hand on his sloping shoulder. He stood up, and my hand slid off, falling to the bed. "Are you going to open your restaurant here in Austin?"

"It's not my first choice. That would be Miami, or even New York. But if I build a reputation here, I might stay," he said. He pulled a T-shirt on over his head and then snapped on a pair of ratty blue sweatpants. "Come on, I'll take you home."

I took a deep breath and tried to suppress the whine I could feel coming: *Why can't I spend the night with you here?* We'd been over this one. I hated being dropped off at 2 a.m. It made me feel like a whore being deposited back on her corner. But Oliver had a demanding job, I knew, and he worked late and then had to get up early to meet suppliers or the owner of the restaurant, or deal with whatever crisis might pop up. And it seemed as though the restaurant was always having one kind of an emergency or another—staff was quitting, competition was edging in, profits weren't up as far as expected.

Someday I'll be handling all of this, I reminded myself.

"Maybe after you open your restaurant, I can come work there. After I finish school, I mean," I said, standing and pulling on my bra and underwear, before retrieving my work uniform from where it lay crumpled in the corner. I'd once suggested bringing some clothes to leave at Oliver's house—sweats or pj's, something I could slip into after work—but he seemed irritated by the idea and dodged the question. I hadn't brought it up again.

Sometimes I felt like my age was putting me at a disadvantage; I simply didn't know the rules for dating a thirty-four-year-old man. All of my previous boyfriends had been my age. Nick would never have minded if I left every stitch of clothing I owned at his place, nor would he have ever asked me to leave in the middle of the night. But then, Nick didn't have a real job, and he spent every afternoon playing Xbox games with his best friend, Fitch.

Now Oliver just laughed and pulled me toward him.

"You're adorable," he said, burying his head in my hair, his hands sliding down until they cupped my ass. I was wearing yet another new lingerie set, this one a solid purple satin, with a lightly padded demi-bra and matching thong bikini underwear. The thong had me wriggling with discomfort all night at work—I couldn't get used to the feeling of a permanent wedgie—but it had really turned Oliver on.

I wrapped my arms around his waist and wondered if he'd want to make love again. I hoped so. That way I'd get to stay here with him for longer, and maybe it would get to be so late, I could just spend the night.

And then Oliver was plucking at the underwear, sliding his hands underneath the waistband. His mouth moved to my neck, kissing the soft skin of my throat in the way that he knew made me melt.

"I thought you wanted to get some sleep," I said, testing him.

"I'm not so tired right now," Oliver murmured. And then he was turning me around, discarding my bra, and leaning me forward, moving the thong to the side, while he pushed into me.

Chapter Thirty-nine

I'm glad you've got the night off," Paige said, pushing the shopping cart through Central Market. "I can't believe I'm going to say this, but I can't take another night of eating alone." She stopped and peered into a glass case filled with prepared food. "The mushroom lasagna looks good. How does that sound to you? We could get some garlic bread and a Caesar salad to go with it."

I looked doubtfully into the shopping cart that already contained a six-pack of double-chocolate cupcakes, croissants, five containers of Yoplait yogurt ("The baby needs extra calcium"), three different kinds of jam, a bag of chocolate chips, two boxes of butter sticks, frozen waffles, and two cartons of ice cream—one strawberry, one mint chocolate chip. Also nestled in the cart was a vanilla-scented pillar candle and satin-nickel candleholder that I'd gotten for Oliver's apartment, thinking it might warm it up. Last week, I'd given him a framed black-and-white photograph of a Paris grocer's market to hang in his living room, and he'd seemed to really like it.

What was he doing right now? I wondered, checking my

watch. The dinner rush had already started, so Oliver was likely at his normal station, a generous worktable in front of him, the six-burner cooktop at his back, where he personally made many of the entrées that were served at Versa. He'd be in his crisp white jacket, his hatless head lowered in concentration over whatever it was he was cooking or prepping. His dark brown hair would be curling down over his forehead, slightly moist with sweat while he worked.

"Who's going to eat all of this food?" I asked Paige, making a good-faith effort to shake off the Oliver obsession.

"We are! Come on, Mick, you always have a huge appetite," Paige said.

"I guess," I said. "But maybe we should get something healthy, too. Aren't you supposed to be watching what you eat?"

"No," Paige said firmly. "This is the one time in my life when I can eat whatever I want. And don't nag me, you sound like Zack."

"I'm not nagging. I just think that maybe we should add in a token vegetable to soak up all of the grease and sugar."

"Ha-ha. Oh, look, crème brûlée!"

"We already have ice cream and cupcakes," I said.

"Maybe you're right. Speaking of dessert, I talked to Kevin today," Paige said in a too-casual tone of voice that I knew all too well. There was a lecture coming. "He said that you seem to be getting cozy with your boss at the restaurant."

"Oh?" I said.

"Don't 'oh' me. You know what I'm talking about," Paige said.

I knew exactly what she was talking about. The night

before, after we thought that everyone had left for the night, Oliver and I made love in his office. It was incredibly uncomfortable, since he wanted me to lie down on his steel desk while he stood in front of me, and the desk had been hard and cold. And then Oliver couldn't get any good traction, and every time he thrust his hips forward, the desk would slide across the floor, screeching loudly while my head bounced on the top.

After we had finished and dressed, and were walking out of the restaurant, Oliver said, "I'm going to just drop you at home tonight," and I was silent, resenting this dismissal, when Kevin walked out of the back kitchen where he did all of his baking.

"Hey, Kevin. What are you doing here so late?" Oliver said.

"Just sorting out some stuff. I think I'm going to make bread pudding soufflés as a special for dinner tomorrow," Kevin said. His eyes flickered from Oliver to me, and self-consciously I raised a hand to smooth down my disheveled hair.

"Did you know Mickey here is an aspiring chef? I'm teaching her some of the ins and outs of the business side of things," Oliver said, lying glibly.

Ins and outs? Was that supposed to be funny, I wondered, glancing quickly at him. Oliver's expression was innocent.

"An aspiring chef? What happened to medical school?" Kevin asked.

"I, um, decided not to . . . well, I'm delaying my admission," I said.

"Really. Wow. Well, I'd better push off. Mick, do you need a ride home?"

"That's okay, Oliver said he'd drop me off," I said.

"It would be great if you could take her. I need to make a few phone calls before I go. Thanks, buddy," Oliver said.

"Oliver . . . ," I began.

"Sure, no problem. Come on, Mick," Kevin said, turning to leave.

I waited a beat, looking at Oliver, but he just winked at me and then turned around and walked back into his office. And I followed Kevin out, feeling disposable and panicking that Oliver was losing interest in me.

And now the only question was, just how much of this little run-in had Kevin shared with Paige?

"I was hanging out with our boss last night—he's really great, very funny. And Kevin saw us, and I think he got the wrong idea," I said.

"Really. Because Kevin told me he heard the two of you having sex in your boss's office," Paige said dryly.

"What? I can't believe he told you that. Oh my God, that's none of his business, and it's none of your business, either."

"He wasn't being a gossip, he was worried about you. And after what he told me about that chef guy, I have to say I'm worried, too," Paige said, wheeling the cart into the checkout. She groaned when she saw how long the lines were. "My feet are killing me, and I'm starving. And look, that guy in front of us has one, two, three . . . *fifteen* items, and this is the twelve-items-or-less line!"

"We have twenty items."

"Yeah, well, they should have a super-express lane exclusively for pregnant women."

I turned toward Paige and noticed for the first time how tired she looked. Her face was puffy, and her eyes were sunken and ringed with dark circles.

"Paige, why don't you go sit down, and I'll finish checking out," I said.

"No, I'm fine. Just a little tired," she said.

"So . . . what did Kevin tell you about Oliver?" I asked, trying to sound casual.

"That he's a womanizer. A *married* womanizer. And he's already had flings with a couple of the waitresses," Paige said.

"He's wrong about that. Kevin saw a waitress leaving Oliver's office in tears like two months ago, but she wasn't crying because they broke up, she was crying because she was quitting," I said, relieved that it was the same misunderstanding that had already been cleared up.

"It was something else. Although I don't know if you want to hear this."

"Tell me."

"Are you sure? Maybe this should wait until we get home."

"No! You can't say that and then not tell me!"

"Well . . . Kevin told me that he walked in on Oliver having sex with another one of the waitresses. In the kitchen. Apparently, he had her up on the kitchen counter and was . . . um . . . going down on her," Paige said.

I felt light-headed. He'd done the same thing with me our first time. Was it some sort of a compulsion for him? Diddling waitresses on countertops?

"Did he say who it was?" I asked. I stared at the magazine rack, trying to ignore the sickly sour feeling spreading through me.

"Yeah, I think he said her name was Sarah. Does that sound right? Do you work with someone named Sarah?"

"Wait, that can't be right. Sarah really likes Oliver, but I know they never got together. She told me so, and I don't think she was lying," I said.

"Mick . . . Kevin said it was just a few nights ago," Paige said.

"But that's impossible," I said. The relief was like fresh air being sucked into my lungs. Kevin had to be wrong. Oliver and I spent nearly every night together.

And then I remembered. Three nights ago, Oliver told me he wasn't going to be able to see me after work. He said the owner, Mr. Kramer, was coming in to meet with him to go over the receipts. Oliver had acted nervous about it, said he was worried that business had been slowing down lately. I'd gotten a ride home with Caitlin that night, and Sarah . . . Sarah was still there when we left. Normally she's the first one out the door, but she'd definitely been there, looking at Oliver with those narrow eyes, and I'd felt a childish pleasure that he'd picked me over her.

Me over her. Her over me.

"I'm sorry, sweetie, I know that must be hard for you to hear," Paige said, putting her arm around me and patting me on the back. "And, God, I should have waited to tell you, instead of dropping it on you in the middle of the grocery store. What was I thinking?"

I began to lean forward and move the food onto the conveyer belt, marveling at how numb I felt.

"You know, Mick, I have tons of candles at home, feel free to use whatever you want," Paige said when she saw me holding up the candle and staring at it.

"It's a present for someone," I mumbled.

Paige sighed. "You're giving him presents?"

And then I crumpled, lifting my hands to my face.

"Oh no. Mickey, don't, he's not worth getting upset over," Paige said, grabbing my arm and pulling one of my hands down so she could clasp it in her own. "And maybe Kevin's wrong. Because for some strange reason, he thought you'd changed your mind on going to medical school, so maybe he was wrong about Oliver, too."

I shook my head and looked at my big sister, the person I'd always looked up to. She'd always been so cool and capable, able to handle anything. Just look at her now—she'd broken up with her live-in boyfriend and the father of her child, and she was dealing with that better than I was handling finding out that my married lover was screwing around on me.

"He wasn't wrong. I'm not going to medical school," I heard myself say.

Chapter Forty

Although I'd already hatched and discarded several revenge plans, I still had no idea how I was going to handle the Oliver situation the next night when I went into work. Should I just quit without explanation? Confront him? Try to embarrass him in front of the staff? None of it seemed to capture the level of vengeance I was going for.

"Whatever you do, just keep it dignified. He's not worth making a scene over," Paige had advised as she dropped me off at Versa the next evening.

I nodded, but wasn't convinced. Oliver hadn't even bothered to call me the night before. Was he with Sarah then, too? Anger choked in my throat, and when I got inside, I headed straight for Oliver's office.

"He's not there," Adam said, appearing behind me while I rapped on the door.

"Where is he?" I asked.

"What do you want to see him about?"

"Something that's none of your fucking business," I said sweetly, and stepped around him.

"Someone's PMS-ing," I heard Adam say behind me.

"No, but if I was, you'd really regret saying something like that. Trust me," I called back over my shoulder, and then went to find busywork that would keep me in the kitchen so I could intercept Oliver when he arrived.

He still hadn't shown up at five-thirty, the time Oliver always held the servers' pre-shift meeting, and everyone was milling around, restlessly waiting. Normally this was the calm before the storm, and we'd be joking around with the kitchen staff, but tonight there was so much tension in the room, even Ansel commented on it.

"Why does everyone look so pissed off?" he asked me.

I shrugged and pulled out some lemons and limes to slice for the water glasses, ignoring Adam when he told me to recheck the tables in my section. Adam stomped off, glowering and mumbling under his breath that he was going to have to have a word with the owner about bad attitudes among the waitstaff, as if that would scare me.

Screwing the boss does have some benefits, I thought.

"Give him my best when you talk to him," I snapped at Adam's departing back.

"What crawled up your butt?" Opal asked me.

"Just leave me alone," I muttered.

"What-*ever*," she said, turning on her heel and walking away.

Sarah also didn't join the other servers in the dining room, I noticed. She was also finding reasons to hang around in the kitchen, folding enough napkins to last us a week. She kept glancing at the back door and at Oliver's office. I tried not to care.

At six o'clock, Adam ran back into the kitchen. "Oliver's finally here, thank God," he said out loud to no one in particular. He just wanted all of us to know that he was on the case, self-important prick that he was. "When people started to come in, I freaked, but it turned out it was Oliver with some friends of his."

"What friends?" Sarah asked.

"His wife and some other woman," Adam said.

At the word "wife," I froze in the middle of slicing a lime. His wife. Here. The one he was supposedly separated from.

"Shit," I said under my breath. "Shit, shit, shit."

I put the last of the lime slices in a rectangular metal container, carefully covered it with plastic wrap, and then plunked it in the refrigerator.

His wife was here. His *wife*.

Adam rounded up the rest of the waitstaff for the meeting, and when I turned to join them, I noticed that Adam, Ansel, and a few of the line cooks were watching me.

Oh my God, I realized numbly. They all knew. They knew that I was sleeping with Oliver, although I'm sure they thought of it in cruder terms than that. They probably made vile jokes about it when I was around, snickering to one another over Oliver's latest conquest.

I could just hear Ansel now, pointing his chin at me as I walked into the dining room, a heavy tray lifted up on my shoulder: *Oliver's banging that one. It's crazy, man, he does her right on his desk.*

Just when I thought this couldn't be any more mortifying, I thought. And who had told them? Oliver, bragging about his exploits? Kevin, maybe, unable to keep such a juicy tidbit to himself? Or had someone else seen us leaving together, or going into Oliver's office and shutting the door behind us?

The door to the kitchen swung open, and Oliver came

striding in. Before, when everything about Oliver was colored with a gauzy romance, I'd mused that whenever he entered a room, the space always seemed a little smaller, as though he filled it beyond his physical dimensions. Now I saw him for what he was—a ridiculous rooster of a man, so cocky and egotistical that every self-important affectation, every temper tantrum made him that much more unlikable.

"Come on, everyone, we have customers here. We need to go over the specials quickly," he said. "The starter is a carmelized-onion-and-goat-cheese torte. The salad's a warm wilted spinach with a mini blue cheese soufflé and bacon vinaigrette. The entrée, roasted rack of lamb with white-truffle mashed potatoes, but push the salmon, we need to move it. For dessert, Kevin's made a chocolate-glazed pecan caramel pie. And that should do it. Any questions? Good, get out of here."

And then without looking at me, or Sarah, Oliver walked back to the prep area, pulled on his white chef's jacket, and began grilling Ansel about whether all of the dinner prep had been completed. As much as I wanted to stalk after him, I knew that Paige was right—I couldn't do it now, not in front of all of these people. I'd just end up looking like an even bigger fool.

Instead, I forced a neutral expression onto my face and headed out toward the dining room.

"Mickey, I told Calla to seat Oliver's wife in your section, you'd better get out there," Adam said, catching me just before I pushed through the swinging door.

"What? No. Adam. No," I said. "Give her to someone else."

"Why?"

So this was what he wanted: a confession.

"You know why," I said.

"It's too late, they're already seated. You'd better get out there," Adam said, and a mean, Grinch-like smile threaded across his face. And then I realized what he was really after: humiliation. A punishment for my unforgivable crime of rejecting him. In a way, it was truly pathetic. This was all he had to lord over—the dining room of a small restaurant.

"You are such an asshole," I said.

"Just do your job," Adam said quietly.

True to his word, there were two women sitting at a table in my section, an open bottle of wine in front of them. I wondered which one was the wife. Certainly not the woman facing me, I thought. She was older than Oliver, a redhead in her late forties, and was pretty in a soft, out-of-focus way. The other had her back to me, and all I could see was long, shiny brown hair that curled out slightly at the ends.

I took a deep, shaky breath and walked to the table.

"Hello, welcome to Versa. My name is Mickey, and I'll be your server tonight," I said.

"Hi, Mickey. I'm Oliver's wife, Laura," the brunette said.

I turned to her, my chest pounding, praying that she wouldn't be able to sense that I was the whore sleeping with her husband—because that's certainly how she'd think of me, as a slut, a tramp, not just a silly girl who'd fooled herself into thinking that the man who was obviously using her actually cared about her as a person. But Laura just smiled at me benignly and said, "It's so nice to meet you. This is my stepmother, Faith."

"Hi," I said to Faith the Stepmother, and then glanced back at Laura.

She didn't look anything like I thought she would. I'd assumed Oliver's wife would be beautiful, but in a cold and distant way. A pouting-blonde-heiress type, who walked around with a small yapping dog stuck in her Hermes bag. The kind of woman who'd married Oliver because she liked the idea of being Mrs. Oliver Klein, wife of the hottest chef in Miami, and not because she truly cared about the man.

But Laura was pretty in a plump, homey way. Her green eyes were kind, and her smile was wide and punctuated by a dimple in each cheek. She looked like she could have been a cheerleader back in high school, the girl-next-door who was friends with everyone. Laura wasn't the slut that men screwed on kitchen counters when their wives were away—she was the one they married.

"Let me tell you about the specials tonight," I began, and then stopped abruptly, because I'd forgotten to write them down. For once I hadn't feared being yelled at as Oliver had done on my first day of work. He'd barked at me a few times since we'd started sleeping together—"If I didn't, people would be suspicious," he'd insisted—but even he had the sense not to target me when his wife was sitting just a few feet away in the dining room. I wondered if he knew I was waiting on her.

That would worry him, I thought. Or at least, it should.

"No, don't bother. Oliver said he was making something special for us. He likes to do that," Laura said, laughing self-consciously.

Jealousy cut through me. When Oliver and I were together, we just ordered pizza, or picked up drive-through, or occasionally he'd bring home leftovers from the restaurant. But other than the omelet he'd made on that first night we'd spent together, Oliver had never cooked anything special for me. But, after all, he was her husband, and I was just his mistress. Who was I to be jealous? I gritted my teeth into a smile.

"Sarah, where are you going?" Adam called out, and I turned around to see what would cause him to shout across the dining room from where he stood at the kitchen door.

Sarah had emerged from the ladies' room, tears streaming down her face, and was storming toward the front of the restaurant. When Adam called out her name, she turned and looked back, first at him, then at Laura. And then, her body shuddering with tears, she flung the glass front door open and fled.

"Sarah?" Calla said to Sarah's departing back, and then shrugged prettily when the waitress didn't respond.

I watched her go, and then turned slowly back around, wondering if Laura had noticed the commotion. She had. Her face had gone gray and her eyes looked moist.

She knows, I realized. She knows her husband's unfaithful.

Suddenly my shirt collar felt too tight around my throat— Adam insisted that we keep them buttoned all the way up— and my ponytail hurt my scalp, pulling and stretching the hair back too hard.

"Um. Can I get you anything else right now?" I asked.

"Who was that?" Laura asked.

"Who?"

"That woman who just left," she said.

"That's, um, Sarah. One of the servers. She's having a bad day, she, um, just broke up with her boyfriend," I said, and then hastily added, "He's in grad school at UT. The boyfriend, I mean."

Laura looked at me, and I could tell that she didn't buy the lie. I didn't know what to say, I felt like the world's biggest hypocrite. Was I supposed to console my married boyfriend's wife over the knowledge that he was screwing yet another woman?

"I'll bring your starter out as soon as it's ready," I mumbled, falling back and practically running for the kitchen.

Adam was standing at the back of the dining room, next to the door.

"What's it like meeting the big guy's wife?" he asked, smirking at me.

"Fuck off, Adam."

Chapter Forty-one

❧ ❀ ❧

Kevin drove me home after my shift. I was exhausted. Sarah's dramatic exit had meant we were one server short, and Adam piled most of the grunt work on me. Turns out he didn't have much of a sense of humor about being told to fuck off.

As Kevin pulled out of the employee parking lot, he glanced over at me.

"Are you mad at me for telling your sister?"

I shrugged. "No, not really. I'm glad that I know. Well, not glad, but . . ."

"Yeah, I know what you mean. I heard that prick Adam sat the wife in your section."

I nodded and sighed. It had been a long night. Oliver had played the part of the devoted husband, cooking his beloved wife her favorite foods for dinner: coconut shrimp, roasted chicken, white-truffle risotto. Laura had oohed and ahhed over each dish and pretended that she had never seen a teary-eyed girl run from the restaurant.

I had managed to avoid Oliver for the most part—which was easy, since we always pretended we didn't know one another during the dinner rush anyway—and then he left early with his wife, entrusting the kitchen to Ansel's less-than-capable hands.

"What was she like?" Kevin asked. "I didn't get to meet her."

"She's nice. Too nice for Oliver," I said honestly. "So . . . how is it that everyone in the restaurant knows about Oliver and me?"

"I don't think everyone does know, and don't worry, I didn't tell anyone other than Paige. Ansel suspected something. He told me that Adam claims to have followed you after work one night and saw Oliver take you to his apartment, but Ansel didn't know whether to believe him. I hate to say this, because I don't want to make you feel worse, but the general consensus was that you were too smart and too well grounded to get involved with someone like Oliver," Kevin said.

"Not that smart. Obviously. I don't know what the hell I was thinking," I said.

"It happens to the best of us. I've gotten involved with guys like Oliver; I think most people have. Just be glad you found out early," he said sagely.

When I got home, all of the lights in the apartment were still on, and Paige was sitting up on the couch, wearing her bathrobe, reading a Maeve Binchy paperback and eating a Butterfinger.

"Why are you still up? Are you feeling okay?" I asked.

"I'm fine," Paige said, yawning loudly. "I wanted to hear how it went with Oliver tonight."

I collapsed on the couch next to her, kicking off my Doc Martens. I glanced at Paige and saw that her eyes were rimmed with red. There were discarded tissues balled up on the table next to her.

"Have you been crying? What's wrong?" I asked.

"Nothing," she said. "I'm just tired. Long day at work."

"Uh-huh. What's really wrong? Is it Zack?"

"Maybe a little."

"He calls all the time, why don't you talk to him?"

"Three days. He hasn't called in three days," Paige said, and her eyes filled with tears. She picked up the Kleenex box and pulled out a tissue. "It's my last one."

"I'll get you more," I said.

"He's probably forgotten all about me and met someone new," she said, sniffling into the precious last tissue.

"Paige . . . you haven't taken any of his phone calls in weeks. He probably figures that you don't want him to keep calling," I said.

"I know," she said miserably. "I think I've screwed everything up."

"What happened? I don't even know why you guys broke up."

Paige sighed and rubbed the heels of her hands against her eyes. "After Zack proposed to me, I thought it over for a few days. I thought about Scott, and how badly our marriage ended, and I thought about all of the crap luck I had with guys before that. And I wondered if maybe I was just cursed when it came to marriage."

"Oh, please. You don't believe in curses."

"I know. Which is why I decided I was being stupid, and

that the worst mistake I could make would be to lose Zack. And so I decided to say yes."

"Paige!"

"I felt awful for ruining his romantic proposal that night, and I wanted to make it up to him. So I made reservations at Fonda San Miguel, which is where we went on one of our first dates. I had it all set up—I bought him a wedding band that I was going to give to him, and I'd arranged for the waiter to bring over a bottle of champagne."

"What happened?"

"I'm getting there. Anyway. When Zack got to the restaurant, he was acting very cool and very distant. And before I even got a chance to tell him my answer or give him the ring, he launched into this big speech about how disappointed he was about my reaction to his proposal—"

"I can see his point."

"And that he thought I was just scared of commitment—"

"You are."

"If you keep interrupting me, I'm not going to tell you the rest of the story."

"Sorry. Go ahead. I'll be quiet."

"So then I got angry at him for pressuring me, when he promised he'd give me all the time I needed to think things through. And I was pissed that he'd ruined what was supposed to be this big romantic gesture—"

"But he didn't know that!" I said.

"Mickey! You promised you'd let me finish."

"I forgot. Please continue."

"Well, that was basically it. We had a fight, and I left, and we've barely spoken since."

I stared at her.

"What?" she asked.

"Let me get this straight. Zack proposed to you, and by your own admission you didn't handle that particularly well. Instead of accepting his proposal, like you wanted to, you left him hanging for a few days."

"A marriage is supposed to last until one of us dies. I don't think it's unreasonable to spend a few days thinking it through."

"Absolutely. But then you decided to say yes, and instead of telling him your decision, you picked a fight with him because . . . what was it again?"

"He was crowding me, pushing me for a commitment."

"But you'd already decided you wanted a commitment!" I said, throwing my hands up.

"Well. Yeah. That's why I think I screwed things up," Paige admitted.

"Paige. You have to call him."

"I can't!"

"Why not?"

"Because . . . because . . . I don't know. I don't want to talk about it anymore," she said.

"That's mature."

"What happened with Oliver tonight?" she asked. "Come on, I need to think about something else. I'm all cried out, and I'm out of tissues."

"It was . . . bad," I said.

"Did you confront him?"

"I didn't have a chance. His wife showed up. And I had to wait on her," I said dully. I slumped back against the sofa and rested my feet on the edge of the coffee table.

"No! What? I thought they were separated," Paige gasped.

"Me, too. Apparently, Oliver had a big blowup with his boss in Miami, and made such a big stink on his way out that he couldn't get a job in another restaurant there," I said.

"His wife told you that?"

"Kevin told me, he just found out today, although I don't know who told him. Anyway, that's why Oliver ended up in Austin—turns out it was the only place he could get a job. But apparently he's hoping to get back in somewhere in Miami, so he didn't want to move his wife and kid out here, just to move them back again," I said.

I sounded amazingly calm even to my own ears as I relayed these tidbits of information. It had been such a weird night, and somehow it felt like it was all happening to another person.

"He's an even bigger asshole than we thought. So, he's just been cheating on his wife all along?"

"Mm-hmm. I'm an adulteress," I said bitterly. "And she was nice, really nice. She deserves better."

"You deserve better. And it's not your fault. You thought he was separated," Paige said fiercely.

"I knew he was married. I didn't exactly go out of my way to find out what the status of their marriage was," I said. I'd been too worried that if I pushed him on any aspect of his life, he'd leave me, and that shamed me even more than Laura's kind smiles and overly generous tip.

"You didn't talk to him at all?" Paige asked.

"I couldn't. He got in late and then left early. The other chick he was seeing stormed out in tears. Laura—that's his wife's name—saw her, and I think she knew," I said.

"Well, I'm sure it isn't news to her that her husband is an asshole," Paige said. "I will never understand why women stay with guys like that."

"I thought I was in love with him."

"Oh, Mick." Paige leaned forward and wrapped an arm around me.

"I'll be okay," I said, although the words sounded hollow to me.

"So what are you going to do?"

"I'm going to go over before my shift tomorrow and quit," I said.

"Good. Tell him to shove it up his ass while you're there. Are you still going to Mom's for lunch?"

That had been our agreement. Paige would let me be the one to tell Mom and Dad about my plans, but I had to do it soon. This weekend. And I was okay with it. I'd been putting it off for long enough.

"Yup. Tomorrow should be a fun day," I said.

"Aren't they all," Paige sighed.

"We make quite a pair, don't we," I said, slouching over and resting my head on my big sister's shoulder. "I've been screwing and getting screwed over by a married man, and you're knocked up and not talking to the baby's father."

"We'll be okay. Cassel girls always land on their feet," Paige said.

"We do?"

"Mm-hmm," Paige mumbled. She sounded sleepy, and her head felt heavy against mine.

"Good to know," I said softly.

Chapter Forty-two

"What are you doing?" I asked as Paige unbuckled her seat belt and opened her door.

"I'm coming inside with you," Paige said, grunting with the effort of heaving herself out of the car.

I flung open my door and scrambled out of the car. "You don't have to do that. I said I'd tell them. What, do you think you have to go inside with me to make sure I'll go through with it?" I asked.

Actually, I had been toying with the idea of not telling our parents the whole truth, and instead softening the news by telling them I was just deferring admission at Brown for a year. Then I'd have the whole next year to slowly ease them into the idea of my switching career paths.

Paige just smiled knowingly and closed the car door. I rolled my eyes. She's so annoying when she acts superior.

"Oh, good God," I said.

"What? I didn't say anything. Mom invited me over for lunch, too. And Sophie."

"So, what . . . the whole family's going to be there?"

"It'll be easier this way. You'll have Sophie and me to back you up," Paige said. "Besides, what do you think they're going to do . . . ground you?"

Actually, the thought had occurred to me.

"Pah. Of course not. Be serious."

"Come on, coward, stop stalling. Let's just go in and get it over with," Paige said.

She turned and walked purposefully up to the house, her rounded belly leading the way. I trailed behind her, feeling like I was twelve years old and about to be punished for shoplifting a lipstick at the mall. Which I didn't really do. My friend Dee Dee Miller did it, only she slid the lipstick into my handbag without telling me, so of course I was the one who got busted.

Paige rang the bell, and then pushed the door open, not standing on ceremony. We could immediately hear them— voices raised, Mom's shrill and fast, Dad's irritated.

"I am not going through this again, Stephen," Mom said.

"You're being ridiculous," Dad replied.

"That's typical. You always have to demean me."

"How am I demeaning you?"

"By calling me ridiculous! It's condescending and patronizing. I won't stand for it."

Paige and I looked at one another, and my sister raised her eyebrows. A sickly mass formed in my stomach. Just like that, I was a little kid again, hiding in my bed, the coverlet over my head, smothering me with safety, while my parents raged at one another a floor below.

"Let's just go," I whispered, pulling on Paige's sleeve.

"No way. If they're going to pull this shit, they're going to face the consequences. Come on, I think they're in the kitchen," Paige said, striding off in that direction.

I hesitated for a minute and then skittered after her. When I got to the kitchen, Mom and Dad were standing on opposite sides of the butcher block island. My mother had her hands on her hips and her eyes were narrowed, and Dad's arms were crossed in front of him.

"What's going on?" Paige demanded.

"It's none of your business," Mom told her. "Hi, Mickey honey, how are you?"

"Fine," I said, my voice faltering.

"Of course it's my business. This is exactly what we've all been worried would start happening when you got back together," Paige said.

Mom lifted her hands up in front of her, palms facing outward. "Paige, don't start with me," she said wearily.

"No, Blair, let's just tell them what's going on. I think they should know," Dad said.

"Fine. You tell them," Mom said. She turned around and poured herself a cup of coffee and then sat down at the kitchen table.

"Your mother told me today that she wants to call the wedding off," Dad said.

I crossed my arms in front of my chest and rubbed my arms, thinking, *I knew they'd screw it up, I knew it, I knew it, I knew it.*

"So we're thinking about going to Vegas for the weekend and eloping instead," Dad continued.

Paige and I turned to my mother.

"Vegas?" I said.

"And what, have Elvis marry you?" Paige asked dryly.

"Are you guys serious?" I asked.

My mother shrugged and sipped some coffee. "I'd love to

get married out in the backyard, with our lovely daughters and Nana and Ben and all of our friends there. But not if you three are going to sulk and act like we're torturing you."

"What's going on?" Sophie asked, walking in the kitchen, Ben in her arms. She was wearing a denim skirt and black T-shirt and had pushed her hair back with a pair of sunglasses. Ben reached up and grabbed the sunglasses and tried to stuff them in his mouth. "No, baby, those are too expensive for you to use as a chew toy. Did you all know that mixing graham crackers with baby spit produces a material that could be used to patch airplanes? Why does everyone look so grim? Mick, did you finally tell them about med school?"

I froze, staring at her in shock. The realization of what she'd done registered on her face.

"Oh . . . oh. Um. Sorry, Mick," Sophie said, looking stricken.

"Tell us what about medical school?" Mom asked.

"Don't tell me, you forgot to send the financial aid forms in. You know that if you don't get them in on time, you can kiss a scholarship good-bye. And then you'll have to take on student loans, and forget about it, you'll be paying those back for thirty years," Dad said.

"Stephen, shhh, Mickey's trying to tell us something," Mom said.

And then they both turned and looked at me, waiting. They didn't look at all apprehensive. After all, it was me, Mickey, the daughter who—the shoplifting incident aside—never gets in trouble. When Paige was a teenager, she'd broken curfew a few times, returning home with the fruity scent of wine coolers on her breath. And on Mom's regular sweeps of Sophie's room, she'd uncovered everything from a half-empty pack of cigarettes to birth control pills. Not me. I didn't have any practice in disappointing them.

Nothing like starting big, I thought.

"I've decided that I'm . . . not going to medical school," I mumbled. I sat down at the kitchen table, to the left of my mother. There was a pen mark on the top of the table, from when I was in high school and making signs for my student government campaign and the purple marker I was using bled through onto the table. I stared hard at it.

"What did she say?" Dad asked Paige.

"Mickey, speak up," Mom said.

"I said . . . I'm not going to medical school," I said louder.

"What? But . . . why?" Mom asked.

"What do you mean you're not going? Of course you're going," Dad said.

"She doesn't have to go if she doesn't want to," Paige interjected.

"Yes she does," Dad said.

"Says who? She can make her own decisions," Sophie insisted.

"No she can't," Dad said. He folded his arms in front of him.

"Stephen! Mickey, we're just a little confused. I thought you wanted to go to medical school. I thought it was your dream," Mom said.

"No. It wasn't my dream. I thought it was something I'd like to do, but . . . I don't know. I liked the idea of becoming a doctor more than the reality of it. I don't like blood," I said.

"So be a dermatologist," Dad said. "They don't have to deal with blood."

"Stephen," my mother said again.

"What? It's the best job in the world. All you have to do is prescribe zit cream to teenagers and you have a license to print money. Tell her, Paige," Dad said.

"Don't look at me. I don't think she should go if she doesn't want to," Paige said.

"Dad does have a point. If Mickey was a dermatologist, she'd be able to give us free Botox treatments," Sophie said.

"That's true," Paige said thoughtfully.

I stared at my treacherous sisters. I couldn't believe they were willing to sell me out just to have some toxins injected into their foreheads.

"Paige! I thought you didn't believe in that. I thought you said you were going to age gracefully," I said.

"That's easy to say when you're twenty-two. Wait until you get to be my age, you'll have a different perspective on such things," Paige said darkly. She pulled a chair out from the table, and the legs screeched against the floor as she sat down.

"We're getting off point," Mom said.

Ben started to hoot with displeasure.

"I think he needs a change," Sophie said, sniffing around his bottom and wrinkling her nose.

"I'll do it," I volunteered, standing eagerly.

"Nice try," Sophie said. She tucked Ben under her arm and carried him out of the room like a football. I sat back down and watched her go, envious. Maybe I should get pregnant, too. A baby seemed the perfect excuse to get out of unpleasant family gatherings.

"What would you do if you don't go to medical school?" Mom asked.

"Blair, don't start. She's going to medical school," Dad said.

"No, Daddy, I'm not. And you can't make me," I said, crossing my arms in front of me. "I'm . . . I'm going to culinary school."

"Culinary school?" Mom repeated. She pushed back a lock of hair that fell in her face.

"But you can't cook," Dad said. "Remember that cake she made when she was little, and she mixed up the baking soda and baking powder? It tasted like a shoe."

"This is so typical. You're still treating me like I'm a child," I said.

"Where is this cooking school you want to go to?" Mom asked.

"Well . . . I was thinking of applying to the Culinary Institute of America. But then the chef at Versa suggested that I take a year off and apprentice somewhere, and then if I'm still serious about it, I should consider going to school in Paris," I said slowly.

"Paris? As in Paris, France? And just who's going to pay for that? Do you have any idea what the exchange rate is over there now? Forget about it!" Dad exploded. His face got very red, and droplets of sweat beaded up on his forehead.

"Stephen, that's enough. You're not helping," Mom said. She took a deep breath. "So, that's your plan? You're going to apprentice at Versa for a year and then apply to cooking schools?"

"No. Not exactly. I'm not going to be working at Versa. In fact, I'm handing in my notice tonight. But Kevin told me he'd help me find a position in another restaurant," I said.

"You're quitting? Why?" Dad asked.

"It's complicated."

"But Mickey, sweetie, if you can't hold down a simple waitressing job, what makes you think you'll do any better working in a kitchen? And would you really rather take on a backbreaking, menial-labor job than go on to medical school? I know it'll be a challenge, but you've always been a wonderful student," Dad said, switching tactics. Now he spoke to me in a soft, reasonable tone, painting a picture of what my life would be like in the restaurant trade—long nights of hard work, minimum wage, no guarantee that I'd ever climb beyond the position of fry cook—compared to the rarified environment of medical school. I knew he was just trying to manipulate me, but damn it if it didn't work. All of a sudden, my mouth tasted sour with fear. Was I making a huge mistake?

"I can hold down a job, Dad. I'm quitting because I'm involved with my boss, and I just found out he was married," I said, and then clapped my hand over my mouth. Where in the hell had that come from? I looked around, and saw that now Dad was staring down at the table, clearly embarrassed, Mom's forehead was creased, and Paige looked distant, absentmindedly stroking her rounded stomach.

Sophie walked back into the room, Ben in her arms.

"What did I miss?" she asked.

"Your sister was just telling us that she's . . . well . . . changing jobs," Mom said slowly.

"Okay. Look. I don't know if I'm doing the right thing. I don't know if I'm meant to be a chef. But right now, at this very moment, that's what I want to do. So I'm not going to rush into anything, I'm not going to make any life-altering decisions. I'm just going to take a year and try it out. If I like it, I'll continue on and go to school. And if I don't, I'll figure something out then," I announced.

"I think that sounds very sensible," Mom said.

"You do?" Dad asked.

"You do?" I chimed in at the same time.

"Yes, I do. Mickey's right, she's young, she should take some time to figure out what she wants in life," Mom said.

"Thanks, Mom," I said. I turned to look at Dad, who was still staring at Mom, his mouth slightly open.

"I guess your mother's right," Dad said finally. "Take a year. See how it goes. Did you by any chance happen to defer your admission to medical school? So you could get in again if you changed your mind?"

"Not exactly. But if I do change my mind—and I'll tell you right now, I don't think I will—but if I do, I'll just reapply," I said, and he looked somewhat mollified at that.

No one said anything for a few minutes. Other than the loud tick-tick-tick of the kitchen clock and Mom's occasional slurps of coffee and Ben's coos, the room was oddly quiet. I looked around. It hadn't changed much since I was a kid. There were the same cream painted cupboards, the tiled countertops, the wide-planked oak floors, even the same white refrigerator that had once been the place where our report cards and pictures were posted. Now it was mostly empty, except for some snapshots and Ben's birth announcement.

"So . . . um. You guys really aren't going to have a wedding?" I finally asked.

"What? What did I miss?" Sophie asked.

"Mom and Dad are going to get married at one of those Vegas drive-through chapels," Paige said.

"Tell me you're kidding," Sophie said.

My parents exchanged a look.

"I think that depends on you girls," Mom said slowly.

It was our turn, my sisters and I, to exchange looks. Paige was contemplative, Sophie serene, and I knew that we were all in agreement.

"I think you should have your wedding here," I said.

"Definitely," Paige said.

"You can't do it without us," Sophie said.

"But . . . will you girls still be my bridesmaids?" Mom asked.

"On one condition," Paige said. "We need to find nice dresses. Because so help me God, I will not stand up in front of everyone we know, fat, pregnant, and wearing shrimp pink satin."

Mom laughed. "Okay, no shrimp pink satin."

"Good, that's settled. Now, what's for lunch? I'm starving," Paige asked, and she went to the refrigerator and began to rummage inside.

Chapter Forty-three

I timed my arrival at Versa for four o'clock so that I'd be able to get in to see Oliver before the rest of the waitstaff arrived. But some of the cooks were already there, chopping vegetables into neat piles, oiling the grill, and scraping their knives against a sharpener, a sound that gave me the shivers.

Ansel shot me a knowing look as I was lifting my hand to knock on the door.

"What?" I asked irritably.

"Nothing. Just stopping by to see the boss man?" Ansel asked. He grinned and stroked the sparse hair of his stupid goatee. In fact, Ansel had entirely too much facial hair, from the overgrown sideburns to the silly little mockery of a beard. His hair was so long, he wore it back in a ponytail when he worked.

"Is he in there?" I asked.

Ansel nodded. "Yeah, he said not to bother him. He's going over the supplier's accounts."

I shrugged this off and rapped my knuckles against the door.

"Go away," I heard Oliver yell. I opened the door and walked in.

"Didn't you hear me, I said . . . oh. Mickey," Oliver said. He put down his pen and looked at me. I could tell he was trying to gauge my mood. Was I going to yell at him? Cry? Offer up a blow job? "Come on in, close the door behind you."

I pushed the door closed and then stood behind the visitor's chair, my hands resting on the back. I wasn't afraid—hell, I wasn't even that angry anymore. The initial rage I'd felt had burned out quickly, leaving me with the sour aftertaste that comes when you realize that not only have you been taken advantage of, you left yourself open to it.

"Go ahead, sit down," Oliver now said, his face opening into a smile, obviously deciding that charm was the way to go. I couldn't really blame him—it was a technique that had worked beautifully on me in the past.

"No, I'm fine standing," I said. The chair felt like a shield, plus it gave me a place to rest my hands, so that I wouldn't undermine what I was about to say by crossing and uncrossing my arms or playing with my hair. "And I'm not going to stay long. I just came by to tell you that I'm quitting. Effective immediately."

The smile vanished. "You're on shift tonight."

I nodded.

"Well, you can't just quit on me, it's unprofessional," Oliver said. Now a frown tugged his mouth down, and his eyes shone with disapproval. Manipulating bastard that he was, I knew it was just another ploy, only now he was playing on my sense of propriety.

"Yes. But not nearly as unprofessional as sleeping with

two of your waitresses," I said, holding up two fingers for emphasis.

"What? Is that why you're upset? You know I'm not seeing anyone but you," Oliver said. He stood up and came around the desk and reached out for me. I flinched.

"Don't touch me," I warned him.

He put up his hands, palms outward, and then leaned back against the desk. The chair was still between us. If I had to, I could knock him in the shins with it, an image I took comfort in.

"Talk to me," he said, the charming smile back.

"Why are you pretending that nothing's wrong? Your wife was here last night."

"So?"

"Jesus, Oliver, I waited on her. It was mortifying, I kept feeling like I owed her an apology," I said.

"I told you—we're separated," Oliver said. "You didn't do anything wrong, and neither did I."

"Are you separated legally, or just by distance? Because when you left together, the two of you looked pretty cozy," I said.

Oliver shrugged and folded his arms together. "It's complicated. We've been married for eight years, we have a daughter together."

"Uh-huh. And how does Sarah factor into all of this?" I asked. I could see that my words surprised him.

"I don't know what you mean," Oliver said. "What does Sarah have to do with anything?"

"You're fucking her," I said.

"She told you that?"

"No. She didn't have to."

"She just likes to flirt with me, that's all, that's the kind of girl she is." Oliver smiled and held out his hand to me. When I didn't take it, he stepped forward, and leaning one knee against the chair, he slid his hands around my waist. Suddenly he was kissing my neck.

I couldn't believe it, but my body was actually responding to him. How was it possible? I knew that he was a bastard, and even so my breath caught as his hands slid up under my T-shirt, stroking higher until he got to the lacy edge of my bra. It was one of the many lingerie sets I'd thrown money away on just to impress him, to turn him on. Remembering this was like being hosed with icy cold water.

"Kevin saw you with Sarah. Having sex with her. On the kitchen counter," I said flatly, and pushed his hands down away from my bra, away from me.

"He's lying."

"No. He's not."

Oliver watched me for a minute, gauging my reaction. I stared back at him levelly, and finally he shrugged and smiled.

"Okay. Fine. Yes, I slept with Sarah. Just the one time, and it really didn't mean anything. She was just there and . . . available," he said carelessly, and it felt as though the breath had been sucked out of me. I realized then that I'd wanted him to deny it, wanted him to convince me that it was all a mistake—Sarah, his wife—and that what he wanted was me.

"Available," I repeated. "And is that what I was, too? Available?"

"What do you want me to say? Come on, Mickey, I think it was pretty clear from the beginning that our relationship is largely physical," he said.

My mouth was dry, and the lights in the office seemed overly bright, starkly boring down into me. But he was right. It had been clear, I'd just been intent on not seeing it.

"I should go," I said abruptly, and I turned to leave, but Oliver reached out and grabbed onto my wrist.

I probably should have fought him, but, perversely, I wanted to see what he'd do, so I let him draw me close to him, pulling me up against him, trying to mold my body against his.

"Come on, this doesn't have to end. We're good to-gether," Oliver said.

I could feel his erection pressing against me, and I stepped back.

"No, we're not, and yes, it does. Good-bye, Oliver," I said.

He didn't say anything, and I didn't look back. I just swung open the door and walked out. Sarah was standing there, hovering just outside the door. Dark circles highlighted her eyes, and her mouth was tight and drawn in. When she saw me, she visibly winced and then drew her arms around her-self, as if protecting herself from me.

I shook my head at her. "He's not worth it," I said softly.

"Yes he is," she whispered back, and her eyes moved past me, into the office behind me.

Only then did I look back. Oliver was focusing his smile on Sarah with the same measured charm he'd directed at me, easily substituting in Girl Number Two. And even as it creeped me out, I was glad I saw it. Because as Sarah lit up, her sal-low face pretty again, and she stepped around me, moving to Oliver, I was completely free.

Chapter Forty-four

"Do I look fat?" Paige asked. She turned to the right and then to the left, examining herself in Mom's full-length cheval mirror. Sophie lifted her camera and snapped the shutter, catching Paige's pregnant reflection in the picture.

"Hey!" Paige said. "Don't do that. I was making a silly face."

"You look adorable," Sophie assured her. "And no, not at all fat. Good job on the dresses, Mickey."

"Thanks, I thought they'd be perfect," I said, feeling very pleased with myself. Our matching strapless navy blue cotton poplin dresses had fitted bodices and A-line skirts that fell just above the knees. I'd found Sophie's and mine at Banana Republic, and then enlisted the aid of a seamstress to make a maternity version of the dress for Paige.

I nudged Paige to the side and examined my own reflection. My mom's stylist had arrived at the house that morning, and after turning Mom's head into an adorable mess of curls, he gave the rest of us casually elegant loose topknots. I touched my hair gently, marveling at how fake and sticky it felt.

"You're going to mess it up if you keep playing with it," Paige said.

I stuck my tongue out at her. "What time is the ceremony starting? And where did Mom go?"

"It's starting soon, like in about fifteen minutes. And I don't know where Mom went—I think she's downstairs, greeting guests," Sophie said. She snapped another few pictures of us: me patting my hair, Paige slicking on lipstick.

"Sophie, so help me God, stop taking pictures of me when I'm not ready," Paige warned.

"The candid ones are always the best," Sophie insisted.

"I'll go get Mom," I said, and slipped out of the master bedroom and padded barefoot down the hallway. I stood at the top of the stairs, peering down to see if I could catch a glimpse of ivory silk among the crowd of wedding guests milling around the house, and feeling shy about going downstairs in my bridesmaid getup.

As I stood there, shifting from foot to foot, trying to decide what to do, I saw Zack standing at the bottom of the stairs. He was slightly hunched over, his hands stuffed into the pockets of his pants. A small torn piece of toilet paper was still stuck to his jaw, covering a shaving nick.

"Zack!" I called softly. He didn't respond, so I grabbed a paperback novel off the table by the stairs and tossed it down at him. It bonked him on the head, and he startled and looked up. I waved.

"Ow!"

"Oops, sorry, I didn't meant to throw it that hard," I said. "Can you see my mom around there?"

"I don't see her. Do you know where Paige is?"

I hesitated and then nodded. "Up here."

Zack bounded up the stairs. "Just so you know, I'm not crashing. Sophie invited me," he said, looking sheepish.

"I think it's great that you're here. And . . . I think Paige will be happy to see you," I said.

His face brightened. "Really? Because I've been going out of my mind, I miss her so much."

"She's been really upset, too," I said, not feeling at all badly that I was breaking Paige's confidence. I was doing it for her own good. "Here, come with me."

I grabbed his hand and led him down the hallway. The door to my mom's bedroom was half open, as I'd left it, and I rapped my knuckles on the door. "Is everyone decent in there?" I asked.

"Of course we are. What, do you think we stripped off our clothes in the two minutes since you've left?" Paige replied.

I rolled my eyes at Zack and then pushed the door all the way open.

"Paige, you have a visitor," I said, leaning against the doorjamb so Zack could pass by me into the room.

Paige looked up, and her eyes widened and her mouth formed an O.

"Hi," Zack said.

"Hi," Paige replied softly. She'd gone very still, and with the afternoon light that filtered through the old-fashioned lace curtains backlighting her, I thought she'd never looked lovelier.

"Hi, Zack," Sophie said, grinning. "Mick, what do you say you and I go downstairs and track down the bride."

I followed Sophie halfway down the stairs before I realized that I was still barefoot.

"Crap. I left my shoes up there," I said.

"Good, that'll give you a reason to go find out what's going on with those two," Sophie said.

I climbed the stairs again, walked down the hall, and knocked softly on the door before pushing it open. Zack was holding Paige close against him, and her head was turned and resting on his shoulder.

"Um, sorry . . . I just forgot my shoes," I said, bending down and retrieving the strappy sandals from just inside the door.

Paige turned and looked over her shoulder at me, and she had a soft, dreamy expression on her face. "I'll be down in a few minutes," she said.

"Take your time," I replied, and then retreated.

Sophie was waiting for me at the bottom of the stairs. Aidan was with her, holding Ben, who looked handsome in a blue poplin Ralph Lauren romper that almost exactly matched the oxford shirt his daddy was wearing. Aidan had his free hand tucked around Sophie's waist, and she was leaning against him.

"So, what's happening up there?" Sophie asked, her face bright.

"I think all is well. They were hugging. And Paige looked . . . peaceful," I said.

"Yes!" Sophie said, pumping her arm.

"I'm going to be the only one here without a date, aren't I?" I said glumly.

"You can be Ben's date," Aidan offered.

"Gee, thanks," I said.

"Don't worry, I have you taken care of, too," Sophie said.

"What did you do?" I asked.

"Vinay! Over here," Sophie called out, waving her hand.

I turned to see who she was looking at, and saw a tall man wearing a khaki poplin suit over a crisp white shirt, open at the neck, walking toward us.

"Is that . . . ," I started to say, and then stopped, glancing at Aidan.

"Hi," Vinay said. A caterer holding a tray of mini crab cakes high over his head passed by us, and Vinay stepped closer to me to get out of his way. His sleeve brushed against my bare arm, and I could just barely discern the spicy scent of his aftershave.

"Vinay, this is my husband, Aidan. And you know Ben, of course. And this," Sophie said, with a game show hostess's flourish, "is my sister Mickey."

"Mickey," Vinay said, smiling. "It's nice to finally meet you. Sophie's been telling me all about you."

I stared up at him, trying to think of something to say. He was absurdly good-looking with liquid dark eyes that seemed to convey so much about him. Kindness. Wisdom. Strength.

"Mickey," Sophie said, nudging me, and only then did I realize how wildly inappropriate I was being just standing there mute.

"Um, hi, very nice to meet you," I said, blushing.

"Hey, there's Mom. I'm going to go get her. Aidan, you come with me, and Mickey, you stay here," Sophie announced, and my skin burned even hotter. Could she be any more obvious?

"Right then. Something tells me she meant to leave us alone together," he said, once Sophie had bustled off.

"I'm so sorry, she's so bossy. Do you have any sisters?"

"One, older than me. Hideous, of course."

"Then you understand."

"All too well. Sophie tells me you just graduated from college," he said.

"A few months ago."

"Are you getting sick of everyone asking what your future plans are?"

"Oh my God, yes. I can't even tell you," I said.

"I took a year off after university, before I went to medical school, and every time my parents' mates were around they'd grill me on when I was going to school, and where, and when was I going to get married," Vinay said. "It got to the point that I'd pop round to the pub whenever anyone was coming over."

"But at least you knew where you were going. I was supposed to go to Brown med school this fall, and then decided not to. Now everyone just acts like I'm one of those kids who moves home after college, lying around on the couch all day and mooching off their parents," I said.

"You're planning to stay in Austin?"

I shrugged. "For the foreseeable near future. I'm thinking about going to culinary school next year, but . . . I'm still working out the details."

"That's good," Vinay said.

"Well, I haven't gotten in anywhere yet."

"No, I meant I'm glad you're staying in Austin," he said lightly.

I looked down at my arms. I actually had goose bumps. Not even Oliver had done that to me.

"You're not married, are you?" I asked.

Vinay looked startled. "Um. No. Not yet," he said, shaking his head.

"No fiancée? Girlfriend in another town?"

"No and no."

"Good," I said.

"I have a feeling there's a story underneath those questions," Vinay said.

"Not a very interesting one," I replied, and when we grinned at one another, I could feel the possibility shimmering between us.

"Mickey, where's Sophie? And Mom?"

I turned around, and Paige was standing behind us, holding tightly on to Zack's hand. They were both grinning, and her updo had shifted wonkily off center.

"I don't know. Sophie went off to find Mom, but now she's missing, too."

"No I'm not. Here we are," Sophie said, cutting through the crowd, Mom in tow. "She keeps trying to get away from me."

"Sophie, stop pulling me. I have to go greet the Johnsons. And Mary Beth is here, I have to say hello to her," Mom said, waving to a friend across the room.

She looked beautiful. The short nipped-in jacket and fitted dress showed off her slim figure, and the happiness shining in her face made her look decades younger than her sixty-three years.

"No way. We're already running late. Aidan's asking people to move outside, and once everyone's out there, sitting down, the ceremony is going to begin," Sophie said firmly. "I had to practically pry her and Daddy apart."

"Isn't it supposed to be bad luck for Daddy to see you?" I asked her.

"It's too late for that," Mom said.

"I guess I should probably go outside," Vinay said. He smiled at me, and the stomach flutters started up again.

"Have we met?" Mom asked him.

"No, I don't believe we have. I'm Vinay Prasad," he said, holding out his hand to Mom.

"He's Ben's pediatrician," Sophie explained.

"How nice of you to come. Thank you for joining us," Mom said so giddily, I wondered if she'd been sampling the champagne.

"Thank you for inviting me," Vinay said. He slid his hand into mine and pressed it gently. "I'll see you after the ceremony?"

I nodded. "I'll find you," I said.

Vinay smiled and moved on, following the throng of people making their way to the backyard. A tent had been set up outside, and the florists had spent the day filling it with candelabras, twinkle lights, and masses of flowers—roses, lilies, hydrangeas. Now that the sun was setting and the candles were lit, it looked magical.

"He's gorgeous," Mom said, nudging me.

"I should get going, too," Zack said, although he looked unwilling to leave Paige's side and she held on tightly to his hand.

"Let's tell them," Paige said.

Sophie inhaled audibly. "Does that mean what I think it does?" she asked.

Paige looked up at Zack. "We're getting married," she said softly.

Sophie squealed and grabbed them both in a hug.

"Oh, Paige," Mom said, clasping Paige's hand in her own, and I saw that Mom had tears in her eyes. Yes, she'd definitely gotten into the champagne. It always made her get misty.

"Congratulations," I said, throwing my arms around Paige and squeezing her hard.

Zack leaned over and kissed Paige briefly.

"I'll see you after the ceremony," he said.

"Bye," she replied.

Zack kissed my mom on the cheek, and then turned back to squeeze Paige's hand one more time before he left.

"It's time," Sophie announced. "Is everyone ready?"

"Wait," Mom said.

"It's too late to be having second thoughts," Sophie said.

"I just wanted to tell you all how much I love you, all of you. And how much it means to me—to your father and me—that you're here today," Mom said.

"Mom, if you start to cry, your mascara is going to run," Sophie warned.

"I'm wearing the waterproof kind."

"Even so, it'll make your eyes puffy," Sophie said, but she leaned forward and hugged our mother carefully. "Careful! I don't want to get lipstick on your suit."

"Come on, Paige, Mickey, give me a hug," Mom said, and she pulled us all to her, until all four of the Cassel women were standing in a huddle.

"As long as we're all here, I have to ask . . . what is Abbey Tyler wearing?" Sophie whispered.

"I know! That awful suit with the loud floral print?" Paige said.

"I thought she looked nice. She has a beautiful figure," Mom said.

"Without a doubt, she wins the ugliest dress contest," Sophie said.

"That isn't nice," Mom said.

"Well, it's true."

"And when did Mr. Walker start wearing a toupee?" Paige asked.

"Is that what's wrong with him? I knew he looked different, I just couldn't figure out what it was," I said.

"I thought he'd gotten plugs," Sophie said.

"Girls. Don't you think that rather than making fun of our guests, this would be a good opportunity to share how much we love one another?" Mom said.

We all looked blankly at her.

"That's not really our thing," Paige said.

"Yeah, we don't do the touchy-feely stuff," Sophie agreed.

"Way too weird," I said.

"I give up. I love you all. Now I'm going to go marry your father," Mom said.

We were laughing as we broke apart and walked down the hallway to the back of the house. The florist had laid our bouquets out on the kitchen table, and we each picked one up—simple nosegays of red roses for the bridesmaids, white for the bride. Sophie ducked out the back door to signal to the musicians, and as the string quartet started to play Pachelbel's *Canon in D*, she reappeared.

"Okay, Paige, I'm going first. And then you, then Mickey, and then Mom. Everyone count to five slowly before you start down the aisle, so we're all spaced out evenly."

"No, wait."

We turned to look at our mother. She was shaking her head.

"I don't have anyone to give me away," she said.

"Do you want me to go get Nana?" I asked.

"No. I want you girls to walk with me," Mom said.

"Are you sure?" Paige asked.

"But I was going to get in front and then take pictures of you as you came down the aisle," Sophie protested.

"I don't care about that. What I care about is that I have my daughters at my side," Mom said.

Sophie opened her mouth to lodge another protest—she'd hidden her camera inside a topiary at the front of the tent—but I shook my head at her.

"Mom's right. We should walk with her," I said.

Paige nodded. "Yeah. It's perfect."

Sophie shrugged and grinned. "Whatever you say, you're the bride," she said, and grabbed one of Mom's hands. I took the other.

"Where should I go?" Paige asked.

"Hold my other hand," Sophie said. "And hold Mom's bouquet for her. I guess we'll just leave ours behind. Okay, is everyone ready? Mom?"

"I'm ready," Mom said. Her voice quavered.

"We'd better hurry, or she's going to start crying again," I said.

"No, I'll be fine. Let's do it."

And then, serenaded by the sweet strains of the quartet, we walked out the back door, hands clasped together, a chain of mothers, daughters, and sisters.

About the Author

Whitney Gaskell grew up in Syracuse, New York. A graduate of Tulane Law School, she worked for several years as a reluctant lawyer before writing her first novel, *Pushing 30*, followed by *True Love (and Other Lies)*. She lives in Florida with her husband and son, and is at work on her fourth novel. You can visit her website at www.whitneygaskell.com.

Don't miss
Whitney Gaskell's
other novels

TRUE LOVE
(AND OTHER LIES)
and
PUSHING 30

Available from
Delta Trade Paperbacks

TRUE LOVE (AND OTHER LIES)
A sharp, witty novel about destiny, friendship, and soul-sucking jobs.

"I've learned enough about the world to have developed a well-established personal rule: *The whole concept of a one true love who completes your soul is total bullshit.*"

Travel writer Claire Spencer doesn't believe in fate, much less any part of that fairy-tale Prince Charming love-at-first-sight crap. Between the boyfriend who first dumped her, then fled the country to get away from her, and her parents' vicious divorce, Claire doesn't exactly have any successful relationship role models.

So when she ends up sitting next to a sexy American expatriate on a flight from New York to London and he asks her out, she figures there has to be a catch. After all, full-figured Claire hardly falls into the current stick-thin beauty deal, and men haven't exactly been beating down her door.

But after years of disappointing dates, nightmare set-ups, and a bastard of an ex-boyfriend, Claire may have finally met the man of her dreams. It's almost enough to make a girl start believing in destiny. The only catch? Someone else got to him first, and Claire can't believe who it is.

"Funny, romantic . . . an entertaining read with all the right stuff."—*RomanticReviewsToday.com*

PUSHING 30

A smart, funny novel about finding Mr. Right when everything is going wrong.

Meet Ellie Winters. She's under a little pressure . . .

"The one thing you should know about me is this: I'm the consummate Good Girl."

Ellie Winters is dependable and loyal and has a near-phobic aversion to conflict. But as her thirtieth birthday looms ever closer, she starts to feel like she's lost the instruction manual to her life. She has just broken up with her boring boyfriend, despises her job, and is the last of her high school friends to remain single. Worse, her dysfunctional family is driving her nuts, and she's somehow become enslaved to her demanding pet pug Sally, who she suspects is the reincarnation of Pol Pot.

One night, after a botched attempt to color her hair at home, Ellie rushes to the drugstore for emergency bleach, Sally in tow. Sally is accosted by a smitten canine admirer . . . but it's the dog's owner who captures Ellie's attention. Television news anchor Ted Langston is witty, intriguing, and sexy. The only catch? He's twice her age— and the only man on the planet who isn't interested in dating a younger woman. And no one, from Ellie's best friends to Ted's ex-wife, wants to see them get together.

This novel asks the question whether a Good Girl can find her happily-ever-after with the one man who's so wrong for her, he's perfect.

"Feisty, poignant, sexy, and packed with delicious comedy."—Sue Margolis, author of *Apocalipstick* **and** *Original Cyn*